INSIDE THE RED CHURCH

"You ain't going in there," Tim said, his eyes wide behind his glasses.

"Now, why in the heck would I want to go in there?"

"You just had a funny look in your eye."

"Shh. Listen . . ."

The singing stopped, and a silence settled over the mountains.

Then, a soft sound. A scratching, fluttering sound.

Not inside the church. Above. In the steeple.

A shadow moved, a lesser gray against the church bell.

Tim gasped. Ronnie swallowed hard, and some of the blood from his nosebleed snaked down his throat.

It smells the blood. The thing with wings and claws and livers for eyes . . .

"Run!" he shouted at Tim, but his little brother was already a step ahead of him. They dashed between the cars and hit the gravel road, rocks flying as they scampered away from the red church. They were exposed, vulnerable in the open, but Ronnie didn't dare head into the forest. The pounding in his ears almost sounded like laughter, but he didn't stop to listen.

Instead, he ran into the night, hunching his shoulders against the monster that swept down from the blackness. . . .

THE RED CHURCH

SCOTT NICHOLSON

PINNACLE BOOKS
Kensington Publishing Corp.
http://www.kensingtonbooks.com

PINNACLE BOOKS are published by

Kensington Publishing Corp.
850 Third Avenue
New York, NY 10022

ISBN 0-7394-2586-2

Pinnacle and the P logo Reg. U.S. Pat. & TM Off.

Printed in the United States of America

To Angela, who saved me more than once

ONE

The world never ends the way you believe it will, Ronnie Day thought.

There were the tried-and-true favorites, like nuclear holocaust and doomsday asteroid collisions and killer viruses and Preacher Staymore's all-time classic, the Second Coming of Jesus Christ. But the end really wasn't such a huge, organized affair after all. The end was right up close and personal, different for each person, a kick in the rear and a joy-buzzer handshake from the Reaper himself.

But that was the Big End. First you had to twist your way though a thousand turning points and die a little each time. One of life's lessons, learned as the by-product of thirteen years as the son of Linda and David Day and one semester sitting in class with Melanie Ward. Tough noogies, wasn't it?

Ronnie walked quickly, staring straight ahead. Another day in the idiot factory at good old Barkersville Elementary was over. Had all evening to look forward to, and a good long walk between him and home. Nothing but his feet and the smell of damp leaves, fresh grass, and the wet mud of the riverbanks. A nice plate of spring sunshine high overhead.

And he could start slowing down in a minute, delaying his arrival into the hell that home had been lately, because soon he would be around the curve and past the thing on the hill to his right, the thing he didn't want to think about, the thing he couldn't help thinking about, because he had to walk past it twice a day.

Why couldn't he be like the other kids? Their parents picked them up in shiny new Mazdas and Nissans and took them to the mall in Barkersville and dropped them off at soccer practice and then drove them right to the front door of their houses. So all they had to do was step in and stuff their faces with microwave dinners and go to their rooms and waste their brains on TV or Nintendo all night. They didn't have to be scared.

Well, it could be worse. He had a brain, but it wasn't something worth bragging about. His "overactive imagination" got him in trouble at school, but it was also kind of nice when other kids, especially Melanie, asked him for help in English.

So he'd take having a brain any day, even if he did suffer what the school counselor called "negative thoughts." At least he *had* thoughts. Unlike his little dorkwad of a brother back there, who didn't have sense enough to know that this stretch of road was no place to be messing around.

"Hey, Ronnie." His brother was calling him, it sounded like from the top of the hill. The dorkwad hadn't *stopped*, had he?

"Come on." Ronnie didn't turn around.

"Looky here."

"Come on, or I'll bust you upside the head."

"No, really, Ronnie. I see something."

Ronnie sighed and stopped walking, then slung his bookbag farther up on his shoulder. He was at least eighty feet ahead of his little brother. Tim had been doing his typical nine-year-old's dawdling, stopping occasionally to tie his sneaker strings or look in the ditch water for tadpoles or throw rocks at the river that ran below the road.

Ronnie turned—*to your left,* he told himself, *so you don't see it*—and looked back along the sweep of gravel at the hill that was almost lost among the green bulk of mountains. He could think of a hundred reasons not to walk all the way back to see what Tim wanted him to see. For one thing, Tim was at the top of the hill, which meant Ronnie would have to hike up the steep grade again. The walk home from the bus stop was nearly a mile and a half already. Why make it longer?

Plus there were at least ninety-nine other reasons—

like the red church

—not to give a flying fig what Tim was sticking his nose into now. Dad was supposed to stop by today to pick up some more stuff, and Ronnie didn't want to miss him. Maybe they'd get to talk for a minute, man-to-man. If Tim didn't hurry, Dad and Mom might have another argument first and Dad would leave like he had last week, stomping the gas pedal of his rusty Ford so the wheels threw chunks of gravel and broke a window. So that was another reason not to go back to see whatever had gotten Tim so worked up.

Tim jumped up and down, the rolled cuffs of his blue jeans sagging around his sneakers. He motioned with his thin arm, his glasses flashing in the midafternoon sun. "C'mon, Ronnie," he shouted.

"Dingle-dork," Ronnie muttered to himself, then started backtracking up the grade. He kept his eyes on the gravel the way he always did when he was near the church. The sun made little sparkles in the rocks,

and with a little imagination, the roadbed could turn
into a big galaxy with lots of stars and planets, and
if he didn't look to his left he wouldn't have to see
the red church.

Why should he be afraid of some dumb old
church? A church was a church. It was like your
heart. Once Jesus came in, He was supposed to stay
there. But sometimes you did bad things that drove
Him away.

Ronnie peeked at the church just to prove that he
didn't care about it one way or another. *There. Nothing
but wood and nails.*

But he'd hardly glanced at it. He'd really seen only
a little piece of the church's mossy gray roof, because
of all the trees that lined the road—big old oaks and
a gnarled apple tree and a crooked dogwood that
would have been great for climbing except if you got
to the top, you'd be right at eye level with the steeple
and the belfry.

Stupid trees, he thought. *All happy because it's May
and their leaves are waving in the wind and, if they were
people, I bet they'd be wearing idiotic smiles just like the one
that's probably splitting up Tim's face right now. Because,
just like little bro, the trees are too doggoned* dumb *to be
scared.*

Ronnie slowed down a little. Tim had walked into
the shade of the maple. Into the jungle of weeds that
formed a natural fence along the road. And maybe
to the edge of the graveyard.

Ronnie swallowed hard. He'd just started develop-
ing an Adam's apple, and he could feel the knot pogo
in his throat. He stopped walking. He'd thought of
reason number hundred and one not to go over to
the churchyard. Because—and this was the best reason of all, one that made Ronnie almost giddy with
relief—he was the *older* brother. Tim had to listen to

him. If he gave in to the little mucous midget even once, he would be asking for a lifetime of "Ronnie, do this" and "Ronnie, do that." He got enough of that kind of treatment from Mom.

"Hurry up," Tim called from the weeds.

Ronnie couldn't see Tim's face. That wasn't all bad. Tim had buck teeth and his blond hair stuck out like straw and his eyes were a little buggy. Good thing he was in the fourth grade instead of the eighth grade. Because in the eighth grade, you had to impress girls like Melanie Ward, who would laugh in your face one day and sit in the desk behind you the next, until you were so torn up that you didn't even care about things like whatever mess your dorkwad brother was getting into at the moment. "Get out of there, you idiot. You know you're not supposed to go into the churchyard."

The leaves rustled where Tim had disappeared into the underbrush. He'd left his bookbag lying in the grass at the base of a tree. His squeaky voice came from beyond the tangle of saplings and laurel. "I found something."

"Get out of there right this minute."

"Why?"

"Because I *said* so."

"But look what I found."

Ronnie came closer. He had to admit, he was a little bit curious, even though he was starting to get mad. Not to mention scared. Because through the gaps in the trees, he could see the graveyard.

A slope of thick, evenly cut grass broken up by white and gray slabs. Tombstones. At least forty dead people, just waiting to rise up and—

Those are just stories. You don't actually believe that stuff, do you? Who cares what Whizzer Buchanan says? If he were so smart, he wouldn't be flunking three classes.

"We're going to miss Dad," Ronnie called. His voice trembled slightly. He hoped Tim hadn't noticed.

"Just a minute."

"I ain't got a minute."

"You chicken or something?"

That did it. Ronnie balled up his fists and hurried to the spot where Tim had entered the churchyard. He set his bookbag beside Tim's and stepped among the crushed weeds. Furry ropes of poison sumac veined across the ground. Red-stemmed briars bent under the snowy weight of blackberry blossoms. And Ronnie would bet a Spiderman comic that snakes slithered in that high grass along the ditch.

"Where are you?" Ronnie called into the bushes.

"Over here."

He was *in* the graveyard, the stupid little jerk. How many times had Dad told them to stay out of the graveyard?

Not that Ronnie needed reminding. But that was Tim for you. Tell him to not to touch a hot stove eye and you could smell the sizzling flesh of his fingers before you even finished your sentence.

Ronnie stooped to about Tim's height—*twerp's-eye view,* he thought—and saw the graveyard through the path that Tim had stomped. Tim was kneeling beside an old marble tombstone, looking down. He picked something up and it flashed in the sun. A bottle.

Ronnie looked past his little brother to the uneven rows of markers. Some were cracked and chipped, all of them worn around the edges. Old graves. Old dead people. So long dead that they were probably too rotten to lift themselves out of the soil and walk into the red church.

No, it wasn't a church anymore, just an old building that Lester Matheson used for storing hay. Hadn't been a church for about twenty years. Like Lester had said, pausing to let a stream of brown juice arc to the ground, then wiping his lips with the scarred stump of his thumb, "It's *people* what makes a church. Without people, and what-and-all they believe, it ain't nothing but a fancy mouse motel."

Yeah. Fancy mouse motel. Nothing scary about that, is there?

It was just like the First Baptist Church, if you really thought about it. Except the Baptist church was bigger. And the only time the Baptist church was scary was when Preacher Staymore said Ronnie needed saving or else Jesus Christ would send him to burn in hell forever.

Ronnie scrambled through the bushes. A briar snagged his *X-Files* T-shirt, the one that Melanie thought was so cool. He backed up and pulled himself free, cursing as a thorn pierced his finger. A drop of crimson welled up and he started to wipe it on his shirt, then licked it away instead.

Tim put the bottle down and picked up something else. A magazine. Its pages fluttered in the breeze. Ronnie stepped clear of the brush and stood up.

So he was in the graveyard. No big deal. And if he kept his eyes straight ahead, he wouldn't even have to see the fancy mouse motel. But then he forgot all about trying not to be scared, because of what Tim had in his hands.

As Ronnie came beside him, Tim snapped the magazine closed. But not before Ronnie had gotten a good look at the pale flesh spread along the pages. Timmy's cheeks turned pink. He had found a *Playboy*.

"Give me that," Ronnie said.

Tim faced his brother and put the magazine behind his back. "I—I'm the one who found it."

"Yeah, and you don't even know what it is, do you?"

Tim stared at the ground. "A naked-woman book."

Ronnie started to laugh, but it choked off as he looked around the graveyard. "Where did you learn about girlie magazines?"

"Whizzer. He showed one to us behind the gym during recess."

"Probably charged you a dollar a peek."

"No, just a quarter."

"Give it here, or I'll tell Mom."

"No, you won't."

"Will, too."

"What are you going to tell her? That I found a naked-woman book and wouldn't let you see it?"

Ronnie grimaced. *Score one for dingle-dork.* He thought about jumping Tim and taking the magazine by force, but there was no need to hurry. Tricking him out of it would be a lot more fun. But he didn't want to stand around in the creepy graveyard and negotiate.

He looked at the other stuff scattered on the grass around the tombstone. The bottle had a square base and a black screw top. A few inches of golden-brown liquid were lying in the bottom. He knew it was liquor because of the turkey on the label. It was the kind that Aunt Donna drank. But Ronnie didn't want to think about Aunt Donna almost as much as he didn't want to think about being scared.

A green baseball cap lay upside down beside the tombstone. The sweatband was stained a dark gray, and the bill was so severely cupped that it came to a frayed point. Only one person rolled up their cap bill that way. Ronnie nudged the cap over with his foot. A John Deere cap. That cinched it.

"It's Boonie Houck's," Ronnie said. But Boonie never went anywhere without his cap. Kept it pulled down to the bushy line of his single eyebrow, his eyes gleaming under the shade of the bill like wet ball bearings. He probably even showered and slept with the cap plastered to the top of his wide head.

A crumpled potato chip bag quivered beside the cap, fluttering in the breeze. It was held in place by an unopened can of Coca-Cola. The blind eye of a flashlight peeked out from under the edge of the chip bag.

Ronnie bent down and saw a flash of silver. Money. He picked up two dimes and a dull nickel. A couple of pennies were in the grass, but he left them. He straightened up.

"I'll give you twenty-five cents for the magazine," he said.

Tim backed away with his hands still behind him. He moved into the shadow of a crude stone monument, made of two pillars holding up a crosspiece. On the crosspiece was a weathered planter. A brittle sheaf of brown tulips stabbed up from the potting soil.

Tulips. So somebody had minded the graveyard at least once since winter. Probably Lester. Lester owned the property and kept the grass trimmed, but did that mean the tobacco-chewing farmer had to pay respects to those buried here? Did the dead folks come with the property deed?

But Ronnie forgot all that, because he accidentally looked over Tim's shoulder. The red church was framed up perfectly by the stone pillars.

No, not *accidentally. You* wanted *to see it. Your eyes have been crawling right toward it the whole time you've been in the graveyard.*

The church sat on a broad stack of creek stones

that were bleached yellow and white by eons of running water. A few of the stones had tumbled away, revealing gaps of darkness beneath the structure. The church looked a little wobbly, as if a strong wind might send it roof-over-joist down the hill.

The creepy tree stood tall and gangly by the door. Ronnie didn't believe Whizzer's story about the tree. But if even half of it were true—

"A quarter? I can take it to school and make five bucks," Tim said.

The magazine. Ronnie didn't care about the magazine anymore. "Come on. Let's get out of here."

"You're going to take it from me, ain't you?"

"No. Dad's supposed to be coming over, that's all. I don't want to miss him."

Tim suddenly took another step backward, his eyes wide.

Ronnie pointed, trying to warn him about the monument. Tim spun and bumped into one of the pillars, shaking the crosspiece. The concrete planter tipped over, sending a shower of dry black dirt onto Tim's head. The planter rolled toward the edge of the crosspiece.

"Look out," Ronnie yelled.

Tim pushed himself away from the pillar, but the entire monument toppled as if in slow motion. The heavy crosspiece was going to squash Tim's head like a rotten watermelon.

Ronnie's limbs unlocked and he leaped for Tim. Something caught his foot and he tripped, falling on his stomach. The air rushed from his lungs with a whoosh, and the smell of cut grass crowded his nostrils. He tasted blood, and his tongue found the gash on the inside of his lip just as he rediscovered how to breathe.

A dull cracking noise echoed across the graveyard.

Ronnie tilted his neck up just in time to see the planter bust open on the monument's base. Tim gave a squeak of surprise as dingy chunks of concrete rained across his chest. The pillars fell in opposite directions, the one on Tim's side catching on the ledge just above his head. The crosspiece twirled like a slow helicopter blade and came to rest on the pillar above Tim's legs.

Ronnie tried to crawl to Tim, but his shoe was still snagged. "You okay?"

Tim was crying. At least that meant he was still alive.

Ronnie kicked his foot. He looked back to his shoe—

No no no

—red raw burger hand.

An arm had reached around the tombstone, a bloody arm, the knotty fingers forming a talon around his sneaker. The wet, gleaming bone of one knuckle hooked the laces.

Deadghostdeadghost

He forgot that he'd learned how to breathe. He kicked at the hand, spun over on his rear, and tried to crab-crawl away. The hand wouldn't let go. Tears stung his eyes as he stomped his other foot against the ragged grasping thing.

"Help me," Ronnie yelled, at the same time that Tim moaned his own plea for help.

Whizzer's words careened across Ronnie's mind, joining the jumble of broken thoughts: *They trap ya, then they get ya.*

"Ronnie," came Tim's weak whine.

Ronnie wriggled like a speared eel, forcing his eyes along the slick wrist to the arm that was swathed in ragged flannel.

Flannel?

His skewed carousel of thoughts ground to a halt.

Why would a deadghost thing be wearing flannel?

The arm was attached to a bulk of something behind the tombstone.

The hand clutched tightly at nothing but air, then quivered and relaxed. Ronnie scrambled away as the fingers uncurled. Blood pooled in the shallow cup of the palm.

Ronnie reached Tim and began removing the chunks of concrete from his little brother's stomach. "You okay?"

Tim nodded, charcoal streaks of mud on his face where his tears had rolled through the sprinkling of potting soil. One cheek had a red scrape across it, but otherwise he looked unharmed. Ronnie kept looking back to the mangled arm and whatever was behind the tombstone. The hand was still, the sun drying the blood on the clotted palm. A shiny fly landed and drank.

Ronnie dragged Tim free of the toppled concrete. They both stood, Tim wiping the powdery grit from the front of his shirt. "Mom's going to kill me. . . ." he began, then saw the arm. "What in heck . . . ?"

Ronnie stepped toward the tombstone, his heart hammering in his ears.

Over his pulse, he could hear Whizzer: *They got livers for eyes.*

Ronnie veered toward the edge of the graveyard, Tim close behind.

"When I say run . . ." Ronnie whispered, his throat thick.

"L-looky there," Tim said.

Dorkwad didn't have enough brains to be scared. But Ronnie looked. He couldn't help it.

The body was crowded against the tombstone, the flannel shirt shredded, showing scoured flesh. The head was pressed against the white marble, the neck arched at a crazy angle. A thread of blood trailed from the matted beard to the ground.

"Boonie," Ronnie said, his voice barely as loud as the wind in the oak leaves.

There was a path trampled in the grass, coming from the underbrush that girded the graveyard. Boonie must have crawled out of the weeds. And whatever had done that to him might still be in the stand of trees. Ronnie flicked his eyes from Boonie to the church. Had something fluttered in the belfry?

A bird, a bird, *you idiot.*

Not the thing that Whizzer said lived in the red church.

Not the thing that trapped you and then got you, not the thing that had wings and claws and livers for eyes, not the thing that had made a mess of Boonie Houck's face.

And then Ronnie was running, tearing through the undergrowth, barely aware of the briars grabbing at his face and arms, of the scrub locust that pierced his skin, of the tree branches that raked at his eyes. He heard Tim behind him—at least he *hoped* it was Tim, but he wasn't about to turn around and check, because now he was on the gravel road, his legs were pumping in the rhythm of fear—*Not the thing, not the thing, not the thing*—and he didn't pause to breathe, even as he passed Lester Matheson, who was on his tractor in the middle of a hayfield, even as he passed the Potter farm, even when geezery Zeb Potter hollered out Ronnie's name from his shaded front porch, even as Zeb's hound cut loose with an uneven bray, even as Ronnie jumped the barbed wire that marked off the boundary of the Day property, even as the rusty tin roof of home came into view, even as he saw Dad's Ranger in the driveway, even as he tripped over the footbridge and saw the sharp, glistening rocks of the creek bed below, and as he fell he realized he'd hit another turning point, found yet another way for the world to end, but at least *this* end wasn't as bad as whatever had shown Boonie Houck the exit door from everywhere.

TWO

"Why didn't you tell me?"

"Like you'd understand? You didn't understand the first time." Linda Day balled her hands into fists. She could smell beer on David's breath.

Drunk at three o'clock, she thought. *Doesn't he know that the body is sacred? If only he were more like Archer.*

David closed in on her. She backed against the kitchen table. He'd never hit her in their fifteen years of marriage. But his face had never set in such a mix of hurt and anger before, either.

He waved the papers in the air, his thin lips crawling into a sneer. "A lie. All those years . . . ."

God, he wasn't going to cry, was he? Mr. Ain't-Nothing-It'll-Heal that time he flipped the tractor and had his forearm bone poking through his denim jacket?

She looked into his wet brown eyes. Who was he? What did she *really* know about him? Sure, they'd gone to high school together, were both in the Future Farmers of America, lost it together one fumbling Friday night in the pines above the Pickett High football field, never really dated anybody else, got married like everybody expected and—after that little California interlude—settled down on the

Gregg family farm after cancer had chewed her father's lungs away.

More than half of their lives. Not nearly enough time to figure David out.

"Don't start that," she said.

"I ain't the one who started it. You said when we got married that all that foolishness was over and done with."

"I thought it was."

"Thought it was?" he mocked. His face twisted.

"I was going to tell you."

"When? After you'd sneaked another hundred lies past me?"

Linda looked away, anywhere but at his burning, red-rimmed eyes. The stick margarine on the counter was losing its sharp edges in the heat. Two black flies were playing hopscotch on the kitchen window screen. The roses that made a pattern on the yellowed wallpaper looked as if they needed watering. "It's not like that."

"Sure, it ain't." A mist of Pabst Blue Ribbon came out with his words. "When a man's wife gets love letters from another man, why, that's nothing to worry about, is it?"

"So you read them."

"Course I read them." He stepped closer, looming over her, six-three and shoulders broadened by lifting ten thousand bales of hay.

"Then maybe you noticed that the word 'love' isn't in a single one of them."

He stopped in his tracks. Linda thought about retreating to the hall entrance, but she was trying hard not to show fear. Archer said fear was for the meek, them that huddled at the feet of Christ.

David's brow lowered. "There's lots of different kinds of love."

She studied his face. Twice-broken nose. A white scar in one corner of his mouth. A strong chin, the kind you could forge steel with. Skin browned by years of working in the sun. Had she ever really loved the man who wore that face?

"There's only one kind of love," she said. "The kind we had."

"The kind you and *Archer* had."

"David, please listen."

He reached out. She held her breath and leaned away. But he didn't touch her, only swept the can of Maxwell House from the table behind her. It bounced off the cabinet under the sink and the lid flew off, sending a shower of brown granules onto the vinyl floor. The rich smell of the coffee drowned out David's sweet-sour breath.

His teeth were showing. Broad and blunt. Pressed together so tightly that his jaw trembled.

Linda scooted along the edge of the table to her right. There was a knife on the counter, a skin of dried cheese dulling the flash of the blade. If she had to—

But David turned away, slumped, his shoulders quivering.

David never cried, at least not in front of her. But since he'd found the letters, he was doing a lot of things he'd never done before. Like drinking heavily. Like leaving her.

"Hon—" She caught herself. "David?"

His work boots drummed the floor as he strode away. He paused at the back door and turned, looking down at the letters in his hand. Tears had shimmied down one side of his face, but his voice was quiet, resigned. "Archer McFall. Pretty funny. Who'd you put up to doing it?"

"Doing what?"

"We both know it ain't Archer, so quit lying. Is it one of your buddies from California?"

Linda shook her head. *He doesn't understand. And I had hopes that he would join us.* "No, it's nobody."

"Nobody? *Nobody* who's been writing you letters while dumb-and-happy David Day runs a hammer and eats sawdust for ten hours a day, only *he* don't mind because he's got a wonderful family waiting at home each night waiting to shower him with love and bullshit?"

His bulk filled the door frame, blocking her view of the barn and the pasture beyond. The room darkened as a cloud passed over the sun. "I told you, it's not the way you think," she said.

"Sure. Archer McFall just happened to walk back into your life at the exact same time that you started to get the letters. That's a mighty big coincidence."

"This isn't about Archer or the Temple. It's about *us.*"

He flapped the letters again. "If it's about us, how come you didn't tell me about these?"

"I was going to."

"When? After hell finished freezing over?"

"When I thought you were ready to listen."

"You mean when I was ready to swallow it hook, line, and sinker. And get reeled into that mess the same as you. I thought you learned your lesson the last time."

The cloud passed, and the sun lit up the mottled spots on the window. She looked past them to the reddish square of the garden, at the little rows of green that were starting their seasonal push to the sky, then looked beyond to the wedge of mountains that kept North Carolina from slopping over into Tennessee. Two hundred acres of Gregg land, every inch of it stony and stained, every ash and birch and poplar stitched to her skin, every gallon of creek water running through her veins like blood. She was as old-family as anybody, and the old families belonged to the McFalls.

"It's only letters," she said. "That doesn't mean I'm going back in."

"Why did you ever have to fall for it in the first place?"

"That was nearly twenty years ago. I was a different person then. *We* were different people."

"No, *you* were different. I'm still the same. Just a mountain hick who thinks that if you say your prayers and live right, then nobody can break you down. But I reckon I was wrong."

"You can't still blame me for that, can you?" But his eyes answered her question by becoming hard and narrow. "Don't you know how terrible I thought it was to be trapped here in Whispering Pines forever? Stay around and squirt out seven kids with nothing to look forward to but the next growing season? To be like my mother with her fingers as knobby as pea pods from all the canning she did? What kind of life is *that?*"

"It's good enough for me. I didn't need to run off to California."

"I must have asked you a dozen times to come with me."

"And I asked you a dozen and one times to stay."

"You were just afraid you'd lose me."

He hung his head and shook it slowly. "I reckon I did," he said, barely above a whisper. "Only it took me this long to find out."

"The kids will be home soon," she said. "Ronnie's been looking forward to seeing you."

He held up the letters again. "You're not going to

drag them into this mess, are you? Because, so help me, if you do—"

The threat hung in the air like an ax.

"Archer's not like that." Linda said it as if she only half-believed her own words.

"You said the group broke up."

"I . . . Most of us left. I don't know. When they said he was dead, I—"

"He's dead. Now, the question is, who's trying to bring back *this*?" David held up one of the letters, more for effect than anything. Because Linda knew perfectly well what was on the letter.

She could see the symbol from across the room, even though it was bunched into the top right corner. It looked like one of those Egyptian symbols, only the cross was topped with two loops. Two suns. The Temple of the Two Suns.

Not that she needed to see it, because she was sure now that it had been seared into her brain, that its power had reached over years and across three thousand miles and through the thick white walls of her renewed faith in Jesus. Because, after all, there was only one true savior. And his name was Archer McFall.

If only David would open his heart. Sure, he'd been born with Baptist blood, he'd been dipped in the river below the red church so that his sins would be washed away, he'd given his ten percent, but there was so much more to faith than the rituals and scriptures and prayers. Her own heart was swelling again, budding, unfolding like a flower under a bright sun. No, under two suns. Twice the love. If only she could share that with David. But he wouldn't understand. He was as blinded by Jesus as everybody else was.

David watched her carefully, waiting for her reaction. She swallowed her smile and let her face slacken.

"The Temple," he said in a sneer. "You promised you were over it. But I guess I'm the fool."

"He's not asking for money."

David laughed, a bitter sound. He rubbed his forehead with his right hand. "Probably the only thing he's not asking for, whoever it is."

"Since you read the letters, you know exactly what he wants."

"Yeah." He held up one of the letters. " 'We've missed you, sister,' " he read.

"And that's all."

" 'There will come great trials, but we bathe in the light of faith.' " He shuffled to the next letter. " 'The stone is rolled away.' "

"Where's the love in that?" Linda was straining to show disinterest. David wasn't from one of the old families. She had been a fool to think Archer would accept him, anyway.

"Where's the love? Where's the *love?* Why, right there on the bottom, where it says 'Forever Yours, Archer McFall.' On every single one of them."

"Maybe he didn't die. Or maybe somebody started up the group again and is using his name. That's all it is. I don't care one way or another."

But I do care. I've always cared, even when you thought you and your Christian friends had "cured" me. There was always a little room in my heart tucked away for nobody but Archer.

David's eyes had cleared a little as he sobered, but kept their bright ferocity. "You don't care so much that you didn't even bother to throw the letters away, huh?"

"Don't matter none to me."

"That so?" David started to crumple the letters into a ball.

Linda's mouth opened, and her arm reached out of its own accord.

David smiled, but it was a sick smile, the kind worn by a reluctant martyr. He crushed the paper into a hard wad of pulp and tossed it on the floor at her feet. "I seen him come around. Last week. Laid out of work just so I could hide up in the hills and watch the house. Just me and a six-pack. Mostly I was curious if you were sending out any letters yourself."

"You bastard."

David licked his lips. "Is ten o'clock the regular meeting time?"

Linda felt the blood drain from her face. How much did he know?

"Got himself a Mercedes. I guess this 'cult' business pays pretty good."

"It wasn't—" Linda started.

David nodded. "I know. It wasn't Archer McFall. Then why don't you tell me who it really was?"

Linda wondered how many times David had watched the house from the woods. Or if she could trust anything he said.

Trust. That was a good one.

David slowly approached her. She was like a deer frozen in the headlights of his hate. She looked down just as his boot flattened the wad of letters.

"How long?" he said, and his eyes were welling with tears again. As if the reservoir had been filling all his life and, finally full, now had to leak a little or bust.

"It's not like that." She looked again at the butcher knife on the counter, close to tears herself.

He took another menacing step. "I wondered why

you been acting strange lately. And why you ain't been up to going to church."

Linda grabbed a gulp of air and scooted from the table to the kitchen counter. David was close behind her and caught her when she spun. His hands were like steel hooks in her upper arms, holding her firmly but not squeezing hard enough to bruise.

She stared at his stranger's face with its wide eyes. She'd never noticed how deep the two creases on his forehead were. The hard planes of his cheeks were patched with stubble. He looked old, as if all his thirty-seven years had dog-piled him these last few weeks.

"Tell me who it is," he said.

She shuddered with the force of his grip. Those hands had touched her so tenderly in the night, had softly stroked her belly when she was pregnant with the boys, had tucked daisies behind her ears when they fooled around in the hayfield. But now they were cruel, the caresses forgotten, the passion in them of a different kind.

She turned her face away, afraid that he'd see the fear in her eyes. The knife was beside a bowl of melted ice cream, within reach. But David grabbed her chin and twisted her eyes back to his.

Archer had warned her what the price of belief would be. Persecution. Pain. The loss of everything human. She could hear Archer's voice now, pouring from the geysers of her heart. *There will come great trials. And great sacrifices. Because sacrifice is the currency of God.*

But the reward was greater than the sacrifice. Belief paid back a hundredfold. Devotion now brought Archer's steadfast love unto the fourth generation. Surrendering to him meant that her offspring would reap the harvest. She had been telling herself that ever since Archer and the Temple of the Two Suns reclaimed her heart. And she reminded herself now, locked in David's grip.

He'd never hurt her before. But Archer said those who didn't understand always fell back on violence, because violence was the way of their God. That was why the world had to end. From the ashes of their heavenfire would come—

"Who *is* it?" he asked.

She grunted through her clenched teeth. David relaxed his grip until her mouth could move. "Ahh— Archer."

"Archer. Don't lie to me, damn it." He clamped his fingers tight again.

She fumbled with her left hand, running it along the edge of the counter. She felt the cool rim of the bowl. If only she could keep him talking. "It is. And he doesn't want me . . . that way."

"It can't be Archer."

"He's come back."

David choked on a laugh. "The second coming. They really *do* have you again, don't they?"

"No, I meant he's come back to Whispering Pines." Her hand went around the bowl and touched wood. Her fingers crawled along the knife's handle. Archer said sometimes you had to fight fire with fire, even if it meant descending down to their level. Even if it was a sin.

"You said he was *dead.*"

"They said . . . I thought . . . I never saw his body."

"It's not Archer."

"It *is.* You know I'd never cheat on you."

He released her arm with his left hand and drew his arm back. He was going to hit her. She snatched at the butcher knife, then had it in her palm, her fingers around it, and all the old memories flooded back, all the energy and power and purity that Archer promised and delivered. She raised the knife.

David saw it and stepped away easily. The blade sliced the air a foot from his face. He lurched forward and caught her wrist on the downstroke. The knife clattered to the floor.

They both looked at it. Silence crowded the room like death crowded a coffin.

A chicken clucked out in the barnyard. Somewhere over the hill, in the direction of the Potter farm, a hound dog let out one brassy howl. A tractor engine murmured in the far distance. The clock in the living room ticked six times, seven, eight. David reached out with the toe of his boot and kicked the knife into the corner.

He exhaled, deflating his rage. "So it's come to this."

"I didn't mean to—"

"Is that what they preach? Stabbing your own husband?"

"I . . . you scared me." The tears erupted from her eyes even as David's tears dried up, probably for good. "I thought you were going to hit me."

"Yeah." He was calm again, walking dead, a man who wouldn't harm a fly. "I guess you never could trust me, could you? Not the way you could trust them."

"I didn't lie to you."

"Which time?"

Archer was right. Pain was a steep price. Faith required sacrifice. "When we got married, and I said I was through. I believed it then."

"And I believed it, too. Guess you're not the only fool in the family."

"Please, David. Don't make this any worse than it has to be."

"Fine." He spread his arms in surrender. "I guess it don't matter none who it is. I just don't see why you had to make up this stuff about the cult."

"It's not a cult."

"And Archer McFall just happens to walk back into your life twenty years after he died. You really must be crazy, or else you think I am."

Archer always said he would return. How could she ever have doubted him?

Easy. You had your world taken away from you, and you came back to this safe, normal, God-fearing life and slipped into it like a second skin. You hid away your heart like it was separate from loving and mothering and living. But this normal life was all a lie, wasn't it? Maybe David was right, even if he was right about the wrong thing.

"I reckon I'll get the kids, then," he said, and a chill sank into her, deep-freezing her bones.

"No." She went to him.

"Any judge in the land would give me custody. Don't worry. I won't make no claim on the farm. That's rightly yours as a Gregg, if for no other reason."

"Not the kids," she wailed. She pounded her fists on his chest. He didn't try to stop her.

The blows softened and she collapsed, grabbing his shirt for support. He kept her from falling. She felt nothing in his embrace.

"How are we going to tell the boys about us?" She sniffled.

"They already know. They ain't dumb."

"I thought . . . I don't know what I thought." But Linda knew exactly what she thought. She thought the children were hers, to love and protect and introduce to the joys of worship in the Temple of the

Two Suns. To deliver unto Archer, so the generations would be spared.

"Now quit your crying. They'll be here any minute."

Damn him for trying to be strong. Acting like she didn't matter. Her eyes went to the knife in the corner.

"Don't do it, Linda. I'd hate for that to come up at the custody hearing."

Jesus-loving bastard. But she wouldn't lose hope. Archer would know what to do. Archer would—

"Did you hear that?" David asked, releasing her.

"Hear what?" She rubbed her arms, trying to wipe away the memory of his rough touch.

David went to the door. Linda thought about the knife. No, if she used the knife, they'd take the kids away for sure. She heard something that sounded like a calf caught in a crabapple thicket and bawling its heart out.

"It's Ronnie," David said, then leaped off the porch and ran toward the creek that divided a stretch of pasture from the front yard.

Ronnie raced across the pasture, moaning and wailing, waving his arms. Tim was farther back, running down the road, and even from that distance Linda saw that her youngest boy had lost his glasses.

Ronnie reached the little wooden footbridge that spanned the creek, a bridge that was nothing more than some pallet planks laid across two locust poles. His foot caught in a gap in the planks and his scream went an octave higher as he plummeted into the rocky creek bed. Her own shout caught in her throat.

David reached the creek and jumped down to where Ronnie lay. Linda scrambled down the bank after him. Ronnie was facedown, his legs in the shallow water. His head rested on a large flat stone. A trail of blood ran down the surface of the rock and dribbled into the creek, where it was quickly swept away.

"Don't move him," Linda shouted.

David gave her a look, then knelt beside Ronnie. The boy moaned and lifted his head. Blood oozed from his nose. His lip was swollen.

He moaned again.

"What?" David said.

This time Linda was close enough to hear what he was saying.

Ronnie's lips parted again. "Uhr—red church."

His eyes were looking past both of them, seeing nothing, seeing too much.

THREE

Sheriff Frank Littlefield looked up the hill at the church and the monstrous dogwood that hovered beside it like a guardian. He'd always hated that tree, ever since he was a boy. It hadn't changed much since the last time he'd set foot in the graveyard. But *he* had, the world had, and Boonie most definitely had.

The young get old and the dead get deader, he thought as he studied the shadowed belfry for movement.

"What do you figure done it?" asked Dr. Perry Hoyle, the Pickett County medical examiner.

Littlefield didn't turn to face the man immediately. Instead, he squinted past the church steeple to the sun setting behind the crippled cross. The cross threw a long jagged shadow over the cemetery green. Somebody was cutting hay. Littlefield could smell the crush of grass in the wind. He scratched at his buzz cut. "You're the ME."

"Wild animal, that's my guess. Mountain lion, maybe. Or a black bear."

"Sure it wasn't somebody with a knife or an ax?"

"Not real likely. Wounds are too jagged, for one thing."

Littlefield exhaled in relief. "So I guess we can't call it a murder."

"Probably not."

One of the deputies was vomiting in the weeds at the edge of the cemetery.

"Don't get that mixed in with the evidence," Littlefield hollered at him. He turned back to Hoyle. "Black bear wouldn't attack a man unless her cubs were threatened. And it'd have to be a mighty big mountain lion."

"They get up to two hundred pounds."

"But they're extinct up here."

"One of them college professors down at Westridge believes mountain lions are making their way back to these parts."

Littlefield resumed rubbing his scalp. He'd just had it trimmed at Ray's, a good clipper job that let the wind and sun get right to the scalp. The department thought he wore the short style to give himself a ramrod appearance, but the truth was, he kind of liked the shape of his skull. And his hat fit better when he went to the Borderline Tavern to kick up his heels to some Friday-night country music. Boonie used to dance at the Borderline, too. Back when he still had feet.

The two men stood quietly and looked at the church for a moment. "Never been many happy times here," Hoyle said.

Littlefield didn't rise to the bait. He was annoyed that Hoyle would fish those waters. Some things were for nothing but forgetting. He hardened his face against the past as easily as if he'd slipped on a plastic superhero mask.

"Who found the body?" Hoyle hurriedly asked.

"Couple of kids who live down the road. They were walking home from school this afternoon."

"Must have bothered them something awful."

"Hell, it's bothering *me,* and you know I've seen a few ripe ones."

"What did they tell you?"

"The older one, he's about thirteen, fell running home and busted his face up. He'll be all right, but for some reason it got to him worse than it did the little one. Kept mumbling 'the red church' over and over again."

"How old's the little one?"

"Nine. Said he saw some stuff laying in the grave-yard and went through the bushes to have a look. He said he saw a cap and a flashlight and a bottle of liquor, but he didn't touch any of it. Ronnie, the thirteen-year-old, came back to see what was taking so long, and that's when the victim must have dragged himself out from the bushes and grabbed ahold of Ronnie."

Littlefield didn't like calling Boonie Houck a victim. Boonie was a good fellow. A little bit creepy and plenty lazy, but he was in church of a Sunday morning and was known to vote Republican. Nobody deserved to die this way.

Hoyle looked like he could use a cup of coffee, maybe with a few drops of brandy in it. "He lived a lot longer than he should have with those kinds of wounds. My guess is he was attacked sometime in the early morning, between midnight and sunup."

Littlefield's stomach rolled a little. How did Boonie feel lying in the weeds, wondering about the wound between his legs, knowing that whatever had ripped him up was somewhere out there in the dark? "You going to send him to the state ME's office?"

"Reckon I ought to. They can do a better job of guessing than I can." Hoyle pulled a handkerchief from his jacket pocket and wiped the sweat from his bald head. "The press is going to want to know something."

"Wonderful."

"Plus, if it is a wild animal, might be some rabies going around. That could make an animal go nuts and do something like this."

"We haven't had that up here in a long time, either."

"Times change."

The sheriff nodded. *You used to have hair, and I used to be worth a damn. Boonie used to be alive, and the red church used to be white.*

"Let me know when you're ready to drive him down," Littlefield said. "We'll get the pieces together."

He didn't envy Hoyle. The drive to Chapel Hill took about four hours. Boonie would be kicking up a mean stench by the time the trip was over. But Littlefield decided he ought to save his pity. Unlike Boonie, at least Hoyle would be coming back.

Littlefield patted the medical examiner on the shoulder and went to examine the articles lying on the grass in clear plastic bags. He bent over the bag that held a porn magazine. He fought an odd urge to flip through the pages.

A camera flash went off. "Could you please move to one side, Sheriff?"

He looked up. Det. Sgt. Sheila Storie waved her arm. She was taking photos of the crime scene.

No, not a crime scene, Littlefield had to remind himself. *An accident. A tragic, violent, unexplained accident.*

The kind of thing that happened too often in Whispering Pines. But Littlefield was relieved that a psycho with a set of Ginsu knives wasn't on the loose in his jurisdiction. They'd had one of those down the mountain in Shady Valley a few years back, and the case was never solved. *Damned inept city cops.*

He already knew he was going to put Storie in charge of the investigation. When they arrived and found the mess, she hadn't even blinked, just got out her clipboard and tape measure and went to work. She was too young to be so unmoved by death, in Littlefield's opinion. But maybe she was a little bit like him. Maybe it was the kind of thing that made them cops.

Got to keep yourself outside of it all. Don't let them get to you. No matter what they do, no matter what the world takes from you.

"What do you make of it?" he asked Storie.

Her eyes were blue enough to hide everything, as unrevealing as her camera lens. "Extensive trauma. Death probably due to exsanguination."

Storie's educated flatland accent always surprised him, even though he should have been used to it by now. Most people took her for a local until they heard her speak. "That's what Hoyle says. Only he calls it 'bled to death.' "

"Unless shock got him first. Same to the subject either way. I haven't seen this much blood since those driver's ed films they show in high school." She took two steps to her right and snapped another picture, then let the camera hang by its strap over her chest.

"Must have taken a while. You looked over in the bushes where he crawled after the attack?"

"Yes, sir. He left a few scraps."

Littlefield swallowed a knot of nausea.

"Footprints go from this grave marker here, where the boys said they found the stuff. They're deep, see?" She pointed to the pressed grass. The smaller prints of the boys were visible as well. But Boonie's were clearly marked by the thick treads of his boots.

"That means he was running, right?"

"He must have seen or heard whatever it was and gotten scared. He was probably attacked just before he started running."

"Why do you say that?"

"Blood here is coagulated almost to powder. The blood over there"—she waved to the slick trail of slime where Boonie had crawled out of the bushes— "isn't as oxidized."

Littlefield nodded and passed his hand over his scalp. The breeze shifted and he could smell Boonie now. A person never got used to the odor of death. The detective didn't even wrinkle her nose.

"Hoyle thinks it's a mountain lion," Littlefield said.

She shook her head. Her brown hair was a couple of inches past regulation and swished over her shoulders. "Wild animals typically go for the throat if they're treating something as prey. There are a few wounds around the eyes, but those are no more devastating than the other injuries. And it doesn't look like the subject had an animal cornered so that it would be forced to defend itself."

Littlefield was constantly amazed by the level of instruction that new officers received. A college degree in Criminal Justice, for starters. Then state training, not to mention extra seminars along the way. Littlefield had long since quit going to those things, at least the ones that didn't help him politically.

Or maybe Storie was a little too educated for her own good. Frank knew that as a female in a rural department, she had to be twice as smart and icy and sarcastic as everybody else. She couldn't go out for after-shift beers.

Pay attention, damn it. In case you're going senile and

need a reminder, one of your constituents is gathering flies long before his natural time.

"So you don't necessarily hold to the wild-animal-attack theory?" he asked.

"I'm not saying that. I'm just saying that if it *was* an animal, its behavior was unnatural." She looked across the stretch of tombstones to where the cemetery ended near the forest. Her brow furrowed.

"What is it?" Littlefield asked.

"The thing that bothers me the most."

If Storie's bothered . . . A small chill wended its way up Littlefield's spinal column and settled in the base of his neck.

"No animal tracks," she said.

The sheriff's jaw tightened. So that was what had been bothering him ever since he'd first walked the scene. An animal's claws would have ripped chunks out of the ground, especially if it were attacking.

"Damn," he whispered.

"No tracks means no easy answers." She almost sounded pleased. "There are no other human footprints, either."

Storie had cracked a big case last year, when an ex-cop had hauled a body up to the mountains for disposal. Perp was a big goofy guy who went around bragging about how he'd never get caught. Well, Storie set her nose on his trail and nailed him so hard that his lawyers had to recite scripture in the courtroom to save him from a lethal injection. The conviction got statewide coverage, and Storie's picture was in both the local papers.

This looked like it might be another of those high-profile mysteries that, if she solved it, would make her a legitimate candidate for sheriff. If she ever ran against him, she'd have him beat all to hell on looks. Her accent would hurt her some, though.

"Tell me, Sergeant. What do you think did it?" he asked.

"I can honestly say I have no idea, sir." She folded her arms over the camera.

"Any chance that somebody did it with a sharp weapon, without leaving footprints that we could see?"

"The pattern of the wounds seems random at first glance. But what bugs me is the ritualistic nature of the injured areas."

Areas? Littlefield wanted to remind Storie that those body parts were once near and dear to Boonie Houck. But he only nodded at her to continue.

"Look at the major wounds. First, there's the eyes."

"We haven't found them yet."

"Exactly. That's an inconvenient spot for a rampaging animal to reach. In any event, it's unlikely that a claw would take both eyes."

"Unless they were shining, and somehow attracted the animal's attention. The moon was over half-full last night."

"Okay. Let's go on to the hand. Seems like an animal would have started gnawing at a softer spot."

"Maybe it did."

"That brings us to the fatal wound."

"Now, that's not been determined yet." Littlefield felt the tingle of blood rushing to his cheeks.

"I saw the rip in the front of his pants." She lifted the camera. "I took pictures, remember?"

"Guess so." His tongue felt thick.

"With the loss of that much blood, I'm amazed he survived as long as he did."

"You said the wounds were ritualistic. What's that got to do with his . . . er . . ."

"Penis, Sheriff. You can say it in the company of a woman these days."

"Of course." His face grew warmer with embarrassment. He looked across the mountains. He would love to be walking a stream right now, flicking a hand-tied fly across the silver currents, the smell of wet stone and rotted loam in his nostrils. Alone. Anywhere but here with blood and the red church and Sheila Storie. "So what does it mean?"

"It may mean nothing. Or it may mean we have a deviant personality on the loose." The flash of her eyes gave away her belief in the latter. Or maybe she was only hopeful.

"Is it because we haven't found the . . . other part, either?"

"I don't know yet."

"Think we ought to call in the state boys?" Littlefield knew Storie would bristle at turning the case over to the State Bureau of Investigation. She would want a shot first.

"That's your decision, Sheriff."

"I suppose we'll have to wait for the state medical examiner's report. Hoyle's sending him down to Chapel Hill."

"Good."

Littlefield tried to read her expression. But the sun was in her face, so her half-closed eyes didn't give away anything. He knew she thought Perry Hoyle had about as much forensic sophistication as a hog butcher. The whole department was probably a joke to her. Well, she was a flatlander, anyway. "Hoyle doesn't think the wounds were made by a weapon."

"You asked for my opinion, sir."

Littlefield looked up the hill at the church. Suddenly he felt as if someone had reached an icy hand down his throat and squeezed his heart. His brother Samuel was on the roof of the church, waving and smiling.

His dead brother Samuel.

Littlefield blinked, then saw that the illusion was only a mossy patch on the shingles.

He sighed. "I'm putting you in charge of the investigation."

Storie almost smiled. "I'll do my best, sir."

Littlefield nodded and stepped over the strings that marked off grids at the scene. He knelt by the toppled monument. "What do you make of this?"

"The boys' footprints lead over here. I'd guess vandalism. Tipping tombstones is an old favorite. Maybe they were messing around when the subject heard them and tried to crawl out of the weeds."

"Seems like they would have heard Boonie yelling." He stopped himself. Boonie wouldn't have called out, at least in nothing more articulate than a groan. Boonie's tongue had been taken, too.

Hoyle rescued him from his embarrassment. "We're ready over here, Sheriff," the ME called. Littlefield winced and started to turn.

"I'll handle it, sir," Storie said. "It's my case, remember? I might see something I missed the first two times."

She was right. Littlefield's shoulders slumped a little in relief. He hoped Storie hadn't noticed, but she didn't miss much. She had detective's eyes, even if they were easier to look at than look through. "Go ahead."

Littlefield headed across the cemetery and up the hill toward the red church. He glanced at the markers as he passed, some so worn he could barely make out the names. Some were nothing more than stumps of broken granite. Other graves were probably forgotten altogether, just the silent powder of bones under a skin of grass.

The ground was soft under his feet—good mountain soil, as black as coal dust. Almost a shame to waste it on a graveyard. But people had to be buried somewhere, and to the dead, maybe the most fertile soil in the world wasn't comfort enough. Maybe his kid brother Samuel had yet to settle into eternal rest.

The names on the markers read like a Who's Who history of this end of the county. Potter. Matheson. Absher. Buchanan. McFall. Gregg. More Picketts than you could shake a stick at.

And three Littlefields off by themselves.

He knelt by two familiar graves. His mother and father shared a single wide monument. He looked from the gray marble to a smaller marker, which had a bas-relief of a lamb chiseled in its center. Its letters were scarcely worn, and the fingerlike shadows of tree branches chilled the stone. Littlefield read the damning words without moving his lips.

Here Lies Samuel Riley Littlefield. 1968–1979.
May God Protect and Keep Him.

His heart burned in his chest and he hurried away, his eyes frantic for a distraction. He stopped by the dogwood. The thing looked like it was dying. But it had looked that way for the last forty years, and every spring it managed to poke a few more blossoms out of the top branches. A memory stirred and crawled from the shadows before he could beat it back.

The red church. Halloween. The night he'd seen the Hung Preacher.

The night Samuel had died.

He shuddered and the memory fell away again, safely buried. The sun was warm on his face. Down the slope, Hoyle and Storie were hauling Boonie's body to the back of the overgrown station wagon that served as the county's nonemergency ambulance.

Littlefield moved away from the tree and put a foot on the bottom of four steps that led into the church foyer. The door was large and made of solid wooden planks. The cracks between the planks were barely distinguishable due to the buildup of paint layers. Over the door was a small strip of colored glass, two deep blue rectangular planes separated by an amber pane. Those had survived the onslaught of juvenile delinquents' rocks.

The sheriff climbed the rest of the steps. The top one was a wider landing, scarred from the tailgate of Lester Matheson's truck. Littlefield examined the thick hinges and the door lock. There was a lift latch in addition to the dull brass handle. Littlefield put his hand on the cool metal.

Wonder if I need a warrant to open it? he thought. *Naw. Lester won't mind if I have a peek.*

There was a small chance that if Boonie had been murdered, some evidence might be hidden inside. Or the door might be locked, but he didn't think Lester would bother keeping up with a key just to protect a hundred bales of hay. People didn't steal out in these parts. The thieves and B&E addicts kept to Barkersville, where the rich folks had their summer homes.

Littlefield turned the knob and the catch clicked back into the cylinder. He nudged the latch up with his other hand, and as the door creaked open and the rich dust of hay hit his nostrils, he realized he hadn't set foot inside since shortly after Samuel's funeral.

Please, God, just let it be a plain old ordinary murderer. Some drunk who got mad because Boonie took two swigs

before passing the bottle instead of one. A Mexican Christ-
mas tree worker with a grudge. I'll even take a crazy if you
got one.

His palms were sweating, the way they had when
he was seventeen and he'd first heard the laughter
in the belfry.

The door opened onto a short, windowless foyer.
A shaft of light pierced the ceiling from the belfry
above.

Where the bell rope used to hang.

The bell rang in his memory, a thunderclap of
angry bronze, an echo of the night Samuel died.

The plank floor creaked as Littlefield crossed the
foyer. Golden motes of dust spiraled in the draft.
What must it have been like a century ago? The worn
wood had endured a hundred thousand crossings.
Trembling and red-faced virgin brides with their best
dresses dragging on the pine, solemn cousins come
to pay their respects to a dear departed, women in
bonnets and long swirling skirts gathering for Jubi-
lee. Littlefield could almost see the preacher at the
steps, shaking the hands of the menfolk, bowing to
the women, patting the heads of the children.

The sheriff peered up through the tiny rope hole,
an opening barely large enough for a child to scramble through. The hollow interior of the bell was full
of black shadow. But that would tell him nothing.
He returned to scanning the floor for signs of blood.

The foyer opened onto the main sanctuary. The
chill crawled up his spine again. He didn't know
whether it was caused by childhood legends, or the
chance of finding a killer hiding among the bales of
hay. For a frantic moment, he almost wished he wore
a firearm.

The bales were stacked to each side, forming a
crooked aisle down the center of the church sanctu-

ary. Lester had left the altar undisturbed, probably because lifting hay over the railing was too much work. The altar itself was small, the pulpit hardly more than a rectangular crate with a slanted top. A set of six wormy chestnut beams, hand-hewn, crossed the open A-frame overhead. The interior walls were unpainted chestnut as well. In the dim light, the woodwork had a rich, deep brown cast.

The bales were packed too tightly against the walls to afford hiding places.

Unless somebody had removed a few bales and made a hollow space inside the stacks.

He'd done that in his family's barn, when he wanted to hide out on an autumn day, or when he and his brother played hide-and-seek or army. But few hours could be stolen back then. Crops, livestock, firewood, fence mending—a long list of chores was waiting at six every morning that never got finished before dark. But back then, Littlefield had slept in dreams and not bad memories.

Nothing stirred amid the hay. The church was silent, as if waiting for a congregation to again fill it with life. Littlefield walked to the dais. The chill deepened even though the air was stuffy. A small wooden cross was attached to the top of the pulpit. Like the cross on the church steeple, it was missing a section of the crosspiece.

Littlefield leaned over the waist-high railing and looked into the corners of the altar. The small vestry off to the side held nothing but bare shelves and cobwebs. He didn't know what he expected to see. Maybe he was just trying to ease his own mind, to reassure himself that old rumors and long-ago strangeness were put to rest. Boonie was dead, and that had nothing to do with the red church or Samuel or the Hung Preacher.

As he was turning to leave, he noticed a dark stain on the dais floor. It was the kind made by a spill. Maybe Lester had stored building materials in here once. At any rate, the rust-brown stain was far too old to have been made by whatever had killed Boonie.

But something about it held his attention. The shape seemed familiar. He tilted his head, as if stumped by an inkblot in a Rorschach test. When he realized where he had seen the form before, he drew in a dusty gasp of air.

The dark shape in the belfry, that long-ago Halloween.

Littlefield strode back through the church, suddenly anxious to be in the sunshine. He was going to go with the animal theory for now. If Storie wanted to play her forensic games, that was fine. But he wouldn't allow himself to believe that something masquerading as human had ripped apart good old Boonie Houck. Not in Pickett County. Not on God's ground. Not on his watch.

As he closed the door and looked across the graveyard where Storie searched the weeds for clues, the chill evaporated. Something fluttered in the belfry.

Bird or raccoon, he told himself without looking up. Not the thing that had laughed as Samuel died.

He hurried down the slope to see if Storie had found any of Boonie's missing parts.

FOUR

Bummer.

That was Ronnie's first thought when the gray blindfold of unconsciousness dissolved into light. And that was the last thought he'd had when the anesthesiologist had pressed the mask to his face. Or maybe not. He'd been so stone-black-buzzed from the injection that he couldn't be sure if he'd had any prior thoughts at all.

His face, at least what he could feel of it, was like a molasses balloon. Pain tingled and teased him through a curtain of gauze. It was a sneaky, funny pain, a bully that skulked around the edge of the playground, waiting for you to chase a stray kickball. Once you were alone, it would jump on you and beat you and kick you and rip you—

More of the druggy haze fell away. Ronnie opened his eyes and the light sliced at his pupils. His eyes were overflowing, but he couldn't feel the tears on his cheeks. His stomach turned crooked flips. Mom and Dad were blurry images beside the bed. A man with a mustache whose eyes looked like licorice drops leaned over him.

"I think we've got somebody waking up." The

man's mustache twitched like a caterpillar on a hot griddle. He wore a white coat.

Doctor. Ronnie's thoughts spun, then collected. *Pain plus doctor equals hospital.*

He opened his mouth to speak, but his tongue was too thick to find his teeth.

"Easy now, little partner," the doctor said. "Take it slow."

Slow was the only way Ronnie *could* take it. His arms and legs felt like lead pipes. He turned his head to look at his parents. Despite the numbness, he felt a warmth growing in his chest. Mom and Dad were *together.*

Well, they weren't holding hands, but at least they weren't yelling at each other. And all it took to make that happen was for Ronnie to . . . What *had* he done?

He slogged through the tunnels of his memory. He remembered the ride to the hospital, Dad holding him in the backseat, Dad's shirt against his face. The shirt should have smelled of sawdust and sweat and maybe a little gasoline, but Ronnie had smelled nothing but blood.

Then, farther back, before that, the little foot bridge, falling, the rocks . . .

Ouch.

Ronnie was old enough to know that the memory of pain could never quite match up to the real thing. Which was a good thing; otherwise, everybody would be running around as crazy as old Mama Bet McFall, or Grandma Gregg down at the Haywood Assisted Care Center back before she slipped into the grave. But even Ronnie's memory of the pain was strong enough to wipe out some of the numbing effects of the drugs.

Dad stepped forward, his lower lip curled, his face

made sickly green by the fluorescent strip lights. Dad never looked quite right indoors, sort of like the tiger Ronnie had seen in a pen down at the Asheboro zoo. Both of them nervous and impatient, pacing, too large for walls or bars.

"Hey, Ronnie," Dad said, unsuccessfully trying to funnel his deep voice into a whisper. "How are you feeling?"

"Muuuuhr." Even Ronnie couldn't translate the sound his vocal cords made.

Mom leaned over him, a tight smile wrinkling her face. The skin under her eyes was dark blue. She reached out and brushed hair away from his forehead with a clammy hand. "It's okay, baby."

The doctor checked Ronnie's pulse. "Coming around fine. You'll be able to take him home in an hour or so. Buzz one of the nurses if you need anything."

The doctor left the room, and the draft from the closing door swept over Ronnie like a tide of water. Being a molasses-head wasn't all bad. His thoughts weren't dropping as fast as usual, but he was thinking *wider* than he ever had before. If not for the pain bully waiting behind the numbness, Ronnie wouldn't mind hanging out in this half-speed dreamscape for a while.

This was almost peaceful. If he closed his eyes, the white walls fell away and the sky got big and he could float on a cloud and no one could bother him, not even dingle-dork—

Tim. What had happened to Tim?

The molasses of his face rippled as his eyes opened wide. Mom and Dad and . . . where was Tim? Because suddenly it was all coming back, the molasses creek turning a bend and flowing into sunlight and, now hot and golden, churning over a precipice in a sugary waterfall. The run home, the hand on his foot, the bleeding thing—*they got livers for eyes*—the toppled monument, the red church, the graveyard.

Had the bleeding thing trapped Tim?

Dad must have sensed his agitation, because a hand on his shoulder prevented him from sitting up. "Now, you heard the doctor, son. Just rest up."

Mom chewed on the skin at the end of her thumb. "You got busted up pretty good when you fell. Broke your nose. The doctor said you were lucky you didn't crack your skull."

Good old Mom. Found the bright side to everything. So he had a broken nose. He thought of some of the players on his football cards, how their noses had great big humps across the bridge or were twisted off to one side. Just what a guy like him needed. Now Melanie would never talk to him.

The molasses mask slipped a little more, and the pain bully chuckled from the shadows, knowing an opportunity was drawing near. Ronnie became aware of a lower portion of his body, where the knot of snakes nested in his stomach. He was going to throw up.

Total bummer. He groaned and his tongue worked.

"What is it, honey?" Mom said, her face now paler and her eyes wider.

"Poooook," he said. His right arm flailed like a water hose under pressure.

"Puke?" She looked at Dad. "Oh, Lord, David, he's going to throw up."

Dad looked helpless. The situation called for quick action and compassion. As a caregiver, Dad made a good pallbearer.

Mom spun and began searching under a counter beside the bed. A mirror ran along the length of the counter, and Ronnie was startled by his own reflection. His nose was purple and swollen, little clots of bloody gauze hanging out of his nostrils. His eyes were like green-brown marbles pressed into ten pounds of dough.

The image accelerated his nausea. He turned his body with effort, and now Dad helped, putting a hand in his armpit to lean him over the steel railing of the bed. The scene in the mirror was doubly disorienting from being reversed. The greasy snakes crawled up Ronnie's throat.

Mom found a plastic pan made of a yucky aqua color, but that was okay because yucky was just what the situation required. She held it under his face, and the snakes exploded from his mouth. His eyes squeezed shut in the effort of vomiting, and drops of something besides molasses beaded his forehead. His abdomen spasmed twice, three times, four, a pause, then a fifth eruption.

"Oh, my Lord," Mom exclaimed to Dad. "Call the nurse."

"He said this might happen. And look, it's stopped now."

"But it's blood."

"What did you think it would be, grits and sausage gravy? They just operated on his nose."

Ronnie looked into the pan and his guts almost lurched again. A thick gruel of blood and mucus pooled in front of his face. And what were those things floating in—

Fingers. They cut off my fingers and made me eat them.

Dad's words came as if through cotton. "What the hell are *those?*"

"Get a nurse." Mom waved her hands helplessly.

The draft of the door opening wafted over Ronnie again, but this time it provided no comfort. He lay back on the raised pillows.

A tired-looking nurse looked in the pan. "Oh, those are the fingers of surgical gloves. The doctor stuffs them with gauze and uses them as packing."

"How did they get in his stomach?" Mom's voice was a thin screech.

"The packing must have worked its way down the pharyngeal opening of his Eustachian tubes. I'm sure it's nothing to worry about."

"Nothing to worry about?" Dad's voice was loud enough to make Ronnie's head hurt. "It's not your kid in the bed, is it?"

The nurse gave a forced smile that Ronnie figured she wore while giving medicine to somebody who wasn't likely to last the week. A smile that plainly said, *If there were another job in Pickett County that paid this well, he could puke rubber fingers until he choked, for all I care.*

But all she said was, "I'll see if I can find the doctor."

After she was gone, Mom said, "You didn't have to raise your voice."

"Shut up."

"David, please. For Ronnie's sake?"

Ronnie wasn't bothered by the argument. The relief of passing nausea was so great that he would have slow-danced with the pain bully, he felt so wonderful. So what if more sweat had popped out along his neck and in his armpits and down the slope of his spine? The stomach snakes were gone.

The act of vomiting also cleared his head a little. That was a mixed blessing. Or mixed curse. Because not only were the good wide thoughts gone, they were being replaced by memories.

Before he'd been wheeled into surgery, the sheriff had talked to him about the things that happened at the red church. It was scary enough just to talk to a policeman, especially one with a crewcut and a face that looked like it was chiseled out of stone. But the sheriff wanted him to remember what had happened, when Ronnie really, really, really wanted to be in the business of forgetting.

Forgetting the wet, slooshing sound his shoe had made as he jerked his foot from the graveyard grip.

Forgetting the raw, bloody arm reaching around the tombstone.

Forgetting the laughter that had fluttered from the belfry of the red church.

The sheriff finally went away, and they had rolled Ronnie to the operating room. Then came the needle and the mask and the wide thoughts and the darkness.

"How are you feeling, honey?"

He looked at his mom. Her hair was wilted and stringy, a dull chestnut color. She looked about a hundred and twelve, older even than Mama Bet McFall, the crazy woman who lived up the road from the Day farm.

"Better," he whispered, and the air of his voice scraped his throat as it passed.

The door opened again and Ronnie craned his neck. The doctor was whistling an uneven tune through the scrub brush of his mustache. Ronnie would bet money that it was a Michael Bolton song. Or maybe something even lamer. Ronnie was almost glad that his nose was clogged. He would have bet double-or-nothing that the man was wearing some sissy cologne. He flopped his heavy head back on the pillows.

"I heard you had a little episode," the doctor said.

Episode? Was that the medical term for vomiting up fingers?

"I'm okay now," Ronnie said in a wheeze, mainly

because the doctor was leaning over and reaching for his nose. And even though the painkiller was still dumbing him down, he was smart enough to know that being touched there would hurt like heck. Even through the molasses that encased his brain.

The doctor backed away at the last moment. "The packing looks like it's still in place where the break occurred. I don't think any harm was done."

Nope. No harm at all to you, was there, Mr. Mustache?

"We could always roll him back into the OR and pack some more gauze up there," the doctor said to his parents, as if Ronnie weren't even in the room.

"What do you think?" Mom turned another shade closer to invisibility.

"I believe he's okay," the doctor said, fingering his mustache. "In fact, I'd say you could go ahead and take him home. Call me next week and we'll schedule a time to take the stitches out."

Dad nodded dumbly. Mom worked at the gnawed skin of her fingers.

Ronnie was eager to go home. By the time the nurse showed up with a fake smile and a wheelchair, he was sitting up in bed, feeling dizzy but no longer nauseated. As the nurse wheeled him to the elevators, he was floating away again. The outside air tasted strange and thick.

Ronnie was surprised to see that the sun was setting. He felt as if years had passed, not hours, since he'd fallen. Pinkish gray clouds wreathed the horizon above the dark mountains.

Mom had pulled her big black Coupe De Ville by the hospital doors. Dad eased him into the backseat and they were on their way home. They had gone about two miles when Ronnie remembered Tim.

"Where's Tim?" he managed to ask. He was sleepy again, a molasses-head.

"At Donna's. They went back to the graveyard to find his glasses."

So Tim had survived the encounter at the red church. *The Encounter.* Sounded like a title for a cheesy monster movie. *Whatever.* His thoughts were getting wide again.

He wanted to be asleep by the time they drove past the red church.

He was.

"Didn't see nothing," Lester Matheson said. His face was crooked from decades of chewing his tobacco in the same cheek. He ground his teeth sideways, showing the dark mass inside his mouth, occasionally flicking it more firmly into place with his tongue.

"Last night, either?" Sheriff Littlefield turned from the man's smacking habit and looked out over the rolling meadows. A herd of cows dotted the ridge, all pointed in the same direction. Like their owner, they also chewed mindlessly, not caring what dribbled out of their mouths.

"No, ain't seen nothing up at the red church in a long time. Course, kids go up there to mess around from time to time. Always have."

Littlefield nodded. "Yeah. Ever think of posting a 'No Trespassing' sign?"

"That would only draw twice as many. I'd never keep nothing out there that I couldn't afford to get stolen."

Littlefield shifted his weight from one foot to another and a porch board groaned. The Mathesons lived in a board-and-batten house on the edge of two hundred acres of land. Even Lester's barns seemed better built than the house. It was roofed with a cheap linoleum sheeting that had visible patches in the material. The windows were large single panes fixed with gray strips of wood. The air coming from the open front door was stale and cool, like that of a tomb.

The sun was disappearing into the angle where Buckhorn Mountain slid down to the base of Piney Top. The air was moist with the waiting dew. Pigs snorted from their wooden stalls beside the largest of Lester's two barns. Crickets had taken up their night noises, and the aroma of cow manure made Littlefield almost nostalgic for his own childhood farm days. "Have you ever seen Boonie hanging around the graveyard?"

Lester scratched his bulbous head that gleamed even in the fading light. His hand was knotted from a life of work, thick with blue veins and constellations of age spots. "Well, I found him in the red church one time, passed out in the straw. I just let him sleep it off. As long as he didn't smoke in there, he couldn't really hurt nothing."

"Have you noticed anything unusual around here?"

"Depends on what you mean by 'unusual.' The church has always been mighty unusual. But I don't have to tell *you* that, do I?"

"I'm not interested in ghost stories," Littlefield lied.

Lester emitted a gurgling laugh and leaned back in his rocker. "Fine, Sheriff. Whatever you say. And I guess Boonie just happened to get killed in one of them gang wars or something."

"Perry Hoyle thinks it was a mountain lion."

Lester laughed again, then shot a stream of black juice into the yard. "Or maybe it was Bigfoot. Used to be a lot of mountain lions in these parts, all right.

Back in the thirties and forties, they were thick as flies. They'd come down out of the hills of a night and take a calf or a chicken, once in a while a dog. But they're deader than four o'clock in the morning now."

Lester was a hunter. Littlefield wasn't, these days. "When's the last time you saw one?" the sheriff asked.

"Nineteen sixty-three. I remember because everybody was just getting over the Kennedy mess. I took up yonder to Buckhorn"—he waved a gnarled hand at the darkening mountain—"because somebody said they'd seen a six-point buck. I set up a little stand at a crossing trail and waited. My stand was twenty feet up a tree, covered with canvas and cut branches. Moon come out, so I decided to stay some after dark, even though it was colder than a witch's heart.

"I heard a twig snap and got my rifle shouldered as smooth as you please. We didn't mess with scopes and such back in them days. Just pointed and shot. So I was looking down the barrel when something big stepped in the sights. Even in the bad light, I could see its gold fur. And two shiny green eyes was looking right back up the barrel at me."

Lester drained his excess juice off the side of the porch. The old man paused for dramatic effect. People still passed down stories in these parts. The front porch was Lester's stage, and they both knew his audience was duty-bound to stay.

The sheriff obliged. "You shot him," he said, even though he knew that wouldn't have made a satisfactory ending to the tale.

Lester waited another ten seconds, five seconds longer than the ritual called for. "About did. I knew what he was right off, even though his fur was about the same color as a deer's. It was the eyes, see? Deer eyes don't glow. They just sop up light like a scratch biscuit draws gravy."

"What happened next?"

"He just kind of stared back at me. Damnedest thing I ever saw. Looking at me like I was an equal, or maybe not even that. Like I was a mosquito buzzing around his head. He drew his mouth open like he was going to snarl, and his whiskers flashed in the moonlight. And I couldn't pull the trigger."

"Scared?" Littlefield asked, hoping Lester wasn't insulted. But Lester seemed to have forgotten the sheriff as he stared off at the mountain.

"In a way I was, but that's not the reason I didn't pull the trigger. There was something about him, something in the eyes, that was more than animal. You might think I'm crazy, and you probably wouldn't be too far wrong, but that cat *knew* what I was thinking. It *knew* I wouldn't pull the trigger. After maybe half a minute of us staring each other down, he slipped into the woods, his long tail twitching like he was laughing to hisself. Like I was a big ball of yarn he'd played with and gotten tired of."

The sun had slipped behind the horizon now, and Littlefield couldn't read Lester's expression in the darkness. All he could see was the crooked shape of the farmer's face.

"I was frozen, and not just from the chill, either," Lester continued. "When I finally let out a breath, it made a mist in front of my face. I was sweating like I was baling hay and racing a rainstorm. I strained my ears for any little sound, even though I knew the cat was gone."

Littlefield had been standing more or less at parade rest, a habit he had when he was on official business, even around people he knew. Now he let his shoulders droop slightly and leaned against the porch rail. As a youngster, he'd hunted at night himself. He could easily imagine Lester in the tree, muscles taut, ears picking up the slight scurry of a chipmunk or the whispering wings of a nighthawk. Like any good storyteller, Lester had put the sheriff in another place and time.

"You're probably wondering why I'm going on so about this mountain lion," Lester said. "You're asking yourself what that's got to do with Boonie Houck's death."

"That mountain lion would have died a natural death long ago."

Lester said nothing. There was a clattering inside the house, then the rusty *skree* of the storm door opening. Lester's wife Vivian came out on the porch. Her hair was in a bun, tied up with a scarf. She had a slight hump in her back, a counterpart to her husband's twisted face. The interior light cast her odd shadow across the yard.

"You done yapping the sheriff's ear off?" she asked, her voice trembling and thin. She must have been a little hard of hearing, because she talked louder than necessary.

"Ain't hardly started yet," Lester said, not rising from his rocker. "Now get on back in the house before I throw a shoe at you."

"You do and I'll put vinegar in your denture glass."

Lester chuckled. "I love you, too, honey."

"You going to invite the sheriff in for pie?"

"No, thank you, ma'am," Littlefield said, bowing a little in graciousness. "I've got a few other people to talk to tonight."

"Well, don't listen too much to this old fool. He lies like a cheap rug."

"I'll take that under advisement."

The door sprang closed. The darkness sprang just

as abruptly. "So you haven't seen a mountain lion since then?" the sheriff asked Lester.

"Nope."

"And you're sure you haven't seen anything strange around the red church?"

"Haven't *seen* nothing. Heard something, though."

"Heard something?"

"Last night, would've been about three o'clock. You don't sleep too well when you get to be my age. Always up and down for some reason. So when I heard them, I figured it was one of those in-between dreams. You know, right before you fall asleep and your real thoughts are mixing in with the nonsense?"

Littlefield nodded, then realized the old man couldn't see his face. "Yeah. What did you hear, or think you heard?"

Littlefield glanced at his watch, about to chalk up his time spent talking to Lester as a waste. The luminous dial showed that it was nearly nine o'clock.

"Bells," the old man said in a near-whisper.

"Bells?" Littlefield repeated, though he'd plainly heard the man.

"Real soft and faint, but a bell's a bell. Ain't no mistaking that sound."

"I hate to tell you this, Lester, but we both know that the red church has the only bell around here. And even if some kids were messing around there last night, there's no bell rope."

"And we both know why there ain't no bell rope. But I'm just telling you what I heard, that's all. I don't expect you to put much stock in an old man's words."

The ghost stories. Some families had passed them down until they'd acquired a mythic truth that had even more power than fact. Littlefield wasn't ready to write *Death by supernatural causes* on Boonie's incident report. Since Samuel had died, the sheriff had spent most of his life trying to convince himself that supernatural occurrences didn't occur.

Just the facts, ma'am, Littlefield told himself, hearing the words in Jack Webb's voice from the old *Dragnet* television show.

"There were no recent footprints around the church. No sign of disturbances inside the church, either," Littlefield said, piling up the evidence as if to convince himself along with Lester.

"I bet there wasn't no mountain lion pawprints, either, was there?"

This time, Littlefield initiated the ten-second silence. "Not that we've found yet."

Lester gave his liquid laugh.

Littlefield's head filled with warm anger. "If you believe so much in the stories, why did you buy the red church in the first place?"

"Because I got it for a song. But it won't be my problem no more."

"Why not?"

"Selling it. One of the McFall boys came by the other day. You know, the one that everybody said didn't act like regular folks? The one that got beat near to a pulp behind the football bleachers one night?"

"Yeah. Archer McFall." Littlefield had been a young deputy then, on foot patrol at the football game. Archer ended up in the hospital for a week. No arrests were made, even though Littlefield had seen two or three punks rubbing their hands as if their knuckles were sore. Of course, nobody pressed the case too much. Archer was a McFall, after all, and the oddest of the bunch.

"Well, he says he went off to California and made

good, working in religion and such. And now he's moving back to the area and wants to settle here."

"I'll be damned."

"Me, too. And when he offered me two hundred thousand dollars for the red church and a dozen acres of mostly scrub pine and graveyard, I had to bite my lip to keep from grinning like a possum. Supposed to go in tomorrow and sign the papers at the lawyer's office."

"Why the red church, if he's got that kind of money?" Littlefield asked, even though he was pretty sure he already knew.

"That property started off in the McFall family. They're the ones who donated the land for the church in the first place. Remember Wendell McFall?"

Coincidences. Littlefield didn't like coincidences. He liked cause and effect. That was what solved cases. "That's a lot of money."

"Couldn't say no to it. But I had a funny feeling that he would have offered more if I had asked. But he knew I wouldn't. It was like that time with the mountain lion, like he was staring me down, like he knew what I was thinking."

"I guess if he's a successful businessman, then he's had a lot of practice at negotiating."

"Reckon so," Lester said, unconvinced. He stood with a creaking that might have been either his joints or the rocker's wooden slats. "It's time to be putting up the cows."

"And I'd best finish my rounds. I appreciate your time, Lester."

"Sure. Come on back anytime. And next time, plan on staying for a piece of pie."

"I'll do that."

As Littlefield started the Trooper, he couldn't help

thinking about the part of Lester's story that had
gone untold. The part about why a bell rope no
longer hung in the red church, and why Archer
McFall would want to buy back the old family birthright.

He shook his head and went down the driveway,
gravel crackling under his wheels.

FIVE

The dawn was crisp and pink, the air moistened by dew. The scent of pine and wild cherry blossoms spread across the valley along with the thin, smoky threads of the night's hearths. Water swept its way south underneath the soft fog that veiled the river. A rooster's crow cracked the stillness of the hills.

Archer McFall nestled against the damp soil, the earth cool against his nakedness. He kept his eyes closed, looking back into the dark avenues of his dreams, chasing shadows to nowhere. The dreams were splashed with red, the color of retribution. They were human dreams, strange and new and chaotic.

The rooster crowed three times before Archer remembered where he was.

Home.

The word, even though it was only thought and not spoken, left a bitter taste in his mouth. The bitterness came from the memory of old humiliations. And an older suffering, one that ran deeper than the expansive surface of sleep.

Archer coughed. Pine needles and brittle leaves pressed against his cheek. He shivered and rolled into a sitting position, opening his eyes. After so long in darkness, he was almost surprised at the brightness of the coming day. The light slashed through the gaps in the forest canopy, sharp and merciless and full of grace.

He gazed down at his bare human flesh. His skin seemed to fit well enough. These human bags of water and bone had always seemed awkwardly constructed to him. But he'd come among these people to take up their ways. Deliverance was more joyful when the victims thought it came from one of their own kind.

More thoughts came back to him, more memories flooded the gray mass of brain that filled his skull. He spat. A reddish clot of half-digested pulp clung to a stump.

As the sun warmed him and his shifting night shapes slithered the rest of the way out of existence, he planned his route back to the Mercedes. He knew the river well. It flowed below the old home grounds, below the church. He'd left his car in the woods a mile away. A Brooks Brothers suit, pinstriped and charcoal gray, was spread out in the trunk, along with leather shoes, knit socks, cologne, a Rolex wristwatch, and a sky-blue tie.

The uniform of the walking dead, the Christian soldiers, the false idol-worshipers. The pretenders. And he would pretend to be one of them.

Archer stood and brushed the clinging loam from his body. A kingfisher swooped and lit on a branch nearby, then either smelled or sensed him and disappeared with a frantic snap of wings. Archer smiled and studied the gray mountain slopes.

Home.

The Promised Land.

Creeks as old as lies, dirt as dark as hopelessness. Stones as cold as the heart of a father who had only enough love for one son. Mountains thrust like angry fists up to the sky, defying the heaven that so many people believed in, including his dear, deranged mother.

The worst part of this incarnation was the emotional turmoil. No wonder these creatures sinned. No wonder they sought refuge in lust and depravity and excess. They were God's mistakes. But God's biggest mistake was jealousy, the craving to build things in His image, the demand for sacrifice.

God demanded love, but had no love of His own to spare. At least not for the second-born. Not for the one destined for dust, while the first earned a high place above. The second son was fit only to rule what he could see, left to find corrupted pleasure here on Earth.

Archer began walking down the rugged incline toward the river. Brambles and branches pricked at his skin, but he soaked up the pain and buried it inside the hollowness of his rage. Sharp outcrops of granite tore at the soles of his feet, and he relished the flow of blood from his wounds.

Jesus had walked in wilderness. So would Archer.

The blood would leave tracks. Others could find his trail, if they were clever. Let them follow. He was born to lead, after all.

And even if they found him, what were they going to do? Kill him?

His laughter echoed through the trees, as deep as the glacier-cut and time-eroded valleys, the human vocal cords vibrating strangely as he threw back his head and chilled the spine of the forest.

Sheriff Littlefield leaned back in his oak swivel chair. Not a whisper of a squeak came from the well-oiled springs. Detective Sergeant Storie shifted uneasily in the chair across the desk from him, her suit jacket rumpled. The morning light on her face showed that she had slept little and poorly. Her eyes were puffy and narrowed from the headache caused by disrupted dreams. Her hair was still wet from a morning shower, and the smell of her conditioner filled the room.

Steam billowed from Littlefield's cup of black coffee. He looked through it, and the steam parted and swirled as he spoke. "I talked to the folks out in Whispering Pines."

"Any eyewitnesses?"

"Nobody saw anything." He put a little too much emphasis on the word *saw.*

"What about knowing? This isn't the big city, where people don't want to get involved. The old woman in the apartment next to mine knows it when my cat breaks wind. And the rest of the neighbors are clued in before the fumes disperse."

Littlefield winced. But he let the wince slip into what he hoped looked like a frown of concern. Storie was always calling him "old school" as it was.

"Well, two people said they heard the bells ringing at the church," he said.

"So the killer celebrated by letting everybody know what he'd done?" Storie asked incredulously.

"Must have been their imaginations. There's no bell rope."

Storie leaned forward, tapping the report that lay on Littlefield's desk. The pages were wrinkled, probably from where she had worried over them in bed while trying to fall asleep. "Nobody heard the screams, either, I suppose."

"All we have is what we had yesterday. I've got Charlie and Wade searching the hills up around the church. Wade brought his dogs. If there's anything to be found, they'll turn it up."

Storie stood. "I guess I'd better get to work. Any word from Chapel Hill yet?"

"Hoyle says they should get around to the autopsy Monday. Ought to have preliminary results by Wednesday or so."

"What if it *is* a psycho?"

Littlefield looked past her to the glass case that lined one wall of his office. He had a collection of confiscated drug paraphernalia that would make a doper weep with envy. Colorful bongs and ornately carved pipes adorned the shelves, along with photographs of a younger Littlefield posing next to marijuana plants. In the center of the case stood a brass cup emblazoned with a badge: the 1998 Law Enforcement Officer of the Year Award, bestowed by the North Carolina Sheriff's Association.

There wasn't much crime in Pickett County. In Littlefield's seven years as sheriff, there had been a total of two murders. In one, the killer himself called the department, and blubberingly narrated how he had just blown his wife's head open with a .38 revolver. He was waiting on the porch when officers arrived, draining the last of his liquor, the gun cleaned and returned to its cabinet. His wife's body was in the garage, gingerly covered with a hand-woven shawl.

The other was Storie's case, the one that had established her as a legitimate detective. In Littlefield's mind, all the technical training in the world was useless until you actually snapped the cuffs on a perpetrator. And Storie had done that with style, making headlines across the region by helping prosecute the cop-turned-killer. After the trial, she gave the press a highly quotable statement: "If I had written the book, the final chapter would have been different. He would have gotten the death penalty."

So Littlefield was left with domestic disputes and civil disturbances. Some kids with a stereo blasting too loud, a drunk breaking windows, somebody rearranging the letters on Barkersville's Main Street Theater marquee to spell out crude words. Or some longhair in an army jacket would sell oregano joints behind the high school. The crime stats looked great on paper, which was part of the reason Littlefield had won his Sheriff's Association award.

But sometimes he was afraid that Pickett County was just a little *too* sleepy, that underneath the shimmering overlay of tight community and good-natured harmony was a layer of moral rot. After all, people were people. Maybe having a mad killer on the loose wasn't really so hard to imagine, not with what played out in other small towns across the country on the nightly news.

"Dogs should be able to track it, whether it's a mountain lion or a human."

Storie put her hands on her hips. "And?"

"And what?"

"The rest of the sentence. I get the feeling that you aren't telling me everything."

Littlefield sighed and rubbed his eyes. Storie was now wide-awake, as if she had magically cast her weariness over to him. He didn't know how to begin, but it would be unfair to withhold the information.

Information, hell. It was flat-out rubber-room stuff. But she would find out sooner or later, if she talked to any of the old-timers in Whispering Pines.

"Well," he started, "it's about the church."

"The church?" Her eyebrows lifted into her wet bangs. "What about the church? Did you find something yesterday?"

"Nothing that you could call a clue," he lied. "Maybe you'd better sit back down."

Storie sat on the arm of the chair, clasping her hands together. Like Wade's hounds, she was excited by the fresh scent of prey. Littlefield pretended to look through a stack of papers on his desk, then cleared his throat.

"The church is haunted."

Littlefield could have sworn he heard his wristwatch ticking in the sudden silence, but that was impossible. His wristwatch was electronic. Even the police scanner, which sat on a stack of manuals in the corner, quit its squelching in response to his statement. He searched Storie's face.

Her eyes were wide, disbelieving, as if she had misheard him. But they quickly hardened back into a cool, professional gaze.

"Okay, Sheriff," she said with an irritated laugh. "That explains everything. A ghost sneaks out at night; maybe it's pissed off because its sheets got mildewed in the wash, whatever. So it finds a drunk in the graveyard with a dirty magazine and a bottle of bourbon and decides to vent its wrath. That explains why we didn't find any footprints at the scene. Case closed."

Littlefield folded his arms over his chest and let the wave of sarcasm sweep over him and die in the corners of the room.

His tight lips must have aroused Detective Storie's curiosity, because she looked as if she expected him to admit he was joking. "What?" Her mouth dropped open. "Sheesh, you're *serious,* aren't you?"

He said nothing. The coffeemaker on a side table gurgled. He walked slowly over to the machine and refilled his cup. "Want some?" he said, lifting the pot in Storie's direction.

She shook her head. Littlefield had been dreading this moment ever since they'd gotten the call yesterday. The thing at the church had never left. All these years of hoping, wishing, and his best attempts at praying hadn't made it go away.

"In the 1860s, the church was the only one in these parts," he began, walking to the closed door of his office. He looked at the hardware store calendar hanging there. The almanac said the moon was favorable for planting root crops.

He continued, keeping his back to the detective. "Back then it was called Potter's Mill Baptist Church, after the old grist mill that operated down by the river. Wendell McFall was the pastor. He was an 'old school' preacher"—he turned to judge her reaction and saw she was carefully controlling her expression, which didn't surprise him—"all fire and brimstone and hell to pay. But during the Civil War, they say he started stretching his interpretation of the Gospel.

"I don't know how much you know about the history of these parts, but the war pretty much made a hard life harder for the people who lived here," he said. "Pickett County men were part of the fifty-eighth North Carolina Troops, and almost two-thirds of them were killed in action. Women were keeping up the fields and home chores at the same time. It was a bad stretch, as you can imagine. And Reverend McFall started preaching that the end of the world was nigh."

"Now, *there's* an original idea," Storie said. "They've been peddling that line for at least four thousand years."

Littlefield gulped his coffee, welcoming the hot sting in his throat. At least Storie hadn't walked out of the office yet. Maybe rank had its privileges after all.

"Some of the soldiers' bodies were shipped back here to be buried," Littlefield said. "Reverend McFall insisted on holding midnight vigils over the graves, because he said they would rise up and walk again otherwise. At the same time, he was preaching some nonsense about how God had two sons, and while the first one was merciful and good and holy, this second son was just the opposite."

"Too bad this guy wasn't around in the 1980s," Storie said. "He could have made a fortune selling cheesy paperbacks."

Littlefield ignored her. "So McFall starts warning the congregation that this second son would return to the earth, come to undo the good done by Jesus. Said the second son demanded love and sacrifice, like God's spoiled little brat. In those times, the preacher was pretty much the leader of the community. While those ideas might seem a little flaky now, people were more imaginative back then, carrying with them all the legends and beliefs of their Scottish and English ancestors. So when a man of the cloth told you he had a vision, then you were bound to believe it. And with their fathers and brothers and sons dying and hunger spreading, the congregation must have felt that they hadn't given enough tribute to God. Or His sons."

Littlefield had never discussed religion with Storie, or with much of anyone else, for that matter. He'd invited her to attend the First Baptist Church in Barkersville, but that was more of a rote politeness than a serious recruiting pitch. Littlefield himself usually went to services about once a month. He'd stopped reading the Bible after he finished his run through Sunday school and there was no longer anyone to force to him memorize verse. But he'd been raised Baptist, and he was going to die Baptist, even if he'd never devoted a minute to finding out what that really meant. Jesus was Lord, and that was that.

His grandmother on his mother's side used to tell the story of the red church while she snapped peas or shucked corn. He would sit at her feet, helping with the chore at his own awkward pace, listening too closely to the story to do much work. Sometimes Littlefield's mother would come in and say, "Don't fill Frankie's head with that foolishness," but Grandma would start right in again the minute Littlefield's mother left the kitchen.

Littlefield closed his eyes and tried to hear her voice in his mind. But it was no use. He fumbled for eloquent words, found none. "McFall was the one who painted the church red. Said that would bring the first son around to save them, to defeat the second son. Plus the congregation had to start meeting at midnight on Sunday instead of in the morning. By this time, according to the way the old-timers tell it, McFall was feverish and white as a sheet. He'd stand in the pulpit, a dozen candles lighting up the old wooden interior of the church, and he'd describe his visions. He'd go into convulsions and rant about sin and violent ways and the punishment of the wicked and false idols and a blight carried unto umpteen generations. And the strange thing was, McFall never did prescribe a remedy for this punishment. No prayers, nothing. He wasn't even passing the plate."

Storie was rapt now, staring at the sheriff. He didn't know if it was because she found the legend fascinating or whether she was transfixed by her boss's making a fool of himself. "So this second son . . . was he supposed to be the devil or something?"

Littlefield shook his head. "McFall believed this

second son had a power equal to Jesus'. And according to my grandmother, McFall had most of the congregation believing it. So the preacher was riding
high, dishing out his revelations while the congregation cowered speechless in the pews. And I guess he
started getting a little delusional after that."

"After *that*? Like he wasn't before?"

"He started taking advantage," Littlefield continued. "Said he was the instrument of the Lord, and
only he could protect them from the second son.
Well, he got a woman pregnant, the wife of a soldier
who was off fighting at Gainesville. People started
whispering then, though they were too afraid to con-
front the preacher. Then, one morning following a
midnight service, one of the parishioners found her
young child mutilated at the altar of the red church.

"Well, as crazy as the preacher had been acting,
they figured he had played Abraham or something.
Only God didn't tell him to stop as he raised the
knife, so he chopped up the child as a sacrifice. That
Sunday night in 1864, the parishioners showed up
for service and hauled the preacher from the pulpit.
Somebody climbed up the bell rope and cut it loose,
threw it out on the ground where the others stood
holding torches."

"They didn't," Storie cut in. Littlefield couldn't
tell if she was still mocking him. He decided to bust
on through the tale and get it over with. He could
feel his neck blushing.

"You know that dogwood by the church door?
They hanged him from it."

"So that was that. Except his ghost still haunts the
church, right?"

"I guess the Potters and the Mathesons and the
Buchanans started feeling a little guilty and decided
that maybe 'an eye for an eye' was all fine and dandy,

but once a sin was paid for, all was forgiven. They buried him out in the woods, covered him with rocks in a place long forgotten. But they said prayers over his grave even if he didn't deserve them. They even took care of the woman he got pregnant."

The police scanner squawked, and a female dispatcher's voice came over. "Ten-sixty-eight. Ten-sixty-eight on Old Turnpike Road."

The tension in Littlefield's office eased slightly. "Denny Eggers's cows got out again," Littlefield said.

A deputy on patrol responded to the call. "Ten-four, base. Unit Four, en route."

"Ten-four," said the dispatcher. The scanner returned to broadcasting its ambient hiss.

The sheriff looked at Storie. She stood and stretched. "Well, I'd better get out to the church and see if I missed anything yesterday," she said.

She was at the door, with her hand on the knob, when Littlefield spoke. "The woman he got pregnant brought flowers to his grave. They say that three days after the hanging, she came running out of the woods with tears in her eyes, her clothes torn by the tree branches. She said, 'Praise God, the stone's been rolled away.' "

Detective Storie didn't turn around. The sheriff continued, his words spilling over each other, as if he were experiencing an attack of nausea and wanted it to pass. "When she said that, the church bell started ringing. Only the bell had no rope. And nobody was in the church at the time."

Storie turned. "So *that's* why you told me all this. That'll really stand up in court." She dropped her voice into a low, professional delivery. " 'Your Honor, I would like to submit as state's evidence thirty-two a tape recording of church bells ringing, made on the night of Mr. Houck's death.' "

Littlefield stared into the black pool of his cup of coffee. "Maybe all that has nothing to do with Boonie's death. I sure as hell hope not. A psycho might be able to hide out in the woods for a few weeks, but the bloodhounds would get him sooner or later. Same with a mountain lion. But I hear that one of McFall's descendants is back in town."

"So you expect me to believe in coincidence?" she said. "They didn't teach paranormal investigation at the academy. As for Reverend McFall's ghost, I'll believe it when you can prove it in court."

"I've got an eyewitness for you," he said, his voice tired now, an old man's defeated voice.

"Who?"

He glanced at the Officer of the Year award, glinting dully in the morning sun that sliced through the parted blinds. Storie approached his desk. She leaned over it in a position of superiority, like a teacher berating a daydreaming student.

"Who?" she repeated. "Who's going to testify that a ghost committed murder?"

"Me."

SIX

"You?" Storie shook her head.

Littlefield sat back, feeling twice his forty years. The good thing about the past was that you left it farther and farther behind each day. The bad thing was that you also got closer to the day when you could no longer hide from the past. A day of reckoning and judgment.

"I was seventeen," he said, his flesh cold. "It was Halloween night. Back then, and probably still to this day, getting drunk and driving over to the red church was the thing to do on Halloween. Me and a few of my high school buddies loaded into a pickup I borrowed from my dad. Well, my kid brother Samuel, he was eleven at the time, saw the beer in the bed of the pickup and said he was going to tell on me."

Littlefield rubbed his eyes. He wasn't going to let himself cry in front of a woman or another cop. He cleared his throat. "So I told him he could come along if he'd keep his stupid little mouth shut. We went out to the church—we only lived about two miles away, up near the McFalls at the foot of Buckhorn—and parked in the trees off to one side of the graveyard. We drank the beer and dared each other to go inside the church, you know how teenagers will do."

"Sure I do," Storie said. "I just never expected you to have been such a scofflaw."

Littlefield wasn't sure if her sarcasm was designed to provoke him or encourage him to continue. But he'd kept the story bottled up for too long. He'd never had anyone to confide in.

"Naturally, we were all too scared to do it. Like I said, the ghost stories were pretty well known in these parts. Which was funny as hell, because that's where most of us went to church on Sundays. During the day, with all the people there and the sun in the windows, it wasn't scary at all. But at night, with the dark shadows of the woods, your imagination had a lot of room to play.

"So then we got to picking on Samuel, calling him a chicken, as if we were any braver. And, damn me, I was as bad as any of the others. Samuel sat in the bed of that pickup truck, his eyes wide and shiny in the moonlight and his lip quivering. What else could he do but go up to the church?"

Storie leaned against the wall. The sheriff glanced at her, but she was staring at the floor, looking uncomfortable. She was a cop. Maybe she was as emotionally inhibited as he was and hated this type of intimacy. Well, she could walk out if she wanted. Now that he had started, he was going to finish the story, even if the walls and God were his only audience.

"He went across the graveyard, wearing a cape that was part of his trick-or-treating getup. He was Batman that year, and the cape was a beach towel tied in a knot around his neck. Maybe as he walked, he tried to convince himself that he was a brave superhero."

Littlefield closed his eyes, and it was as if an October wind had carried him back to that night. He could almost smell the freshly fallen leaves, the sweetness of the late autumn grass, the beer that had spilled in the truck bed, the smoke from the cigarettes one of the boys smoked. He continued in a monotone.

"By the time he passed those lonely tombstones, I started feeling a little guilty. I jumped out of the truck and ran across the graveyard to get him and drag him away. I hollered, and I guess he thought I was going to do something to him. He ran up the steps and lifted the latch to the church door, then went inside. The rest of the guys were hooting and moaning, making ghost noises while trying not to snicker.

"I followed Samuel inside the church and closed the door behind me. That's when I got the idea. 'Let's scare the bejesus out of them,' I said, mad at the other guys mostly because I was so much like them. The entryway was dark, but the moonlight spilled through the belfry and lit up that little square where the bell rope used to hang. The hole was about two feet by two feet, too small for most people to squeeze through. But Samuel was slender and wiggly, so I knew he could slip through there if I boosted him up."

Unit Four's voice came through on the police radio and interrupted Littlefield's story. "Come in, base. Found the cows, all right. Denny's getting them rounded up. I'll be ten-ten for a few—"

Storie crossed the room and cut off the radio, then turned back to Littlefield. Her eyes flicked to the sheriff's face, then away, as if she were as ashamed of his vulnerability as he was.

He continued. "I told him, 'Get up there and hide, and I'll run out screaming and say that the Bell Monster got you.' He must have been scared, but I'd always been his hero, and I guess he trusted me that everything would be okay, that nothing bad could happen while I was there. So I boosted him up, and he scrambled through, then I saw his pale face framed in the rope hole. 'When I wave my arms, you kick the bell,' I said. He nodded, and I ran outside, waving my arms and screaming like a crazy man.

" 'It *got* him, it *got* him,' I yelled. 'The Bell Monster got him.' And all those drunken guys jumped out of the pickup and took off running down the road. I turned and pointed to the belfry, signaling Samuel to ring the bell. I saw his eyes, his white forehead, and the dark mess of his curly hair. And behind him, behind him . . ."

Littlefield took three swallows of cold black coffee. He looked at the sunlight sneaking around the window shade. He'd never told anybody this part. Except for himself. He'd relived it during a thousand sweaty, sleepless nights.

"The Bell Monster was there," he said, his whisper filling the room.

"It was really just a shadow, but it was there. It had sharp edges, and it moved toward Samuel. I screamed for real then, and I guess Samuel thought it was part of the act. Then he turned around and saw the thing, God only knows what it looked like from that close up. He scrambled over the edge of the belfry and started to slide down the roof. It was a short drop, he should have been fine. But that stupid cape got caught on a nail or something, and I heard the pop from clear across the graveyard." Littlefield's whisper dropped a notch quieter. "His neck broke."

Littlefield could still see Samuel's startled expression, his eyes and tongue bulging as his body spun beneath the eave of the church. The image had been burned into his retinas, coming to him in dreams and while awake, crisper than a high-definition television signal, more vivid than any movie.

Storie came to him and put a hand on his forearm. "I'm sorry."

The tears came now, hot and wet and stinging, but not enough to flush away the image of his dead brother's face. "We buried him there at the church. Sometimes I think that's the worst part, that we left him buried there forever. The place got what it wanted. The place got *him.*"

Littlefield wiped his nose on his sleeve. "And here I am, blubbering like an idiot."

Storie came closer. "It's okay, Frank," she said, and for a moment he thought she was going to hug him. That would be the final humiliation. He spun so that the back of his chair was facing her.

"I saw him," he said.

"I know. It must have been awful."

"No, not Samuel. I saw *him*. Right when Samuel's neck broke, I saw the Hung Preacher. Just for a second. He shimmered there at the end of a rope, hanging from that goddamned dogwood tree that I've never had the nerve to chop down. He was looking at me like he knew what he'd done. And he was mighty damned pleased with himself."

Littlefield was deflated, tired. He was sorry he'd said anything. How could he expect anyone to believe what he barely believed himself? He knew what had happened that night. He'd *seen* it with his own eyes. But that night existed as if in a separate reality, a private hell, apart from the safe and sane world of Pickett County.

"Did any of your drinking buddies witness anything?" Storie asked.

Damn her. Of course she'd want hard evidence. A

broken soul wasn't enough to convince her. His anger dried his eyes.

"No," he said, staring at a drug-prevention poster on the wall. "Officially, it was a prank that turned into a tragedy. Freak accident. Of course, the old-timers muttered and added Samuel's death to the legend of the red church. The rest of the world went on with the business of living."

"Except you," Storie said.

Except me. Storie *did* have a detective's eyes. Littlefield ran his hand over his scalp and stood. "Well, now you know your sheriff is apeshit crazy."

"The eyes can play tricks. In my psychology classes, they taught us that bad memories can trigger—"

Littlefield sliced his palm across the air to silence her. "I don't give a damn about theories. I know what I saw."

She clenched her fists and looked at him, the hurt clear on her face. She hurried out of the office, and he did nothing to stop her. She slammed the door, and Littlefield's Officer of the Year award rattled in its case.

Elizabeth McFall, known to the old families as Mama Bet, knelt in the damp forest soil.

The dead belong to the dirt. And the dirt belongs to Him that shaped it all.

The dirt would have her soon enough. She was nearly eighty, suffering from diabetes, cataracts, and high blood pressure. But at least God allowed her legs to work still, and her mind was a lot clearer than her eyesight. She looked through the treetops, at the blue sky and the invisible kingdom waiting behind it.

A hand touched her shoulder.

"You done yet, Mama Bet?"

It was Sonny Absher, the biggest small-time thief this side of Tennessee. She hoped his sins didn't jump onto her, like lice or fleas jumping to greener pastures.

The worst part of this whole business was that the Abshers were in on it. The Buchanans were bad enough, what with their moonshining and wife-beating and chicken-stealing ways. But at least the Buchanans knew how to get down on their knees and say they were sorry. The Abshers would just as soon spit at God, even if the saliva fell right back onto their oily faces.

But the Abshers couldn't be culled from the congregation. All the families had a hand in the original persecution, and they all carried a common debt in their hearts. After all these years, they were practically of the same blood anyway. And that blood would have to spill, and spill, and spill.

"I'll be done shortly," Mama Bet answered. "Gotta suffer a little, get right down here on my knees and feel a little pain."

"So this is where they buried him?"

Mama Bet bowed over the small pile of stones. "Yeah. But without a body, a grave's just a hole in the ground."

Sonny Absher snorted. She could smell the white lightning on his breath, in his clothes, strong enough to drown out his rancid sweat. "You mean you believe all that bullshit about Wendell McFall coming back from the dead?"

"You better hush yourself," Mama Bet said, shrugging his hand away from her shoulder. "God might strike you down. Look what He done to Boonie."

"God's done and struck me," Sonny said. "He got me born here. Why in hell else would I be part of this bunch?"

Sonny drew a cigarette from his stained shirt pocket, lit it, and blew a gray cloud of smoke to the sky. He retreated to a stand of laurels, where his brother Haywood and Haywood's wife and teenage daughter waited. Stepford Matheson sat on a stump, whittling on a little chunk of white ash.

Haywood had tried to aspire to a little dignity, taking up with the Baptists and selling insurance in Barkersville. His hands were folded in reverence, but he didn't fool Mama Bet. A person of true faith didn't believe in insurance. But Haywood was all show anyway. His retail-rack suit swamped his skinny frame.

You put a weasel in a forty-dollar suit, and you get a forty-dollar weasel. And Nell ain't quite got all the ingredients to be a trophy wife. I mean, a quart of makeup and a weekly trip to the hair salon ought to give better results than that. Why, I've seen better eyeliner jobs down at Mooney's Funeral Home.

Mama Bet turned back to the loose pile of stones that marked her great-grandfather's former resting place.

Forgive me, God, for thinking ill of others. I guess I suffer the sin of pride. I'm just a little shaky, is all. Scared. You can understand, can't You?

Sure, God could understand. God was really the blame for this whole mess, when you got right down to it. God was the one who put those fool notions in Wendell McFall's head. God was the one who put temptation in Wendell's path. God was the one who sat right up there in the clouds and didn't lift a finger while Wendell sliced up that pretty little girl.

God sat right there and laughed. And God laughed the night He slipped His seed into Mama Bet's belly. Oh, yes, God was a sneaky little devil, all

right. Came to her in the dark and made her forget
all about it after.

Until she missed a few of her monthlies. Her belly
had started to swell and her breasts grew heavy with
milk. Everyone thought she had suffered a sin of the
flesh, had fallen in with one of those door-to-door
Bible salesmen who had a reputation for rutting like
stallions going after a pent-up mare. And so the little
hens clucked, Alma Potter and Vivian Matheson and
all the other no-good gossips of Whispering Pines.

She didn't tell anybody she was still a virgin. Then,
now, and forever, as far as she could tell. Virgins
couldn't get pregnant, could they? Only one had in
the whole history of the world, the way the Bible told
it.

Mama Bet delivered the baby without help, had
strained and groaned and screamed for twenty
hours, as her water burst and her uterine walls spasmed. God forgive her, she had even cussed that
baby's Father. Borrowed every bad word in the Absher repertoire, then added a few of her own. Finally
that slimy head popped through, followed by little
shoulders and arms and belly and legs.

*Can a body love something so much that her heart aches
with the loving?*

She had often wondered. Because she fell in love
with that child, she pulled him onto her belly and
then hugged him against her face, her tears running
like whatever was leaking from her broken place
down there. Her whole world, her whole reason for
living, was realized in that moment after birth.

"How long you going to pray over that damned
old pile of rocks?" Sonny called.

"Shut up," Haywood said.

Mama Bet slowly rose to her feet, pushing on the

mossy stones for support. Haywood started forward to help her, but she waved him away.

"I get my strength from God and Archer," she said.

Oh, yes, it was strength, all right. The strength born of stubbornness and determination. God was the worst absentee father of all time. Because He never really just showed up and did His business, never made this or that happen directly, though He had His hand in every little breath that human beings took. He kept Himself invisible, because He wanted nary bit of the blame when things went wrong. That was why He'd planted the seed and sneaked away in the night without even leaving an instruction manual on how to raise a messiah.

Mama Bet peeled her scarf back and let it rest around her neck. The sun was high enough to break through the canopy of forest. The leaves weren't at full size yet. Otherwise, the grave would be in the shadows all day. Mama Bet took a deep swallow of the fresh mountain air. She could taste the past winter's ice and the coming summer's oak blooms in the same breath.

Round and round these dadgummed seasons go. Seems like they get faster and faster, mixing together and not stopping to rest, like the world's in a great big hurry to get to the reckoning.

She hobbled across the damp leaves of the forest clearing until she reached the others. The congregation. Only they didn't know it yet. They knew only that they had to come, had to join in, had to open their hearts. Mama Bet was the only one who knew that the Second Son was back, and now there would be hell to pay. But she had never whispered a word of the truth, except to Archer. Darned if she couldn't keep a secret as good as God could.

"I reckon we ought to pray," she said. She held out her wrinkled hand to Stepford, who folded his pocketknife and put away his carving. He wiped the wood chips from his hand and clasped it to Mama Bet's. Noreen took her other hand, smiling. She was a pretty girl, not as moonfaced as the rest of the Abshers. Maybe she had Potter blood in her. Zeb Potter had been known to cat around a little, back before his health started failing. Maybe Nell had succumbed to old Zebulon's sinful charms.

There I go again, God. Thinking ill of others, as if I got no sins of my own to worry about. Strike me down if it be Thy will. Just please don't plant another seed in me. I don't think I could take another go-round as bad as the last one.

Well, that, plus she had no more love to spare for another child. Archer Dell McFall took up every square inch of her heart. Archer had given her more joy than she ever thought heaven could hold. Archer was the most beautiful creature under Creation. Darned if God couldn't produce a fine offspring when He set His mind to it.

The others gathered in a circle and held hands, though Sonny gave another of his little grunts of annoyance. Mama Bet shot him a wicked look. He blinked and went cow-eyed. The gathered bowed their heads.

"Dear God, give us the strength to do Your will, and to accept our part in Your work," she said, her voice taking on a tremulous quality. "We know we have sinned and come short of the glory, but we know You love us anyway. Lead our eyes from evil visions and lead our ears from the call of false prophets. Allow us to make whatever sacrifices You require, that we may not stray from the one true path. Keep us and protect us unto the fourth generation. Amen."

And may Archer do this thing right, she silently added, as the others echoed "Amen."

"Are we done now?" Sonny said, pulling out another cigarette.

"We might not ever be done," Mama Bet said.

"When the Lord Jesus gives you a mission, you follow it to the end," Haywood said.

Poor Haywood. Swallowing that New Testament tomfoolery hook, line, and sinker. Well, Archer will shine the light on him soon enough.

Stepford spat onto the trunk of a poplar. "Come on, Sonny. I'm thirsty," he said. He turned and started down the path that led to the rutted dirt road. They had parked their cars at the foot of the trail.

"Wait a second," Sonny yelled. He turned to Mama Bet. "Do we got to go to the red church tomorrow night?"

"I said so, didn't I?"

He frowned at the forest floor. "It's getting so a body ain't got time to pitch a good drunk, what with all this bowing and scraping and worshiping."

"Well, Mr. Absher, you're welcome to go straight on down to hell if you want, but this ain't about you, is it?"

He looked at the small overgrown grave.

"The stone's been rolled away," Mama Bet said. "We all got sacrifices to make."

Sonny's thin lips curled. "Well, we may have to follow the call, but we sure don't have to like it none."

He turned and hurried after Stepford, his boots kicking up a wash of leaves. Haywood came to Mama Bet's side and took her arm. "Come on, Mama Bet," he said. "Let's get you home so you can rest up."

She smiled at him, at Noreen, even at Nell. The

congregation. Well, part of it, anyway. That Noreen was so pretty, there in her Easter dress the color of robin's eggs. Almost a shame that beauty such as that would have to fall by the wayside.

Because all a pretty face does is hide the ugly underneath, don't it?

"Yeah, I guess we all better rest up," she said. "There will come great trials."

The sky seemed to darken a little at her words, or maybe God took up into the trees and reached His fingers out to throw a shadow in her eyes. He liked to keep things confusing, all right. She sometimes wondered if He loved her, if He really loved any of them. Or was He just pretending so He could get the things He wanted, like love?

Haywood led her down the mountain path to her home, to the birthplace of the Second Son.

SEVEN

Linda watched the sun crawl down toward the ridge of Buckhorn Mountain. Just a few more hours. She was wondering how she could slip away without the boys noticing. She almost wished David had stayed. He swallowed lies more easily than the boys did.

She turned from the door and went back to the kitchen. Timmy would be hungry when he got in from his chores. She could see him through the window above the sink, chopping at the brown garden soil with his hoe. The cabbage and peas and potatoes were in the ground, and soon it would be time to plant corn and cucumbers. She didn't know how she was going to manage the farm alone. Even though the fields were leased out for growing hay, the garden took a lot of backbreaking time and sacrifice.

Sacrifice.

Archer always said that sacrifice was the currency of God.

Linda bit her lip. Tears stung her eyes, and she didn't know whether they were brought by regret or joy. The fold would prosper in the next life and unto the fourth generation, but letting go of the things in this life was hard. There were joys to be had here:

her children and sometimes even David, a walk in the wet grass of a morning, standing in the barn during a rainstorm with the music of the drops on the tin roof.

No, that was mortal thinking, covetous and vain and destructive. But she *was* a mortal. Still. A mother of two wonderful boys. Until Archer demanded it, she wouldn't forsake them.

Linda stopped at the refrigerator. One of Ronnie's poems from school was hanging from a banana magnet. His teacher had circled a large red *A* on the corner of the page. "The Tree," it was called.

> The tree has arms
>   that hug,
> not as warm as Mother's.
> Sometimes when I walk by,
> the tree waves
> and I run away.
> The tree barks at me.

Ronnie was doing okay. He had slept most of the time since coming back from the hospital. His face was pale and his nose was lost in gauze and padding. Once he had vomited blood and stained the carpet in the boys' room. The place smelled like carpet-cleaning spray, but luckily it was warm enough that she could leave the windows open.

Linda pulled some hamburger from the refrigerator. They had killed their final cow the previous fall. Linda wondered if the dead cow counted as a sacrifice. Maybe for the God of cows. Let Archer worry about that kind of stuff.

Tim came in the back door.

"Go wash your hands, honey," she said over the rush of water as she rinsed some potatoes.

"They're sore." Not too much whine in his voice.

"I know. You'll get used to it."

Tim came to the sink and saw the hamburger. "It looks like that guy's face."

"Hush, honey."

"I dreamed about him last night."

"Was it scary?" She searched his face, looking for weakness. All she saw were David's eyes, the stubborn gift of genetics. She moved over and let Timmy wash his hands.

The sink turned brown-red from the dirt. "No. In my dream, the graveyard was sort of dark, but not a bad dark. A fun dark, like a carnival or something. And the dead man was all ripped up and stuff, but he was walking around the tombstones."

"You're a brave boy. That sure would have scared me." Was Archer coming to the boys? Or had it just been the usual trick of dreams?

Tim turned off the taps and wiped his hands on the dishcloth that hung from a cabinet knob. "There was another person, a boy, up at the church. Except the church wasn't a church, it was lit up like a spookhouse. This boy was up in the place with the bell, just laughing and laughing and laughing and ringing the bell. And the dead man danced around the tombstones, pieces of him falling off the whole time."

Archer. It had to be Archer. *The truth has many faces,* he always said. "Well, you've been through a lot. It's no wonder you had such a weird dream," Linda said, pressing out two patties and placing them in a black iron skillet on the stove. The heat made the meat sizzle, the white noise of energy transformation.

"That dream was nowhere near as scary as talking to the sheriff. Or seeing Ronnie in the hospital."

The sheriff. No wonder Tim had thought the man

was going to arrest him. The sheriff had stood like an army man in the hospital lobby, asking Tim questions in his deep, patient voice. He was a threat. But he was of the old blood, and had his own debt to pay. Archer could handle him.

The burgers popped as she flipped them, sending tiny sparks of pain up her bare arms as hot grease spattered on her skin. The bell rang on the microwave. "Dinner's ready," she said.

While Tim ate at the kitchen table, Linda took some apple juice to Ronnie. She turned on the light, and he moaned. "It's okay, honey," she said. "I brought you something to drink."

He was feverish and pale against the pillow. His nose was still plumped by packing, and a stray bloody thread of gauze dangled from one nostril.

"N-not thirsty," Ronnie said.

She sat beside him on the lower bunk. As the oldest, he usually slept in the upper bunk, but she didn't want to risk his falling during the night. Archer would want him mended, healed, whole. Not like this.

Why did you have to go and break your nose? He looked so small, with his hair brushed back and the *Star Wars* sheets pulled up to his chin. Theo, his stuffed bear, had fallen to the side, the stiff arms providing no comfort.

For a split second, she blamed Archer for the injury. Of course, she knew that Archer had taken Boonie Houck, had made the drunkard pay for his sins at the same time Archer rejuvenated himself for holy work. Boonie's worthless life had culminated with a great act of giving. Serving as a sacrifice was Boonie's highest possible purpose in this world. He should have been whimpering in gratitude as Archer took his wicked eyes and tongue and other sinful parts.

Ronnie's accident was only a down payment, she knew. Many innocents would fall so that none of the guilty escaped. That was the Word, that was the Way. She had accepted the testament long ago.

Archer warned that some choices would be difficult. But he reminded the fold that earthly love was only another vanity, another sin. All love must be directed to the Temple of the Two Suns. And none of that love could be wasted on the First Son, Jesus.

Jesus, the plague maker. The damning one. The liar. A mask of light and peace covering a devil's scarred and pocked face. Linda shivered, recalling how deeply the Baptists had brainwashed her. And to think that she'd been making the boys go to their church.

A Jesus trick, Archer had explained. Using David, to trap her. To "save" her.

She shuddered and put the apple juice to Ronnie's lips. He strained his head forward and took a swallow, then collapsed back against the pillow. "How are you feeling, sugar?"

"Hurts," he whispered.

"I know, baby. It'll be okay soon."

"I just want to sleep."

"Sure." She kissed him on the forehead, careful to avoid the purpled flesh around his eyes. "Sweet dreams."

Timmy was finished eating by the time she got back to the kitchen. She sent him to wash his face and brush his teeth, and then to bed. She turned on the radio, the local station. A Beatles song was playing, "Strawberry Fields Forever." Sinful. But she was strong. She could withstand this test of faith.

Yes, Archer, I am strong. I am worthy. The music can't touch me, because I know it for what it is.

She listened as the song segued into its second fadeout, the backward-tape effects filled with secret messages. The taunts and seductive whispers of Jesus. Something about burying Paul, the cursed apostle. Dozens of people across the county, maybe hundreds, were being exposed to this depraved Christ-worship. She said a quick prayer to Archer for their souls.

Another song came on. The Culture Club, a band she used to like. Back before she met Archer. "Karma chameleon," Boy George sang. Karma chameleon. More sacrilege, more perverted celebrations of the spirit, another false Way.

The boys would be asleep now. She turned off the radio and silently crept out the door. The sky was charcoal gray in the west, where the waxing moon hung bloated and obscene. But the ground, the earth, the mountains were black as absolution. As near Archer's promised peace as one could hope, at least in this mortal world.

Crickets. The chuckle of the creek. The wind soughing through the trees, hiding the noises of nocturnal creatures.

She didn't need light in order to see.

She needed only faith.

And darkness.

Archer's darkness summoned her, a beacon so righteously black that it was blinding.

She crossed the damp meadow and slipped into the forest.

Zeb Potter cradled the shotgun across one flannel-wrapped arm. He shined the flashlight into the belly

of the barn. The cows were banging against the walls
of their stall, uneasy lowing coming from their throats.
The air was thick with the smell of fresh manure.

Something's scared 'em bad.

Zeb had been getting ready for bed, had taken out
his chewing tobacco and his teeth and was deciding
whether or not he could go one more night in the
same pair of long johns when the bawling of a calf
filled the night. A calf could wail its lungs out if it
wanted, but hardly ever cut loose without a good reason.

Most people thought cows were dumb as dirt, but
they had peculiarities that none of those genius
"agronomists" from NC State would ever be able to
explain. A healthy cow, you hit it in that place just
between and a little above the eyes with a sledgehammer, and it dropped dead on the spot, ready to turn
to steak and hamburger. But a sick cow, you had to
hit it five or six times before it went down. And why
was that? The sick cow was living to get healthy, but
the healthy cow was about as well off as it could hope
to be. So the healthy cow didn't have as much to
look forward to. Cows knew a thing or two about life.

So they always kicked up a fuss when they smelled
something bad. Though all the big predators had
died out, once in a while a pack of wild dogs came
over the hills from Tennessee-ways, where people let
such things go on. But on this side of the state line,
people took care of their problems. They didn't wait
for problems to do their damage and move on.

After the first commotion, Zeb had cussed once
and slipped into his boots without bothering to find
his socks. He'd stopped by the door and put on his
hat and collected his twenty-gauge and his spotlight.
If Betty were still alive, she would be waiting by the
door in her nightgown, telling him to be careful.

And he would have patted the shotgun and said, "This is all the care I need." But Betty had gone to be with the Lord, and the farm was big and lonely and the house made noises at night. And the damned hound had probably skulked away into the woods at the slightest scent of trouble.

The shotgun was heavy, and Zeb's muscles ached from tension. He flicked the light over the barn, its yellow beam bouncing around among locust posts and old wire and rotted feed sacks. Hay dust choked the air, and the crumbs from last fall's tobacco snowed between the cracks in the loft floor above. Something was moving around up there.

That ain't no damned wild Tennessee dogs.

Zeb clenched his bare gums together and moved as smoothly as his old bones would let him over to the loft stairs. A chicken was disturbed from its nest under the steps and almost got its knobby head blown off when it erupted into Zeb's face. Zeb picked up the flashlight he had dropped. The cows were noisier now, their milling more frantic.

Zeb put a trembling foot on the stairs. "Who's up yonder?" he hollered, hoping he sounded angry instead of scared. Nothing but moos answered him.

He'd heard what had happened to Boonie, and there was no way in hell that it was going to happen to him. The sheriff had even been out, asking if Zeb had seen or heard anything unusual. But the only thing Zeb had heard was those damned bells in the middle of the night, what was probably some of them high school kids finding a way to bug as many people as possible.

He thought now about going up to the house and ringing the sheriff's department. Littlefield told him to call if anything "unusual" happened. Littlefield sure liked that word. But Zeb had known Littlefield when the boy was knee-high to a scarecrow, and he didn't want the sheriff to think that he couldn't take care of his own problems. That was why Tennessee and the rest of the damned country was in such a mess. Everybody closed their eyes when the bad stuff came along.

John Wayne never even blinked.

Zeb played the spotlight into the darkness at the top of the stairs. He put a boot on the second tread, and before he could decide whether he was really going to or not, he had taken another step, then another, and he was halfway up before he even started thinking again. He laid the barrel of the shotgun over his left wrist so he could shine the light while still keeping his right hand at the trigger. If he fired the gun in that position, with it held beside his hip, the recoil would probably break his trigger finger. That was one worry that John Wayne never had.

"Might have been somebody with a knife or an ax," the sheriff had said. "Either that, or a wild animal."

Sure, it could be somebody with a blade. City folks had moved into Whispering Pines, up from Florida or down from New York, come to escape those streets that were full of maniacs with drugged-out eyes and hands that would rather slap you than lift in greeting. But guess what? The city folks had brought the bad things with them. A killer's instinct was as easily packed away in a U-Haul as a fitness machine or a golf cart was.

He'd told the sheriff in no uncertain terms that there wasn't an animal around here big enough to mutilate a man like that. Maybe off in Africa or something, but things were tamed over here. So when Littlefield said Perry Hoyle had mentioned a mountain lion, Zeb laughed out loud. The idea of a touched-in-the-head killer running around was way easier to swallow than believing a mountain lion was on the loose.

But right now, Zeb was in no mood to laugh at anything. His stomach was a wet sack of cornmeal, tied closed by the knot in his throat. He had ascended enough to poke his head into the loft, and the spotlight jittered from corner to corner, too fast for him to really see much.

Hay, stacked crooked like a child's wooden blocks.

The bright metal glint of his tools hanging on the wall by his workbench.

Night, cool beyond the chicken wire that covered the open windows.

Posts, the dull underside of the tin roofing, the hewed stakes where the tobacco hung to dry, the—

The dark thing, swooping, a sudden papery rattle breaking the strained quiet.

Zeb jerked the spotlight and his trigger hand tensed.

Bat.

Goddamned no-good mouse with wings.

Zeb exhaled, his heart pounding in his eardrums. A small, warm ache filled his chest.

Easy now, Zebulon. Don't be putting yourself in no hospital.

He'd been in the hospital last year, and that was as close to prison as he ever wanted to be. Doctors sticking things inside every hole in his body, nurses seeing him naked, people in white coats telling him when to eat what pills. Couldn't have a chaw, no, sir. *Have you ever had this, this, or this?*

Finally, they'd cut him open and taken out his gall bladder. He suspected it was just for the hell of it, that they really couldn't find anything wrong but didn't want to admit it. But he figured the surgery would make them happy, and he'd never needed the damned gallbladder anyway. At least they didn't take anything important, and he got to go home again, even if he still felt like warmed-over liver mush about half the time.

Zeb was mad at himself for shaking. And to prove to himself that he didn't close his eyes to problems, and that, by God, *he* didn't have no sorry Tennessee blood in him, he walked across the loft, careful to avoid the black squares cut in the floor where he threw down hay to the cattle in the winter months.

If anybody was up here, they were trespassing, plain and simple.

And if it was a touched-in-the-head druggie escaped from the city, Zeb could handle him.

No matter the ax or knife.

A shadow of movement caught his eye, and he brought up the light to see that it was only a piece of hemp rope, swaying in the breeze that leaked in from the windows.

A metallic squeak came from behind him. Zeb spun, the flashlight beam crawling over the workbench. A short piece of stovepipe rocked back and forth. *Wasn't no wind blowed* that.

He crept toward the bench, the pump-action shotgun leading the way. It occurred to him that the flashlight was giving away his position. The druggie or whatnot knew exactly where Zeb was.

Nothing to do but walk brave and proud. He stood John Wayne straight and said, "Come on out where I can see you."

Only silence and the muted ruckus of the cows.

"Got a gun here."

A cricket chirped somewhere amid the hay.

Zeb played the light along the wall above the workbench. Something wasn't right.

There was the pitchfork, hanging by two rusty nails. A pulley, used for raising cows so they could be properly gutted. A cross-saw. An ax. A crop sprayer with a shoulder strap. A loop of harness. A shovel. Two hoes. An old mowing bar for the tractor. Three different thicknesses of chain.

And what else? What was missing?

The wall went dark and it took Zeb a second to realize that the light had been blocked.

Druggie.

A face filled the circle of light, a face that looked familiar but unreal. Zeb's chest was boiling, as hot as a chicken-scalding cauldron.

Not a druggie. A . . .

Zeb's finger tightened on the trigger, and the roar of exploding gunpowder slapped against the tin roofing, then echoed to give Zeb's ears an extra deafening blow. Pellets ripped scars in the wormy chestnut walls. And the thing that had been standing before him was blown back to hell where it belonged.

Except . . .

Sweet merciful Jesus.

The thing was still there, the face split into a sharp grin as the features around it rippled between skin and scale and fur and a shapeless, slick gray. But the eyes were the worst, those green stabbing rays that loved and hated worse than any dream or nightmare, eyes that owned, eyes that blessed and cursed, eyes that—

Zeb could hear himself whimpering as he tried to pull back the pumping stock. He'd been right: firing the gun *had* broken his shooting finger, but no time to worry about the pain in his heart and hand. He might have missed the first time, but the thing was closer now, only he was too weak to reload—this would never happen to John Wayne.

The spotlight had fallen in the hay, but its beam was angled upward. The bright-eyed thing filled the circle of light like the star of a demented puppet show. It raised the sledge, Zeb's cow-killing hammer, and as the eight-pound metal head began its downward stroke, aimed for that place just between and a little above the eyes, he realized that maybe those Tennessee-born bastards were right.

There *was* a time to close your eyes until the bad stuff went away.

EIGHT

Frank Littlefield topped the hill in his Trooper, blinking against the dawn as he threaded his way into the valley of Whispering Pines. He had the window rolled down because the smell of green spring was so much sweeter this far from town. The few houses were set away from the road, with stretches of pasture and tobacco fields broken by stands of hardwood forest. Below, the silver and brown of barn roofs made tiny rectangles along the plain of the river. Cows ambled near the fence lines, moving as sleepily and lazily as the river, their heads all pointed in the same direction.

A few vehicles passed, their occupants in dark suits and starched dresses, with hair respectfully combed or brushed. They were headed toward Barkersville, toward church. Sunday was supposed to be a holy day, a day of rest and fellowship, of fried chicken and televised sports. Not a day of death.

He reached the valley floor and turned onto the gravel road that he knew too well. A boy was fishing off the one-lane bridge, and Littlefield slowed to minimize the dust raised by the Trooper's passing. The sheriff checked the boy's stringer line to see if the trout were biting. The stringer was slack. Even the fish were lazy today.

He rounded a bend and the red church came into view. From this distance, the structure seemed to have a face. The windows were like flat eyes, the eaves a brooding brow, the uneven stone foundation a cruel grin of broken teeth. The church glowered, smug and hateful on its cemetery hill. Littlefield looked away to rid himself of the image of Samuel hanging from the eaves.

A strip of yellow plastic at the lower edge of the cemetery marked off the scene where Boonie Houck had died. DO NOT CROSS, the police line commanded. Funny how those words always came a little too late. If only the barrier had been in place a week ago. Then Boonie might be waking up with a hangover instead of sleeping on a metal gurney in the state medical examiner's meat locker.

All we have to do is mark off the whole world. Little yellow strips for everybody.

A truck was backed up to the church's door. It was Lester's farm truck, a big black Dodge two-ton. Bales of hay were stacked in the cattle bed. Lester had never worked on Sundays. The only time he missed a morning worship service was when he had to make a November run to the tobacco market in Durham.

Littlefield decided to have another talk with Lester. Storie would be waiting for him at Zeb Potter's place, but from what the detective had told him over the phone that morning, there wasn't much Littlefield could do for the old farmer. And the sheriff had a feeling that whatever was going on at the red church might have some connection to last night's murder. Because Zeb Potter most definitely had not been attacked by a mountain lion. Unless mountain lions had learned how to swing sledgehammers.

He pulled into the twin ruts that served as the church's driveway and parked by the Dodge. Lester was standing at the church door, a bale of brown-yellow hay in his gloved hands. "Howdy, Sheriff. You're getting to be a regular around these parts."

"A mite *too* regular," Littlefield said, getting out of the Trooper. He looked up at the dogwood, at the thin black branches that never died. He started to glance at the belfry, but caught himself and turned his attention back to Lester. "I guess the sale went through okay."

"Sure did. I ain't seen that many zeroes since my last report card, way back in the fourth grade." Lester drained the excess tobacco juice from his mouth.

Someone came out of the sanctuary. It was the Day woman, the mother of the boys who had found Boonie's body. A red kerchief held her hair out of her face, and her shirt-sleeves were rolled halfway up. Bits of straw clung to the flannel.

"Hi, Sheriff," she said, tossing a bale of hay into the truck and starting back inside the church.

"Good morning, ma'am. How's your boy this morning?"

She looked confused at first, as if she didn't know who he was talking about. "Ronnie? Oh, he's fine. Just fine. They bounce back fast when they're that age."

Fast enough so that you can go out and leave them unattended? "Glad to hear it, ma'am. What about the little one?"

"Timmy's okay, too. He's at the house, keeping watch for me."

"Did he remember anything else about finding the body? Anything that might help us?"

She looked at Lester, then into the dark belly of

the church. "I think it's best that he forget all about it, don't you?"

"Maybe so." Who or what was inside the church that was making her so nervous? And what was she doing here in the first place? To Littlefield, the chore seemed like something more than just a case of neighbor helping neighbor.

Lester squinted up at the sun. "Excuse us, Sheriff. We got work to do."

"Sure. One thing, though. You hear anything last night?"

Lester's eyes flicked almost imperceptibly to the belfry. Almost. "No. I slept like a hibernating log. Why?"

"I thought you might have heard something. What about you, Mrs. Day?"

The woman was leaning against the door frame, biting her lip. "Heard something? What do you mean?"

"Like maybe something from over your neighbor's way? On the Potter farm?"

She shook her head. "Why, no, Sheriff."

He eased closer to the steps that led into the red church, veering clear of the dogwood. The air coming from the church was cool, even though light slanted through the windows. Lester and Linda stepped side by side as if to block his way.

"Somebody killed Zeb Potter last night." The sheriff watched for any reaction. Lester quickened the pace of his tobacco chewing. Linda Day looked in the direction of the Potter farm.

"I guess it for sure wasn't no mountain lion this time, was it?" Lester said.

"That's what my deputies say. Zeb was killed with a sledgehammer."

"Huh. They know who done it?"

"Not yet. We're trying to lift some fingerprints." But Littlefield suspected they would find no clues. No fingerprints, no footprints, no clothing fibers. And no eyewitnesses. "I was wondering if you heard the bells ring last night?"

Littlefield had learned from long experience how to tell if a person was about to lie. And Lester fit the profile. The old farmer's nostrils flared slightly with indignation, he drew in a sharp breath, his eyes shifted left and right, and he stood a little straighter. "Like I told you, I was sleeping like the dead."

The sheriff nodded. "What about you, ma'am? Or your husband?"

She was a better liar than Lester. Maybe she had done it too often. "Well, I had the radio on most of the night, at least till I fell asleep. I wouldn't have heard nothing. David was . . . asleep."

"I see. Well, I guess I better get over to Zeb's."

He started to turn, then quickly looked up at the pair, trying to catch them off guard. "You mind if I have a quick look inside the church? You know, in case the killer stopped by. I'm kind of figuring that the same person that killed Zeb killed Boonie."

Sweat glistened underneath Lester's eyes. He pulled at the straps of his coveralls. "Well, Sheriff, I don't mind a bit, but it ain't my property no more. I don't know if I can give permission like that unless you got a search warrant."

A smooth voice boomed from inside the church. "Now, now, Lester. Our church is always open."

Lester and Linda parted, standing one on each side of the door like concrete lions at a library entrance.

A man stepped into the light. He was tall, with dark curly hair and healthy, tanned skin. He had a slight touch of gray hair at the temples. His cheeks crinkled when he smiled, but his deep brown eyes were unreadable. He wore a white cotton shirt and a gray tie, slacks, and a pair of leather shoes that cost about two weeks' worth of Littlefield's salary.

"A church should turn away no one, especially a man who seeks the truth," the man said. An aroma of cologne wafted from him, but underneath the spicy musk was a disturbing smell that Littlefield couldn't place. The man stooped and extended a hand. "Sheriff Littlefield. I'm glad we have a capable man on the job in these uncertain and dangerous times."

The sheriff climbed to the landing. The preacher's hand was as cool as a fish. "Pleased to meet you, uh . . ."

"It's been a long time. Nearly a lifetime ago."

Now his face was familiar. McFall. Except he didn't have that typical McFall slump, that devious way of moving, the almost cowering attitude that ran in the McFall family as a result of being snubbed and kicked around. "I'm Archer McFall," he said, in that used-car-salesman voice of his.

"Archer. Lester told me you were moving back here." Littlefield glanced at Lester, who had suddenly become highly interested in the flaking paint of the truck's cattle bed.

"Well, Sheriff, everybody loves these mountains," Archer said. "It gets in your blood."

"And you bought this here church?"

"Yes, sir. I'm going to open it up again. God's work has been sorely neglected in these parts. People are in desperate need of the Word and the Way. That we have a murderer in our midst is only one more sign of how far we've fallen."

Littlefield nodded. He never knew how to conduct himself in the presence of a preacher. He always felt a flash of guilt for his sins and his irregular church visitations, but usually an aura of forgiving calm emanated from someone of the cloth. With Archer, though, he felt nothing but the guilt.

"Come on inside, Sheriff. Make sure there's no killer here. We can't have a devil hiding out in the house of God."

Suddenly the sheriff didn't want to step inside. In his mind, he could hear the fluttery Halloween laugh from his childhood. The boards were clapping, clawing, the church door was a mouth, he was going to be swallowed, like Jonah into the belly of the whale. Like his brother Samuel.

He swayed dizzily and felt the preacher's strong grip on his forearm. "Are you okay, Sheriff?"

"Uh . . ." Littlefield rubbed his temples. "Not getting much sleep lately. These damned—excuse me, Reverend—these doggoned murder cases must be getting to me."

"There's peace in prayer, Sheriff. You will find your killer. All things in God's good time."

Littlefield felt his feet shuffle forward, almost against his will, and then he was inside the church. Most of the hay was gone. The handmade pews that had been stacked against one wall the day before were now lined unevenly across the floor. Brooms, pitchforks, mops, and buckets were scattered across the sanctuary. The room smelled of candle wax. They had accomplished a lot this morning.

Or had they been working all night?

Behind him, Lester and Linda resumed their work. A woman emerged from the small wing at one side of the dais. Littlefield recognized her face but didn't know her name. She gave a short nod and began dusting the lectern. Littlefield thought he might sneeze, but he rubbed his nose until the urge passed.

"Looks like you'll soon be ready for a service," Littlefield said.

"There are different kinds of service, Sheriff. I work for God, you work for the people. But we're a lot alike, in a way."

"What way?"

"We both know there's more to this church than just nails and chestnut and rippled glass."

Littlefield tried again to read the man's eyes. The irises glittered like muddy diamonds with many facets, each facet hiding a different secret. Archer surely was well versed about the legends, handed down in his family for generations. Those were the sources of his childhood beatings. That he could maintain faith in God after such suffering was a miracle in itself.

"My father used to say, 'It's people what makes a church,' " Littlefield said.

Archer smiled, showing perfect white teeth. "He was a wise man."

"Aren't you afraid of what people are going to say when you open the church again?"

"God delivered Daniel from the lion's den. He delivered Isaac from Abraham's sacrificial altar. Why should I expect any less?"

"Well, for one thing, push never came to shove for Abraham, because he never had to deliver the knife blow. And Daniel didn't have a great-great-grandfather named Wendell McFall."

The preacher let out a laugh that rolled from deep inside his diaphragm. The sound echoed in the wooden hollow of the church, the acoustics amplifying the power of Archer's voice. "Ah, the scandals and the ghost stories," he said. "There's only one ghost here and that's the Holy Ghost. As for the rest of it, I hope that the legends might draw a few curiosity seekers to our services. There are many paths to the one true Way."

"Amen to that." Littlefield walked to the dais, the fall of his boots resounding in the hollow of the church. He leaned over the railing that fronted the pulpit. The stain was still there. Littlefield's dizziness returned as he tried to attach an image to the random shape.

And he saw that it was the shape of an angel, or a Bell Monster, winged and fierce, with jagged claws and . . .

Yeah, sure. Sounds like something a murderer's lawyer would make up. It's nothing but a stain, old paint or something.

It was larger than it had been the day before, yet still retained its weathered quality, as if the stain had been embedded in the floor ages ago. And Littlefield wondered if it had been even smaller before Boonie's death. As if . . .

He didn't want to give legitimacy to his superstitious turn of mind. Telling Detective Sergeant Storie about the ghosts had been foolish enough. But now that the thought was trying to form, he held it outside himself, examined it rationally.

. . . as if the stain is made from the blood of its victims.

There. Now that he admitted it, it seemed safe and perfectly silly. A psychotic killer wasn't on the loose. Something worse was on the loose, somehow finding legs and hands and a pair of eyes and a soul.

A soul.

"See anything unusual, Sheriff?"

Archer's voice pulled him from a pool of dizziness. He met those brown eyes again, eyes that were now as dull and faded as the ancient woodwork of the church. Some famous person had said that eyes were the windows to the soul. Well, Archer's windows needed a good washing. Except then, you might be able to see inside.

"I don't believe you have anything to worry about," Littlefield said. "Now that you've cleaned up, there's no place for a killer to hide."

Except right out in the open.

Archer smiled, standing with his arms crossed. He was taller than the sheriff. "I never worry. I have God on my side, remember?"

"Yeah, but isn't that what the other side always says, too?"

Archer laughed again. "So they do, Sheriff. So they do."

Littlefield walked back through the church, Archer following. "I used to come to services here when I was young," the sheriff said. "Back when it was Potter's Mill Baptist Church."

"Oh, is that so? Being inside it must bring back a lot of memories."

Littlefield didn't respond. He paused in the foyer to look up at the square hole in the ceiling. "You going to get a new rope?"

"Sooner or later. And I hope none of the congregation gets a crazy notion to hang their preacher."

"God stopped Abraham's knife." Lester and the Day woman were standing in the doorway. They drew back as he went into the sunshine. "Thanks for your time. Guess I'd better get on over to Zeb's."

As Littlefield was getting in the Trooper, Archer called to him from the steps: "Say, Sheriff. Why don't you come back sometime for a service?"

"When?"

"First one's tonight at midnight."

Midnight. It figured. Nothing could be ordinary about this church.

Maybe he *would* come to a service, Littlefield

thought as he drove away. Crazy as it was, maybe he would.

The thing with wings and claws and livers for eyes clicked sharp bone against Ronnie's window. *Can you hear him aknocking?*

Ronnie was trapped by the weight of blankets, frozen in sweat, clenched around the tight fire in his belly. *Close your eyes and it will go away. Close your eyes—*

His eyes were already closed. He opened them.

The sunlight coming through the window made his head hurt. He'd been asleep for so long that he couldn't remember where he was for about a minute. Plus he'd been having really weird dreams about the red church and a walking bloody thing and something to do with Mom.

"Mom?" he called, his throat dry.

His nose wasn't as sore today, but he felt as if somebody had taken a hand pump and blown his face full of air. He licked his thick lips. "Mom?"

Tim came into the room, still wearing his pajamas. And he was eating chocolate-chip cookies. Mom was going to kill the little dork if she caught him eating cookies so early in the day. But, after the scary dreams, Ronnie was actually kind of glad to see his brother, though he'd never admit it in a million years.

"Where's Mom?" Ronnie asked.

Tim shrugged. His belly button showed below the fabric of his top. "Ain't seen her this morning."

"What time is it?" Ronnie groaned as he tried to sit up, then fell back onto the pillows.

"Almost eleven."

"Eleven?" That meant that Mom was skipping church again. It was the first time she'd missed

church two weeks in a row since Tim was a baby. Not that Ronnie minded, because his Sunday school teacher, Preacher Staymore, usually told him he needed to be saved, then made him wait after class while everybody else went to the main sanctuary for worship service.

Preacher Staymore would sit beside Ronnie and ask the spirit of Jesus to move into Ronnie's heart so that the child might be spared, and though Jesus loved the little children, there was only one path to salvation and that was through the blood of the Lord. And Preacher Staymore would tremble and put his palm on Ronnie's head and invoke the mercy and the power and the goodness, then ask Ronnie if he could hear the Lord aknocking. And the whole time Ronnie would be thinking about how Preacher Staymore's breath smelled like a basket of rotten fruit.

"Can you hear Him aknocking?" the preacher would say, his eyes shining and glassy. "He's awanting in. And all you got to do is say, 'Come on in, Jesus. Come right on into this sorry sinful heart of mine and clean house.' If you won't do that one little thing, then don't go crying to the Lord when the devil comes to drag you into the pits of hell."

And Ronnie would always be afraid. That message, along with the preacher's pungent breath, made him hastily agree to be saved, to let the Lord shine His everlasting light into the darkness of Ronnie's heart, to throw the door wide open and say, "Come in, come in, come in."

Getting saved always filled him with a kind of warmth, as if something really *had* come into his heart. But the feeling always faded, and he'd slip back into his sinning ways. Preacher Staymore said there were two kinds of sin: the kind of the flesh, and the kind of the spirit. Ronnie suspected that sins of the flesh had something to do with the naked women like those in Boonie's magazine, but his own sins were mostly those of the spirit. Still, any kind of sin made his heart beat faster, and maybe that drove the Lord away, what with all the noise and commotion in his chest.

So every few weeks, Preacher Staymore would sense that Ronnie needed another saving. Ronnie was scared enough of the hellfire not to take any chances, even though sometimes he wondered, if the Lord was merciful, why would He make people go to such a bad hot place? And if sinners went to hell, what was the point of Jesus dying for them in the first place? And if the Lord was all-powerful, why didn't He just make people so they didn't sin? And if He already knew what happened in people's hearts, why did there have to be a Judgment Day when all the sins were revealed?

But those kinds of thoughts were sins of the spirit, and led to a fresh need to be saved. Ronnie didn't want to think about that right now. He had enough troubles, like a broken nose and his parents separated and a scary red church and bad dreams.

"Have you seen Mom?" he asked Tim.

Tim bit a crescent of cookie and shook his head. "Not since last night," he said, spraying cookie crumbs onto the floor as he spoke.

"Dang."

"The police are out again."

Ronnie sat up. *"Here?"*

"No. They're over at Mr. Potter's."

"Mr. Potter? I guess maybe the sheriff wanted to ask him some questions."

Tim shook his head. His bowl haircut made him look like a turtle. "I don't think so. Their blue lights were flashing when they drove up. And I saw the ambulance over by the barn."

"You're fooling."

Tim's eyes widened behind his spectacles. "No, I ain't. You can go look."

Ronnie rolled himself out of bed with a groan. He leaned against the railing of the top bunk, dizzy from spending nearly two days in bed. Through the window, he could see two police cars on the Potter farm. The sheriff's vehicle was parked by the house. One of the deputies walked toward the barn, the sun glinting off his handcuffs and black shoes.

"You don't suppose . . . ?" Ronnie said.

"That whatever got Boonie Houck got Mr. Potter?" Tim sounded almost pleased at the prospect. "That would be cool. Like one of those movies Mom won't let us watch."

Ronnie remembered his dream. Maybe it was just his overactive imagination again. "Did you hear anything last night?" he asked, trying to sound like he didn't care one way or another.

"Not really. I heard some bells ringing. I don't know what time, except for it was dark."

"I hope Mom is okay." Sure, Mom would be okay. Nothing would get her.

Not even the thing with wings and claws and livers for eyes.

Ronnie thought of Preacher Staymore's words: *Can you hear Him aknocking? He's awanting in.*

No way in hell would Ronnie let *that* thing come in. He shivered in the sunlight.

NINE

Sunday. A holy day, at least to the Protestants and Catholics and Mormons. Fools all. But Mama Bet comforted herself with the knowledge that they'd be burned by the light in due time.

It was almost as if God had roped off a little section of the Blue Ridge and saved it for the Potters, Abshers, McFalls, and the rest. The original families came from Scotland and England, as white as the driven snow, though their hearts were as dark and Jesus-laden as any of their ancestors' hearts. And somehow those families had managed to protect this piece of valley at the foot of Buckhorn from invaders and outsiders. Kept it pure, except for the original taint that they brought with them when they settled in the 1780s.

You can't ever shake the blood.

She sat in her front porch rocker, looking out over the mountains she loved so much. Heaven ought to be this nice. A fresh spring breeze cut through a gap, working up from the foothills to stir the jack pines and locusts and poplars. The sky was clear enough for her to see the gray face of Grandfather Mountain forty miles in the distance. Even with her cataracts, she could make out the features that looked like a brow, a nose, and a long granite beard.

Her goat bleated below the porch. She kept a few chickens, too, but they were free-ranging up in the woods. She was getting too old to track down their eggs, and plucking their feathers was too rough on her fingers. Come to think of it, she didn't know why she bothered with a goat, either. She hated the taste of goat's milk, and she didn't know how to cook the animal up even if she could bear to kill it.

"What are you thinking about, Mother?" asked Archer. He sat on the porch swing, uncomfortable, his face rigid, as if holding his earthly flesh together took all his concentration. He was a fine boy, handsome and respectably clean-shaven, with the whole world laid out before him. All a mother could want for her son.

She felt a tug in her heart, or maybe it was a spell of the murmurs. The murmurs were coming on a lot more often lately. God was priming her for a trip up to the kingdom, striking her with all the little ailments that added up to the miseries of old age. God could be downright cruel when He set his mind to it. But He allowed good stuff to happen, too. Like Archer.

"I was just remembering," she said. "When you was little, you used to go up yonder on that knoll and pick gooseberries. You'd eat them things till you turned green and got sick to your stomach. And I'd lay you down in bed, tuck you in, and give you a nice cup of peppermint tea."

"And you'd tell me stories," Archer said. His voice was different from the one he'd used on television. It was softer, more down-home, a little of his Carolina mountain accent creeping in between those California words.

"Sure did. You probably don't remember any of them silly stories."

Archer leaned forward, sniffed the air. "I remember them all."

"All of them?"

"Yeah. The Old Testament. Jack tales. Ghost stories. And the real story of Jesus. Except that one always gave me nightmares."

"I hope I done right. It wasn't easy, raising you by myself. I reckon I made some mistakes along the way, but I always acted out of love."

Archer left his porch swing and knelt before her rocker. He took her hands and looked up, his brown eyes shining with that same radiant depth they'd had when he was a baby. As he grew older, those eyes got him in trouble. They made the other kids suspicious and made adults uncomfortable. Those eyes, plus the fact that he was a McFall, pretty much brought the persecution on him. Many were the times he came home from school with a black eye or a skinned knee or his little shoulders shaking with sobs.

All she could tell him was that the lamb must walk among wolves. He seemed to accept that he would be persecuted, that the human hatred was all part of God's plan. He came up with that bit about "There will come great trials" all by himself. What willpower it must have taken to keep from lashing out, what patience and understanding Archer had possessed even from an early age. Of course, he always knew that he was the Second Son. She was up-front about that right from the moment he could speak.

"You did everything perfectly," Archer said. "God should be proud."

"Well, I ain't so sure about that. If I was so all-fired perfect, maybe I'd be out of this place by now."

"Why don't you let me buy you one of those chalets at Ski Village?"

Mama Bet looked at the scar that ran up Wellborn
Mountain. The steel threads of the lift cables arced
along the barren slope. The snow had melted weeks
ago, leaving nothing but a mud patch. She despised
those ski people. "No. People best stick to their own
kind. Besides, I reckon God put us here for a reason."

*And that reason just might have something to do with
that little hellhole in back of the root cellar, the one I got to
keep plugged with prayers. But I ain't going to worry you
with that.*

Something beeped in Archer's pocket. Mama Bet
looked at him suspiciously.

He smiled. "Cellular phone. You ought to let me
get you one, Mother."

"That's the devil's tool," she said, frowning. "I
don't even trust words that come over wires. When
it's invisible, there's no telling where the messages
are coming from."

Archer pulled his phone from his jacket pocket
and flipped it open. He put it to his head. "Archer
McFall."

He listened for a moment, then put his hand over
the mouthpiece. "Excuse me, Mother. It's the foundation offices in California."

She nodded. She'd been against his exodus to California from the start. Nothing out there but hea-
thens and hippies and all manner of strange cults.
Archer had no business among that sort.

But children had to learn on their own, didn't
they? All you could do was fill them up with love,
and let them wander the path. You couldn't hammer
faith into them. You couldn't drive goodliness and
grace into them like nails. You couldn't *make* them
believe the things God wanted them to believe. They

just had to search in their own hearts, and, God willing, come up with the truth.

She watched him as he carried on a conversation, something about stock splits, portfolios, and divestitures. She didn't understand why God kept Archer meddling in such affairs. But then, there was a lot she didn't understand about God. And she had to admit, that black Mercedes looked awfully shiny and clean down there in the driveway.

She rose from her rocker and headed for the door. Archer glanced at her questioningly, but she waved him back to his phone conversation. She entered the house, walking over the same boards that the McFalls had trodden for more than two hundred years. The main room was the original cabin, thick hand-hewed logs chinked with yellowed cement. Not much had changed in the room since her great-great-great-grandparents Robert and Hepzibah McFall had first blessed these walls with love and devotion.

The old stone fireplace was black from ten thousand fires. The room was dark, the small wooden windows nailed shut. Three sides of the cabin were partially underground, built that way to cut down on the wind leaking through the cracks, though the room always stayed as cold as a Christian's heart. Water was piped from a spring up the hill, and a leak dripped steadily into the freestanding ceramic sink in the corner.

A few rooms had been added onto the south side of the cabin, and these had glass windows. The sun poured through, God's pure light, but it barely touched what had once served as kitchen, bedroom, and living room combined. When electricity first reached these parts in the 1950s, Mama Bet wouldn't allow them to hook up the original part of the house. Some things were to be kept sacred, untouched by the progress that marked the spread of the devil's influence.

Mama Bet went past the rough hemlock table where Wendell McFall had once taken his meals. She parted the gingham that curtained off the pantry. She took a candle from a counter and lit it, and looked to make sure Archer was still outside. She stepped inside among the shelves and rows of canning jars, dried beans, and sacks of cornmeal. The chill from the back of the pantry crept over her like a live thing, a giant shadow, an ice-cold invisible lover.

She pushed aside the rotted boards that lined the back of the pantry. A fungal, earthy smell filled her nostrils. She extended the candle into the root cellar, peering over the rows of potatoes and red apples into the darkness. The candle shrank from the stale, still air, its light swallowed by the dirt walls of the cellar.

"I'm getting too old for this, God," she whispered in silent prayer. God said nothing, but she knew He was up there, watching, biting His tongue to keep from laughing. She wiggled the base of the candle into the red clay until it stood without her holding it. She could see the stone that blocked the narrow tunnel, a tunnel that wound down and down and deep into the earth.

This was the one secret she had spared Archer, the one that had been passed down through eight generations of McFalls. The Appalachians were the oldest mountains in the world, had risen from the hot magma when God crushed the world together. And she knew exactly why God made the Earth. He had trapped the devil inside it, wrapped billions of tons of rock and dirt and molten lava around the beast. And, oh, how the devil must have kicked and struggled to get free, shoving up mountains and causing the rifts that became the oceans.

She knew this as surely as she knew that Archer was a savior. You didn't question universal truths. You accepted them on faith. You tucked them in your heart and made the best of them. You fought for them. You made the sacrifices that kept those truths alive.

Who knew when the devil had first wormed its way finally to the surface of the world? It could have been tens of thousands of years ago, or a few hundred. All that mattered now was that the devil was loose upon the face of the Earth, and Archer had to defeat it.

That had to be why Archer had returned to Whispering Pines, why God had called His son back home. The devil was still here, tied to this mouth of hell, living in those original families. The devil had hidden behind the faces of the Littlefields, worn the masks of the Houcks, slipped into the blood and meat of the Mathesons.

Archer would have to perform the cleansing. And she had to help. Even though she was as worn as these mountains, eroded by time and tides, by the forces of God's tireless punishment. Even though she was only mortal.

She crawled to the rear of the root cellar and rolled away the flat stone. In the weak light, she could see the small crippled cross that had been carved into its surface. She stuck her face near the black opening. She never understood why the path to hell was so bone-chillingly cold. It should have been blazing hot, and smelling of sulfur and brimstone and smoke instead of dirt. But God worked in mysterious ways, and the devil worked just as strangely.

She cast her prayers into the pit. She could hold back the hordes. With her faith, she could win the battle below. Let God and Archer take care of the devil up here.

Mama Bet finished her prayers, the same ones the

McFalls had been saying for over two centuries. She replaced the stone, sweating with effort even though her fingers were stiff from the cold. On aching knees she backed her way to the pantry, retrieved the candle, and replaced the boards along the back wall. She wiped the dirt from her hands and cussed God for burdening her with this holy work. As if filling her up with a messiah weren't bad enough. No, He made her crawl on her belly like a serpent.

She blew out the candle and peeked through the gingham curtains. Archer was still outside. She could hear him carrying on with his business deals over the telephone, acting for all the world like an ordinary person. Well, Jesus had taken on work as a carpenter before starting up his career as a liar. Archer might as well be a rich preacher as a poor one.

She turned on the kitchen tap and stuck her hands under the frigid springwater. The dirt ran red down the drain. She put the candle away and wiped her hands on a towel. Her dress was stained at the knees, but she didn't like to change clothes in midday. That was wasteful, the kind of thing a Christian might do.

She heard voices outside. *They ain't supposed to gather here, not with Archer around. The church will be ready soon enough.*

She hurried onto the porch. Archer folded his phone and put it away. At the edge of the yard, in the shade of the trees, stood some members of the congregation: Stepford Matheson, Sonny Absher, Donna Gregg, and Rudy Buchanan. Rudy carried a shotgun and a Bible.

They started forward, Rudy's broad face split with a grin, Sonny and Stepford red-faced from drink. Donna Gregg hung back, tugging Sonny's sleeve. He brushed her away and scowled.

"What do y'all want?" Mama Bet called, shading

her eyes so she could see them better. Archer stood beside her, looking down on them.

"We been thinking," said Rudy, apparently the leader of this shoddy crew.

"Well, there's a first time for everything."

Rudy's thick lips curled. Mama Bet could almost hear the gears churning rustily inside his head as he tried to think of a comeback. He soon gave up, and settled for raising the shotgun barrel until it pointed at the sky.

"We've been hearing a lot about the red church, and the day of reckoning, and all this foolishness about 'great trials,' " Rudy said. "Now all of a sudden you're telling us that Archer's the Second Son of God. And that somehow we're all part of it, because of what our kin did way back when." He looked at Stepford and Sonny.

Stepford swayed a little, and Rudy pressed the Bible against him until he regained his balance.

"Yeah," Stepford said. "You're telling us that *this*"—he pointed to Archer—"is the earthly face of God? Then God must be one hell of a practical joker, I say."

Mama Bet started to speak, but Archer raised his hand. "I don't blame you for your doubts," he said to them. "I know some of you were raised as Christians. But people use God for their own purposes, they twist His ways to benefit themselves. People build up the idols that are easy to accept. And they always destroy what they can't understand."

Sonny spat. His eyes were bloodshot and bright. "We didn't hang Wendell McFall."

"You don't think it's fair that you have to suffer for the sins of your ancestors. But blood sins require payment in blood. And sacrifice now will protect your blood unto the fourth generation."

Rudy elbowed Stepford. "Tell him."

Stepford moved reluctantly closer, until he was at the foot of the porch steps. Mama Bet's goat, which was tied to the porch rail, came over and sniffed his dirty jeans.

Stepford shooed the goat away and looked up at Archer. "We decided we ain't so sure you're a messiah after all."

Rudy nodded, his courage bolstered by the shotgun. "Yeah. All we hear is fancy talk. Sure, Boonie Houck and Zeb Potter got killed. But how do we know that has anything to do with these 'great trials' we keep hearing about?"

"Getting killed sure don't take no sacrifice," Stepford said. "It ain't like they were asking to die, or anything."

Donna Gregg pressed close behind Sonny, her chest against his back.

Dirty sinners, Mama Bet thought. *It's a wonder that God and Archer don't strike them down on the spot. And Sonny married, at that. Of course, his wife took down to Raleigh after she got tired of getting beat up every time he got drunk. I can hardly wait to see them adulterers get cleansed.*

"This *is* about sacrifice," Archer said, his voice lifting now, resounding with the power of his faith. Mama Bet's heart swelled with pride.

"More big talk," Sonny said. "But we ain't seen no signs."

"Yeah," taunted Rudy. "Why don't you whip us up a miracle? Maybe break us up some loaves and fishes?"

"To hell with that," slurred Sonny. "Do something worthwhile, like changing some water into wine."

The drunken trio laughed, Donna smiling uncertainly behind them.

"True faith doesn't require proof," Archer said.

"Exactly what I'm saying," Rudy said. "I can't rightly call my faith 'true.' It's more like it's been shoved down my throat. And I don't much like the taste of it."

Mama Bet saw that Sonny and Stepford wore similar expressions of rebellion.

The devil's in them so deep they can't even separate it out from their own selves. Can't they just accept that the time for the cleansing is here, that God's back and ready to do the job right this time?

"Archer?" Mama Bet said. Her son was holding his head in his hands, his knuckles white from the pressure of squeezing. He bowed forward, wobbling unsteadily, and nearly fell against the porch rail. Mama Bet hurried to catch him.

My poor baby.

Muffled moans of anguish came from behind his hands. His legs and shoulders quivered. She touched him, and her fingers felt electrified. Suddenly the moans turned into roars and Archer threw his arms wide.

The sky darkened as if a large cloud had passed over the sun.

Donna screamed, and Sonny joined in. Rudy dropped the shotgun and clasped the Bible to his chest. Stepford fainted dead away, his legs folding up like a wet stretch of rope and his eyes rolling up to stare at the top of his skull.

Mama Bet looked on her son with love. Archer smiled, all wings and claws and livers for eyes.

Detective Storie knelt in the hayloft of the Potter barn. The sledgehammer lay on the warped boards of the floor, its handle slick with blood, the eight-pound head clotted with grue. A few strands of gray hair clung to the shredded matter that had once been encased in the delicate shell of Zebulon Potter's skull.

The sheriff's face turned ashen as he looked at the body. "Zeb was a friend of my parents," he said, looking out the window as though the mountain slopes were a movie screen and the past were being projected onto them. "I used to help him bale hay during the summer. He even gave me a hound puppy a long time ago. So long ago that Samuel was still alive."

Storie didn't like the vacant look in the sheriff's eyes. She'd seen that look once. During a criminal transport, in her first week on the Charlotte Metro force, she had met evil, if such a thing could possibly be embodied. She'd been green then, a rookie who thought that police officers could actually make a difference simply by caring.

The middle-aged suspect in the back of the car had allegedly raped an eight-year-old girl. He bragged about it as they drove to the Mecklenburg County jail, his unshaven face broken into a satisfied grin, his eyes afire with some secret madness. Storie was riding shotgun, fuming and helpless. *Innocent until proven guilty, even if they're guilty.* That was what they taught in cop school.

"The puppy was named Roscoe," Littlefield said quietly, rubbing his scalp. "Got run over before it was barely big enough to bark."

Perry Hoyle knelt and examined the open cavity of the victim's skull. Storie took another photograph and the camera's flash glinted off Hoyle's bald head. She pulled a metal tape measure from her jacket pocket. "You mind holding that end?" she asked the sheriff.

He started as if jerked from a dream and took the

end of the tape. Storie pointed to the hammer. The sheriff held the tape near the handle and Storie let the tape unwind until it stretched near the body.

"Seventeen feet," she said, though she doubted the sheriff was listening. He was so damned hard to figure out, at times friendly, at times cold and distant. But she didn't need friends, and she didn't need to waste thoughts on Frank Littlefield. She wrote the measurement in her notebook.

Long ago, the child rapist had put his face near the wire screen that separated the front seat from the rear. His breath smelled like sardines and gasoline. "Hey, good-looking, what you doing after work?" he'd said.

Storie had clenched her fists, fighting the urge to pull her nightstick from her belt and drive it into the rapist's face. But, no, he was a suspect and he had rights. No matter that he'd already pulled three years for two separate indecent-liberties raps. No matter that he'd be out on the street in two years. No matter anything but that the world was absolutely, hopelessly insane. God had made a pretty good stew, then He'd screwed it up by mixing in humans and giving them free will and brains.

Brains. Zeb Potter's brains were as gray as the old oak boards that covered the barn walls.

"I can finish up here, Sheriff," she said. He nodded absently and moved to the workbench. Deputy Wade Wellborn helped Hoyle put the body on a stretcher. The body made a sticky sloughing noise as it was lifted from the pool of blood.

"Guess I'm not helping much," Littlefield said quietly. Storie didn't want to show him up in front of the others. She understood that vacant look. Because she knew it well.

She'd seen it herself, in her own eyes, in the mirror

of a Charlotte Metro police car. As she was transport-
ing a rape suspect with a familiar face and secret mad
eyes. It was the same suspect she'd arrested a few
months earlier. Purest evil wearing meat. This time,
he'd gone for a six-year-old. The girl had died on
the way to the hospital.

The rapist recognized Storie. "Hey, honey, you can
lock me up, but I'll be back. One of these days, I
might even get around to *your* part of town."

Storie had nearly pulled the car over and shot the
creep in the head. But she did her job and took him
in, handed him over to a judicial system that was fair
but overmatched.

That was when Storie made two decisions: she
would leave the Metro force and get a job with a
rural department. And she would try her damnedest
to make a small difference, even though the world
was absolutely, hopelessly insane. Even though God
was insane.

Or was God, like the serial rapist, also innocent
until proven guilty?

She watched Littlefield follow Hoyle, Wellborn,
and the cold body of Zeb Potter down the loft stairs.
Outside, a small breeze played through the trees, the
sound she imagined gave Whispering Pines its name.
Somewhere out there, a killer was harboring a secret
madness in his eyes. Storie didn't like secrets.

TEN

David Day watched from the hills as the sunset threw bands of orange over the dark lines of the horizon. The air was moist and smelled of damp leaves. Normally, being alone in the woods gave him a sense of peace. But under these trees where he had spent some of the happiest hours of his life, he felt like an intruder. Because now the forest belonged to something else.

Below him, the old Gregg farm was spread out like a wrinkled green carpet. He still thought of it as home, even though he hadn't slept there in weeks. But all the things that made the place home were still behind those white walls of the house: the boys, the bed, the maple gun cabinet, the trophy heads on the wall. Everything but her.

He hated that the boys were alone. But they were safer at the house than with Linda at the church. She would give them to Archer sooner or later, unless David could find a way to stop Archer again. But this time would be more difficult.

The red church was crouched on a little rise to his left, above the road and the curve of the river. Six or eight cars were parked by the old building. People milled around the cemetery grounds, going into and out of the church. They moved like ants on a sugar hill, heads meeting, seeming to communicate silently from that distance. One of those ants was Linda.

The police were finally finished at the Potter farm. David had seen them carrying a stretcher from the barn. From the way the deputies' backs stooped, the load must have been heavy. The sheet-draped load was marred by a dark stain. They'd slid their burden into Perry Hoyle's station wagon. Then the vehicles had driven away one by one, including the sheriff's Trooper. The cruiser driven by that woman deputy was the last to leave, about an hour ago.

Poor old Zeb. And Boonie before him. In California, the killing hadn't seemed as brutal, as casual. But David hadn't known any of those victims. Boonie and Zeb were mountain folks. These were *his* people who were dying this time, not nameless longhairs and drifters.

Archer was gathering a flock, just as he had done in California. And David had learned that there were only two kinds of people who followed Archer McFall: the dead and the about to be.

David lifted his Marlin rifle and peered into the scope, the odor of gun oil comfortingly strong. Through the magnifying lenses, he saw Lester at the church door. The crosshairs were centered on the man's beet-red face. David shifted the scope and saw Becca Faye Greene, her smile a rapture of lipstick. Another shift, and Linda's face filled the small circle of the scope.

Linda.

They'd met in the ninth grade, a Buckhorn Mountain boy and a valley farm girl. Most of the families, including the Days, who lived on the back side of Buckhorn were the descendants of Union sympathizers. Some people in these parts still held a grudge, the ones who had Rebel-flag license plates and considered summer tourists to be invaders. In seedy bars at each corner of the county, the Civil War was renewed every Friday night.

But, Day or not, Linda had let him pick her books up that time she'd dropped them in the mud getting off the schoolbus. She had thick books, math and social studies. All David had was an auto-repair manual and a set of plans for a wooden desk.

She had pushed her hair back with one hand and actually looked into his face. Her eyes were deep and blue and seemed to penetrate his skin so that she could see everything he kept hidden. He looked back and grinned like a sick mule. His hands felt as if they were made of wood as he wiped the books clean against his pants.

"Thanks," she said, smiling. Her teeth were only a little crooked, just enough so that David didn't feel self-conscious. He gave her the books. She walked away, her figure shifting attractively inside her knee-length dress.

He had solved the mystery of those curves, though it had taken years. But the waiting was far from a waste. David knew that she liked yellow squash better than butternut, and she hadn't laughed at his big dream of owning a sawmill. She liked Bob Seger, and David liked him a little. She cried every time they slaughtered a beef steer. He cried when each of the boys was born.

Through the scope, her blue eyes were damp and bright. But the depth had been replaced by a flat glaze, her pupils large. She was scared or excited or aroused. Or maybe all three. Just the way she had looked in California.

David swiveled the rifle barrel slightly to the right. Archer smiled into the crosshairs of the scope. The preacher was looking through the lenses at David, the magnifying process somehow reversed, David the prey and Archer the hunter. David shuddered and blinked and the illusion passed.

He couldn't hold the rifle steady. From this range, the .30-06 round would drop only a few inches in trajectory. The hot bullet would pierce Archer's chest, chew up his heart, and shatter his ribs. And then what?

He pictured Linda, screaming, spattered by the gore of her messiah. She would kneel by Archer, the other disciples crowding around as his death tremors passed and his blood cooled. Then their wailing would lift and fill the darkening sky, the moon would moan, the red church would howl in anguish. Just as legend said happened the last time one of the McFall preachers was killed. And those buried in the cemetery would . . .

David closed his eyes and let the barrel of the gun tilt slowly to the ground. Sweat stung his eyes, and the metallic stench of his fear overwhelmed the green smells of the forest.

Forgive me, Lord, for I am weak.

He leaned against a cold hickory and waited for midnight.

"It'll be dark soon," Sheriff Littlefield said, turning from the window in Storie's cramped office. Papers were piled high on the sofa, crime reports and DARE brochures and gun magazines. He had nowhere to sit. He couldn't be comfortable in front of Sheila anyway, even if he were lying in a feather bed. "You coming?"

"Afraid not." She didn't look up from her cluttered desk. "I'd better go over these reports one more time."

Littlefield sagged against the wall, the years heavy on him, the last two days heavier still. "I guess you never thought you'd get a serial killer here."

She looked up. "I guess you didn't, either."

She hadn't mentioned Littlefield's confession, the way he'd broken down in front of her about Samuel. Whether it was kindness or embarrassment that kept her off the subject, he hoped it would continue. "We'll be calling in the SBI."

Storie's lips tightened. "I want this bastard."

Littlefield contemplated the black sludge in the coffeepot. "No witnesses. No prints. No suspects. No motives. Probably no DNA evidence."

"Let's wait for the state lab to have a look. Or did I forget that ghosts don't have DNA?"

Littlefield slammed his fist against the wall. Storie's framed copy of a newspaper article trembled from the blow. "Look, forget what I said about the ghosts. I wouldn't expect you to understand, anyway. You're not from around here."

Storie stood, the wheels of her chair squealing in the rush. She parodied a hillbilly accent. " 'Cause I ain't mountain, I don't know nothin'. Well, Sheriff, I wouldn't believe in ghosts or boogiemen or haunted churches even if I lived in Transylvania County. I'm sorry about your brother, and I know his death must have . . . *upset* you. But this is the twenty-first century, even in the Appalachians."

They stared each other down. Littlefield finally looked away, out the small window to the lights of town below. "You do it your way. I'll solve it mine."

Storie held up some papers. "The answer's here somewhere. And we'll get the coroner's report back in a few days."

"A few days might be too late."

"You think there's going to be another one?" She sat down, her anger deflated.

"Maybe more."

"You really *do* think the church has something to do with all this, don't you?"

"There's no such thing as coincidence."

"What's the background on this Archer McFall character? You think we should bring him in?"

Storie was interrupted by the receptionist's voice paging from the speakerphone: "Sheriff, you have a call on line two."

"Who is it?"

"The radio station. Wants to know about reports of murders in the county."

"That's all we need, getting everybody worked up," he said to Storie, then louder, to the dispatcher, "Tell them we'll have a press release going out next week. In the meantime, they can make do with the obituaries."

"Yes, Sheriff." The static was silenced.

"I'd better get to the church. It's going on midnight," he said.

Storie called to him as he reached the doorway. "Sheriff . . ."

Her face was hard, but her eyes were soft. "Sorry I lost my temper," she said.

"We all want to solve this case. And I hope I'm wrong about the church. Lord only knows how wrong I want to be."

"What kind of crazy has a church service at midnight?"

"The kind named Archer McFall."

"Well, be careful."

"I'm going to church. What's the worst that could happen?"

Littlefield was relieved that she didn't prod him for an answer.

"I got to go," Ronnie said.

"You're crazy." Tim was still in his pajamas, watching television with the living room lights off. A half-empty bag of cookies and a bottle of Pepsi were beside him on the couch. The flickering from the screen strobed over him and made his movements jerky. Twin reflections of the on-screen action played themselves out in his glasses as well as in the false eyes of the deer heads mounted on the walls.

"You can either stay here by yourself or come with me." Ronnie's dizziness had passed, and he'd taken one of the pills that made his nose stop hurting. But the pill also made him feel as if he had pillows under his feet.

"What if Mom comes back?"

"Mom won't be back. Not until morning."

"How do you know?"

"I just *know,* dingle-dork."

"I'm scared."

"The moon's out and we can take a flashlight." Ronnie didn't know why he wanted to go to the red church. Especially at night. But maybe he didn't want to. Maybe something was *making* him go.

Like the thing with wings and claws and livers for eyes.

He swallowed invisible dry needles. Tim was looking at him, waiting. Maybe it would be better if Tim stayed here. But then the thing might get him. No, better to stick together.

Ronnie went to the closet by the front door. Tim reluctantly followed. "Better take a jacket," Ronnie said.

He rummaged in the closet for a flashlight. His

heart stopped for a moment when he saw Dad's fishing pole, leaning all thin and lonely in the corner. A pair of hip waders flopped bonelessly against the wall.

If only Dad were here . . .

But Dad wasn't here, for whatever mysterious reason people got mad at each other. Mad enough to hate. Maybe Jesus was paying Ronnie back for all those sins of the spirit, all those questions he asked himself that Preacher Staymore said would lead to eternal damnation.

"The answer is Jesus," Preacher Staymore said, every time Ronnie was getting saved and asked one of those questions. But Jesus was the question. How could He be the answer to His own question? But Dad said the Baptists were the true religion, and Dad was smart enough to catch a trout in four inches of water.

Ronnie found the flashlight and put on a jacket and they went out the door. The driveway and the gravel road were pale under the big moon, like white rivers in the night. But the wooded hills rose black around them, filled with the chatter of a million restless insects. Across the meadows, the Potter farm was dark and still. The stars above were far and cold with great spaces between them. Ronnie wanted so much for there to be a Jesus behind the stars.

"I'm scared," whispered Tim.

"Shh. It's okay. I'm here."

"I want Dad."

"Me, too. But Dad's not here."

"Even Mom."

"We'll get to Mom."

"Are you scared?"

"No," Ronnie lied.

"Then why are you whispering?"

Ronnie looked off the porch into the thick shadow of the barn, then down along the creek bank. The thing with wings and claws and livers for eyes was nowhere around, or else was really good at hiding.

"I'm not whispering," he said aloud. He hoped Tim didn't hear the tremble in his voice. "Now come on," he said, stepping off the squeaky porch.

"Where are we going?"

"You know."

"Do we *have* to?"

"Yeah."

"How come?"

"We just have to, that's all. Remember what Dad says: 'Some things, a man's just gotta do.' " Ronnie didn't want to point out that Dad could do anything, wasn't scared of anything, and was a man, and they were only boys.

They started down the driveway, Tim huddling close and Ronnie not minding a bit. When they reached the road, Ronnie looked back at the house and its squares of yellow light. For a moment the light beckoned, promising safety and warmth and the possibility of love. But love wasn't found behind walls. It was found in Mom and Dad and Jesus.

He switched on the flashlight when they reached the road. It made an orange circle in the gray gravel. Ronnie shifted his head back and forth, studying the dark roadside weeds for any movement. The sounds of the forest were smothered by their footsteps crunching on the gravel.

"I thought you didn't like the church," Tim said.

"I don't. But we have to go anyway."

"Do you think whatever got Boonie Houck and Mr. Potter—"

"No," Ronnie said too quickly. "There's nothing out here now. It's . . ."

It's what? Eaten its fill and flown home to the belfry?

"We'll be okay," Ronnie said.

"Do you think it was the thing that lives in the church steeple?"

"What thing?"

"You know. What Whizzer says. The thing with wings and claws and livers for eyes."

"Whizzer's a dork."

They went around a bend and were out of sight of the house. Ronnie couldn't smell the river, but he could feel its fishy dampness on his face. They passed the last of Zeb Potter's pasture. The barbed-wire fence ran into the forest, and the trees pressed close on both sides of the road. The moon sliced through a narrow gap between the treetops.

"How come Mom's at the church so late at night?" Tim asked. There was a note of complaint in his voice.

"What am I, Einstein or something? And do you have to ask so many stupid questions?"

"Talking makes me not as scared."

They walked faster now, the exertion driving away the moist chill of the spring night. They hit an incline and slowed. One side of the road sloped away into blackness. The river rushed over rocks below, the water gurgling like a choking victim trying to breathe.

They rounded another turn, and the red church stood on a hill, black under the moonlight. The moon glinted off the windshields of cars that were huddled around the church. Behind the cars, the pale slabs of tombstones stood like soldiers. The dog-wood was all black bones and sharp fingers and reaching hands of wood.

The church's front door was open, a gray rectangle against the darkness of the church structure. Yellow light flickered from the church windows, tiny pin-pricks that would flash and then disappear. *Candles,* Ronnie thought. The church had never been wired for electricity.

Singing drifted from the church, a choir of several dozen voices. The music was nothing like the songs they sang at First Baptist. This singing was hollow and creepy, as if half the people were singing off-key on purpose. But if they were singing about Jesus and God's love and mercy and salvation, that would make the music not so creepy. Ronnie listened but couldn't make out the words.

"That song is creepy," Tim said.

"Shh." Ronnie grabbed the sleeve of Tim's jacket and led him toward the edge of the woods, where the nearest cars were parked. He wanted to be as far away from the dark wall of forest as possible, but he also was reluctant to approach the graveyard. He pulled Tim down to the ground and they crawled between the cars until they could see into the church. The singing stopped.

"Do you see Mom?" Tim whispered. Ronnie el-bowed him in the ribs.

A man's voice resonated inside the church and spilled into the night.

"My fellow worshipers," the voice rang out. During the pause, someone coughed. The voice continued. "We are gathered here tonight to honor the one true God. For He is a jealous God, and many are the lies that fall on our ears. Many are the promises made to us by those who wear faces of evil. Many are the paths that lead from the true Way."

Ronnie peeked over the hood of the vehicle they had hidden behind. The engine was still warm. He saw the rounded light on the dashboard. It was the sheriff's Trooper.

Ronnie felt a little better. Nothing bad could happen if the sheriff was here. Ronnie knew that the cops on the TV shows were all fake, but the sheriff had seemed like a nice guy when he'd asked Ronnie about finding Boonie. So if both the sheriff and Mom were here . . .

". . . and the First Son was a carpenter," came the voice. "The First Son went among the people, among the sick and the outcast and the poor. The First Son taught of love and peace and salvation."

Salvation. So the man was a regular preacher after all. Though he spoke more like an actor than any of the preachers Ronnie had ever heard, the man's voice made Ronnie less afraid.

"And God called the First Son back to heaven, letting Him die on the cross so that we might find grace," the preacher said, his voice rising. "But God always promised that the Son would return. And the Son has returned. The Son walks among us. But it's not the First Son that God has sent. God gave Jesus a chance to save the world, and Jesus failed. Jesus with his false miracles and lies. So now the job goes to the Second Son."

"Second Son," murmured a few in the audience.

Second Son. That didn't sound like something a Baptist preacher would say. But now that he thought about it, it kind of made sense. Why should Jesus be an only child, when God could make as many offspring as He wanted? Jesus certainly hadn't made the world a perfect and sinless place.

And the red church wasn't as scary anymore. In fact, Ronnie felt a kind of warmth radiating from the structure. How silly and dumb and third-grade he had been, thinking the church was a bad place. The church was a *good* place.

The preacher increased his cadence. "The Second

Son spares no one from His love. This one needs no money, asks for no servitude, demands no tribute. The Son has found the path, and it leads through people's hearts. The Son wants to take us all home. But every journey begins with a single step. Tonight, in this house of the Lord, let us begin."

"Let us begin," echoed twenty voices.

"Let us begin," Ronnie whispered.

"Why are you saying that?" Tim said, still crouched behind the Trooper.

"Didn't you hear?"

"Hear *what?*"

"The Second Son."

"What about it?"

Tim wouldn't understand. All he cared about was cartoons and comic books and miniature action figures and sweets. Preacher Staymore hadn't made Tim get saved yet. Tim didn't know the warm feeling of something moving into your heart. And this warmth—spreading from this preacher's voice straight into Ronnie's blood—was better than anything Ronnie had ever known. This time he was saved for real.

Ronnie felt light, as if made of cotton candy. Even his broken nose, which had been throbbing with every beat of his heart, was forgotten in the rush of purest love. And love was what was between the preacher's words, love was what filled the wooden cavity of the church, love was what emanated like a welcoming fog from the red church and crept out across the hills of Whispering Pines. Love was more numbing than the pain pills.

"Let's go in," Ronnie said.

"Are you crazy?"

"It needs us." Ronnie started around the front of the Trooper. Tim grabbed his shirt from behind and pulled him backward. They fell on the ground, and Tim's flailing hand struck Ronnie's nose. Pain flashed behind Ronnie's eyes in streaks of bright purple and electric lime green. He yelped in agony.

"You dork." He grunted at Tim between clenched teeth. He pushed Tim away and rolled to his knees. He put a hand to his nose and felt something warm and wet.

The people inside the church had started singing again, but Ronnie scarcely heard it. He shivered and realized the night was chilly. The warmth of love had left him, as if he'd been asleep and someone had yanked the winter quilts off his body. An empty ache filled his chest. Something had been taken, and he couldn't remember what it was.

"You ain't going in there," Tim said, his eyes wide behind his glasses. The moon gave Tim's eyes a feral, eager quality.

"Now why in the heck would I want to go in there?"

"You just had a funny look in your eye."

"Shh. *Listen.*"

The singing stopped. A silence settled over the mountains. The wind waited in the tops of the trees. Not an insect stirred. Even the river seemed to pause in its twisting bed.

Then, a soft sound.

A scratching, fluttering sound.

Not inside the church.

Above.

In the steeple.

A shadow moved, a lesser gray against the church bell.

"Holy crud." Tim gasped.

Ronnie swallowed hard, and some of the blood from his nosebleed snaked down his throat.

It smells the blood. The thing with wings and claws and livers for eyes . . .

"Run!" he shouted at Tim, but his little brother was already a step ahead of him. They dashed between the cars and hit the gravel road, rocks flying as they scampered away from the red church. They were exposed, vulnerable in the open, but Ronnie didn't dare head into the forest. The pounding in Ronnie's ears almost sounded like laughter, but he didn't stop to listen.

Instead he ran into the night, hunching his shoulders against the monster that swept down from the blackness.

ELEVEN

Ronnie ducked low, sensing the cold shadow sweeping down over him and blocking out the moon. Ahead, Tim stumbled in the gravel and veered toward the ditch that ran along the edge of the road. Tim looked back at his older brother, his mouth a round well of fear. Ronnie saw a fluttering shape reflected in Tim's glasses.

Then Tim hurdled the ditch and headed into the trees.

No, no, no, not the forest, Ronnie silently screamed.

But Tim was already out of sight, lost amid thrashing branches. Ronnie followed, sizing up the dark gaps between the trees, each like a door to nowhere. Something brushed his shoulder, and he bit back a shout. His body was electrified, sweat thick around his ankles and armpits and trickling down the ladder of his spine.

The monster is going to get me.

Ronnie thought of Boonie Houck, eyeless and mutilated and groping for a handhold to drag himself back to the ordinary, sane world.

Going to get me get me get me.

He held his breath and jumped the black ditch. A pine branch whacked him across the face, and he yelped in pain, then fell to his knees. Blood was flowing steadily from his nose. It made a warm rope down his chin.

Tree limbs snapped above and behind him in the dark.

The trees had arms, would hug him and hold him. The trees were part of the nightmare.

He scrambled to his feet, throwing damp leaves and dirt as he regained his balance. He ran ten steps, twenty steps, blind, his arm raised over his face to fend off the branches. His heart spasmed like a trapped animal in his chest.

Ronnie didn't know where the road was, and couldn't hear Tim above the noise of his own passing. He dodged between the trees, unaware of his feet.

Run, dingle-dork.

Maybe if the Bell Monster follows me, you can get away. If the thing's not too hungry, maybe one boy will be enough for it.

Shards of moonlight cut into the forest canopy in places, creating a mad strobe as he ran from darkness to light, darkness to light. Then all was dark as he moved under the thicker canopy of old oak and hickory, and the branches were higher, no longer beating at his sides.

He was going downhill now, skidding in the mud. He stepped on a flat rock and fell on his rear, sliding and then rolling back to his feet.

A damp chill overlaid his sweat, and he knew he was near the river. Though his nose was blocked, he carried the river's fishy and muddy smell in his memory. The rushing water roared faintly in his ears.

Follow me, but not too close, Ronnie silently willed the Bell Monster.

The trees opened and he reached the river. Moonlight glinted off the black water. The froth of waterfalls sparkled like ten million eyes. The air was colder here, fresh and heavy in Ronnie's gasping lungs. The earth vibrated under his feet as he dodged among the gray rocks along the riverbank.

He huddled in a gap between two boulders, peering back up the slope. The tops of the trees moved, all big black creatures, live things, hostile and bristling and in league with the Bell Monster.

Ronnie didn't know how long he had been running, but it felt like years. He breathed with his mouth open, his throat sore. His nose had stopped bleeding. He wiped his chin with his hand.

If the thing smells blood . . .

Ronnie crawled along the rocks until he reached the water. He stuck his hand in the current and a frigid shock ran up his arm. But he cupped his palm and brought the water to his face, wiping, then repeating the process until he thought his face was clean.

The front of his jacket was wet. He drew himself into a ball and waited for the Bell Monster to find him.

Waited.

Waited.

The river roared on, sweeping down below him past the red church and under the bridge into the valley.

A few thin clouds drifted across the sky, made silver-gray by the moonlight.

Did Tim make it? Or did the Bell Monster lose track of me and go after him?

Ronnie suddenly felt ashamed, remembering how he ran away when they'd found Boonie Houck. He'd left Tim behind to face the red, raw horror alone. And now he was abandoning him again.

Big brothers were supposed to take care of little brothers. Even if little brothers were dorks.

Dad was gone, and Mom was at that weird meeting in the red church. Tim had nobody to help him. Except Ronnie.

"Danged rocks are getting cold anyway," he whispered to himself. He stood on trembling legs, his bones aching and stiff. The trees around him were still, their leaves wet and heavy.

He eased his way from behind the boulders, his back to the river. If he went upstream he would eventually come to Buckhorn Mountain, where a series of creeks ran together. If he went downstream he'd reach the bridge near the red church. If he went back into the woods, he would have to climb a hill to see where he was.

The river wasn't too deep to cross, only waist-high in most places, but he was already nearly frozen. Besides, Tim wouldn't dare cross the river. Tim had fallen into it once, and had been scared of deep water ever since.

Ronnie hunched low and headed back the way he thought he had come. His nose was not hurting much but, like the river, pulsed steadily under the bandages. He moved quietly through the trees, the way he did when he was playing Indian scout. He kept his palms up to push the branches from his face.

Once away from the river, he found an old hunting trail. A little moonlight splashed along the clearing, and he paused to listen for Tim. The Bell Monster probably hadn't found Tim yet, or screams would be shattering the night silence.

Ronnie gulped at that thought. What if the thing had gotten Tim while Ronnie was cowering by the water? What if the Bell Monster had come aknocking on Tim's rib cage? What if the thing with wings and claws and livers for eyes was even now scooping out Tim's guts and having a late-night snack?

No. Think happy thoughts.

When you have one of those waking nightmares, when you think bad things in the dark and can't go to sleep, you think happy thoughts. Cartoon dogs, fat clowns, things like that. Except sometimes the cartoon dogs bite and the fat clowns grow sharp smiles.

Happy thoughts.

Ronnie kept walking, using those words as a mantra, falling into their rhythm.

Think happy thoughts, think happy thoughts, think happy thoughts. . . .

He tried to picture those stupid yellow smiley faces, but the faces kept turning into Preacher Staymore from Sunday School, lips pursed and asking, *Can you hear Him aknocking?*

Ronnie staggered on, tripping over roots and stones, mentally clinging to his happy-thoughts mantra.

He was nearly on his hundredth repetition when he first heard the twigs snapping.

He froze.

Whatever had been following him rustled some low bushes to his left.

A whisper of wings.

A soft clicking, like that of claws meeting in anticipation.

A wet flutter, like that made by liverish eyes opening and closing.

Ronnie's limbs turned wooden, his feet grew roots, he was part of the dark soil he would die on. As the bushes exploded with movement, Ronnie's last thought was that maybe Tim got away.

And then the monster had him, in a fury of tooth and wing and razor hatred.

The monster had smelled his blood in the dark.

The monster embraced him, eager and sharp-fingered.

The monster—

Ronnie kicked and screamed, flailing his elbows. He pressed his eyes closed, not wanting to watch the thing open his insides and pull out his dripping wet heart.

Ronnie balled his fists.

The creature growled in his ear.

"Ronnie, it's *me.*"

Dad?

Yes, it was. Ronnie imagined Dad's smell, all after-shave and sawdust and boot leather.

He relaxed in his dad's strong arms, finally opening his eyes. Dad's face was pale in the weak wash of moonlight.

"The . . . the thing," Ronnie said, fighting back tears.

"Shh," Dad said. "It's okay now. Nothing's going to get you."

Ronnie shivered against his Dad, burrowing close for warmth. Ronnie was relieved to note that Dad had a gun with him. He suddenly pushed away. "Tim. Where's Tim?"

"Right here." Tim came out from the shadow of the trees.

"Did you see it?"

Tim's glasses flashed as he nodded.

"What *is* it, Dad?" Ronnie asked.

"I'll tell you later. Right now, let's get to the house." Dad put an arm around each boy and led them up the hill.

"Is Mom going to be okay?"

"I hope so, son. I hope so."

They walked past midnight and into safety.

* * *

Midnight.

Linda was lifted by invisible loving arms. The singing, the sermon, the pure love of her fellow worshipers, all flowed through her like the charged juice of her blood. Every cell of her body glowed in the warmth of Archer's glory. Her mouth was flooded with the sweetness of the communion they had taken.

She felt as if she had returned from a long sleep. But it *had* been a long sleep, years and years and years of religious tyranny, licking at the pierced feet of David's foolish Jesus. But now Archer was back, and everything would be the way it was before.

She would belong again.

She looked to her right, to the owner of the hand she was holding. Sheriff Littlefield. Of course. The Littlefields were one of the old families. They, like the Greggs, Mathesons, Potters, and others, had attended the church back in Wendell McFall's day. Now the families were reuniting, answering a call that was deeper than flesh and blood.

Archer McFall leaned over the lectern, spent from his rampaging sermon. His eyelids fluttered and the muscles in his shoulders twitched. He lifted his head and smiled. The sweat on his face glistened in the candlelight. He reached out with a trembling hand and caressed the broken wooden cross that jutted from the top of the lectern.

"He has found us worthy," Archer said, in a drained voice that had none of its earlier thunder.

"Amen," echoed the parishioners.

Linda turned from her front-row pew and looked at the others. Lester Matheson smiled at her, his teeth yellow. His wife Vivian swayed as if in rhythm to an inaudible hymn, her eyes closed. Old Mamie Pickett was beside Vivian, her wrinkled and spotted hands folded carefully across the waist of her blouse.

Nell and Haywood Absher sat erect in the back row, Nell in her blue hat with the diaphanous netting. Their daughter Noreen wore a blissful, vacant expression. Others filled the church, their eyes bright with joy. Mama Bet sat in the last row, her wrinkled mouth pressed in solemn joy.

Abshers. Mathesons. Greggs. Picketts. McFalls. Only one family was missing. No, two. The Potters and the Houcks.

The sheriff had said that old man Potter had died. And Boonie Houck had lost his sinful eyes and tongue and penis. Linda couldn't mourn their loss. They had found their own path to the everlasting glory that Archer spoke of. They had paid in blood so that the other families might live unto the fourth generation.

Nobody gets anything without a little sacrifice. Archer needed them. He just sent them home ahead of the rest of us, that's all.

Archer lifted his head, his brown eyes as intense as truck headlights. Linda quit thinking. He was about to speak.

"We have done God's work," Archer said, swiveling his head to indicate the refurbished interior of the church.

"We done Him proud," Lester shouted.

"Amen," Vivian said, not opening her eyes. A clamor of approval spread across the room. Linda glanced at the black world outside the windows, momentarily sorry for all the blind, misguided fools who had been led astray by that devil, Jesus. Even her very own sons had fallen for the devil's tricks.

Her eyes welled and spilled over.

I'll bring them. They should know of the true path before it's too late.

She looked back at Archer, so grateful for his rescuing her from the flames of Christianity. She slid from her hard pew and knelt on the floorboards, bowing to Archer. Her heart was a tortured mix of love and regret. She had found Archer, then had lost him, and now she had found him again.

Archer says that the truth will always win out. Faith will beat Satan and Jesus both.

She bent lower, her head near the floor she had spent hours cleaning.

Faith is sacrifice. And sacrifice is the currency of God.

She kissed the floor, tasted the red church. And she knew—*knew*—that Archer would need her children.

Ronnie and Tim.

But what were their sins?

A voice came to her, unbidden: *They don't pay for their own sins. They pay for yours, Linda.*

She looked up from where she was kneeling on the floor. Archer smiled at her, eyes moist and arms spread in supplication.

Remember Abraham from the Old Testament? When God asked him to kill his beloved son Isaac? Do you think Isaac was the one who had sins to pay for? Of course not. Abraham was the one who needed to suffer a little, who needed to prove his faith.

Around her, the parishioners stood and began to file out, talking quietly among themselves. Their words were joyless now, muted, as if the gathered had given all their emotions to the walls of the church. Outside they went, shuffling sacks of skin and fluid and organs, while within, the wood seemed vibrant, soaked with light and energy and the ghosts of prayers.

Archer stepped off the dais and came to Linda. He offered her his hands. For a moment she thought she saw stigmata, tiny red pocks in the white palms. *The mark of Jesus.* She recoiled in horror even as the image faded.

"What's wrong, my child?" Archer said. He was the Archer of old, aged and ageless, wise and innocent, his eyes sparkling with love and hate.

"I-I'm . . ." she stammered, looking back down to the floor. She couldn't meet his eyes, couldn't stare into the hot hells inside them, couldn't bear his gracious cruelty. Because she knew she would see the threat in them, the hunger, the need for her children.

But then, Archer was a divine incarnation, the flesh of God, sent among the mortals with a mission to perform. What were her needs next to the needs of Archer?

She felt Archer's strong arms pulling her to her feet.

"Do you doubt?" he asked simply. There was no anger in his voice, no accusation.

Linda shook her head. She could hear the others talking outside, seemingly revived by the fresh spring night. A few cars started and drove away with a crunch of gravel.

Archer cupped her chin and tilted her head up until their eyes met. "You're as lovely as you were in California."

Linda thought for a moment that he was going to kiss her. *If only* . . .

But she was mortal and he was the Second Son. He didn't need love the way that others did, the way that David did. For Archer, love was a fuel, a human juice that would propel the world to heaven. Love wasn't for the soul, not a contract between two people in defiance of death; no, to Archer, love was for the *Soul*, the collective, the glory. Not an ounce of it could be spared on carnal yearnings.

Oh, she had loved him. Archer with his long hair and his Volkswagen bus with peace signs painted on the rear and sides. Archer who could never fit into the small-town mountain life. Archer who had dreams, who saw visions, who accepted the taunts and jeers with equanimity.

It was just after her high school graduation, when she and David had been busy planning their marriage and their careers and their future together. And that was when Linda first recognized the glass walls that surrounded her, that would forever keep her caged in the mountains. Oh, she could leave, she could go to Charlotte or the Outer Banks, but only for days at a time. Her life was here, as bound to the mountains as the granite foundations of the Earth were. That long-ago summer, she had carried the certainty of it like a lump in her throat.

She was waiting tables at the Mountaineer Diner when Archer came in. She'd noticed Archer in high school, but he kept to himself, carrying at times a Bible or thick books that weren't required reading. That in itself was enough to mark him as an outcast. But coupled with the fact that he was the great-great-grandson of the Hung Preacher, he might as well have had a sign that read KICK ME stuck to the back of his shirt.

He sat in a corner booth that day, under the fake antique Pepsi-Cola sign. Linda looked around, hoping Sue Ann, the other waitress on duty, would take the "weird one." But Sue Ann was leaning over the counter, showing her cleavage to some red-eyed trucker. So Linda pulled out her order pad and walked over to the booth.

"What do you want?" she said, sizing him up as a lousy tipper in addition to being a long-haired creep. He fumbled with the menu and scraped a bit of gravy away with his thumb.

"Coffee," he said.

"That all?" She was irritated by the way he watched her, as if she were a piece of chocolate cake.

He nodded. She turned to hurry back to the kitchen.

"Your name's Linda, isn't it?" he said.

Maybe he would tip after all. "Yeah," she said, giving him her two-dollar smile.

"My name's Archer."

"I know. You go to Pickett High, don't you?"

"Did. I graduated."

Linda didn't remember him from the ceremony. Of course, she and David had hit a little Jim Beam before crossing the stage. Suddenly she felt guilty, as if his stare saw through her, into her. Then she was angry at herself for feeling guilty. Who cared what some longhaired bum thought?

His eyes were brown, vibrant yet distant. She felt dizzy looking into them.

"Uh . . . coffee, coming right up."

She brought the coffee but he didn't drink it. "The body is a temple," he said. "And sacrifice is the currency of God. For He is a jealous God, and He punishes children for the iniquity of the parents."

What a weirdo, she thought, but within fifteen minutes she was taking a break and sitting across from him in the booth, on the edge of the cheap vinyl seat. He talked matter-of-factly, and damned if he didn't know just what he was talking about.

"You're tired of this place," Archer said. "You're tired of these people and all this arguing over whether Chevy is better than Ford and what caliber bullet takes down a deer the fastest. You're about to be married, your union blessed by God, and you think that this is your dream come true, that it's happily-ever-after from now on. But scratch the surface"—he leaned forward as he said this, their faces only a foot apart—"and you find that you're scared to death that this is *it,* this is all there is to life."

She tried to protest, tried not to show that he had completely peeled back the layers of her soul like an onion. But she was already enthralled, already hooked, already mesmerized by the cadences of his speech. And by the time Sue Ann was calling Linda to get back to work, she had agreed to meet Archer for dinner.

She had to lie to David, but sinning was much easier back then. She and Archer ate at the Chick'n Shack over the line in Tennessee. She didn't resist when Archer took her out behind the old red church after dinner. They rode back through town in his van, her with her head down, hoping no one would see her. At the same time, she was thinking that this was it, she was going to do it, she was going to cheat on David and damn the consequences. It was time to finally get around to the business of taking chances.

But Archer only wanted to talk. She thought at first it was just another come-on line. He wasn't really her type. She was no longer sure just what *was* her type, even though she had always thought it was David. So they sat in the dark and Archer talked, and even though she was aching with lust and the fire of her flesh would lead her to the fires of hell, she somehow couldn't get up the courage to touch him.

Archer talked of strange things. He made her look at the stars. He pointed to the church bell and the dogwood and told the story of the Hung Preacher. Linda thought at first he was trying to spook her so that she would slide close and he could put his arm around her. But he told the story wrong.

In Archer's version, the Hung Preacher was a victim of persecution. "It was all a conspiracy of Jesus," he said. His eyes seemed to gather the scraps of stray light and glistened like oil. "Jesus got in the heads of all those people and made them kill my great-great-grandfather. And Jesus had to pay nothing for his own sins. Because God loved Jesus more than He loves the entire world."

Linda knew she should be getting the hell out of the van, that he was insane, but he spoke so reasonably and kept his voice level. So she listened to the rest of it, how Jesus hated the McFalls because they would bring forth the holy child. And that child would rise up and reveal Jesus for the fallen angel that he was. By morning, when the first timid rays of the sun peeked over the hills, she was more than in love; she was devoted.

She went through that summer with a bounce in her step, seeing David throughout the week but saving every Sunday night for Archer and his private sermons. When she found out that Archer had others, like Mandy Potter and Esther Matheson, she got jealous. But Archer explained how each had a part in the Divine Plan and that Linda would always hold a special place in his heart.

They moved to California at the end of the summer. Linda wrote a good-bye letter to David, three pages. At the end, she'd written, *I hope you understand, but there's a larger mission that I must attend to. I love you.* Archer helped her write that last bit, and she cried until Archer made her stop.

They headed west in the van, Archer driving, the

seven girls taking turns sleeping, singing silly songs by the Eagles and the Beach Boys, at least until Archer pointed out the sinful subtexts in the lyrics. Then they passed the time wondering aloud what California would be like.

"What are we going to do out there?" Linda asked from the front passenger seat. They were halfway across Tennessee, and the hills were rounded and green. Archer was hunched over the steering wheel, wearing a faint, peaceful smile.

"Get delivered," he had said.

Now, with his face only inches from hers, Linda wanted so very much for Archer to deliver her once and for all.

TWELVE

Sheriff Littlefield looked around the churchyard at the trees. The moon bathed the open hill with light, and the tombstones were like silver sentinels, mute and mocking. Littlefield took a deep breath of the chilly air, trying to clear his head. His tongue was fouled with a sweetly putrid aftertaste. He felt as if he had just walked out of the long tunnel of a dream.

He had come to the church to see if he could learn more about Archer McFall. His plan had been to keep a polite smile on his face and sit quietly through the service. He would shake hands if necessary and bow in prayer at the right time. But his eyes would always be slightly open.

His plan had failed. The green digital display on his watch read 1:57. Somehow he had lost nearly two hours. He leaned against the front of the Trooper and tried to remember what had brought him to the red church.

The others had gone already, shaking hands with each other and saying "God bless," and driving back to their dark farmhouses. Linda Day and the preacher were inside the church. He could hear them talking.

The sheriff was hit by a sudden wave of nausea that almost drove him to his knees. The candlelight dancing from the open church door blurred in his vision. The huge, twisted dogwood swayed, as if moving to invisible music. His head roared with the first soul-ripping toll of the church bell.

He covered his ears and looked up at the bell tower, his mind scattered by the noise.

No rope. It can't be ringing.

The dull cast iron of the bell glinted under the moon. As the note pealed through Littlefield, vibrating every nerve ending in his body, he fought to keep his eyelids from snapping shut in agony. The bell hadn't moved an inch.

Archer was at the mouth of the church now, arms spread to the sky. The preacher was a dark shape shimmering in Littlefield's tears. Behind Archer, Linda was bowed in reverence or else hunched in an agony that echoed Littlefield's own.

With the second toll of the bell, Littlefield knew the deep resonance had driven him insane. Because the night *walked*.

A shape fluttered from the forest and settled in the belfry, a ragged black thing, an insult to the swimming beauty of the stars. The red church took on a glow, as if consumed with bright fire. A rope dangled from a strong, high limb of the dogwood. Pulling the rope taut was a body, full and heavy and limp.

It's him.

The thought came to Littlefield along with a flood of other broken thoughts and images. The cemetery ground buckled and swelled, and the turf beneath the headstones rippled like boiling water. Archer grew in Littlefield's vision—*grew*—until he filled the church door, and the edges of Archer's body sharpened. The nearby trees leaned forward as if to ogle the unreal spectacle before them.

Littlefield surrendered to gravity and fell to his

hands and knees. With effort, he lifted his head, transfixed by the still form of the Hung Preacher shimmering twenty feet away. The man's face was waxen, and the skin reminded Littlefield of the way Freeman Harper had looked after floating dead in the river for two weeks. The tongue protruded like a blacksnake's head. The eyes bulged, maniacally gleaming as if lit by strange suns.

The Hung Preacher wore a vested suit of ill-cut cotton that draped about the body like burlap, the ivory buttons resembling teeth. The dull leather square-toed shoes dangled inches above the ground. A leaf stirred between the feet, and Littlefield watched the leaf's shadow skip across the grass on the breeze. He visually traced the shadow of the tree, thrown long across the hill by the candlelit church. But the Hung Preacher cast no shadow.

Littlefield stared the illusion full in the face. But he knew the Hung Preacher was no illusion. He had almost been able to convince himself that the first time had been a trick of the mind, the night that Samuel died. Now here was the ghost again, dangling like a slip of lost light, back to prove that the long-ago Halloween was as horrible as Littlefield remembered.

But in some small part of himself, he knew that such things were impossible, irrational. *Dead people don't come back.* Samuel had died, and was as dead or deader now than he had ever been. This hideous vision hanging before him had no right to be here. Dead people belonged in the dirt.

He focused on the Hung Preacher's bloated, wan face.

See? It can't be real. You've let it build up in your mind, giving shape to your guilt over Samuel. You've just heard too many stories, that's all.

And the stories are wrong. Because in the stories, right

*after the Hung Preacher comes back, the congregation gath-
ers around him—*

The bell rang a third time, louder and more jarring than before, and the Hung Preacher blinked
and smiled.

The black tongue flitted back inside the swollen
head. The dead arms trembled and raised as if testing
the gravity of a new reality. The Hung Preacher parted
his blood-engorged lips and laughed. It was the Halloween laugh, the terrible and unforgettable sound
from Littlefield's childhood. All the fear came flood-
ing back, all the memories, only this time he couldn't
run away.

Around and behind Littlefield, the cemetery came
alive.

His screams sheared the damp silence of the night.

"Do you smell that?" Tim said.

David Day *did* smell it. He knew the smell inti-
mately. He was a hunter. Death had its own essence,
a thick, heady quality that went beyond the olfactory
sense. Death seeped inside of you like a mist.

"Smell what?" Ronnie said, his voice nasally because of his bandages. David looked down at the wide
eyes of his oldest son. Ronnie was lucky that he
couldn't smell. The coppery odor of blood and a
sickly-sweet aroma of decay mixed in the night air,
tinged with an underlying pungency.

David looked down the gravel road, then back to
the woods. He didn't know what was safer, being out
in the open stretch of moonlit road or sneaking
through the dark forest. Their house was still half a
mile away, and the only nearby houses, those of the
Potters and the Mathesons, were dark. He gripped

the gun more tightly. The weapon probably wouldn't do any good, but it made him feel better.

Tim kept trying to run ahead of their little group. He didn't seem scared anymore, just excited, as if he had sneaked out past bedtime to play some silly chasing game. David tried to keep his fear to himself, but Ronnie was smart. Ronnie knew that something bad had come to Whispering Pines.

"Hey, looky," Tim said, pulling his hand from David's. He pointed into the tall grass along the side of the road ahead. "There's somebody."

It could just as easily have been a sack of grain or a pile of rags, except for the pale hand that extended from the weeds onto the roadbed. Even in the dimness, there was no mistaking the fact that it was a human hand, its fingers curled upward in motionless begging. The hand was slender, feminine.

"Stay here," David whispered, taking a quick look around. The breeze that had steadily risen and fallen was now in a lull. The stillness was almost more unbearable than the flapping of leaves and the groaning of trees bending in the wind. He crept toward the body, his rifle tilted in front of him.

David fought back the vomit that tried to leap from his stomach. He recognized the woman's blouse. He thought at first that her blouse was unbuttoned and that she was wearing a dark, rumpled shirt underneath. But now he realized that her chest was open, not her blouse, and that someone or something had parted her rib cage. Blood pooled in the cavity, a slight steam rising toward the moon.

Her heart was gone.

David glanced at the woman's face. Her eyes were open, her mouth gaping in an endless, voiceless scream. It was Donna. Linda's cousin.

Linda had given Donna the blouse for Christmas

two years ago. David hadn't liked Donna because he always got the sense that she didn't approve of Linda's marrying a redneck. But nobody deserved to die like this, to be ripped open like a cow at the slaughterhouse. Horror and sorrow and fear welled up in David's chest, fought each other for space, and then settled into a miserable mixture.

"What is it, Daddy?" Ronnie called.

"Somebody. . . ." He fought to keep his voice calm. "Somebody had an accident."

"Are they dead?" Tim asked.

David knelt in the grass and looked at the boys waiting thirty feet behind him. They would have to walk past the body, and he didn't want them to know that it was Donna. He settled his fingers on her eyelids and pulled them closed, the way he had seen soldier buddies do in war movies. He tried to nudge her mouth closed, but her jaw muscles had locked in an everlasting scream.

He pulled the blouse closed across her wound, careful not to get blood on his hands. He took off his deerskin jacket, even though the night was chilly. Then he whispered a quick prayer.

"Dear Lord, I know she took You into her heart. And I know she was messing around at that awful church. But please don't hold that against her. The Devil spins a mighty good yarn, and I don't think it's fair if she got tricked off the path of salvation. Judge her by the way she was before Archer got ahold of her. So if it be Thy will, please take her away from him and bring her up into the heavenly fold where she rightly belongs. Amen."

David looked into the woman's face. Death was supposed to be peaceful. But there was no peace in those rigid features. Worst of all, the thin nose and the sharp cheekbones and the rounded eyebrows were Gregg family characteristics. Exactly the same as Linda's. He laid the jacket across Donna's face.

"Are they dead?" Tim repeated, coming forward despite David's order to stay put. Ronnie followed, hesitantly.

"Looks like it, son," David said, standing. "We'd best get home and call the sheriff."

"The sheriff?" Ronnie said. "We saw his truck back at the church."

Tim tried to peer at the body. David put his arm around Tim and led him to the far side of the road. "Come on. Let's get home."

They walked in silence past the forest and into the open stretch of pasture and fields. The Potter farm sprawled dark and empty at the foot of the mountains. The farmhouse and barns were like tiny boats in a rough sea. Nobody let their lights burn all night in Whispering Pines. That was wasteful and expensive. But somehow the darkness in Zeb's windows was more desolate and final than if the occupant had been merely sleeping.

Boonie, Zeb, and now Donna. It's starting again, getting faster. Just like Archer done in California. Except this time I don't know if I can even slow him down, much less stop him.

"How come people are dying, Daddy?" Tim asked.

David thought about how to answer.

The devil's setting up revival camp in Whispering Pines? A preacher got hung over a hundred years ago and he's been pissed off ever since? We've all collected on the wages of sin and now it's payback time?

"I don't rightly know, son," he finally said. "I just know it's going to be all right."

Lying, like marksmanship and tomato growing, got easier with practice.

He could see their house ahead, the mailbox shining in the moonlight. It somehow made him feel safer, even though he knew that mere walls wouldn't keep the Bell Monster away. The lights were off in their house, too.

"Is Mama home?" Tim asked.

"Don't believe so," David said, hoping he could keep his worry hidden.

"How come she was at the church?" Ronnie asked. "We always go on Sunday morning, not late at night."

"Well, she was just being neighborly, helping out," David lied for the third time. Well, it wasn't a complete lie. She was helping out, all right, just not the kind of help a person usually gave to their church. Her service went way beyond bake sales and sending get-well cards and arranging flowers.

She would be out with Archer, taking part in whatever crazy ritual the freak thought up next. She was helping him bring death and fear and hell's madness into their little valley. His chest tightened, this time hot with failure.

He'd rescued Linda once, led her back into the Baptist fold, into the love and light of the Lord. But maybe that wasn't good enough for her, because she'd taken a second taste of the devil's temptation and found it to be sweeter than Christ's redeeming blood.

He clenched his hands tight around his rifle. He tried to offer a prayer, to ask for God's strength, but he'd run out of words. He glanced at the sky, ink-dark and star-filled and stretching from mountaintop to mountaintop.

Just exactly who owns this damned world?

David shivered at the slight weakening of his faith.

He led the boys up the driveway and into the house. He was momentarily afraid that, even if he managed a prayer, it would fall on deaf ears. Or worse, ears that heard but just didn't plain care.

* * *

When the bell rang, Linda didn't cover her ears, though the church shook with the vibrations.

That was part of the ritual, Archer had said. The bell had to ring to drive away that crazy Jesus and all the other demons that clouded people's minds. The bell must toll as a reminder of the iniquities of murderous ancestors.

So she welcomed the sound, and each rich resonance washed over her body like a cleansing wave of holy water. Archer folded his hands together and bowed his head.

"Stronger," he whispered after the third toll. "It's getting stronger."

What's getting stronger? Linda wondered. But she dared not break his reverie to ask. She craned her neck to peer outside the church. That was when the sheriff screamed.

Archer ran down the church steps and stood over Littlefield's prostrate form. Linda followed slowly, waiting for a sign from Archer. The sheriff had been looking at the tree. Linda wondered what he had seen that was so frightening. The churchyard was a place of peace and beauty, not a place of fear. Perhaps the sheriff was faithless, weak, unworthy.

Archer knelt on the ground beside the sheriff and lifted his face to the sky.

"O Father," he intoned in that preacher voice that sent shivers of rapture up Linda's spine, "see me take this sinner into my church. He has joined us in communion and has eaten of the host. O Father, watch him join us in the battle against the unrighteousness and evil that masquerades as salvation, so that he may walk into light forever, amen."

"Amen," Linda echoed automatically. She felt a

piece of the communion between her teeth. She worked it free with her tongue, then swallowed the soft flesh that Archer had consecrated and administered. The sense of well-being expanded in her chest, swelled her head, made her light with love.

And then she *saw.*

The Hung Preacher rolled his eyes in her direction, looking at her appreciatively. Then the thick apparition turned his face back to Archer.

The Hung Preacher's black lips parted, and insubstantial things wiggled inside his mouth. "More," he said, moving his lips again, but the second time he made no sound.

A vision, Linda told herself. *An honest-to-God vision. Just like Archer always promised.*

The Baptists had raved on and on about Elijah and the burning bush, about how such-and-such was revealed to God's chosen, but nobody at First Baptist had ever had a vision of his or her own. Well, Boonie Houck had laid claim to a few, but his revelations never seemed religious in nature, especially since they usually came after a week of the trembles. But this . . . *this* . . .

The Hung Preacher dangled in full glory before her. But even now he was shimmering, fading back into his holy realm beyond this earth. Linda felt her heart leap with uncertain loss.

Archer clutched his hands together and edged toward the dogwood tree on his knees. "Don't go, oh sweet prophet," he pleaded, his voice almost childlike.

The Hung Preacher mouthed the word *more* a final time, the dead face contorted in rage. His arms fell limp at his sides, and he drifted into invisibility.

Archer stood and ran to the spot beneath the tree. He reached his arms out and hugged the empty air to his chest. "Come back," he said softly. He had a lost look on his face.

Linda had never seen Archer appear in any way vulnerable. It made her heart soar with joy. She could be of use to him. He *did* have needs. He needed *her*.

Archer had given her so much, opened her eyes to the follies of Christianity, saved her soul. The least she could do was comfort him now in his time of trouble. At last she had something to offer. She touched his shoulder. His coat was so hot that it almost burned her fingers.

He spun. Linda drew back, her hand covering her mouth in shock.

Archer's face contorted as if the bones of his skull had broken and the fragments were trying to push through his skin. His forehead flattened and elongated, the lower part of his face funneled together, the nose broadened over the mouth. His eyes widened, and a fierce golden color ringed the black, marble-sized pupils. Archer's eyes glittered, capturing the moonlight and turning it into green and yellow diamonds.

A low animal growl came from his throat, and triangular ears pricked up at the top of his head. Whiskers like silver wire sprouted from the sides of the black-gummed mouth. The eyes narrowed, catlike, and Archer fell onto his hands.

No, not his hands. Paws.

Archer's suit ripped, and reddish brown fur sprouted over the preacher's flesh. The creature stepped forward, out of Archer's shoes, its thick claws curling into the ground through the socks.

A mountain lion.

David had told her stories about them, her father had hunted them, and the Appalachian settlers used to fear them so much that they became the stuff of fireplace scare stories. But all the mountain lions were dead.

She had never doubted that Archer could work miracles. Now, with this undeniable proof, she gave the last of herself to him. She fell before the great cat and bowed her head, trembling, awaiting the mighty gnash of its teeth or the swift stroke of its talons, whatever method Archer deemed most fitting. Salvation was all about sacrifice, Archer had told her, and she was willing to make the ultimate one.

Jesus divided loaves and fishes and walked on water. *Big deal.* Jesus had never been anything but Jesus. This proved that Archer was better, the true savior, the real Son of God. This proved that Archer was master of the atoms and cells and all that other invisible stuff that made things what they were.

The animal growled again, a low rumbling noise in its chest. It moved forward and sniffed at Linda. Despite herself, she shivered as warm, moist breath passed across the back of her neck.

Please make it not hurt, Archer.

The mountain lion waited. The sky was a shade lighter now, a deeper blue from the east pushing away the black. The forest was still, hushed in that moment just before dawn when the diurnal and nocturnal animals changed shifts. The great cat's soft breathing was the only sound besides the pounding of Linda's heart.

The cat moved away, toward the still-unconscious sheriff. Linda felt a small surge of disappointment, but also a rush of relief.

So I'm to be spared. I promise to have a purpose if you only let me live, God. You need me here to serve Archer, to help him do whatever he needs done to save the world. To beat Jesus and Satan forever.

She watched as the cat lowered its head toward the sheriff's neck.

THIRTEEN

The house was dark when Linda drove up. That meant the boys were asleep. She hated to neglect them the way she had been, but Archer needed her more than the boys did. A servant should have only one master, Archer always said. And God was a jealous God.

She had passed the body that had been lying on the side of the road. Some of the other parishioners had probably passed it as well, though all would murmur to themselves, "There must be great sacrifices." Linda recognized David's jacket draped across the body. So her husband had been out nosing around.

She hoped he would stay out of the way. If David left her alone, maybe Archer would spare him. David had married into the Gregg family, not earned the birthright with blood. The Days weren't one of the old families, so they owed no tribute to the red church and had no iniquities to pay for.

She got out of the car and took a breath of fresh air. The smells of the farm, freshly tilled soil, hay, and chicken manure always comforted her. That was one of the ironies of her life: she'd always been afraid that she'd wind up trapped in Whispering Pines, yet she had never really felt comfortable anywhere else, especially in California. Not even Archer's wonderful presence there could totally erase her homesickness.

The moon was low in the sky, three-quarters full over the uneven mountain ridges. The deep indigo of the night and the scattered pinpricks of stars were beautiful. She would miss this world. It was hard to believe that a better one existed, but Archer said he had a place for her waiting in heaven. The *real* heaven, not that mock-up illusion that the Christians peddled.

Harps and white robes. What a laugh.

She went into the house, careful not to make any noise. She would go in and kiss the boys good night and make sure the blankets were tucked under their chins. Her hand fumbled along the wall until she found the light switch, and she flipped it up.

"Well, well, well . . ." David said. She jumped back against the door.

". . . if it ain't the whore of Babylon," David finished. He sat on the couch, still in his work clothes, eyes alert. His rifle was across his lap.

"What in the world do you think you're doing here?" she whispered, as loudly as she could without waking the boys.

"Taking care of my own." His eyes narrowed as he patted the gun barrel. "Somebody's got to do it."

"Get out."

"Not while that . . . that McFall bastard is on the prowl."

"Leave Archer out of this."

"I wish I could."

"You think this is all about you? This doesn't have anything to do with you, so just mind your own business."

David watched her as she stepped away from the open door and eased toward the kitchen. Only his eyes moved. The rest of him remained rigid. "What's going on up at the church, Linda?"

"Nothing. Just getting services going again." Linda looked away to escape his gaze. "How are the boys?"

"Oh, they're just fine. Ain't nothing like being scared to death and having their mother taking up with a touched-in-the-head bunch of midnight worshipers."

"Those are good folks. You know most of them. They're our neighbors."

"Yeah, at least the ones who are still alive."

"You saw her?"

"Yeah."

Linda's eyes grew moist. She had not allowed herself to mourn for Donna. But now that David had reminded her, she couldn't fight the mortal weakness of tears.

"Boys saw her, too." David's voice was sharper now that he saw he could cut her with his words. "Lucky for them, they didn't find out who it was."

Linda leaned against the jamb of the entryway that led into the hall. The guilty had to die. But why did it have to be Donna? Her cousin had never really done anything wrong, except maybe committing a little adultery. Was Donna's heart really that tainted, just because she liked to love other women's husbands?

"That makes three," David said. "One every night. Just like in California."

Linda slammed her fist against the cheap paneling, and the trophy heads on the wall shook. "Why didn't you just let me stay in California?" she said, louder than she wanted to.

"You're going to wake the boys."

She crossed the room and stood over him. "Why

didn't you leave me out there? I was happy. Maybe for the first time ever."

David took his hands from the rifle and cupped them over his knees. "Because you turned your back on the Lord. And on me. I couldn't let Archer McFall and that bunch rot your soul."

She snorted, her nose red from crying. "Soul? What do you know about having a soul?"

"I know what's right. And Archer ain't right. He's the devil. He's worse than the devil. At least the devil plays by God's rules, and knows good from evil. Your precious preacher seems to get them a little mixed up."

"You're crazy, David."

"I ain't the one praying to a murdering monster."

"Archer has nothing to do with the killings."

"Sure he don't. Mighty big damned coincidence, wouldn't you say? Archer goes to California, people die hard. Archer comes back to Whispering Pines, people die hard."

"Sometimes the innocent must die—"

"I got news for you. None of us are innocent."

Linda shook her head. "You don't get it, do you? I've been praying and praying, asking God to throw some light on you so you'd see that Archer is the real savior. But I guess that ten-dollar-a-week Jesus is all you've got the brains for. Serves you right to follow him to hell."

David stood suddenly, the rifle thumping to the floor. He glared down into her eyes, but Linda wasn't afraid. *There will come great trials,* Archer said. She would be strong. Her faith would not waver.

"You can follow that fool," David said between clenched teeth. "But I'll be damned if you're going to take the boys with you."

"That's right. You'll be damned," she said, angry

now that David was taking her greatest possessions, the greatest tithe she could make to Archer. The boys were her ticket into Archer's heart, into the kingdom of God.

David bent and picked up the rifle, holding it across his chest between them. "Then let the son of a bitch come and get them. But he'll have to come through *me* first."

David's eyes were hard. She knew how stubborn he could be. He had worn that same expression in California, when he came into the temple after Archer had disappeared. He'd carried her out to his pickup, then drove back to the mountains, stopping only for gas and food or when exhaustion forced him to nap for a few hours. Now, as then, Linda realized just how much she loved him. But love was a trick, a scare tactic that led to desperation. Archer said that earthly love was just another vanity, didn't he?

Love in its way was a false idol. Love was as hollow as a golden calf—all shiny and bright on the outside, nothing but bad dark air on the inside. Love gave you nothing, but took every little thing that you had.

Human love was an altar that you crawled on and then asked to be slaughtered.

Love was Jesus' greatest lie.

She would be strong.

"I hate you," she said, her chest cold, her heart coated with the iron will that Archer had instilled.

David held up a hand, glanced at the front door and then the window. "Did you hear that?"

"Hear what?"

David thumbed the rifle's safety off and tilted his head to listen. "Shh."

"It won't come here," Linda whispered, trying to reassure herself. Archer would send his heavenly agent for the boys. But he'd promised to wait until they'd become part of the fold. That would ensure their place in Archer's eternal glory, and secure her place by Archer's side.

Something rattled at the front door.

It can't be. Tonight's sacrifice has already been made.

In the silence, the ticking of the clock was like raindrops on a coffin.

David put his cheek to the gunstock and waited for whatever was outside to enter.

Can you hear Him aknocking?

Ronnie pulled the covers over his head, but the suffocating darkness made his fear grow instead of disappear. Mom and Dad had stopped arguing, so maybe they had heard the noise, too. Tim was snoring, but Ronnie hadn't been able to close his eyes since they'd arrived home. He was afraid that if he slept, he'd dream about the black shape that flapped across the sky like a jaggedy kite.

And now it was here, the Bell Monster, the scary thing from the church that had wings and claws and livers for eyes. It had followed them home, and Ronnie knew—*knew*—that it had come just for him. Because he had sinned in his heart, and the devil had sent a demon from the pits of hell, just the way Preacher Staymore had threatened in Sunday school.

The claws clicked on the glass. Ronnie chewed nervously on the blankets, and a stray fiber got in his throat and made him cough. The clicking stopped. The monster had heard him. In the stillness, Ronnie listened to the wet mist of its waiting breath.

Ronnie tried to pray. The preacher said that the Lord forgave all sins and protected the children. If

God had control over the heavens and the earth, then surely He controlled the demons as well.

Dear Jesus, please forgive me for my sins of the heart. I know I've suffered bad thoughts, and I haven't been saved in three weeks. But I want you in my heart and not the thing with livers for eyes. Please, please, get me out of this and I promise I'll get saved every week from now on, even if Preacher Staymore's breath smells like rotten fruit. Amen.

Ronnie opened his eyes under the blankets. It was working. The wet noises went away. The prayer had sent the demon back to hell, or maybe back to the red church.

Thankyou thankyou thankyou, O Jesus—

The clicking started again, and Ronnie felt as if the door to his heart had slammed shut. Across the room, Tim rolled over in his sleep. If the Bell Monster came in through the window, it might get Tim.

And maybe if it gets Tim, it will leave me alone.

As soon as he had the thought, his face warmed with shame. Didn't Jesus say to love thy brother? Or was that one of the Ten Commandments? Either way, he had suffered another sin of the heart, and Jesus would punish him even more.

The brave thing to do would be to go out and face the monster. To let the thing rip him open and gnaw on his sinning heart, the way it had ripped up Boonie Houck and probably Zeb Potter and that person on the side of the road.

Mom said that Archer McFall said that sacrifice was the way to heaven. If Ronnie sacrificed himself, maybe Jesus would take him instead of letting the demon drag him down to the hot place. But Archer McFall was weirder than any preacher Ronnie had ever heard of. Who else would hold services in a haunted church? And the memory of those strange hymns that Mom and the others had been singing made him shiver with strange, sick pleasure.

The claws were on the windowsill now, exploring the crack at the base of the window. Ronnie couldn't remember if the window was locked. Mom had raised it yesterday to let in some fresh air, and Ronnie went right after she left and latched it again. But maybe she had unlatched it again while he was asleep.

Footsteps came down the hall, heavy footsteps. Dad's boots. Ronnie pulled the covers off his head and sat up, braver now that Dad was coming to the rescue. He couldn't help himself. He had to glance at the window.

Through the curtains, Ronnie saw the Bell Monster pressed against the glass. It was moist, changing shape as he watched, the lesser gray of its mouth parting in some kind of anger or longing.

And he saw the eyes.

Livers.

Wet, drippy, slick, and red.

Eyes that looked right into Ronnie's, that seemed to crawl down his eyeball sockets and into his brain, to reach from his brain to his heart, as if to say, *You're mine now, you've always been mine, can you hear me aknocking?*

Then the door to the bedroom crashed open and light from the hall spilled across the room and Dad's long shadow filled the doorway.

"Get down," Dad yelled, and Ronnie fell back against the pillows as the first shot exploded from Dad's rifle.

Glass shattered as the percussion echoed off the walls.

Dad yanked the bolt back, reloaded, and fired again.

Gunsmoke filled Ronnie's lungs, and though he

couldn't smell it, he could taste it, as acrid as car exhaust on his tongue.

Tim woke up screaming. Mom ran into the room and hugged him, pausing for a moment to look at the window.

Dad hurried across the room and looked through the broken panes. Jagged glass framed him, sparkling in the moonlight like sharp teeth.

"Is it gone?" Mom asked. Tim cried into her chest, his shudders shaking them both.

"I don't see it," Dad said, the rifle at his shoulder.

"Did you kill it?" she asked.

"Who the hell knows?"

"Will it come back?"

Dad turned from the window and glared at her. "You tell me. You're the damned prophet."

Prophet? thought Ronnie. Like Ezekiel and Abraham and all those? Was Dad committing a sin of the heart?

Dad bent over Ronnie's bed. "You okay?"

Ronnie nodded.

Yeah, I'm as okay as I'm ever going to be, considering that the thing with livers for eyes is after me because I've sinned in my heart, and now it's after you, too. And my nose hurts and you and Mom are fighting again and I'm not going to cry, I'm not going to—

Dad sat on the bed and wiped Ronnie's tears away. "It's gone now. You're safe. I won't let that thing get you."

"P-promise?"

"Yeah."

"Will you stay here?"

Dad tensed, then looked at Mom. Ronnie felt their hatred in the air, a black electricity, as mean as the Bell Monster and almost as scary.

Tim had stopped crying, and now whimpered a

little into the folds of Mom's shirt. Ronnie knew his little brother was waiting for what would happen next. They both knew what was at stake. If Dad left again, they would be helpless against the Bell Monster. And despite the promises, Dad might just be angry enough to leave them all, to go somewhere in his truck and drink beer and do other things that he'd never done before.

This was one of those turning points, like when the Lord came aknocking, and you either opened the door or you didn't. Where everything changed, either for better or worse. No going back to last week, when life was nearly normal and all Ronnie had to worry about was homework and Melanie Ward. This was for all the marbles.

Dad looked at Mom again, then at Tim, then at the shattered window. The sky had settled into that deep blue of early morning and even the crickets had quit their chirping. Somewhere in the hills, a hound dog bayed, a lost, lonely sound in the pre-dawn stillness.

"I'll stay," Dad said, staring out the window at the black slopes of the mountains.

Ronnie admired the muscles in his dad's jaws, the way Dad held his head up proudly, without a bit of back-down in him. Dad said that a man ought to draw his strength from the Lord, that nobody who trusted the Man Upstairs needed to be afraid of anything. And Dad made a pretty good case for it, too: Why should you be afraid of dying if dying only brought you into the presence of everlasting glory?

When Ronnie thought of heaven, he always imagined that color illustration in Dad's Bible, right before the New Testament. The picture showed Jesus at the top of a set of golden stairs that rose up into the clouds. Jesus had long hair and a brown beard and the saddest eyes Ronnie had ever seen. He had his arms out and his palms lifted in welcome, but there was nobody on the stairs. Heaven looked like a lonely place.

And besides, no matter how wonderful heaven was, new things were always scary. Like the first day of school, the time he'd given that poem to Melanie, the first time he'd been inside the red church, this business about Mom and Dad being mad at each other. So he'd rather stay right here in bed, with Dad sitting beside him and Mom and Tim under the same roof. He'd rather just go on living, thank you very much.

Even with a broken nose and a monster after him and schoolwork and Mom hanging out with that creepy preacher.

Even with all that.

He closed his eyes and waited for the sun to come up.

Archer crouched in the forest near the church. He had dragged the sheriff under the trees after sending Linda away. She wouldn't understand why the sheriff should be suffered to live. She was a good disciple, and she would willingly sacrifice herself, but she wasn't prepared for the truth. None of them were.

Archer surveyed the landscape, his great cat's eyes piercing the darkness. God ruled the kingdom of heaven, but He had given Archer the kingdom of Earth, along with dominion over all of its creatures. Archer's brother Jesus had misused that power, had wandered among the humans and confused them with messages of love and hope. Before the rise of Christianity, heaven was attained only through pain, trials, and sacrifice. After Jesus' blasphemy was erased from the earth, people would again turn to those true tests of faith.

Of all the ludicrous Christian beliefs, the most laughable was that being forgiven would earn the sinner a ticket to heaven. Yet it was so utterly human. Why bother living right and enduring the rigors of true faith when all you had to do was say, "Come into my heart" and Jesus would be right there tricking you with lies?

Archer would also grant forgiveness. But his would be delivered after the sinner got on bended knee and begged, begged, even as the dark claws of justice performed the cleansing. Deliverance must be paid in blood. Redemption must be earned the hard way.

And Father above would burn with jealousy as Archer succeeded where Jesus had failed.

Archer felt a brief twinge. Bullets passed through the manifested spirit that lurked at the Days' house three miles away. Archer threw back his head and growled a laugh at the moon, then sent the manifestation back to its home in the belfry. Let it eat the shadows there until the next night's work.

Dawn would be breaking soon. The forest was in the held breath between the changing of the guards, the nocturnal animals returning to their nests and burrows and the morning songbirds shaking sleep from their heads. What a beautiful world God had made. Except for the blight of human hearts, a blight born of God's insecurity, the Earth nearly approached heaven in its glory.

But Archer was here to erase the blight. All that sinned must be destroyed, so that a new, pure world could emerge. And all on Earth had sinned, even Jesus. Especially Jesus. All except the Second Son.

Archer licked his fur, patient in the knowledge that

he had forever. In the meantime, he would continue the cleansing right here in the place of his mortal birth. Here where Wendell McFall's soul had been trapped, where Archer himself had suffered the taunts and abuses of the unrighteous. Here where the sinless ones could come forth in an exodus of blasphemy and mockery.

Archer brought his teeth to the sheriff's collar and gently closed his mouth around the cloth. The sheriff's eyelids twitched as Archer's warm breath tickled his neck, but he didn't awaken. The smell of the man's sin, and those of all the generations of Littlefields, crowded Archer's sensitive nose.

Before Littlefield paid for his own sins, the sheriff first had to suffer for the sins of his ancestors. Archer dragged Littlefield across the churchyard, to a special place of punishment. Littlefield thought that the death of his younger brother had been enough to atone for Wendell McFall's hanging. But he would soon learn that sacrifice was the currency of a jealous God, and of jealous sons as well.

There was joy in being a messiah.

FOURTEEN

Det. Sgt. Sheila Storie looked at the clock above her office door. It was one of those old round clocks of the kind that hung in elementary schools, with a black casing and plain, oversize numerals. The second hand didn't sweep smoothly. It locked into place on each tiny mark, then twitched over to the next. She watched twenty-three of the spastic seconds pass before she took her eyes away.

She had spent the night in the office, napping a few hours in her chair. Now her back was stiff. She stood and stretched and made another pot of coffee, even though her stomach ached from the abusive night of caffeine and snack food from the machine in the hall. Just before the midnight shift change, Deputy Wellborn had called in to report that the hounds had found nothing.

Somehow, she wasn't surprised by the negative report. Hounds might be okay for chasing down runaway convicts, but this was the twenty-first century. Sifting forensic evidence and poring through criminal databases were the ways to solve crimes, not sniffing around the woods. But she had to admit that a night spent at the desk with her reports had brought her no closer to solving the two murders.

Where was the motive?

That was one of the first lessons of homicide investigation: find the motive, and you find the murderer. But she had a near-penniless drunk mutilated in a churchyard and a farmer with his head caved in by a sledgehammer. As far as anyone could determine, robbery was not a motive in either crime. In fact, the only connection between the two victims was that both lived in the Whispering Pines area.

No, that wasn't the only connection. There were more of what she called the BDCs—big damned coincidences. And most of the coincidences seemed to center on the old church.

McFall's buying of it. Frank's spilling his guts about the childhood tragedy he'd endured there. Even the ghost stories seemed to be a red flag of some kind, though she would never in a million years admit that she gave them any credence at all.

Storie looked out the window. The sky was just turning pink behind Barkersville. The two blocks of Main Street were shadowed, the brick buildings cold and empty in the gasp of dawn. A few vehicles were on the road, most of them pickup trucks with tools in the back. People were heading to work, another week to get through before another payday, and then another two days to forget that they had to do it all over again on the following Monday.

The Chamber of Commerce mailed out glossy brochures that said, *Up here, life moves at a different speed.* The idea was to lure rich tourists with the promise of front-porch rockers and lazy river breezes. Of course, once they got here, they were bored out of their minds after two days and then dumped a few thousand dollars in the area craft shops and restaurants. Some different speed.

Then why are you here?

She chewed her pencil. Why the hell *was* she here? Running from the Metro force and big-city crime, she had wanted as rural a life as she could find. Maybe she thought this would be an easy place to cut her teeth, move up a little in rank, and then make a run for sheriff.

She'd always wanted a department of her own. Storie wanted it the way other people craved sex or fame or a family. Solving high-profile cases was just the means to that end. But she also had developed this very scary need to understand Frank Littlefield, to get beneath his professional veneer and his good-ol'-boy act and figure out just what in the hell he was about.

She didn't know much about him. She didn't know enough about the red church or Archer McFall, either. It was time to change that. She pulled her keys from her desk and poured herself a last cup of coffee.

She pressed a button on her two-way. "Unit Two will be in service."

"Ten-four," came the third-shift dispatcher's voice.

She strapped on her shoulder holster before putting on her blazer. The .38 revolver was comforting against her rib cage. As she went outside, she was struck by the moist scent of life: lilies crawling out of their night pajamas, the wild cherry in front of the library snow white with blossoms, birds chattering from branches and utility poles. She took a deep breath and gazed over the mountains.

On those hills were houses, filled with people who were as deeply rooted as the old-growth hardwoods. Smoke curled from a couple of the chimneys, despite the warmth of the morning. These people were no different from the urbanites she had grown up with. They slept with dreams, and the dreams dissolved

when they awoke. Time passed for them as rapidly
as it passed for everyone.

Yep, some different speed, all right.

She got in her cruiser and headed for Whispering
Pines, staying just under the limit all the way.

Frank.

Get up.

Frank didn't want to get up. He was lying under
some hay, and the sun was coming through the open
loft door and warming his bones until they were like
cooked noodles.

"Get up, Frankie."

Frank opened his eyes. The world was yellow, all
sunlight and straw dust. The straps of his overalls dug
into his neck, making him itch. But that was only a
minor problem. He could endure the itch, and he
could ignore Samuel. Samuel was about as minor a
problem as a little brother could be.

"Come on, let's go fishing."

"Go away," Frank murmured. If Grandpa or Dad
found him lazing off, they'd wear out his rear end
with a hickory switch. He could hear Grandpa's
crotchety voice now: *Corn to be hoed and hogs to be
slopped and the goldurned dinner chicken's still wearing
its feathers.* The chainsaw buzzed like a drunken bee
where the two men were cutting firewood on one of
the hillsides.

Something poked Frank in the side. He reluctantly
rolled over and saw Samuel with a cane pole in his
hands, feet bare and an Atlanta Braves cap perched
on his head. A grin filled with crooked teeth threatened to split Samuel's freckled face in half. "Come
down to the river, Frankie."

Frank sat up, dazzled by the sun. Outside, the

fields were a brilliant shade of green. The mountains were sharply in focus, as if each individual tree and rock had been carefully etched onto a fine cotton paper. The sky was so vividly blue that he rubbed his eyes, because the air was like water, thick with currents and eddies and languorous coolness. He stood on wobbly scarecrow legs.

"Got your pole, too," said Samuel. He held out another bamboo cane. A round red-and-white float and a small silver hook dangled from the monofilament line. Frank took the pole without a word, then followed Samuel across the hayloft. His feet felt as if they were wrapped in fat clouds and scarcely seemed to touch the ground. Then they were down the ladder and out of the barn and crossing a long meadow. The grass was alive, like the crisp hair of the earth.

The chainsaw stopped and its echo fell like smoke across the valley and dissolved. In the sudden silence, a bird cried from the trees near the river. Samuel led the way across the meadow, below the garden with its tomato vines and leafy cabbage heads and corn stalks tipped with golden buds. He felt as if he were attached to an invisible line, being reeled toward an unknown shore.

Samuel hummed a church hymn that was a little too somber for such a bright summer day. And Samuel should be skipping, laughing, beating at the thistles with his cane pole. He should be running ahead of Frank to find a hiding place under the cottonwoods. Instead his little brother walked solemnly, watching his toes.

The sky pressed down and Frank swam against it. They were at the river now, and its sparkling silvery eyes watched them.

"We're going to catch the big one," Samuel said, standing on a sandbar and freeing his line. He sneaked a look at Frank and put his hand to his mouth. Then he held out his palm to Frank, showing a writhing mass of thick, glistening nightcrawlers. Frank took one and speared it on his hook. Samuel took one for himself and returned the rest of the worms to his mouth. Frank's stomach tightened in nausea.

The boys launched their baited hooks almost in unison. Dragonflies scooted along the riverbank, their green wings beating against the air. Water splashed over stones, snickering.

"It's almost like Sunday," Samuel said.

"Yeah. Here we are being lazy when there's chores to be done. Dad will get ill as a hornet if he finds out we're fishing." Frank moved down the sandbar a little so the sun didn't flash off the water into his eyes.

"Lazy Sunday. Makes you want to go to church, don't it?"

"Church?"

Samuel smiled and his head lolled limply to one side. "Fun place to hang around, know what I mean?"

"We don't have time for that," Frank said, his hands sweating and his heart pounding.

"I got all the time in the world," Samuel said, as a thick worm crawled from his mouth. The brown tip of it squirmed as if sniffing the air, then the worm inched down Samuel's chin.

"I don't go the church anymore," Frank said. "Not since . . ."

"Since *what,* brother?"

Samuel's float bobbed once, twice. Then he jerked his pole and it bowed nearly double. "Got one, got one," he squealed in delight.

Frank dropped his own pole and lay on his belly

so he could reach into the water and land the fish. In the calm water near the shore, he saw the reflection of the sky and the high white clouds. His own face was dark on the water, unwrinkled, unworried. Young.

"Pull him in," Samuel said. Frank reached out and grabbed the taut line. As he tugged, the river erupted in a silver avalanche.

The Hung Preacher rose from the water.

The fishing line was a rope, the hook a noose that encircled the preacher's neck. The pale figure clawed at the strands, and the skin was purple where the rope dug into flesh.

The Hung Preacher's mouth parted in a suffocated scream, except—no, that wasn't the river, that was the *preacher*—he was laughing, gurgling, a font of morbid merriment.

Frank's own scream was a dull fist in his throat, a mossy stone, a cold fish. He tried to scramble up the bank, but a hand on his arm held him down.

"Time for a baptism, Frankie," came Samuel's voice, only it wasn't the voice of a child. It was a low voice from beyond the grave, a putrid exhalation of hate, the words rustling and slithering like snakes through a catacomb.

Frank looked up at his dead brother, into the eyes that had once been mercifully sewn closed by the funeral director, eyes that now stared accusingly, filled with the hot hunger of vengeance delayed. Samuel's crooked teeth were sharp, moldy, the spaces between them filled with quick darkness.

Samuel was knee-deep in the water now, his gaunt hand tight on Frank's arm, drawing him across the mud and soggy roots into the lapping, laughing tongue of the river. The Hung Preacher tented his hands in a prayer, and his bowed head was smiling, smiling.

Samuel tugged, and Frank was in the river, his dead little brother pushing down on the top of his head, submerging him, and the water tasted like death; the water was crypt air and flooded his lungs even while he struggled toward the surface that was so far away. He fought, even though he knew he deserved to die for what he had done to Samuel.

The hands tugged, pulled. He felt himself going under, deeper—

"Sheriff, wake up."

Littlefield kicked and flailed, moaning.

"Get up, you're having a bad dream."

Littlefield tensed, his muscles spasming from the struggle. "Sh-Sheila?"

"Yeah, Sheriff. Are you okay?"

He opened his eyes. The morning sun was painful. He blinked up into Detective Storie's face. She was so close that he could smell the coffee on her breath. Her hair fell softly about her cheekbones, but her mouth was lined with worry.

What a pleasant sight to wake up to, Littlefield thought. His head felt as if Zeb Potter's murderer had done another sledgehammer job. A sweetly foul aftertaste coated the inside of his mouth. He could smell his own body odor.

Storie helped him sit up. His uniform was moist with sweat and dew. Or maybe baptismal water . . .

"What happened?" Storie asked.

"I don't know," said the sheriff, shaking his head. "Last thing I remember . . ."

He looked across the churchyard. The Trooper was where he had parked it the night before, but that was his last memory. Had he been inside the church?

Gravestones surrounded him, the marble and granite bright in the sun. He knew this area of the cemetery. He had brought flowers here many times. He turned and glanced at the marker where his head had been resting.

A small lamb was engraved on the top of the tombstone. The etched symbols beneath the image pierced his heart, just as they had always done:

Here lies
Samuel Riley Littlefield
1968–1979
May God Protect and Keep Him

May God protect him. Because Frank Littlefield sure hadn't. Frank had practically sealed Samuel's coffin shut through stupidity and indifference. A big brother was supposed to be his brother's keeper.

The dream.

"Look," said Storie, pulling Littlefield from his reverie. She pointed to a flattened path in the grass that led from the forest.

"Something dragged me here."

"Something?"

Sure. The Hung Preacher, the Bell Monster, the Tooth Fairy. Maybe even the Bride of Frankenstein. Take your pick. She'll believe any of them, won't she?

"The back of your shirt is dirty," she said. "And your collar's torn. You look like you pulled an all-night drunk."

"Gee, thanks. I feel like it."

"Must have been a hell of a church service. What did they do, make you go back for second helpings of the wine until you blacked out?"

Communion. Vague images floated through his head, images of taking something into his mouth from Archer McFall's fingers. He swallowed and probed his mouth with a thick tongue. He wanted to spit but couldn't muster enough saliva.

The red church stood silent at the top of the rise. The belfry was black with shadows. He watched for a moment, but the shadows didn't move. His fingers explored the shredded fabric of his collar. Whatever had made the wounds had stopped inches from his neck. He had been spared, but why?

He wasn't sure he wanted to know.

"Looky," said Tim. "There's the sheriff and that lady cop. Out in the churchyard."

Ronnie looked past his dad to the two police officers. The sheriff was sitting in front of a tombstone, his hair all messed up. The woman waved at them. He started to wave back, then remembered what Dad had said.

Dad glanced over into the cemetery, then back to the gravel road. He kept his hands clenched around the steering wheel. Ronnie knew that when Dad set his jaw so that it creased, he didn't want to be bothered.

"Shouldn't we tell them about the dead person we saw last night? And the monster?"

David glanced into the rearview mirror and froze Tim with a hard look. "Those things are best not talked about."

"Is it because the sheriff was at the church with Mom? Is he one of the bad people?" Tim didn't know when to shut up.

"Let the Lord sort that out," Dad said. "Our job is to keep our eyes on our own paths."

They rounded the bend and the church was out of sight. Below the road, the river raced them, losing by a wide margin. The water was low because no rain had fallen in weeks. Ronnie looked for places that might make good swimming holes. Anything to avoid thinking about you-know-what.

"Why do we have to go to school, Daddy?" The motor of Tim's mouth couldn't idle for long.

"The best thing to do is to keep everything as normal as possible."

"Is that why we can't tell anybody what happened?"

"Yep. So you two are going to school and I'm going to work."

"What about Mom?"

Oops, Ronnie thought. *What a dingle-dork.*

"Your mom will be okay," Dad said. "Just took a fool notion. We all do that once in a while. Now let's talk about something else."

Ronnie looked out the window. He didn't mind going to school, even if his nose was still a little sore. The swelling had gone down, and the only problem was that the packing in his nose muffled his speech. Kids would be making fun of him. But at least at school, the Bell Monster had plenty of victims to choose from if it came aknocking. Ronnie wouldn't mind seeing two or three of his classmates come face-to-face with whatever the thing was. But that wish sounded like a sin of the heart, and Ronnie couldn't risk any more of those.

"Got your medicine?" Dad asked. Ronnie nodded.

Yep. A good old pain pill. He would go through the day with a dorked-up brain, that was for sure. He wondered if that was why Whizzer Buchanan smoked those stinky pot cigarettes he brought to school. If so, maybe Whizzer wasn't as loony as Ronnie thought.

Because there was something to be said for going through life in a fog. In the fog, you couldn't see the monsters coming. In the fog, they got you before you knew what hit you.

They reached Barkersville Elementary about a half hour late. Dad said he would pick them up in the afternoon. Ronnie was relieved he didn't have to spend all day worrying about having to walk past the red church. He and Tim got excuse notes from the principal's office and went into the hall.

"See you, Tim," said Ronnie.

"Are you going to tell anybody?"

"Tell anybody what?"

Tim just didn't get it. If Dad said do something, you did it. Dad had his reasons.

"You know. The monster."

"Lock it and throw away the key," said Ronnie, imitating turning a key against his tight lips and tossing the invisible key over his shoulder.

"Even about finding Boonie Houck?"

"If anybody asks, just say the police told you not to talk about it."

"Cool," said Tim, his eyes widening behind his glasses. "We're sort of like heroes."

"Yeah, sure." Heroes. Brave as hell, that was Ronnie, all right. Ran from Boonie Houck and busted his nose. Left Tim to fend for himself when the monster had chased them both. Chickened out when something came scratching around the bedroom window.

At least here at school, the biggest horror was Mrs. Rathbone's prealgebra class.

"Meet me out front after school," Ronnie said. He turned toward the upper-grade wing. He'd taken about six steps before Tim called.

"Ronnie?" The word echoed off the cinder-block walls. Ronnie looked around, hoping none of the teachers came out in the hall to shush them.

"Yeah?"

"Is everything going to be okay?"

"Of course it is."

"With Mom and Dad? And everything?"

Ronnie walked back, made sure no one was in the hall, and gave Tim a quick hug. "Sure. Your big brother's here. I'll make sure nothing happens to us."

Tim almost looked convinced.

"Now get to class, squirt," Ronnie said. Tim hustled down the hall. Ronnie got his books from his locker, then went to Mrs. Rathbone's room. He hung his head as he walked to his assigned desk near the back of the class.

"Why, Mr. Day, we're fortunate that you have graced us with your presence today," Mrs. Rathbone said, folding her arms, stretching her ever-present acrylic sweater over her sharp shoulders.

Ronnie stifled a groan and glanced at Melanie in the next row. He slid into his desk and said, "Sorry, Mrs. Rathbone. We . . . had an accident at home."

"I see," she said, touching her nose in derision. She imitated his stuffy tone as the class giggled. "I trust you have your homework, nevertheless?"

"Uh, yeah, sure." He shuffled through his papers. He hadn't done his homework. Who else but crazy Mrs. Rathbone assigned homework over the weekend?

"Then would you share with us the answer to problem number seventeen?"

Ronnie gulped and pretended to scan down a piece of paper. Mrs. Rathbone was almost as scary as the Bell Monster. Sweat collected along his hairline. He was about to blurt a random answer when, out of the corner of his eye, he saw Melanie wiggling her fingers. He rolled his eyes toward her while holding up his paper to hide his face. Melanie had scrawled something and angled her paper toward him so that Mrs. Rathbone couldn't see it.

$X = 7$.

He looked over his paper at Mrs. Rathbone. "X equals seven?"

The teacher frowned. "Very good," she said, unable to hide the sour disappointment in her voice. She turned her attention to the next victim.

After class, Ronnie caught up with Melanie at her locker. With his heart pounding, he said, "Thanks."

"It was nothing." She smiled. Ronnie grew about two feet and felt as if he'd already taken the pain pill. "Besides, you've helped me a couple of times."

He nodded, unable to think of what to say next.

"What happened to your nose?" she asked.

"Broke it."

"Ouch. Does it hurt?"

"Yeah."

Around them, kids slammed lockers, and the intercom ordered somebody to the office. Ronnie checked the clock on the wall. He'd better hurry to his next class before he'd have to think of something else to say.

"How did you break it?" she asked, her eyes blue and bright and her pretty lips parted in waiting.

He swallowed. Better to stare down Mrs. Rathbone than to talk face-to-face with Melanie. But she was looking at him as if what he had to say actually mattered.

It was now or never, one of those stupid turning points again. Did everything require bravery?

We're sort of like heroes.

Well, maybe.

He lowered his voice conspiratorially, his heart fluttering as she leaned closer to listen. He wished his nose worked so he could smell her hair. "You ever heard of Boonie Houck?"

She shook her head. The warning bell rang.

"I got to go," he said.

She put her hand on his arm. "Sit with me at lunch and tell me about it," she said, then disappeared into the bustle of students.

Ronnie floated to his next class. He'd just learned that fogs came in different flavors.

FIFTEEN

Sheila stood on the steps of the red church and stared it down.

Just a building. Wood and nails and stone and glass. A little shabby, the roof bowed in the middle from age. Walls that creak a little when the wind blows, and mice probably skittering around under the foundation. Nothing but a building.

Then why all the ghost stories? Sure, the Scottish and English and Irish settlers brought their folk legends to the mountains, something to spook the children when gathered around a winter's fire. Maybe preachers were always a favorite target of gossipers, and gossip turned to whispered legend. If Frank could fall for that "Hung Preacher" nonsense, then that was a testament to the power of a whisper.

Even in the flatlands, every town had a haunted house or two. There was one in Charlotte, an old brick house a few blocks from where she had grown up. She had pedaled her bike past it several times, searching the darkness of the broken windows for movement.

One bright autumn morning, Sheila saw something move in the dead space behind a shutter. She stopped her bike and looked up from the edge of the overgrown yard. Something or someone was watching her.

She had shivered and pedaled madly away. She hadn't believed the place was haunted, yet she had never accepted her friends' Halloween dares to enter it.

Now, after all her derision of Frank's stories, she hesitated at the church door. Of course this place held horrors for Frank. His brother had died here while Frank watched. A memory like that would haunt anybody. But did that explain why the hair on her forearms tingled erect when she touched the doorknob?

Sheila looked around the churchyard. Frank was at the edge of the forest, searching the ground. Other than the noise of his moving through the brush, the hill was quiet. Though the sun glared down, she was chilled by the shadow of the huge old dogwood. Its branches hovered over her, long bony fingers, reaching, reaching. . . .

Nonsense. You're just catching whatever craziness is infecting everybody else in Whispering Pines. You deal in facts, and don't you forget it.

She went inside. The foyer was dark, since it had no windows. She blinked and headed into the sanctuary. The handmade pews were lined neatly on both sides, even though the heights of them varied slightly. Storie admired the woodwork of the beams and the carved railing that marked off the dais. Once upon a time, somebody had put a lot of love into this church.

The church smelled of hay and her nose itched from dust. The church had been used as a barn, Frank had said. The church had undergone a haphazard cleaning job since the Houck murder. She wondered if the intent had been to hide evidence, and regretted not ordering the church sealed off with yellow crime scene tape. But Frank said he'd checked the church thoroughly.

She approached the pulpit, aware of her footsteps and heartbeat intruding on the stillness of the church. She wasn't religious, but she was respectful of houses of God. Still, the Christian God was all about getting to the truth, right? So maybe Jesus wouldn't mind her snooping around a bit.

Nothing seemed amiss in the sanctuary and a quick look in the vestry revealed only cobwebs and dark corners. She crossed the dais and stood at the lectern, looking out over pews and imagining what it would be like to have a congregation to address. If she were going to understand Archer McFall's motives, she had to put herself in his place. All murderers had a motive, however senseless in the eyes of sane people.

A preacher as prime suspect? That's about as loopy as a murderous ghost.

She put her hands on the lectern and realized her palms were sweating. Was this the power that lured McFall from California, to leave a life of sun and cash to preach in these cold mountains? Did McFall have a messiah complex or something? No, that was giving him too much credit. The only reason he was a suspect at all was that she couldn't come up with anything better.

She checked over the dais one more time, and on the second pass she saw the stain. It was old and brown, faded into the oak floorboards. It looked like a bloodstain, though too ancient to be from Boonie Houck's murder. She knelt and traced her finger around the edges of it.

The stain made a pattern. She stood and studied it. If you looked hard enough, you could imagine it was an angel, all wings and . . .

She smiled to herself. Yep, she'd failed her own Rorschach test. So much for those criminal-psychology classes. It was time to see if Frank had found anything.

She touched the railing as she stepped off the dais, and something clung to her hand. At first she thought it was dust, but she held her hand to the light coming through the windows. Rust-colored flakes glistened against her skin. Dried blood.

Sheila stooped and looked at the rail, wishing that she'd brought a flashlight. A few flakes of dried blood were scattered across the wood. How had Frank missed seeing them? She thought maybe she'd better be more discriminating about the things Frank said. After all, he believed in ghosts.

She had a solid clue at last, something the labs could work with. They could at least determine whether the blood was Houck's or, if she were lucky, the killer's. She wondered how many fingerprints were lying about the church. Even if they were from fifty different hands, at least she would have a suspect pool.

Sheila backtracked down the aisle, scanning the floor for more bloodstains. No luck.

She went through the foyer, better able to see this time because her eyes had adjusted to the dimness. A coat rack was nailed to one wall, wooden pegs angled out like deer antlers. Sheila bumped into the bell rope and it swayed against her blazer with a whispering sound. The rope led up into the belfry.

Wait a second. Frank said there wasn't a bell rope. Why would he lie about something like that? And what else has he lied about?

Well, at least this explains why those witnesses had reported hearing bells on the nights of the murders. Probably some kids messing around in here.

She hurried from the church to share her news with Frank. She wanted to see his face when he was confronted with his lies. "Hey, Sheriff," she called.

He stepped out from a laurel thicket. He looked a little better now, though his eyes were bloodshot and his hair unkempt. "I didn't find anything," he said with a shrug.

Big surprise.

"Well, I did. Bloodstains."

"Bloodstains?"

"In the church."

Frank's eyebrows raised. "I'll be damned."

"I thought you would be. And another thing. You know the ringing bells that you kept talking about?"

"Yeah?"

"Well, I have a simple explanation for that."

"How simple?"

"Follow me."

She jogged to the church steps and waited for Frank. "In here. I thought you said there wasn't a bell rope because of—"

"Right. There hasn't been a bell rope for over a hundred and thirty years. Because people wanted to forget that mess about the Hung Preacher."

Sure. That's why the legend is alive and kicking today, isn't it? Because they did such a damned good job of forgetting?

She smiled to herself as she followed Frank up the steps. This *will show him.*

She blinked. The rope was gone.

She gazed up into the small hole that led to the belfry. Nothing. Had someone pulled it up? If so, whoever it was would still be up there. They would have seen anybody running from the church.

Frank had his hands on his hips, looking at her.

"I swear. There was a rope here."

"Ha, ha. Very funny."

"I'm serious. Give me a boost up to that hole."

The sheriff shook his head. "No way in hell, Sheila. The last time I did that, I lost a brother. I'm not about to lose you."

She balled her fists. "Damn it, I saw a rope. Are you going to tell me one of your ghosts tied it to the bell?"

"There's no rope."

"Do you think I imagined it? That I'm catching whatever craziness seems to be spreading around these parts?"

The sheriff sighed. "Look, maybe I've been a fool. Forget all that crap about the ghosts. If I really believed in ghosts, why would I bother to investigate the case?"

"Because you're the sheriff. You *have* to act like you know what you're doing."

"You're not going up in the belfry."

"There's no way *you're* going to fit. One of us has to look. We can't just sit back and cower while people keep getting murdered."

Sheila grabbed two of the coatrack pegs and pulled herself up, then positioned one foot against the doorknob. If the murderer was dumb enough to play stupid tricks, he was just begging to be caught. She wondered if she should draw her revolver, but her hands were occupied. If the murderer was waiting with a weapon . . .

She poked her head through the belfry, her anger giving her strength despite the poor grip she had on the wood.

Nothing.

Nothing in the belfry but a cold, tarnished cast-iron bell. A few leaves skittered in the breeze, caught in the corners since last autumn. Nothing else.

After a moment she jumped down, the impact jarring her knees. Frank caught her and helped her regain her balance. Their eyes met at the contact and they both looked away.

"Satisfied?" asked the sheriff.

"I swear I saw a rope," she said, failing to convince even herself. *Had* she seen it?

Well, at least there was the blood. That was real

enough. She vividly recalled the texture of the coagulated flakes. Good, hard forensic evidence, with none
of the problems caused by haunted eyewitnesses.

She brushed past Frank and hurried to the rail.
The blood was gone.

"So where's this blood?" Frank asked when he
caught up with her.

She stared at her hand, thinking of that Shake-
speare play. *Out, out, damned spot.* Had she imagined
it, just as Lady Macbeth had?

"It was right here," she whispered.

"Maybe it was ghost's blood."

From the windows, shafts of sunlight sliced across
the church. Golden dust spun slowly in the air. Wood
and nails and stone and glass. The building, the walls,
waited.

"Are you ready to call in the SBI?" Frank asked
after an awkward stretch of silence.

"Why? So they can certify me as insane as everybody else in these mountains?"

She went outside and sat on the church steps,
alone with her confusion.

Linda drove up the narrow dirt road that led to
Mama Bet's house. The driveway became so rutted
that she had to park along the fence beside the other
cars. She walked the last hundred yards, up the hill
to a little glen in the forest. She heard the music
before she saw the house. Sounded like a fiddle and
a guitar playing "Fox on the Run."

Mama Bet's house was one of the oldest struc-
tures in Whispering Pines, and generations of
McFalls had been born, grew old, and died behind
those warped gray walls. It was a perfect place for
a good old-fashioned revival, away from the snoop-

ing eyes of the cops and those brownnosers from
Barkersville. It was only fitting that the church
members congregate here. After all, besides Archer,
Mama Bet was the last of her line. Though Linda
had always thought the old woman was strange, a
little bit haughty and holier-than-thou.

Lester Matheson had brought his four-wheel-drive
truck all the way up to the house. The truck was
parked under a half-dead apple tree. Two of the
Buchanan sisters sat on the sidewalls, moonfaced and
dull-eyed. The oldest wore a red plastic clip in her
greasy hair.

A goat was tied to the apple tree, browsing along
the banks of the creek. The goat stared at Linda, its
dark eyes knowing and cold. It sniffed the air. The
goat's jaws worked sideways, then it shook the flies
from its ears and dipped its head back to the brush.

Jim Potter and Stepford Matheson continued their
counterpoint melody on guitar and fiddle. Vivian,
Lester's wife, sat in a rocker beside them, tapping
her toe in time to the music. Rudy Buchanan stood
at one end of the porch, nodding his head, though
he was about a halfbeat off the rhythm.

Sonny Absher leaned against a corner post, smok-
ing a cigarette. His eyes moved to the woods behind
the house, then fixed on Linda. "You're late," he said,
smoke drifting through his ragged mustache as he
spoke.

"I got here as soon as I could."

"The reverend don't like people to be late."

"Archer says, 'Everything in God's good time,'
brother," she answered.

The Abshers were a bunch of inbred ignorants,
and Sonny was the worst of the lot. That was one of
the things that burned her up about some of her
neighbors: they were on the doorstep to heaven here

in Archer's mountains, but instead of reveling in the glory, they lived off food stamps and bootlegging and selling the occasional beef steer. Archer would cleanse them, though. She could hardly wait.

She entered the house without knocking. Mama Bet sat in an overstuffed armchair, a shawl over her lap. Her lower legs were thick-veined below the hem of her dress. The woman smelled of smoke and salt, like a cured ham.

"Hi, Mama Bet." Linda bent and kissed the woman's cheek.

"Hey, honey. How's that man of yours coming along?"

"Not real good. I was hoping he would see the light and be spared, but—"

The old woman cut her off with a hard look, her eyes misted by cataracts. "Ain't for us to decide such as that."

Linda lowered her head.

"Only Archer knows the proper time and place for each man's death," Mama Bet continued. *"You* ain't the one turned David into a sinner, are you? You ain't the one packed him off to the Baptist church when he was a boy and too young to know any better. So Jesus is to blame for leading David astray, not you."

"Amen to that," said Nell Absher. Her husband Haywood nodded in solemn agreement. Their daughter Noreen went to the window and looked out over the clouded mountains.

"Here come Hank and Beulah," Noreen said.

"Good," said Mama Bet. "Is that everybody?"

Becca Faye Greene came in from the kitchen, a cup of coffee in her hand. She gave it to Mama Bet and stood beside the old woman's chair. She flashed a smug smile at Linda.

Becca Faye was a Potter by blood, but had married

and kept the Greene name after her husband ran off to Minnesota. She was part of Archer's circle back in high school, but had chickened out when Archer asked her to help found the Temple in California. Since Archer had returned, Becca Faye was doing everything in her power to stay in the reverend's good graces, perhaps to make up for her earlier betrayal.

Or perhaps for something more. Becca Faye's blouse was low-cut, and she was flashing enough cleavage to earn her a severe spiritual cleansing. Linda had seen the way Becca Faye had sidled up to Archer at last night's service. She wondered if the woman had had better luck than Linda in Archer's parked van.

Jealousy. One of the greatest sins of all. Forgive me, Archer.

"Call them on in," said Mama Bet. She put the coffee cup to her wrinkled lips and took a sip.

One of the Mathesons went outside, and the music stopped. The others filed in, silent Potters, Abshers, Mathesons, Buchanans, and two Greggs, both Linda's cousins. One of them met her eyes, then turned away in shame.

Linda wanted to shout, *There will come great trials, cousin. Archer says sacrifice is the true test of faith. Donna needed cleansing as much as anybody.*

But she kept her tongue. No words would bring Donna back from the dead. Except perhaps Archer's words.

About thirty people packed the living room, lined along the stone hearth and against the corner cupboard, filling the kitchen entrance. Some of the Mathesons skulked in the hall, looking into the room over Lester's shoulders. Mama Bet scanned the waiting faces. She worked her mouth in approval.

"You all know why we're here," she began. "The time's almost upon us. We prayed for the return, and now He's returned. We have all sinned and come short of the glory of heaven. Our ancestors came unto these mountains to worship in peace, but then their hearts turned hard and cold and went to Jesus. We thought saying 'I'm sorry' would make all the old sins go away."

The assembled crowd grew silent at the mention of that foul name, Jesus. Linda's stomach clenched in anger. Mama Bet nodded in appreciation of their revulsion, then continued.

"We got away from all the good things we worshiped," she said. "We strayed from the one true path. We needed the savior to return and deliver us from evil. So God sent Archer into the world of us mortals. And God punished us by making our seed go barren and letting our families die out, punishing the sinners unto the fourth generation."

"Amen," said Lester, and a smattering of others echoed the sentiment.

"We are wicked," said Mama Bet.

"Amen," said Haywood and Nell in unison. Haywood adjusted the knot of his red silk tie.

"We deserve God's wrath," the old woman said, her voice trembling as it increased in volume.

Becca Faye raised her hands and threw back her head. "There will come great trials."

The woman's breasts swelled against the fabric of her blouse as she arched her back. Linda sneered, wondering who the hussy was showing off for. Archer wasn't here, and God could care less.

The air in the room was electric, thick with the odor of sweat and tension. "Some of us have suffered loss," Mama Bet said.

Linda looked at her cousins. They lowered their heads. The Potters also looked at each other. Old Alma Potter, Zeb's sister, choked on a sob.

"But don't mourn those who have gone before," Mama Bet said, finding her rhythm. "Sacrifice is the currency of God. It's part of Archer's work. We'll all have to make sacrifices before it's done."

Mama Bet's eyes brimmed with tears. Archer was her son, the last of the McFalls. Linda knew that all the families had suffered losses. But the losses were justified, because all of them, the Greggs, Abshers, Potters, Buchanans, and Mathesons, were touched with sin. All of them had a hand in the murder of Wendell McFall.

"What do we do about the sheriff?" Lester asked. The room grew quiet.

Mama Bet clutched the worn arms of her chair. Her fingers crooked as if she were suffering a spasm of pain. "Archer can deal with the sheriff."

"There's others that are against the church," said Becca Faye, staring at Linda.

Linda's face flushed with anger and shame. "He's my husband. The Old Testament says to honor your husband."

Not that you would know about honoring a husband. The only thing you honor is whatever big-spending cowboy picks you up at Gulpin' Gulch on Friday night.

"What about your boys?" Becca Faye said, her eyes half-lidded with pleasure at Linda's discomfort. The other members of the congregation looked on with interest. Ronnie and Tim were the youngest descendants of the families that had committed deicide more than a century ago.

Linda looked out the window, at the trees green in the sun, at the dark ridges, at the creek winding between the slopes toward the river. She wished she had stayed in California. Then Ronnie and Tim would have never been born. But she couldn't imagine a life without them, even a life spent in Archer's divine arms.

"I pray for Archer's mercy," Linda finally said. Becca Faye had no response to that simple plea.

Sonny Absher broke the silence. "They got to pay like everybody else."

"But they're innocent," Linda said, angry now.

"Ain't nobody innocent."

Especially you, Linda thought, but she shouldn't pass judgment on a fellow sinner. All were equal in the eyes of Archer. All were equally guilty, and all would pay the same price.

No, not exactly the same price. Sonny would lose only his own miserable life. Linda was more than ready to give Archer her life if that was required to complete his sacred work. She even understood that David would have to die if he insisted on interfering. But the boys . . .

The boys shouldn't have to pay for sins that only barely touched them. Their blood was nearly pure. But so had Isaac's blood been pure, and Abraham still had to lay him on the altar.

Mama Bet tried to stand and fell back into the armchair. Two of the Potter brothers moved forward to help her rise. She wobbled slightly in their grip.

"Archer be praised," she said. "Y'all go on now. I'll see you at church tonight."

"Archer be praised," said Haywood Absher. He had been one of the last to leave the Baptist fold, but he had embraced Archer's gospel as wholeheartedly as anyone. At least, he put on a good act of believing.

Linda joined the others in a closing "Amen."

The families began filing out, their heads down. Linda thought they should be joyful, but instead they were worried about their own mortal flesh. Death wasn't the end; death was the beginning of a new life in the kingdom. The coming deliverance was a time of celebration and exaltation, not punishment. God had blessed them by sending Archer to serve as His mighty sword.

Then why did she so dread giving her boys away?

Linda waited on the porch for the crowd to thin. Becca Faye brushed past, leaving a trail of dimestore perfume. Sonny Absher flashed his four-toothed grin and nodded good-bye, then took Becca Faye's arm. He escorted her to his rusty Chevelle, where they would probably spend the afternoon sinning in the backseat.

"You coming to the church early tonight?" asked Lester.

Linda chewed at her thumb. "If it's Archer's will."

"Don't worry none about your boys. Mine went to God years ago, and I've come to accept it." Lester nervously chewed his tobacco.

"What if Vivian is the next sacrifice? How would you feel then?"

"Sins got to be paid for."

"Why can't we just pay for our own sins?"

Mama Bet was listening from the screen door. "It don't work that way, child. Sacrifice is the true test of faith. Remember the lesson of Abraham? It ain't a sacrifice unless you lose something dear."

"And what are you losing, Mama Bet?"

The old woman looked out across the mountains, squinting her milky eyes. A small breeze was blowing from Tennessee, carrying with it the smell of sourwood blooms and pine.

"Flesh and blood," Mama Bet finally said. "Just like everybody else."

SIXTEEN

The last bell rang, and Ronnie ran to his locker, holding his books in front of his face so that no stray elbows would bump him in the nose. The injury throbbed a little, but he'd decided not to take the pain pill. After he'd spent lunchtime with Melanie, pain barely touched him. He felt bulletproof, especially because she said maybe they should eat lunch together every day.

He was mentally going over the poem that he'd given her last month. He had tried to be funny and sweet at the same time, so that maybe if she read between the lines, she'd see that he thought she was the most beautiful flower in the whole garden. Dripping in the rain. Soaking color from the sun. Flashing beauty in the breeze.

Plucking petals. *She loves me. She loves me not.* Well, he'd left out that last part. No way was he going to say *love* in a poem. Plus, she might think that, since she was the flower, that would mean he wanted to pull her arms and legs off.

The best thing about the poem was that she didn't giggle and show it to all her girlfriends. Ronnie didn't think he could stand that. A lot of the other kids already thought he was weird because he carried around books that weren't even assigned. He also wore bargain-brand blue jeans and sometimes his T-shirts didn't even have messages on them. He wasn't cool: he didn't play sports, hang around the Barkersville mall, or watch MTV.

But right now, he didn't care what people thought or how far out of it he was. All he cared about was that Melanie would sit with him at lunch. He recalled the breathless way she had said, "I promise," when he told her not to tell anyone else about Boonie Houck and the Bell Monster. His heart was made of helium.

A commotion in the hall pulled him from his pleasant thoughts. Shouts erupted, and a gawking ring of students had gathered in the math wing. Something was happening, possibly a fight. Most likely a fight. That was about the only thing that drew people's attention these days.

"Leave me alone," came a scared voice.

Tim! Ronnie fought through the circle. He heard Whizzer Buchanan's smoky, snickering voice.

"Tell us about it, goober-head," taunted Whizzer. "Tell us about the thing with wings and claws and livers for eyes."

"No," whimpered Tim. "Let me go."

Ronnie shouldered past the eighth graders in the front row. Whizzer had Tim by the shoulders, shaking him. Tears trailed down Tim's cheeks. His glasses were on the floor, and books were scattered around his feet.

"Tell us, Tim," said Whizzer. "Inquiring minds want to know."

This drew a laugh from the crowd. Ronnie threw down his books and shoved Whizzer in the back. The crowd gasped and grew silent. Whizzer turned, all five-feet-ten of him, jaw muscles twitching. Ronnie imagined the bully's muscles tensing under his camouflage jacket.

"Well, well, well," said Whizzer. "If it ain't Mr. Hero himself."

Whizzer's eyes half closed, as if Ronnie were a bug that he wanted to squash with one big lace-up boot. Ronnie looked around the looming hulk at Tim, who was pressed back against the lockers that lined the hall. "You okay, Tim?"

Tim sniffed and nodded.

"Get your books, then. Dad's waiting."

"And what if I say it ain't time for you to go yet?" said Whizzer.

Ronnie looked at the faces in the crowd. Their expressions were eager, expectant, relieved that they weren't Whizzer's victims of choice this time. If only a teacher would come. He'd even be happy to see Mrs. Rathbone.

"We didn't do anything to you," Ronnie said.

"Yeah, you did. You got born, didn't you?" This drew another laugh, but Whizzer wasn't smiling.

Tim stooped to pick up his books. Whizzer kicked them away.

"Heard you been to church," said Whizzer. "And you got a little friend there. Something with wings and claws and livers for eyes. Everybody likes a good ghost story, Mr. Hero-Man. Tell us about how you saved Tim from the Bell Monster."

Ronnie's heart lodged in his throat. "Did you tell anybody, Timmy?"

Tim shook his head, then knelt and found his glasses and put them back on.

If *Tim* hadn't told, then . . .

Ronnie spun and searched the crowd. Melanie was on the edge of it. To her credit, she was a little pale. She looked away in shame.

He would not cry. Oh, no, Ronnie would not cry, at least not here and not now. He balled his fists, and a sigh of satisfaction rose from the crowd.

"Tell us about the rest of it," said Whizzer, looking down at Ronnie, his smile like a possum's. "Tell us about your Mama and the temple in California."

Temple? California? His mom had never been to California. "You're crazy, you . . . you"—Ronnie was aware that he could never take back what he would say next—"you gap-toothed redneck."

A murmur rippled through the hall. Some of the kids had buses to catch, but the crowd had grown larger. Sweat trickled down the back of Ronnie's neck.

Where were those teachers?

Whizzer shoved Ronnie in the chest. Ronnie stumbled but kept his feet.

"Now you done it, you sissy," said Whizzer. "The reverend says everybody got to pay for their sins in blood. So maybe I'll just let you make an advance payment."

The reverend? Ronnie's head spun in confusion. His ears rang because of the pulse throbbing in his head. He was scarcely aware of the crowd now. It was just him and Whizzer and hate and pain.

Whizzer drew back a fist that looked the size of a football. Ronnie heard the whisper of air just before the fist crashed into the side of his head. His vision went black for a moment, and when it returned, he was looking at Whizzer's boots only inches away.

One of the boots nudged him on the shoulder. "Get up, weasel. Or you want me to step on you a little?"

Ronnie struggled to his knees, then stood on wobbly legs. He realized that the crowd was roaring, shouts and laughter and jeers. Tim had slipped to safety. The blood hunters had bigger game now.

Ronnie pretended to be hurt. It wasn't a far stretch of his imagination. His ears rang and the side of his face throbbed.

"Come on. Archer says there will come great trials," taunted Whizzer. "Archer says it's high time for a cleansing."

Did none of the other kids realize Whizzer was a raving lunatic? No. They didn't care. Reasons didn't matter. Only entertainment at someone else's expense.

Ronnie stooped and bulled his way into Whizzer's belly. He heard the wind rush from Whizzer's gut, and they both slammed into the lockers. Whizzer pounded on his back, but he could hardly feel it. He held on and squeezed, his nose pulsing now. He tasted blood on his lips.

An authoritative voice boomed through the hall. "What's going on here?"

It was Mr. Gladstone, the principal. The one everybody called either Glad-Stoned or Fred Flintstone. The students backed away, and Ronnie relaxed his grip on Whizzer, though he didn't let go. The principal grabbed Ronnie by the collar and finally dragged him to his feet. Whizzer stood and smoothed his jacket, his face red.

"Ah, Mr. Buchanan," Mr. Gladstone said. "Why am I not surprised?"

He turned to Ronnie. "And you are . . . ?"

Lying was useless. Everything was useless. "Ronnie. Ronnie Day."

"Okay, gentlemen. Let's take a trip to my office."

Ronnie and Whizzer marched down the hall like prisoners at gunpoint. The crowd had broken into lines on each side of the hall, whispering among themselves, already expanding the fight into a bloody schoolyard legend. Ronnie realized he was the first person stupid enough to stand up to Whizzer Buchanan. He wiped his nose with his hand. At least Whizzer hadn't punched him there.

Sins paid for in blood. Well, how much freaking blood does it take?

He looked behind him. The kids were juiced on adrenaline, dispersing now, a few shadowboxing to re-create the fight. Tim's tears had dried and he followed Mr. Gladstone as if in shock, carrying an armful of books. Melanie was behind Tim, and Ronnie looked back into her blue eyes.

So this is what it feels like when the Bell Monster rips open your chest and takes your heart. Except this way, you don't die. This way, your heart keeps working, and you get a dose of nails and barbed wire and broken glass with every beat.

Melanie opened her mouth as if to explain, then looked down at the floor and shook her head. Her lip quivered and her eyes were moist.

She loves me. She loves me not.

At least that was one less thing to worry about. The principal nudged Whizzer and Ronnie into his office and closed the door.

"Another one dead." Sheriff Littlefield let the deerskin jacket fall back over the face of the mutilated woman. "One of the Gregg girls."

"You know her?" Detective Storie asked.

"Used to date her sister back in high school." Littlefield looked up the road, where it wound into the hills. He knew this area well. A half dozen houses were tucked away in the shadowed folds. Behind them, Buckhorn Mountain rose so steep and rocky that no one could settle there. The mountain was the end of the world, a great wall that imprisoned as much as it protected.

Littlefield had grown up in one of those old houses. He still owned a couple of acres of sloping timberland at the foot of the mountain. He had visited the land only twice since his mom had died some ten years ago. She had gone to her grave still heartbroken over the deaths of her husband and youngest son.

Frank was the last of the Littlefields. Maybe that wasn't a bad thing. Seemed all the old families were dying out. The world had changed under them, time had left them in the dust, and all that remained was the demolishing of homesteads and the erecting of monuments. Stone markers that read, *May God Protect and*—

"Sheriff?" Storie called from the ditch.

He rubbed his eyes and looked up from where he was kneeling over the body. Whatever haze he'd been in last night still affected him. He felt as if he were moving underwater. "Did you find something?"

She held up a yellow receipt, gripping it carefully by the edge so that she wouldn't smudge any fingerprints. "This must have fallen out of the jacket."

"What does it say?"

"It's from Barkersville Hardware. Made out to Day Construction."

"David Day. He lives about a mile up the road."

"We couldn't be that lucky, could we?"

"David ain't a murderer. I've known him since we were kids."

David sometimes wore a jacket like the one over Donna Gregg's body.

"How well do you know him?"

Littlefield stood, his knees sore. "Well enough."

"As well as you know Archer McFall?"

The sheriff looked up the road, then at Sheila. "I'd better go question him."

"I'll call for Perry Hoyle," Sheila said.

The county's station wagon was putting on a lot of miles these days. Sheila headed back to her cruiser, which was pulled off the side of the road behind the sheriff's Trooper.

Littlefield checked around the body. Chest ripped open. Heart gone. No mountain lion had performed that particular atrocity.

How about the Bell Monster, Frankie?

Samuel's voice. Littlefield glanced into the forest on both sides of the road. His ears rang, a high-pitched buzz that ripped like a jigsaw blade through his brain.

He tried to blink away the darkness that seeped from the corners of his vision.

Not another blackout. Not in front of Sheila.

He wouldn't allow himself to go insane. Too many people were counting on him. Samuel was dead. So were Donna Gregg and two others. More, unless he did something.

A car came down the road and slowed as it approached the scene. Littlefield forced himself to stand erect and wave the car past. One of the Absher boys was driving. Becca Faye smiled at him from the passenger's side. Neither of the pair looked at the body lying in the weeds, though it was visible from the road.

The sheriff waited until his hands stopped trembling, then walked to Sheila's cruiser. She was just hanging up her radio handset when he reached her open door.

"Another unit's on the way, and Hoyle will be out

in a half hour." Her eyes narrowed. "Are you okay, Sheriff?"

He nodded, hoping she didn't notice the sweat on his face. "I'm going to ride up to the Day place."

"Good. I'll wait here for backup; then I'm going to pay a little visit of my own."

"Who to?"

"The Reverend Archer McFall."

He came around the door and leaned over her. "Listen, Shei—" He started to say her first name, then caught himself. "Sergeant. We got nothing on him."

"In that case, he won't mind answering a few questions."

"Maybe we should go together."

She shook her head. "We don't have time. Who knows when the killer's going to strike again? We need to jump on every lead we've got."

"Then let me take Archer."

Her eyes shone with defiance. "This is my case, remember? You assigned it to me. What are you so worried about, anyway?"

Ghosts don't exist. Archer McFall is just another preacher, another ordinary person who took up the Bible and found something in its pages that meant something. That doesn't make him dangerous. That doesn't even make him that unusual.

He didn't want to admit that he was scared. The detective would perform a better interrogation without him around to muddy the waters. After all, Littlefield had taken his chances with Archer the evening before, and had nothing but a gaping hole in his memory to show for it. Littlefield was losing faith in his own abilities, and that was even scarier than the Hung Preacher's ghost.

"Do you know where he's staying?" he asked.

She nodded. "I checked around. He's rented a room down at the Holiday Inn."

"That's funny. His mother has a place up the road. Wonder why he's not staying with her?"

"With his money, you'd think he'd rent one of those chalets by the ski slopes. You're the one who's supposed to know him, remember?"

He looked at Donna Gregg's cold body. "No," he said quietly. "I *don't* remember."

"Maybe after you talk to David Day, you should get some sleep." Sheila went past him and continued her search of the scene. Littlefield got in his Trooper and started the engine. He rolled down the window as he pulled away. "Be careful," he called over the motor's roar.

She nodded absently, her mind already consumed with analyzing the victim's ragged flesh. Littlefield swallowed hard and headed toward Buckhorn Mountain.

It was past four o'clock. David and the boys should have been home by now.

I hope Archer didn't take them early, Linda thought. The angel of God would be coming for them all sooner or later. She couldn't help but hope it was later. She was going to miss the boys when they were gone. But at least the reunion would be sweet and everlasting.

For the tenth time, she peered anxiously through the curtains. The sheriff's Trooper turned off the river road onto their packed dirt driveway. Linda dropped the curtain, heart pounding. Even though he'd attended last night's service, she didn't trust him.

She waited by the front door until she heard his

feet on the porch. She swung the door open and forced a smile. "Hey, Sheriff. What brings you out to these parts?"

The sheriff bobbed his head in greeting. "Bad news, I'm afraid."

Was there any other kind?

She cleared her throat. "It's not the boys, is it?" Hoping, hoping.

Please, God, don't take them yet.

"No." The sheriff looked at her closely, as if they had once shared some secret that he'd forgotten. Then he pointed to the side of the house, where David had nailed a piece of plywood over the window. "Looks like you got a broken window."

"Yeah. Those darned blue jays, they see their reflection and just got to pick a fight. One of them hit it just a little too hard."

"Is David home?"

"He went to pick up the boys at school. Should be back any minute."

"Mind if I wait for him?"

Linda opened the door all the way and stepped aside. "Please come in."

The sheriff sat on the edge of the easy chair and leaned forward. Linda sat across from him, not knowing what to do with her hands. She straightened the magazines on the coffee table, wrinkled copies of David's *Field & Stream* and her *Woman's World Weekly.*

She sat back and cupped her hands over her knees, then pushed her hair away from her forehead. "Wasn't that a wonderful service last night?"

"Reverend McFall sure knows how to preach up a storm. I'll say that for him."

The sheriff's eyes focused behind her. She turned to see what he was looking at. It was a knitted sampler, one Grandma Gregg had made for her, which read MAY GOD PROTECT AND KEEP THIS HOUSE. A little farm scene was stitched below the words.

"We're mighty blessed that he came back," she said.

"Came back?"

"To the mountains."

The sheriff nodded. The room was cramped with silence. The air smelled of the trout she had cooked for lunch.

"So what do you think of this weather?" she asked.

"Pretty nice."

"Yeah, we've got to get our pole beans planted. Been in such a commotion lately, we got behind on our chores."

"How's Ronnie?"

"Ronnie? Oh, he's fine. Good enough to go back to school today. I got to take him to the doctor next week to get his stitches out, but he won't have a permanent hump on his nose or anything."

"That's good."

Another long silence. The sheriff looked at the wall again. "What's that?" he asked.

Linda's heart warmed as she looked at the small metal ankh on the wall. She had put the symbol of the temple in place of the old wooden cross David had nailed there. "It's a joyous time, isn't it?"

"Linda, what's going on at the church?"

She swallowed some air and nearly choked on it. "You heard Archer last night. It's time for a cleansing, time to pay for iniquities."

"People are getting killed."

"Archer says sins have to be paid for in blood."

"Jesus did that for all of us by dying on the cross."

Linda held her breath. *Blasphemy.* Archer had allowed this nonbeliever into the church?

Archer must have his reasons. Who was she to doubt his holy ways?

Outside, a vehicle pulled up. She jumped up from the sofa and ran to the door. The sheriff followed her out onto the porch. David and a glum-looking Ronnie and Tim got out of the Ranger.

David cast a hostile look at the sheriff. "What do you want?"

The sheriff looked at the two boys, then back to David. "It's about Donna Gregg."

Linda put her hand over her mouth. David turned to the boys. "Why don't y'all go play in the barn for a while?" he said to them.

"What's wrong?" Tim asked. His glasses sat askew on his nose. He pushed them up with a thin forefinger.

"Come on," Ronnie said to Tim. "Let's get out of here."

As Ronnie turned, Linda saw the large bruise on his temple. "What happened?" she asked David.

"He got in a fight."

Ronnie? In a fight? He wouldn't hurt an earthworm.

"Something bad happened, didn't it?" Tim said to Linda. "You always send us away when you want to talk about bad stuff."

Ronnie took his brother's arm and led him across the uneven stretch of green lawn. The sheriff waited until the boys had disappeared inside the barn, then said, "Donna's dead."

David looked at Buckhorn Mountain as if he wished he were walking its ridgeline. He always wanted to be away, alone, in troubled times. Linda tried to fake a sob, but failed.

"I found your jacket at the scene," the sheriff said to David. "And a receipt made out to Day Construction. That kind of evidence is enough for me to take you in for questioning, but I'd just as soon do it here."

"She was still warm when I found her," David said, his voice as hollow as a potato barrel in spring. "Must have been about two in the morning."

"Why didn't you report it?"

"You were around. I figured you knew about it before I did."

"Did you see anybody?"

"Depends on your definition of 'anybody.' "

Linda tried to signal David with her eyes. Then she realized she didn't know whose side to be on. The sheriff was one of the flock, but somehow *wrong*, Jesus-tainted and closed-hearted. And David was . . . well, she didn't know what David was.

"Tell me what you saw," the sheriff said.

"Probably the same thing you saw." David folded his arms. "After all, you're one of them, ain't you?"

"One of what?"

He nodded at Linda. "Them. Archer's little angels. I saw you at the church last night."

Linda looked from the sheriff to David, as if she were watching a badminton match being played with a live grenade. She chewed at her fingernail. Blood rushed from the ragged quick and filled her mouth with a brassy sweetness.

"Three people are dead," the sheriff said. "All of them were somehow connected to the church."

"It's not Archer," Linda said too quickly and forcefully.

"The old families," Littlefield said. "Houck. Potter. Gregg."

"They needed cleansing," Linda said. "Archer says we all need cleansing."

"Shut up," David said. "I'm sick to death of

'Archer this' and 'Archer that.' I had enough of that the first time.''

"The first time?" the sheriff asked.

"Yeah," David said. "In California."

"What's California got to do with what's happening now?" Linda asked.

David slowly shook his head. "You don't get it, do you? He was a lot smarter out in California. Or maybe he just didn't know his own power."

"Don't bring your blamed old jealousy into this."

"You didn't see him," David said, his voice rising in pitch. "You didn't see him carry the bodies into the so-called temple."

"What are you talking about?" Linda said.

"The Temple of the Two Suns," he spat. "You didn't hear about the murders out there. Who misses another lost drifter on the Santa Monica freeway? Even a half dozen. Plenty more where they came from. Now I just got to figure out why Archer came back."

Linda shook her head. What was he saying? Archer didn't kill anybody. It was *God* who performed the cleansings. Archer was merely the savior, the earthly vessel.

"You're saying that he committed murders in California?" she heard the sheriff ask David.

"Saw it with my own eyes. How do they taste, Linda?"

Linda looked in horror at the gnawed flesh of her fingertips.

"How do they taste, Sheriff?" David asked.

"What the hell?" the sheriff asked.

"Communion. The body. The bread of life." David walked to the Ranger.

The sheriff looked questioningly at Linda, then called to David, "I'm not through talking yet."

"Well, I am." David pulled his rifle out from under the Ranger's seat.

"Don't do it," the sheriff warned. He fell into a crouch, like one of those television cowboys in a showdown. Except Linda saw that the sheriff wore no firearm.

David laughed. "Don't worry. I won't waste good bullets on the likes of you and her. These are for Archer. I'm going to kill him as many damned times as it takes. This time, I'm going to blow him back to hell for good."

SEVENTEEN

"What's going on?"

"Shh." Ronnie pressed his cheek against the board so that he could see through the knothole. The air was thick with dust. He wondered what would happen to the packing in his broken nose if he sneezed. Could he even sneeze if he couldn't smell?

Dad strode back to the Ranger, leaving Mom and the sheriff standing on the porch. When Ronnie saw the rifle, his heart stuttered in his chest. "No," he whispered.

"What?" Tim said.

Dad went into the house. Mom said something to the sheriff that Ronnie couldn't hear. The sheriff got in his Trooper and drove away. Mom looked around, then also went into the house.

Ronnie moved away so that Tim could look through the knothole. Tim stood on an overturned bucket to get eye-level with the hole.

"I don't see nothing," Tim said.

"They're in the house."

"Is it bad?"

Tim's not dumb. He knows what's going on. I guess this is the part where I have to play brave big brother.

Ronnie tried to sound nonchalant. "Dad's home, isn't he? How bad can it be?"

"I'm scared."

"It's daytime," Ronnie said, though the shadows and dusty cobwebs and the creaking planks of the barn made him nervous. "Monsters don't get you in the daytime."

"No, I mean scared about Mom and Dad." Tim stepped off the bucket and sat on a bale of hay.

Ronnie stared into the row of wooden stalls that lined the far side of the barn. They didn't keep cows anymore. Dad said with beef prices being so low, it was cheaper to buy meat at the supermarket than to raise it. Ronnie almost missed taking care of the animals, putting them up at night and making sure they had hay in the winter. Dad and Ronnie had slaughtered cows, too, hung them up by a chain and cut them open, the steam rising from the animals' insides. Ronnie didn't miss that part of it.

"Mom and Dad will work it out," Ronnie said. "They have to."

"What if they don't? What if she makes him mad again and he leaves? Who will protect us then?" Tim's lower lip trembled.

"Look, I saved you from Whizzer, didn't I? You have to trust me."

"Yeah, right. Like you're going to be able to beat up the Bell Monster?"

Ronnie coughed from the dust. "I'll think of something."

"Anyway, how do you kill a ghost? Dad shot it, but I know it's coming back."

Ronnie had been wondering that himself. Why would a ghost want to kill people? It didn't make sense. If a ghost were crazy, maybe, but just a plain old ordinary ghost?

Whatever it was, the red church was to blame. He'd read books about hauntings. Supposedly, "psychic imprints" could be projected into the walls if a person suffered great emotional turmoil. That seemed kind of stupid to Ronnie, but the Bell Monster was real. What if the Bell Monster was the spirit of the preacher who had been hanged there? Surely having a rope around your throat would cause some emotional turmoil.

But then, everything that had ever died would leave a ghost. What living thing hadn't suffered a little emotional turmoil in its life? A lot of cows had been killed right there in the middle of the barn, shot in the brains with a rifle and cut into pieces and their guts hauled away in a wheelbarrow. But you didn't see ghost cows lurking around everywhere.

Maybe God was trying to take the preacher's soul to heaven, but decided halfway up that the preacher was too evil to enter the kingdom. Maybe the devil didn't want the preacher, either, because the preacher knew too many Bible verses and would tell them to the other people in hell. Maybe the preacher would try to save people who had already been condemned to the everlasting fire. No way the devil would want something like that going on. So the preacher got stuck in the middle, and killed people because he was lonely and wanted some ghosts for company.

That was dorky. He was thinking like a third grader.

"You don't have to kill a ghost," Ronnie finally said. "It's already dead. The trick is to make it *stay* dead."

"How do you do that?"

"By giving it what it wants."

They looked at each other. "What it wants is to kill us," said Tim.

"Yeah." Ronnie sighed. "A real kick in the rear."

"I don't want to die."

Ronnie didn't either—no matter how many times Preacher Staymore tried to tell him that God had a special place for children. The preacher had also introduced him to the idea of committing sins of the heart. It was bad enough back when doing something bad would get you scratched out of the Big Golden Book. Now he'd learned that just *thinking* about bad stuff would damn him to hell.

He'd asked Jesus into his heart every few weeks, just like Preacher Staymore wanted. How long did your heart stay clean after Jesus washed away the sins? What if you died while you were thinking a bad thought, and didn't have time to ask forgiveness? The whole business sounded pretty risky to Ronnie.

And he was in no hurry to find out for sure.

"You're not going to die, Tim," Ronnie promised, hoping he sounded more reassuring than he felt. He was about to say something else when the shot rang out.

The Holiday Inn was off the only four-lane highway through Pickett County, just outside the Barkersville exit. Sheila Storie pulled into the parking lot. The lot was nearly empty. Tourists were rare between the ski season and summer, when Floridians came to escape the heat and New Yorkers came to escape New York.

Archer McFall's room was on the first floor, just beside the motel's drained pool. McFall's black Mercedes was parked in front of 107. Storie parked beside it and got out, checking her watch and wondering how the sheriff was coming along. She glanced through the driver's side window of the Mercedes. The interior was spotless. She knocked on the door of 107.

A tall man answered the knock. He was handsome, but a little slick-looking, like a lawyer on a television show. He had strong cheekbones and a wide face that was freshly shaven. He smiled at her.

"Archer McFall?" she asked.

"Yes, my child. How may I help you?"

The way he called her "child" irritated Storie. He couldn't have been more than ten years older than she was, about Frank's age. He smelled faintly of cologne and a more pungent odor that she couldn't identify. The room behind him was dark, the shades drawn.

"I'm Det. Sgt. Sheila Storie, Pickett County Sheriff's Department," she said, not bothering to dig her badge out of her jacket.

McFall blinked, but his smile didn't waver. "It's a pleasure to meet you, ma'am. Your sheriff and I go way back."

How far back?

Storie looked into his eyes, trying to read them. He gave nothing away. "I was wondering if I could ask you a few questions."

"Oh, about Mr. Houck." His eyes went colder, darker. "That poor, unfortunate man. I hope you've caught his killer."

"No, sir, but we have a few leads."

"I'm glad. What kind of perverse notion leads someone to commit such an act on holy ground?"

"Well, sir, at the time, the red church was being used as a barn."

McFall laughed, a low sound that started in his abdomen and shook his entire body. "That's true.

Without a congregation, a church isn't much of a church, is it? Without people, and what they believe—"

"Did they believe in you in California?" Storie said. She gave him her "sunglasses stare," the kind of cool look that some of her fellow cops gave only when hidden behind the safety of tinted shields.

"The people of Whispering Pines need ministering as much as anyone else."

"Badly enough to make you give up an easy life in California?"

"Why, Sergeant," he said, tugging at his tie. "I do believe you are interrogating me."

"Not really. Just dropped by for a chat."

"In that case, please come in." He showed his capped teeth and pushed the door wide.

Storie went inside. The bed was neatly made, with no clothes or suitcases in sight. A Bible lay open on the bedside table. McFall shut the door and flipped the shades. Afternoon sunlight striped the room.

She sat in the stiff-backed chair by the desk. McFall sat on the edge of the bed, looking uncomfortable. "So why did you come back?" she asked.

"I'm of the mountains. My heart has always belonged here. My mother still lives in Whispering Pines, in a little farmhouse at the base of Buckhorn Mountain."

Storie nodded at him, encouraging him to continue.

"I felt the calling as a child," he said. "As you may know, my family has a long history of serving God and spreading the Holy Word. Even as a child, I always knew I was going to be a preacher."

"Like your great-great-grandfather?"

McFall looked out the window, his jaw twitching. "Wendell McFall was an unpleasant twig on the family tree. Still, I don't think he deserved hanging, do you?"

"I don't know anything about him but the legend."

"Oh, the so-called 'ghost' story. Let me assure you that the only spirit that walks the church is the Holy Spirit. I should know. I spent a lot of time there as a teenager, praying to God for direction."

Storie shifted in her chair. "Tell me about California."

"I thought I would start a church out there. A few local girls went with me. We were a fine bunch, not a sinful thought among us, our hearts as pure as the sun. We were going to start a commune and live a simple, ascetic life."

"Seven girls went out there, I hear." Storie had traced the seven. Of them, only Linda Gregg, now Linda Day, had ever been heard from again.

"When we got there, most of the girls wandered off to Los Angeles and San Francisco. I guess the big-city life was more enticing than a life spent in the service of God."

"How come your church out there failed?"

McFall smiled at her. "It didn't fail. The Temple of the Two Suns prospered, thanks be to God. I had a television show that ministered to thousands. I opened a music store, a religious bookstore, and some other businesses. Even with the success, even though I was reaching the people, my heart held an emptiness. I prayed for guidance, and God told me to go home. So here I am."

Storie watched his face carefully. "If you don't mind my saying so, the Temple of the Two Suns sounds like an unusual name for a church founded by someone from the Bible Belt."

"There are many paths to God. The true path is

to follow your own heart. My heart says that what I do is right."

"What denomination is your religion?"

"Christian, in a manner of speaking. Of course, every sect or order has its unique qualities. 'Two Suns' comes from the idea of God sending a second light into the world. That's one of God's promises, you know."

"It certainly didn't take you long to get a church up and running here," she said.

"I was fortunate that Lester Matheson let me buy the property and return it to the family. And the people of Whispering Pines opened their hearts and welcomed me into their community."

"You have to admit, it's something of a coincidence that murders started occurring as soon as you came back to the area."

"I came because God called." He leaned forward. "He calls all of us. He asked to be invited into our hearts. Is He inside you?"

Storie shifted in her chair. "That's not important."

His mouth twisted. "It's the *only* thing that's important. What's in your heart?"

"Look, Mr. McFall—"

His eyes were bright, feverish. *"What's in your heart?"*

Storie stood and headed for the door. A hand fell on her shoulder. She spun, instinctively crouching into the defensive judo stance she had learned in cop school. For a long second, her muscles froze.

His face.

McFall's chin elongated, and his teeth sharpened between his wide black lips. His eyes were feral, so glitteringly yellow that they seemed to float in front of his face. His nose lifted in a snarl.

Just as suddenly, the illusion passed. McFall stood

before her, his hands up in apology. "I didn't mean to startle you, my child," he said in a calm voice.

Great. As if seeing bloodstains and ropes that don't exist wasn't bad enough, now I'm starting to think . . .

She put her hand to her forehead. Stress, that was what it was. Three murders to solve before more people died. *Her* people, the ones she had sworn to protect.

"What's troubling you, Sergeant?"

His voice soothed her. She had a sudden urge to break down in front of this man who was unruffled by life's traumas and worries. He was like the sun on the smooth surface of a lake. His serenity radiated in almost palpable waves.

"It's nothing, Reverend. Nothing at all."

"You don't have to keep it inside," he said, taking a step nearer. She backed against the door.

"Just turn your troubles over to a higher power," he continued in his soft, firm voice. "Open your heart and trust in God."

That sounded like a good idea. And as soon as she realized it sounded like a good idea, a warning flare rocketed across her mind.

Wait a second. I don't trust antbody, much less a man who's on a suspect list for three counts of murder.

But there was something about his tone, the gentleness and concern in his dark eyes. He was close enough so that she could smell mint mouthwash on his breath. For a moment, she thought he was going to lean forward and kiss her, and the worst part was that she didn't think she would stop him.

Instead he said, "Don't be afraid. Open your heart. Have faith."

She looked into his eyes, and her skin tingled with mild electricity. Such warmth, such promise, such *peace* emanated from his eyes. Such humanity.

Oh, yes. She had faith. She believed. Her heart felt swollen and warm in her chest, like a balloon on a summer day.

I believe. Just tell me what *to believe.*

This was insane. She should have called for back-up, told Communications what her 10-20 was. The only person who knew what she was doing was Frank. She tried to picture his face, but all she could see was the golden light that emanated from Archer.

He touched her face. His fingers were hot. She couldn't look away from his eyes, though part of her wanted to vomit, to punch him, to claw at the corners of his smile.

"Faith comes with a price," he said. "All you have to do is give me everything. But the rewards are great, too. The kingdom of heaven can be yours, which contains all the world and more."

She would give and give and give. No, she wouldn't. She served only the taxpayers and law-abiding citizens. She—

"The congregation must have communion," he said. "One bread, one body. And sacrifice is the currency of God. All I ask of you is that you serve."

She nodded. She could do that. Faith required a little sacrifice, but the rewards were everlasting, weren't they?

"Please," she said, lowering herself to her knees. She gazed up into that beatific face. "Let me serve."

He gave a benevolent nod. "You're not one of the old families. But you are working against the purpose of God."

I have fallen short. I am unworthy. I deserve punishment.

What could she offer that would compensate for her sins? What did she have? She could offer her soul, but that was nearly worthless. She did have flesh. She could sacrifice that, and perhaps appease the God she had so callously ignored all the days of her life.

"Take me," she said, her voice hoarse and her eyes moist. So great was the glory of God. And equally great was the glory of Archer McFall. "Use me any way you need."

McFall cocked his head, as if he were consulting God, listening to a divine command that would determine her fate. He knelt quickly and lifted her by the shoulders of her jacket, then wiped the tears from the corners of her eyes.

"Don't cry, my child," he said.

She smiled at him. How could she bury the happiness that filled her and brimmed over, the joy and rapture that he had delivered unto her?

He pulled her away from the door. "Say nothing of this. Tonight you will serve, and thus gain a place in the bosom of God."

Oh, glory! Oh, how merciful is God in his wisdom! She would make the sacrifice to earn her place, to please Archer, to pay for the sin of pride that had shadowed her life.

"Come to the church tonight," he said, then turned and crossed the room, again sitting on the bed.

He adjusted his tie, then clasped his hands lightly in his lap just as someone knocked on the door. "Would you get that, please?" Archer said.

Storie spun, fumbling with the doorknob in her haste to serve. She opened the door and Frank Littlefield stood before her, his fist held sideways, preparing to knock again.

"Hi, Sergeant," Frank said, no surprise in his voice.

She blinked against the sudden rush of sun, annoyed by this trespass into her spiritual communion with Archer. "What are you doing here?" she said.

He looked past her to the reverend. "I came to get some answers, same as you."

"Come in, Sheriff. We've been expecting you," McFall said.

David lowered the rifle and smiled.

The front door burst open, and David thought the sheriff might have returned to sneak up on him and jump him. He swiveled the rifle toward the door, his finger tight on the trigger. Ronnie stood in the doorway, Tim small behind him.

David sniffed the comforting aroma of gunsmoke. Linda was facedown on the living room floor. Tim ran to her and got on his knees, touching her hair, murmuring "Mommy" over and over again. Ronnie stared at David, his eyes wide with shock, his face pale.

"Did you . . . did you shoot her?" Ronnie asked.

David leaned the rifle against the coffee table. "I ain't that crazy yet."

Linda groaned and Tim helped her sit up.

Ronnie clenched his hands, a tear running down his cheek. "What in the hell's going on, Dad?" he said, shuddering with sobs. "Why are you trying to kill her?"

"I'm not the one trying to kill her," he said, looking down at his wife. "It's that damned Archer McFall."

"Archer McFall's the *preacher*. The preacher's supposed to be the good guy."

"Don't believe everything you hear in Sunday school, son."

"You're scaring me, Dad. You told us a family's

supposed to stick together when times get bad." Ronnie helped Tim lean Linda against the easy chair. She had a welt above her eye. Ronnie looked at it and then glared at David.

He looks so damned much like his mother.

"I didn't touch her," he said. "She fell when I shot that damned thing."

He pointed to the little symbol that hung on the wall, the lopsided cross that Linda had kept from her days in California. She'd told David she'd thrown it away, that all the old nonsense was over. Well, the devil's hooks sank deep. All it took was a little whiff of sulfur and brimstone to fan the embers in a sinner's heart.

The bullet had penetrated the center of the mock cross. The metal arms had twisted outward, curled by the impact. Gypsum powder trickled from a hole in the sheet rock. David nodded in satisfaction at a good shot.

"Hell followed her from California," he said.

"California?" Ronnie said. "She's never been to California."

David wiped sweat from his forehead. Maybe some secrets were best left buried.

"Are you okay, Mommy?" Tim sounded like a four-year-old.

"Yeah, honey," she said, pushing her hair away from her face and looking at David with mean eyes. "There will come great trials, but we keep on walking."

David was filled with renewed rage. So this was what Archer had driven his family to. Linda, ready to give up everything she owned, including her own flesh and blood. Tim, not knowing which of his parents to trust. Ronnie, learning too young that the world was a screwed-up and hard-assed place. And he himself wondering if faith was enough, if he could single-handedly take on the devil that wore lamb's clothing.

No, I won't be single-handed. I've got God and Jesus and a rifle and everything that's right on my side. Surely that will be enough. I pray to the Lord that will be enough.

"What are we going to do, Dad?" Ronnie looked pathetic, his eyes red and moist, his swollen nose a bruised shade of purple.

"It's high time for a cleansing," Linda said, her voice distant. She rocked back and forth as if tuned into an invisible gospel radio station.

David looked out the open door. Dark mountains huddled on the horizon, cowering before the sinking sun. Even the trees seemed to dread the coming night. The shadows held their breath, waiting to send out an army of monsters under cover of darkness.

Linda's eyes focused on a high spot behind the wall. Tim and Ronnie looked at David, expectant and fearful.

Maybe it *was* high time for a cleansing.

"We're going to beat that thing," he said, more to himself than to the boys.

"How do you kill a ghost?" Tim asked.

David rubbed the stubble on his chin. "Hell if I know, Tim."

"Ronnie says the trick is to make it stay dead. By giving it what it wants."

"Maybe so. We're just going to have to trust in the Lord."

"The *Lord,*" Linda said with a sneer. She stiffened and contorted her features. She resembled the wrinkle-faced bat that David had found dead in the barn one morning. The old Linda, the pretty wife and loving mother and good, sin-despising Christian, was as dead as Donna Gregg.

David knew Linda had been saved. He had knelt with her at the foot of the pulpit and held her hand while she tearfully asked Jesus into her heart. Once Jesus was in there, He belonged forever. Or was being saved a privilege that He could take away, like the court took away your driver's license if you drove drunk?

David was getting a headache thinking about it. That was God's business, and not for him to worry about. His mission was to protect the innocent, and let the guilty be damned.

"Get out," he said to Linda, trying not to raise his voice.

She lifted her face to him, her eyes wild. The boys wore twin masks of terror.

"Get out," David said more firmly. He gripped the rifle. "Go to the red church or Archer McFall's bed or straight to hell if you want. Just as long as you stay away from the boys."

Linda trembled as she stood.

"Don't hurt her, Daddy," Tim yelled.

David felt a smile crawl across his face, and a chill wended up his spine. He was sickened by the realization that he was enjoying this. A Christian was supposed to hate the sin but love the sinner. A man was supposed to honor his wife. The Lord's number one lesson was that people ought to forgive trespasses.

But the Lord also knew that the human heart was weak.

David pointed the rifle at her.

Tim jumped at Linda and hugged her, his face tight against her chest. "Don't go, Mommy," he pleaded.

David motioned with the rifle barrel toward the door. Linda glared at him, then leaned down and kissed Tim on top of the head. "Shh, baby. It will be okay."

She gently pushed Tim's arms from her waist. Her blue blouse was dark with Tim's tears. She rubbed Ronnie's hair and smiled at him. "Take care of your brother, okay?"

Ronnie nodded. Linda pulled the mangled cross from the wall and clenched her hand around it. She paused at the door. "It's tonight, you know," she said to David.

He swallowed hard. He started to tell her that he still loved her, despite it all. But he could only stare numbly, his fingers like wood on the rifle.

"Lord help us all," he whispered as she headed into the shroud of twilight. His prayer tasted of dried blood and ash.

EIGHTEEN

The sunset threw an orange wash over the ribbed clouds in the west. The strong green smell of the day's growing died away on the evening breeze. The river's muddy aroma rose like a fog, seeping across the churchyard so thick that Mama Bet could almost taste it. She eyed the shadows in the belfry, clutching her shawl tightly across her chest.

This was bad ground, here at the church. She didn't know why Archer insisted on holding services in this marred house of worship. Wendell McFall had died right there at the end of a rope, one end of it tied high in that bedeviled dogwood. The tree's branches stretched both high and low, toward the sky and the ground, like fingers reaching to grab everything and everybody.

"What's wrong, Mama Bet?"

She turned and looked into the dirty face of Whizzer Buchanan. Fourteen and already in need of a shave. He was all Buchanan, wall-eyed and his hands as plump and clumsy as rubber gloves filled with water. And to think his family used to be fine whittlers, back in the days when people made what they needed instead of buying it down at the Wal-Mart.

"Why, nothing's wrong, child." She smiled at him.

Whizzer smelled of sweet smoke, probably that wacky weed she heard some of the hippies were growing up in the mountains. Archer would cleanse them, sure as day. Archer held no truck with such trash. Hippies were as bad as the hard-drinking Mathesons and Abshers. Sins of the flesh, sins of the heart. All sins led down one road, down one tunnel, into the dark heart of hell.

"How come we ain't seen the Bell Monster yet?" Whizzer asked. Like the Bell Monster was some kind of video game that you could switch on and off at your convenience. The boy had a lot to learn about the workings of God.

"We got to be patient," she said.

Whizzer nodded and ran into the church, his boots thumping across the wooden floor. She looked across the cemetery. Stepford was relieving himself against a tall granite statue. The faded angel accepted the insult with nary a peep.

In the woods, shadows moved and separated. Becca Faye and Sonny came out from the trees, holding hands and giggling like kids at an Easter egg hunt. Crumpled leaves stuck to Becca Faye's blouse, and the top button was undone. Mama Bet hoped the hussy enjoyed her sweaty little frolic. Because soon she would be sweating the long sweat, the devil riding her back, until forever ate its own sorry tail.

Mama Bet walked across the gravel to the church steps. Diabetes was making her feet hurt something awful. She slowly went up the steps, keeping a grip on the worn handrail. She figured she might as well get used to taking them one step at a time, because she just knew that God had a mighty high set of golden stairs for her to climb to get to heaven.

She rested in the windowless foyer, in the cool darkness. Voices came from the main sanctuary, scattered and echoing in the hushed hollow of the church. She overheard Haywood telling Nell about the benefits of a high deductible with a low copay.

"You see, honey," he said, as Mama Bet entered the main body of the church, "odds are that if you do get sick enough to meet your deductible, it's going to run into the tens of thousands of dollars anyway. And the way hospitals charge these days, a body pretty much meets their deductible just walking in the door. So you might as well save that money up front with the cheaper plan."

Nell nodded and put the back of her hand to her mouth to hide her yawn. A couple of pews in front of them, Jim and Alma whispered about Zeb's funeral arrangements. Rudy Buchanan knelt near the lectern, on both knees, practicing his Archer worship. Almost as phony as a boot-licking Christian.

Mama Bet chewed her lower lip between the nubs of her gums. She didn't want to have one of her spells, not on Archer's night. She took slow, deep breaths until her rage subsided.

Some congregation this was. As addle-brained as fish-head stew. But it wasn't Archer's fault. Her boy worked with what material God gave him. If anybody was to blame for this shoddy bunch of backwoods nonbelievers, then you had to turn your eyes upward—to Him that would plant the seed and then laugh until the skies busted open. And all you could do was let your belly swell until you busted open yourself, until the child crawled out from between your legs and took its rightful throne.

"It's going to be tonight, ain't it?" said Jim, pulling her from her reverie.

"That's for God and Archer to know," she answered. "It ain't for the likes of us to worry about."

"Can't help but worry," he said, sweat under his

eyes. "It might be any of us up on the chopping block."

"Pray that you're worthy." She couldn't abide such selfishness in the face of a great moment, the moment the whole world was born to see, the reason God clabbered the mud together and shaped the mountains and spit the seas and breathed life into dust. This one shining moment of glory. This end to everything, and the start of the business beyond everything.

She gazed upon the dark stain on the dais. The thing was taking shape, drawing on the sacrificial blood spilled onto its wooden skin. It had slept for 140 years, fighting free once in a while to drift across the night hills or to spook up some teenagers. But now it was awakening for real, busting loose of whatever kind of invisible chains bound the past.

Archer said the red church had to feed, so let it be fed. Let the juice of these sorry souls soak into the floorboards. Let this church absorb all their human blood and sweat and sin. Let them be cleansed for the final journey. Because Archer so ordained.

A tear collected in the corner of her eye. Jim stood and gently clasped her hand, thinking she was afraid or mournful. No, she was *joyful,* grateful to be allowed to hobble into the church, though it was tainted with the sins of their ancestors. Even aching and stiff, her bones as brittle as chalksticks and her blood vessels as narrow as flaxen threads, even with eyes that could barely tell day from night and fire from ice, even with all the crush of eighty-odd years weighing down and crooking her spine, she could stand proud before the altar.

Here, she could surrender. In this sick house of God, she could give up her flesh and blood.

* * *

Frank Littlefield looked around the motel room. Sheila appeared dazed, her eyes wide and her pupils unnaturally large. Archer McFall sat on the bed like a patient king who was deigning to accept tribute from a minor subject.

"Did you learn anything from David Day?" Sheila asked, though judging from the tone of her voice, she could care less.

"He pulled a gun on me, mostly just for show," Frank said. "He's crazy, but not the kind of crazy that kills three people."

"David Day?" Archer said. "I believe his wife is a member of the congregation."

"Linda," said Frank. "And if I remember right, she was one of the ones who took off to California with you."

Archer looked from Frank to Sheila, and back again. "California has nothing to do with what's happening here. Please put your minds at rest about that. We're all home now, and that's what's important. We're all fulfilling God's plan."

"God's plan," said Frank. "God's plan has left three innocent people dead, assuming that God is the one who pulls the strings."

"Nobody's innocent," said Archer. "And God doesn't pull the strings."

"Sure," Frank said. "I forgot. *You* do."

"Have you been talking to my mother?" Archer smiled. Shadows flitted in the corner of his mouth, or maybe it was worms crawling from between his lips. . . .

Frank blinked away the illusion. "Oh, no, Mr. McFall. I don't have to talk to your mother. Because on the way over here, I was thinking back on a night a long time ago. One night when you and me were both younger and, I reckon, more innocent."

"Nobody's innocent," Archer repeated.

"Samuel was," Frank said.

"What's your brother got to do with this?" Sheila asked, her voice hesitant. She put a hand to her head, then rubbed her face as if wiping away sleep.

"That Halloween night at the red church," Frank said hurriedly. His blood raced, his face grew warm, his stomach clenched around a bag of hot nails.

Archer's eyes widened in interest, his face passive and unconcerned, his hands in his lap. As if he were watching a bug in jar, curious to see what it would do next. "Halloween? There've been so many Halloweens."

"When Samuel climbed up into the belfry, something came up behind him. A shadow. Except the shadow laughed." Frank balled his hands into fists.

"Please, Sheriff, not the ghost story again," Sheila said. She seemed to have recovered from her daze, and was probably worried that Frank would make a fool of himself in front of the public. Probably thought that Frank would blow his law enforcement career, maybe his whole future in Pickett County. But right now, Frank wasn't thinking about the future. He was thinking about the past. About the dead and buried. And about a familiar laugh.

"I recognized that laugh," Frank said. "Sent a chill through me, the first time I heard it again—at the red church, the day after Zeb Potter was killed."

The Halloween laugh. Frank had heard it hundreds of times, keeping him awake at 4 A.M. or jerking him from nightmares. He heard it in the squeal of car tires, in the wail of a police siren, in the rush of the cold river. He heard it in the howl of the wind, and he even heard it in silence. The laugh was loudest in silence.

"You were there." Frank raised his fist toward

Archer's face. Archer ignored the threatening gesture.

"Sheriff," Sheila said, in her stern cop voice.

"You were in the belfry that night," Frank said to Archer.

He'd heard assault suspects talk about being so mad they "saw red," and now Frank knew what they meant. It was a real thing, the red brighter than the blood of the sun. It poured down over his vision, blocking out Sheila, blocking out the Bible on the nightstand, blocking out the consequences.

"You scared Samuel." Frank was trembling now. "You made him jump. You killed him."

"Sheriff, Sheriff, Sheriff," Archer said, shaking his head slowly as if having to explain an obvious truth to a child. "I didn't kill Samuel. *You* did."

Frank leaped at Archer, the red in his vision now completely obscuring everything but the smile on Archer's face. Frank wanted to tear that smile from the man's face, to hear the satisfying rip of flesh and crack of bone. Frank wanted to feed the man his own smile, shove it down his throat until he choked.

His hands snaked around Archer's neck, squeezing. Frank looked at his own fingers, white from the pressure. He felt removed from the attack, as if it were someone else's hands shutting the air from Archer's lungs. As if he were watching a movie. The thought angered him. He didn't want to be distanced, removed, cheated of his satisfaction.

Hands pounded on his back, pulled at his shirt. He barely felt the blows. Sheila's voice came to him as if through a thick curtain of dreams.

"Stop it, Frank," she shouted. "Damn you, you're killing him."

Killing him.

A wave of pleasure surged through Frank, almost

sexual in its intensity. At the same moment, he was repelled by his joyful vengeance. He was no better than Archer, no better than whoever had killed Boonie Houck, Zeb Potter, Donna Gregg.

Sheila had one arm hooked under his right bicep, the other pressing on his neck, her weight full on his back. Frank kept his grip on Archer's neck, watching the carotid artery swell from the stifled circulation. Throughout the attack, Archer had made no move to defend himself. As if he were submitting, a willing victim. A sacrifice.

Frank stared into Archer's eyes. He saw nothing human, no fear, no anger, no pity.

"If he did it, we can take him to trial." Sheila grunted, levering her body against his, trying to break his chokehold. "Let the justice system make him pay."

Justice system.

God supposedly ran a justice system, one where the meek and the just earned a place in the kingdom of heaven. One where the guilty paid for their sins eternally. But eternity was a long way away, and revenge was like chocolate on his tongue, the taste sweet and rich and consuming.

Frank pictured Samuel in his mind as he pressed his fingers tighter. The gristle of Archer's throat popped and clicked, his breath coming in shallow, whistling gasps. Still Archer endured his own murder without raising a finger to protect himself.

Sheila's knee pressed against Frank's lower spine and he shouted in pain. Sheila seized the opening, bending him backward and jerking one of his hands from Archer's throat. She twisted her hip against Frank, and the sheriff slammed against the nightstand as Archer fell back onto the rumpled bed.

Sheila drew her .38 and stood in cop stance, both

arms extended, legs spread, jaw tense. Frank looked up at her. His shoulder throbbed. He ignored it, and rubbed his scalp instead.

"Are you okay, Reverend?" Sheila asked, her hard gaze never leaving Frank's face. Archer didn't answer.

"Reverend McFall?" she said, her voice rising in both pitch and volume. Still she didn't look away from Frank.

The sheriff tried to stand.

"Don't do it, sir," she ordered.

Archer rose slowly from the bed behind her. Floated up without bending his legs. As if God were pulling invisible strings.

"Look out, Sheila," Frank yelled. "Behind you."

She gave him a disbelieving look, as if use of this oldest trick in the book was proof of his utter madness.

Behind her, Archer came to full life, the skin of his neck unblemished, his face contorted.

Changing.

Archer's smile returned, a curved gash of bright, sharp teeth that dripped hate. His wings filled the room behind Sheila, stretching themselves and stirring a wind to life.

Something broke inside Frank's head, some thin threshold was breached, and his thoughts spilled out into dark places where thoughts should never go. He sprang at Sheila, trying for her knees in a perfect flying tackle.

Her gun went off, and the blood spilled along with his thoughts.

It all happened at once, distorted in jerky slow motion, as if the filmstrip of reality had jumped its sprockets and was jamming the projector.

Frank had cracked. Sheila had no doubt at all about that. Attacking a suspect like that, trying to choke Archer, trying to . . .

She still felt groggy, and barely trusted her own thoughts, but now she was acting on instinct. She heard a whisper of movement behind her at the same time that Frank jumped at her knees.

Aiming to wound instead of kill was also instinctive, the product of countless hours of training. Still, she was surprised when the revolver roared in her ears and twitched in her hands. Frank shouted in pain as a red rip erupted in his left shoulder. Frank slammed against the nightstand, the bedside lamp and Bible knocked to the floor, his head bouncing off the edge of the mattress as he crumpled to the floor.

The sulfurous tang of gunpowder reached Sheila's nose at the same moment she realized what she had just done. She had shot Frank. Her sheriff and the man she cared about most in the world was bleeding at her feet. And Archer was laughing.

The source of the laughter was so close that she could feel its wind stirring her hair. The preacher's breath was cold on her neck, sending icy rivers down her spine. Or maybe it was the quality of the laugh itself that chilled her. The voice was scarcely human, a cross between an animal's growl and an asylum inmate's demented cackle. Or maybe Archer's windpipe was so damaged that he could scarcely breathe. It was a miracle he could stand at all.

She stepped backward and pivoted to face Archer, expecting to see red fingerprints around the preacher's throat. She nearly dropped her revolver.

The thing hovering before her was not real. *Not real, not real, not real.* She had cracked, same as Frank. Too many murders to solve, not enough sleep, too much processed food; she shouldn't have watched *Rosemary's Baby* as a child, yeah, that was it, that was why she was crazy, and she began laughing herself.

Because this just ain't happening; this thing's got wings and nothing that big has wings and oh my what big teeth *you have, the better to eat you with, my dear and oh God your* eyes, *what have they done to your* eyes *they look like split meat in a butcher's counter and where's Archer and hee hee since I'm absolute apeshit crazy it's okay if I shoot you, especially if you don't exist.*

Sheila pulled the trigger, the firm metal beneath her finger her only link with reality. The .38 flashed a second time, and the window exploded. Still the impossible vision hovered before her, the hideous face gleaming with a wet, sharp smile. She fired again, and Frank groaned from the floor. The sheriff's hand gripped her pant leg as if he were trying to pull himself to his feet.

"Nice try," said the thing, only now it was using Archer's voice, and the flesh rippled and changed and became the preacher again. His suit had three holes in the breast. He fingered them and smiled. "This is a three-thousand-dollar suit," he said.

Yeah, Judge, I swear to tell the truth the whole truth and nothing but the truth, if only I could figure out what it is, *but I testify that one Archer McFall turned into a . . . a thing . . . yeah, right in front of my eyes, it had big teeth and gray wings and you could smell the rot in the wrinkles of its meat and . . . no, of course I didn't sneak into the evidence room and sample the contraband drugs, hee hee, I'm just apeshit crazy, that's all—*

"And I would be a good boy and lie down and die, but that isn't the way this works," Archer said. "Is it, Frank?"

Archer's face changed again, the body quivered and shrank, and a young boy of about eleven stood before her, his hair mussed and his eyes sparkling blue above his freckled cheeks. Beneath the freckles, his skin was as pale as milk. A beach towel was tied around his neck and hung down his back like a cape.

"Tell her, Frankie," said the boy in a rural mountain accent. "Tell her how it's got to be done."

Frank leaned against the bed, his right hand pressed against the gunshot wound, his left arm dangling limply. "Suh . . . Samuel?" he whispered, his voice cracking.

Sheila looked in disbelief from Frank to the pale boy, then to the revolver in her hand. A small trail of smoke wended from its barrel.

I killed him, Judge. I swear, as God is my witness. I shot Archer dead, but you know the rules. Innocent until proven guilty.

"Tell her how it is, Frankie," said the boy, his eyes darkening. "What the legend says. The gospel according to the Hung Preacher."

"Sacrifice is the currency of God," Frank said in a hiss.

"And everybody pays," said the smiling boy. The gap between his top front teeth did nothing to dampen the corruption of his smile.

"Not you, Samuel," Frank said, struggling to his knees. Tears pooled in his eyes. "You're innocent."

The boy's face changed yet again, became that of a balding middle-aged man with sweat beading his upper lip. "Innocent until proven guilty," he said. "Just ask your lady-cop friend."

Storie recognized that voice, the one that sometimes slithered into her own nightmares. *Hey, honey, you can lock me up, but I'll be back.*

Years ago in Charlotte, she couldn't ram the nightstick into the kiddie-rapist's face or pull the car over and shoot him in the head. But she was already a murderer now, so one more victim wouldn't matter. She pulled the trigger, then again, then again, only the last time the hammer clicked on a spent shell. And still the pudgy man licked his lips and leered at her.

"Except nobody's innocent," the man said, his shape shifting again, growing taller and becoming Archer McFall.

"What have you done to Samuel?" Frank shouted.

"I told you, it's not what *I've* done to Samuel," Archer said. "It's what *you've* done."

Archer touched the spot on his forehead where Sheila had aimed the revolver. "Not bad," he said to her, in his calm televangelist voice. "But you have some deep sins in your heart, Sheila Storie. If only you would open up and let God come inside, give over all your troubles, then you'd find the one true Way."

Sheila stumbled slowly backward, away from this insane vision, away from the black pit of madness that threatened to swallow her whole.

If I close my eyes, it will all go away. Criminal Psych 101: "Psychotic episodes can be triggered by extreme emotional stress, leaving the subject temporarily displaced from reality," yeah, that's a good one, I'll have to remember to tell that to my defense lawyer, because when I open my eyes, Archer McFall is going to be lying dead on the floor of a Holiday Inn motel room, unarmed, with five bullet holes in his body.

And with luck, I'll only get six to ten for manslaughter, only I've got the funny feeling that this is a life sentence. Innocent until proven guilty? Hell, we're all guilty, just like the man says.

She sat on the bed, eyes still closed, the .38 in her limp fingers. She could smell Frank's blood and her own sweat. A breeze seeped through the broken window, raising goose bumps on her neck. A hand touched her just above the knee, and she tensed. Frank's voice broke through the knotted fabric of her thoughts. "Sheila? Are you okay?"

"She'll live," Archer said. "At least for a while."

Sheila's eyelids fluttered open despite her best efforts to keep them clamped tight. Archer smiled at her with his most benevolent and beatific expression.

"I'm sorry to have misled you earlier, Detective," the preacher said. "You will not serve me, nor God, nor the church. That's only for the old families, right, Sheriff?"

Frank's lips pressed tightly together, as if his anger would crawl up his throat and erupt in sharp claws and needles of fire and silver blades.

"Now if you two will excuse me, I have a congregration in need of tending." Archer turned and walked to the door. Three holes formed a triangle in the back of his jacket. Archer opened the door, and the darkening hills were behind him, the security lights in the parking lot blinking on. A car whisked by on the highway beyond the lot. A siren, probably from a patrol car responding to reported gunshots, bounced off the high, hard mountains.

"See you at church, Frank? It's the Third Day, you know." Archer stepped into the twilight and closed the door.

NINETEEN

Night.

It pressed down on the whole world, stretching out and smothering the trees, crushing the mountains, swallowing the weak light of the stars. The night pressed against the remaining bedroom window, and Ronnie knew it was equally thick outside the walls. The scariest thing about the night was that it always came back. You could shine the universe's brightest light into it, make it run away, but the second you switched that light off—*whoosh*—the night came swooping back in blacker than ever.

"We're going to be okay, ain't we?" Tim said. He was in the bottom bunk, bundled in blankets.

Ronnie nodded in the bunk above him, not trusting his voice. Then he realized that Tim couldn't see him, though Dad had left the light on. He took a quick breath and spoke. "How many times do I have to tell you it's going to be all right?"

His anger had no force, like a bad actor's in those stupid daytime soaps that Mom used to watch, back before she joined the red church.

"What about Mom?"

Ronnie rolled over and stuck his head over the

edge of the bunk. "She'll be fine. Things will work out. You'll see."

"I don't like it when they fight." Tim squinted, his glasses put away for bedtime.

"They don't like it, either."

"Then why do they do it?"

Why? That was the big question, wasn't it? Why did the Bell Monster want to eat Ronnie's heart? Why did Mom have to join the red church? Why did Melanie turn out to be the queen of mean girls?

And there was always the big question: Why did God let bad things happen? God let Boonie Houck and Mr. Potter and that woman by the side of the road get killed. He even let people kill His only begotten son. What sort of all-merciful God was that? Maybe Ronnie would ask Preacher Staymore that one, if Ronnie were lucky enough to live until the next Sunday school meeting.

"Ronnie?"

Ronnie realized that Tim had been talking for at least half a minute, but Ronnie had just zoned out. Better to keep the kid occupied, so he didn't completely lose it. "I'm listening."

"We have to give it what it wants."

"Give what to who?" Ronnie said, though he knew *exactly* what Tim was talking about.

"To . . . you know."

"Yeah, yeah. The thing with wings and claws and livers for eyes."

Tim pulled the blankets up to his chin. His eyes were wide now, his lip quivering from fear. Ronnie swung down off the bunk and got in bed with him.

"I won't let it get you," Ronnie said. "No matter what. Dad will beat it somehow."

Tim didn't look like he believed Ronnie, but he didn't say anything. He closed his eyes and Ronnie told him the story of Sleeping Beauty, and he was halfway through "Hansel and Gretel" when Tim fell asleep. Ronnie lay beside him in the cramped bunk, trying to figure a way out of this mess.

Then it struck him, the revelation like an icicle in the chest: God was sending all these trials down on Ronnie as some kind of test. If there was one thing that stood out clearly in the Bible, it was that God liked to test the faith of His people. Job, Daniel, Abraham, why, heck, even Jesus got tempted by the devil, and if God was all-powerful, surely He pulled the devil's strings, too.

Imagine that. Jesus was God's own son, His flesh and blood, His earthly incarnation, yet even Jesus had to measure up. And with Ronnie committing all these sins of the heart lately, it was no wonder that God wanted to visit some great trials on him. And that was the scariest thing of all.

Because Dad said that when the night was dark and the pain was great and you were all alone, then you turned your eyes up to God and you opened your heart and let Jesus come on inside. You let God take away the fear. You let Him work out your problems, you let Him push back your enemies. But what if *God* was the enemy? What if God was the source of your fear?

Even as he thought it, he knew it was wrong. The idea of God as the bad guy was just too awful. You had to have faith. If you didn't, you might as well curl up in a ball and let the Bell Monsters of the world eat your insides. You might as well roll away the stone and head down into hell. So Ronnie tried to picture the face of Jesus from those color plates in the Bible, that man with the beard, long brown hair, and sad, loving blue eyes.

Something clicked against the window.

A rap on the glass at the good window, the one that hadn't been boarded up.

Can you hear him aknocking?

Oh, yes, Ronnie could hear the knock. Only this wasn't Jesus. This was the Bell Monster, come back to finish the job.

This was what God wanted—for Ronnie to get up out of bed and open the window and give himself away. Then the dead would stay dead, ghosts would stay in the ground, and Tim would be saved. And Ronnie would have passed the test.

Ronnie almost yelled for Dad, so Dad could come in with the rifle and kill the thing again. But what good would that do? You could kill it a million times, but still it would come back night after night, forever. Until it had what it wanted.

Until it had Ronnie.

He slid out from under the covers, looked at Tim's face relaxed by sleep, and crossed the room. Even though he was wearing pajamas, he shivered. The thing rapped on the glass again, and Ronnie heard slithery whispers. He hoped the claws were fast, so that he could die without pain.

He was carrying plenty of pain already. His broken nose, the welt on his face where Whizzer had punched him, the stone lump in his chest. At least all those would pass away. Soon Jesus would come and take his hand and float with him up to heaven, where there was a cure for every pain. Because Ronnie believed.

Don't you, Ronnie?

He took another trembling step to the window. He couldn't see through the blackness beyond the glass. All he saw was his own reflection and the lighted bedroom. It was better this way. If he saw the Bell Monster, he would scream, Tim would wake up, Dad would come in, and the Bell Monster would get all of them. Or Dad would kill the Bell Monster and they'd have to do it all again, every night forever, until the test was taken.

So he pulled back the sash-lock and held his breath and slowly slid the window up. It squeaked in its frame, and the cold night air poured through the crack and chilled his belly. He tensed for the claws to his gut, his eyes closed. Nothing happened, so he lifted the window another few inches.

"Ronnie," came the whisper.

Mom.

Relief surged through his body, a warmth similar to the one made by Jesus coming into his heart. But what was Mom doing out there with the Bell Monster?

Confused, Ronnie opened his eyes. The light from the room spilled on Mom's face. She didn't look scared at all. She smiled and put her finger to her lips. "Shh. Where's your dad?"

Ronnie stooped until his head was near hers. "In the living room. He thinks the Bell Monster will come through the front door this time."

"Let's go," she said, waving at him to come outside.

"Where are we going?"

"The church."

The red church. At night. Maybe Dad was right. Maybe Mom really was crazy.

"Get Tim," she said.

"Tim?" Ronnie glanced back at his brother. Tim moaned in his sleep from a bad dream. "Why does Tim have to come?"

"He's of the blood." Her eyes were strangely bright. "We all are."

"What about Dad?"

Mom's eyes narrowed. "He's not a member of the church."

Ronnie started to add that he and Tim weren't, either. Mom smiled again, and it was the old Mom smile, the one that said *Everything's going to be all right* and *Mom will kiss it and make it better* and *I love you more than anything in the world.*

"I'm scared of the red church," Ronnie said.

She took down the screen, reached through the window, and gently squeezed his shoulder. "Honey, it's so wonderful. You know how good it feels to be in the First Baptist Church?"

Ronnie nodded.

"Well, this is a hundred times better. This is like having God right in the same room with you. No more pain, no more anger, no more earthly worries. Nothing but everlasting peace."

Being in the red church was starting to sound a whole lot like being dead. But Ronnie thought that if he went with Mom just this once, he could figure out why she loved the place so much. Besides, she wouldn't let anything happen to her sons. She would protect Tim from the Bell Monster and other bad things, and she'd help Ronnie pass the test.

He woke Tim, putting a hand over Tim's mouth before he could yell out. "Mom's here," he whispered. "We have to go to the church."

Tim's lips moved beneath his palm, so Ronnie moved his hand away. "Why do we have to go to the church?" he said drowsily.

"Why do we ever go to church? Because we *have* to, that's why. Mom's here to take us."

At the mention of Mom, Tim came fully awake and sat up. "Is she here?"

"At the window."

"Hi, sugar," she said. "Now hurry, before Dad

hears. Don't worry about changing clothes. We won't be there long. Just put your shoes on."

"Don't we need to tell Dad?" Tim asked.

"He'll only get mad, honey. He'll yell at me. You don't want him to yell at me, do you?"

Tim rushed to the window and hugged her. Ronnie locked the door and the boys put on their sneakers. Then Ronnie helped Tim slip through the window. Ronnie followed, taking a last look into the lighted room before heading into the night.

The siren was louder now, closer. Frank shut his eyes and leaned against the bed. His shoulder throbbed, but he could still flex the fingers of his left hand. No major nerve damage, at least from the bullet wound. But Archer McFall had damaged his nerves plenty.

Sheila's fingers explored the area around the wound. "Does it hurt?" she asked, her voice as spaced-out as it had been when he'd first entered the motel room. He thought about trying to make a wisecrack, like Bruce Willis in *Die Hard,* but he gave up. Bruce Willis had a writer to feed him lines. All Frank had was a jangled-up nest of thoughts and red wires of hurt in his brain.

He grunted and opened his eyes. Sheila's face was corpse white, as white as Samuel's had been.

Samuel.

Anger and hate pushed Frank's pain away. That bastard Archer had killed Samuel. Whoever or whatever Archer was, ghost or demon or the best damned magician this side of Houdini, the "preacher" was to blame for Samuel's death. And for Frank's long years of guilt.

"You know what's funny?" Frank said.

"Nothing's funny," Sheila said. "I just shot you."

"No, really, it *is* funny," he said. "Once you throw away all the old rules, all the things you thought you knew and that you counted on, then you can believe just about anything."

"What in the hell are you talking about?"

"Ghosts. Archer McFall. Whatever he is, he's real. Not some trick of the mind, or a vision to fit in with your criminal-psychology theories."

"He's real, all right," she said, though she sounded unsure. She folded back the bedspread and yanked the sheet free. She tore a long strip from the sheet and wrapped it around Frank's shoulder and upper arm. He winced at the fresh pain.

"Damn, it's only a flesh wound," she said.

"That's good."

"No, it's not. I was aiming for your heart."

"I'll take that under advisement, for the next time you threaten to shoot me."

She tied off the bandage as the wailing patrol car pulled up to the door. It skidded to a stop, tires squealing, and Wade Wellborn shouted from the parking lot.

"Sheriff? Detective Storie?" He had seen their vehicles.

"It's all clear, Wade," Frank yelled back.

Wade rushed through the open door, gun pointed to the ceiling. "What in the holy heck happened?" he said, eyes wide.

"We had us what you call an 'incident,'" Frank said. His blood stained the makeshift bandage, but the spreading seemed to have slowed. He stood, Sheila taking his good arm and helping him up.

As he struggled to keep his balance, he said, "Maybe it was more of an 'encounter' than an incident."

"Sir?" Wade said.

"Call in backup. Then stay and secure the scene."

"Who done it?" Wade gaped at the bandage, then at the broken window and the holes in the motel's Sheetrock wall.

"You'll have to wait for the incident report like everybody else," said Frank. "I won't even know what happened until I make it up."

Wade hesitated, a confused expression on his face. Then he obeyed Frank's command. When Wade left the room, Frank said to Sheila, "You up for a church service?"

"I don't know. I always thought I'd believe in ghosts when I saw them. Only now I've seen one, and I still don't believe it."

"You ought to have a little faith, Sergeant."

"Faith?"

"Yeah. I *told* you the church was haunted. I just didn't know what was doing the haunting."

"Like I was supposed to believe you when you babbled on about the Hung Preacher?" Sheila seemed to be coming around, emerging from her daze and regaining her sarcastic edge. Frank was glad she was her old self again. He kind of liked her old self. Maybe the old Sheila wouldn't shoot him next time.

They went out the door, Frank taking a last look at the bloodstain on the carpet, the mussed bed, the Bible on the floor. "You drive," he said to Sheila.

"Yes, sir."

"Stop calling me 'sir.' If we're going to try to kill a ghost together, we might as well be on a first-name basis."

The few motel tenants had left their rooms and stood in clumps of two or three, whispering to one another in the parking lot. Blue lights strobed off the windows, adding to the disorienting power of the experience. The Holiday Inn's night manager stood at the far end of the parking lot, half-hidden behind a concrete planter.

"Everything's under control," Frank shouted to him.

"Don't look so damned under control to me," said the manager in a squeaky voice. "Where's Mr. McFall?"

"Checked out early," Sheila replied. She got in the driver's side of her patrol car and opened the passenger door for Frank. As he settled onto the seat, Wade ran over to their car.

"Where are you going?" he asked, his face red from exertion.

"Following up on a lead," Frank said. "We'll radio in the details."

Sheila gunned the engine to life, backed up, then fishtailed out of the parking lot. When they were on the highway and accelerating smoothly, Sheila pulled her revolver from her shoulder holster.

"You're not going to finish the job, are you? Shoot me for real?" he asked.

She handed the gun to him. "Need to reload."

"Why? We already know that bullets can't stop him. Or *it*. Whatever the hell it is."

"There's still such a thing called 'proper procedure.' It might be the last thing I can do by the book." She hit eighty and held steady, running without siren or blue lights. He watched her face as she drove.

He liked her.

Crazy as it was, he liked her. Hell, the world was touched-in-the-head crazy anyway, with its haunted churches, shape-shifters, Hung Preachers, and Looney Toons sheriffs. Why couldn't he like a woman

he had worked with for years? So what if she'd shot
him? He knew men who'd been treated worse.

Sheila glanced at him for a moment, and must
have seen his strange expression. She glanced again.
"What are you looking at?"

"You."

She gave a tired smile. "Just reload the gun."

"Yes, sir," he said, struggling to open the box of
shells she'd flipped onto the seat. She turned off the
highway onto a narrow road that was paved but un-
marked. Frank looked up at the dim stars. A high
haze belted the sky, and the three-quarters wedge of
moon was wreathed with electric-blue clouds just
above the mountains.

"Sheila?" he said, the first time he'd said her name
aloud. At least to her. He'd tried it on his tongue a
few times, back in his small apartment in the wee
hours between nightmares.

"What?" she said.

"What are we going to do when we get to the red
church?"

"You're the sheriff," she said.

"I mean, how do you kill a ghost?"

"Good question," she said.

They rode in silence as Frank clumsily dumped
the spent shell casings and reloaded the revolver using his one good hand. He passed it back to Sheila.

"Feel better?" he asked after she'd returned it to
its holster.

"No," she said. "What about you?"

His shoulder still throbbed with every beat of his
heart, but the pain was just a background distraction
now, mental white noise. "I'll live. More or less."

The dispatcher's voice fuzzed from the radio.
"Base to Unit Two, come in, Unit Two."

Frank turned the radio off.

Sheila glanced at him, her hands still tight on the steering wheel. "Guess we do this without backup?"

"Seems like those are the rules."

Her next question made his breath catch. "Do you believe in God?"

"Sure," he said without thinking. "Jesus is our Lord and Savior."

"No," she said. "I mean *really* believe."

"Look, if you think Archer is the devil and this is the ultimate battle of good and evil—"

"Don't be a jerk, Frank."

"I don't think it's ever that simple," he said. "I mean, God is good and the devil is evil. One's right and one's wrong. You ever known anything that clear-cut?"

"Well, we're only human," she said with some sarcasm. "What the hell do we know?"

"Archer says it's the flesh itself that leads to sin," Frank said, wondering where he'd picked up that little nugget of wisdom. "The heart is pure, but the flesh gets us in trouble."

"Archer says a lot of things." Sheila slowed the cruiser and turned onto the gravel road leading to Whispering Pines. The river glinted below them, the silver of the moon dappled across its surface. They rounded a bend and the dark shape of the church stood out on the hill above them.

"Here goes nothing," Frank said, his voice barely audible over the gravel crackling beneath the wheels.

"What's the plan?"

Frank looked at the long dark fingers of the dogwood, at the black belfry, at the white bones of the tombstones. Figures moved around the church, and cars were clustered in the driveway. Archer's fold was gathering.

"If I come up with one, you'll be the first to know," he said.

It happened so fast that it seemed like slow motion.

He yelled, Sheila braked, and the cruiser slid sideways. Her elbows flailed as she fought the steering wheel, trying to avoid the boy standing in the road. The momentum slammed Frank against Sheila's side and she lost control. The car skated across the loose gravel onto the soft dirt shoulder, then slipped down the embankment to the black river below.

Frank's head bounced off the dashboard, then rammed into the roof, and he reached for Sheila as metal twisted and glass shattered and the world turned cartwheels. As his thoughts turned black and blue, he held on to the image of Samuel in the road, arms spread in welcome, worms dripping from his smile.

Then, wet darkness.

TWENTY

"Where's your car?" Mama Bet asked in the dimness of the vestry. Not that a car mattered much to her, but few around these parts had raised a son who made good in the world. Maybe she suffered from sinful pride, but a flashy luxury car just flat-out said, *I done proud.* Soon cars and pride and such wouldn't matter, but you clung to life's little joys while you had them.

"I won't need a car where I'm going," Archer said. "Where *we're* going."

Archer lit a candle. Waxy smoke mingled with the smell of the communion. The reverent murmurs of the congregation filled the wooden shell of the church, anticipation in the air as thick as flies on roadkill.

Archer's suit was a little rumpled. Mama Bet frowned and straightened his tie. A messiah had to look the part. People didn't fall in for just any old body.

"You going to make me walk into the kingdom on these tired old feet?" she said, trying to get Archer to smile. He was so blamed serious all the time.

"We each must make the sacrifice," he said.

Mama Bet worked her shoulders so that the lace

of her dress collar stopped tickling her neck. "Guess we'd best get on with it."

"Yes . . . you go ahead. Give me a moment to commune with God the Father," Archer said without a hint of irony.

That was one part of this deal that worried Mama Bet. She was finally going to come face-to-face with that low-down, sneaky thing. The one who'd planted the seed and left her with all the pain and trials of raising a messiah. Well, He couldn't properly claim any of the benefits. *She* was the one who had made the hard decisions, the sacrifices, endured the whispers. Even though the reward of heaven was great, she felt she deserved a little something more.

Like maybe God ought to get down on His knees and beg her forgiveness.

She smiled at the image, though she had no clear picture of what God should look like. She remembered that night of sweaty pleasure, but His flesh had been moist and cool as clay. She hadn't glimpsed His face, but had felt his mouth slick on her neck, her shoulders, her chest. She shuddered in a mixture of remembered pleasure and revulsion.

Everybody knew that saying, "An eye for an eye," from the Old Testament. But not many knew the part right after, Mama Bet's favorite verse: "A stripe for a stripe, a burning for a burning."

You got what was coming to you, what was due, the very thing you deserved. That was the best thing about God. He was fair. What you dished out to the world, He fed back to you, over and over, for an eternity.

And her heart swelled at the thought of her part in it, of Archer's part. They were doing holy work. Nothing so dirt-common as fulfilling a prophecy, but rather they were guiding people onto the True Path. Every nutcase who ever took a knife to little girls and boys claimed they had a hotline to God. But Archer was the real thing, the Second Son, God in the flesh.

She paused at the threshold of the vestry. Archer stood with his head bowed, eyes closed, the candles throwing golden light on his peaceful face, the deep brown of the wooden walls busy with shadows. Tears came to her eyes at the beauty of the scene. She could give him up.

See, God, how strong I am? I know You need to take him, that's the Way and the Word. But I hope You got some idea just how much it pains me. If I didn't know the stone would soon be rolled away forever, I'd throw myself down at Archer's feet and not let him go through with it.

Then Mama Bet realized she hadn't been totally truthful to God. She was actually looking forward to the cleansing. Sure, most of the old biddies who had whispered about her unexpected pregnancy were long dead, were under the cold dirt and damp grass of the cemetery. But she had a feeling that those long-dead weren't out of the woods yet. They still had a part in Archer's plan. Archer would sink his claws into them, one way or another.

Thy will be done, amen, she silently added as a catch-all apology to God. Just in case He was one to hold a grudge. He had a long memory, that much was plain. The whole history of the human race was one everlasting bout of suffering.

She opened the door and slipped into the sanctuary of the church. The murmurs quieted, then picked back up again as the parishioners realized Archer wasn't coming out. She glanced at the dark shape on the floorboards of the altar, saw that it had grown larger and sharper, that the Death's Angel was nearly formed. Just a little more blood and it would be whole. Mama Bet lifted her skirt so that the hem didn't brush the floor, then raised her chin proudly and walked across the dais to take her place in the front row.

Nearly thirty of the faithful had gathered. The candles mounted on the wall bathed their faces in unsteady shadows. Mama Bet was pleased to note that the Abshers lined the pew in the second row, Sonny looking uncomfortable in a button-down shirt and bow tie. Becca Faye sat beside him, the vee of her dress offering up the pillars of her flesh. At least the slatternly hussy had worn a bra, even if it was one of those push-up kinds that made a woman look more womanly than was proper.

Becca Faye was wasting her time. Archer had no need for such offerings, and Mama Bet wouldn't let him sample the vile fruits even if he was of a mind to. Sonny could drool over that harlot all day, but Sonny would pay and pay and pay for the privilege, maybe with his tongue, maybe with his eyes, maybe with other things, according to God's will.

"Don't see why we have to put up with this foolishness," Sonny muttered just loudly enough for Mama Bet to hear. "I got better things to do than hobnob with you God-fearing folk."

"Shush," Becca Faye said, though she giggled. Haywood cleared his throat uncomfortably.

Mama Bet turned around and looked Sonny in his oily eyes. "You'd best open them big ears, mister," she said. "You don't get many chances at salvation in this life. So you best be ready when the light shines on your stupid greasy head."

Becca Faye looked around nervously, like a cat caught in a hedgerow, a whiff of her fear carried on the scent of department-store perfume that probably went by the name of Passion Flower or Wild Meadows or such. Sonny's eyes grew bright and fierce.

"I ain't the one that hung Wendell McFall," he said. "None of us are. So why do we got to pay for it?"

Mama Bet shook her head, her mouth wrinkled in weary amusement. "You ain't heard a single word Archer's said. Sacrifice is the currency of God. It ain't a sacrifice if all you're doing is paying what you owe. No, you got to pay *more* than you owe."

Haywood tried to change the subject. "Did y'all hear about the car that run off the road? Jim Potter says it just went over the side for no good reason. Probably a drunk or something."

"Nobody went to help them?" his wife Noreen said.

Haywood glared at her. "They ain't of the old families, so what's it to us?" He added, as if to himself, "Wonder if they had insurance?"

Mama Bet glanced past them to the other rows, at Alma Potter, Lester and Vivian and Stepford Matheson, the Buchanans in the back row, where their barnyard smell barely reached her, Whizzer sullenly chewing on the stump of a half-smoked cigarette. And across the aisle, oh, yes, there they were.

The Day family, minus that meddling David, the boys wide-eyed and fidgeting, the mother glowing with an expectant pride.

There *he* was, the one Archer needed.

A warmth expanded from Mama Bet's chest to the rest of her body. Let the cleansing begin.

Icy coffin black.

Drifting, on beyond black. So easy.

So cold.

At Samuel's viewing, Frank had touched his little brother's hand. Samuel had looked lost in the splendid folds of the casket, a little too pink-skinned and hollow-cheeked. His lips were unnaturally red, a shade they had never been in life. But worse than the interrupted smile was the coldness of Samuel's skin, colder than November air, colder than shaded marble.

That same coldness gripped Frank now. It flowed through his veins, clasped him in its shocking dullness, enveloped him in its numbing shroud. He was dimly aware of the currents around him, the water softly swirling around his skin. The river murmured in his ears, telling him to drift, to surrender, to submit to the embrace of long sleep.

Years passed in that near-perfect state, years in which Frank remembered the roughness of his father's hands, callused and cracked from farm work, hands that could break a locust rail if they had to. Those same hands had met, tucked under chin in desolate prayer, during Samuel's funeral. A week after, those same hands had threaded and looped one end of a thick rope. Then the hands' owner joined his youngest boy in whatever afterlife they each deserved.

And Frank's mother followed six months later. She also killed herself, though she wasn't cowardly or brave enough to take a direct route like her husband. No, she was subtle. She went into the darkness by fading a little at a time, losing appetite and health and soul to the great erosion of apathy. And only Frank had carried on, the weight of all their deaths on his shoulders, pressing down on him as heavy as a cross, the guilt a constant, cold lump in his heart.

And now he followed them into darkness. He could almost hear their whispers drawing him forward, pulling him more deeply into the numbing cold. They were waiting.

He almost smiled in his sleep. So many years of waiting, so many more years of journey ahead.

But what would be waiting?

The bright light of heaven, as promised by his parents and the Baptist preacher and practically everybody in Pickett County.

But if heaven was bright and warm and welcoming, then the change should start occurring any moment now. Because if God and Jesus wanted the eternity of worship they deserved and demanded, then they were being robbed of Frank's servitude by this extended dark purgatory. This cold and peaceful drifting. This slow suffocation.

He was aware of hands reaching, hands darker than the darkness, gentle hands. He relaxed, glad for the end to this interim end. Anxious for heaven. Anxious for the love and light and heat.

Then the hands clamped onto his wounded shoulder, and he screamed into the darkness.

His eyes snapped open against wetness, and he realized he was underwater. Then he remembered the crash. He struggled against the current as the years of drifting became seconds of chaotic tumbling and thrashing and pain. His body was trapped in the submerged car.

The hands on his shoulder . . .

Sheila.

The hands worked down his arm, and Frank stopped flailing, realizing she was trying to help him. The seat belt loosened across his chest. He reached for her, and his fingers brushed her softly flowing hair, and then she was gone.

He blinked into the blackness, his limbs stiffening from the intense chill. His right hand found the door, then the opening of the shattered window.

The water he'd inhaled burned in his lungs as he kicked through the window. A small pocket of air in his chest told him in which direction the surface lay, and he fought toward it.

The car had tumbled into a deeper part of the river, so the current was sluggish, but the weight of his wet uniform limited his progress. Bright streaks of lime and fluorescent orange rocketed across the backs of his eyelids as he paddled upward. Then he broke through the skin of the river, his lungs greedy as he gulped at the night air.

The air tasted of muck and mud and fish, and he spat to clear his mouth, then drew in another gargling gasp. The current tumbled him lazily against a boulder, then another, the rush of the river like white noise.

In the glimmer of the moon, he saw the scarred ground and broken saplings where the car had rolled down the bank. He spun around in the water, looking for Sheila. Nothing but black stones and the white phosphor of the current.

He spat once more, took a deep breath, and dove toward the twin streams of yellow light that rippled ghostlike in the riverbed.

The current pulled him away from the underwater lights. He frantically paddled toward the bank until his feet hit bottom, then waded back upstream, his teeth chattering. He'd been up for nearly a minute. Could Sheila hold her breath that long?

When he reached the spot where the car had gone under, he dove in headfirst. His hand hit smooth metal and he opened his eyes. Judging from the position of the swirling headlight beams, he was on the roof of the car. He let the current drag him to the driver's side. Luckily, the car had settled nearly flat on the riverbed, so he didn't have to worry about the door's being jammed.

Frank forced himself deeper, his lungs already

longing for a taste of oxygen and nitrogen. He found the door handle, opened his eyes again, and thought he made out a shadow in the front seat. But the water was dark, as dark as his drifting dream of death.

He yanked the handle up, and the dented door opened with a burp of released air. Reaching inside, he felt the vinyl of the seat, the warped steering wheel, the freely drifting seat belt.

He probed deeper, holding himself suspended in the cold water with his left hand on the chassis. He found her draped halfway across the seat, her legs dangling limply.

How long had she been under? Had she reached the surface, then come back to rescue him? Or had she been submerged all along? Frank was losing track of time, his thoughts gone fuzzy from lack of air, and he knew they were in trouble.

He squirmed his body into the cab and reached for her torso. Wrapping his arm around her, he tugged her toward the door. His knee caught on the steering wheel and the horn emitted a pathetic, drowning bleat. He pulled again, and the current nudged them out of the vehicle. Vomit and fear forced Frank's mouth open, and rank, muddy water rushed between his teeth.

He spun lazily and acrobatically with Sheila in his arms. He thought of Friday night hoedowns at the Gulp 'n' Gulch, how he'd never had a partner this graceful. He nearly laughed. Choking on Potter's Mill River, with the ghost of his dead brother waiting for them up on the road, with the red church owned by whatever nightmare inhabited Archer McFall's transient flesh, with everything he'd ever held as sane and right and normal now as distant as the sweet night air above, he'd finally found a dance partner.

At least I'll die in somebody's arms, and not all alone, like I always figured would happen.

And he almost surrendered again, almost opened his mouth and let the river sing its song, almost let the cold black in-between sweep them both away to the endless sea. But just as he thought of it, just as he realized that your life doesn't flash before your dying eyes, only the very end of it does, he pictured Sheila. He pictured her behind her desk, and him standing before it, explaining to her why he'd given up.

A little bit of pain? she would say. *You were cold and tired and just wanted to rest? It was easier to give up than face a world where things were topsy-turvy gone-to-hell, where spirits walked and shape-shifters drove luxury cars and you had to stare your embodied guilt in the eyes? You gave up on me, you gave up on yourself, you gave up on us, just because you didn't have faith?*

And her imagined anger flooded his wet and scalding chest, lit a fire in his rib cage, made *him* angry. Frank kicked until his feet found solid purchase. He shoved upward, his arms tightly clutching Sheila around the waist.

He silently prayed as they rose through the water, though he could not decide to whom to send his prayers or what he should ask for. His limbs were so numb he wasn't even entirely sure it was Sheila in his grasp. It could easily have been an old sodden stump.

And then they broke the surface, the air as sweet as a ripe plum, the moon as welcome as a smile, the million bubbles of froth on the river joyously whispering in Frank's ears.

He tilted Sheila's head back so that her mouth and nostrils were clear of the water, then half swam, half drifted to a sandy shallow. He carried Sheila to a flat outcropping of rock and laid her gently on her back.

He had learned CPR as part of his officer certification, and leaned over her face, ready to pinch her nose and force breath into her lungs and reach inside her shirt to massage her heart back to action.

But suddenly she coughed, spat, and blew a clear viscid fluid from her nose. She coughed again, and Frank called her name, then rolled her onto her side so that she wouldn't choke. Her skin was white in the moonlight, almost glowing in its bloodless pallor.

"Sheila?" he called again, louder this time, so that his voice carried over the rushing waters. Her eyelids fluttered weakly, and she coughed again. Then her eyes snapped open and she raised herself on one elbow, her hair trailing water onto the gray stone.

"C-cold," she said, teeth chattering. That reminded Frank of his own chill, settling as bone-deep as a toothache. But he brushed aside his discomfort in the face of this miracle. How long had she been under? Two minutes? Three? Five?

"Are you okay?" he asked, knowing how stupid his words sounded even as he said them.

"Next time . . . you take me for a swim . . ." she said, panting, her throat rattling with trapped liquid, "can you make it . . . a heated pool?"

She sat up, tucking her knees against her chest and hugging them. Her body trembled, and Frank pressed against her, even though he had little body heat to offer.

"You saved my life," he told her. She felt good in his arms, even with cold flesh.

"No . . . *you* saved *my* life," she said. Her shoulders rose and fell with her deep, even breathing. She was recovering quickly.

Too quickly.

There must have been a pocket of air trapped in the car, perhaps near the back windshield where her head had been. That was the only explanation.

That, or else maybe there really was a God, prayers sometimes *did* get answered, sometimes miracles happened.

Frank glanced at the deep black sea of sky overhead, at the winking blue-white stars that stretched out and out forever. Then he cleared the brackish aftertaste of the river from his mouth and spat into the dark water. Sure, God just happened to break from His constant job of keeping the stars burning to actually save a human being. That was a laugh.

God hadn't bothered with saving Samuel, or Frank's father and mother. He hadn't saved Boonie Houck or Zeb Potter or Donna Gregg. Hell, if you got right down to it, He hadn't even saved His only son, Jesus. God was cold and uncaring, as distant as the blue behind stars. God didn't even deserve Frank's hate, only the apathy He showered upon those who would love Him, so Frank spat once more and turned his attention to Sheila.

"Are we dead yet?" Sheila said, her eyes bright with her old sarcasm and verve and maybe that little glint that comes only from seeing the light of life's end.

"No, but you're going to have so much paperwork, you might wish you were," he said. "You wrecked a Pickett County patrol car, and the taxpayers are going to want an explanation."

"And the worst part is, you're only half joking," she said, followed by a laugh that turned into a cough.

"That Frankie, he's a laugh a minute," came a voice from the shadows along the riverbank.

Frank's blood temperature plummeted the rest of the way to zero. Sheila tensed beneath his embrace.

A milky shape came out from the dark trees.

"Samuel?" Frank said.

"Thought you were going to get baptized for sure

that time," the dead boy said. "Somebody up there must like you."

Frank had often dreamed of the apologies he wished he could make to Samuel, all the ways he could try to put things right, a hundred ways to say he was sorry. But now that he had the chance, all he could do was respond dumbly to his brother's ghost. "You mean God?"

Samuel's laughter drifted across the river like a mournful fog.

"No," came the hollow voice. The ghost turned its head up the embankment toward the hill, where the orange lights of the church windows flickered between the trees. "I mean Archer McFall. Him what owns God."

"Samuel?" Frank held up a quivering hand as if to touch the thing that couldn't be there, that couldn't possibly exist. "Is that really you?"

"What's left of me."

Sheila squeezed Frank's forearm. Frank wanted to ask Samuel so many things. But his dead brother spoke before he could think of anything to say.

"Why did you let me die, Frankie?" The hollow eyes became part of the greater night. The wispy threads of the ghosts rippled as if fighting a breeze. Then the ghost turned away.

Samuel drifted up the steep bank and disappeared between the mossy boulders. Frank stood, his wet clothes hugging him like a second skin. He was to follow. He knew it as surely as he knew that all the roads of his life led to the red church, led back to that night of his greatest failure, led forward to Archer and the Hung Preacher and the Bell Monster with its Halloween laugh. As surely as he knew that even the dead weren't allowed to rest in peace. Until Archer said so.

And the thing behind Archer?

Did it have a name, or did it have its own Archer, its own God to obey?

No matter. All that counted now was the arrival of midnight. He took Sheila's hand and helped her to her feet. Wordlessly they began the climb to the red church.

TWENTY-ONE

Ronnie's nose hurt.

Not so badly that the pain drove away the throbbing in the side of his head where Whizzer had punched him, but plenty bad enough. Whizzer had glared at him when the Day family entered the church, had even tried to stand, but one of Whizzer's moronic brothers held him back. Whizzer grinned around his cigarette butt in an *I'll see you after church* expression.

Ronnie flipped him a secretive finger and followed Mom to the second row. Tim sat between Ronnie and Mom, looking around the church with an awestruck expression. Tim wasn't that hard to impress. Ronnie had trembled a little coming up the church steps, but now that he was inside and could see this was just a church like any other, only a little bit older, he was able to bite back his fear.

He recognized most of the people in the church, though he didn't know everybody's name. There sat creepy Mama Bet McFall, who had stopped by last week to sell Mom a few jars of pickled okra. Anybody who ate okra at all, much less pickled it, must be batty. Plus she was Archer McFall's mother, and Ronnie knew that Archer had something to with the trouble between his parents.

"Sit still," Mom whispered to Tim, who had been kicking his legs back and forth in his excitement. He sat back in the pew and held himself stiff for about twenty seconds, then started swinging his legs again.

Ronnie looked at Mom. She seemed happy, her eyes shiny in the candlelight, a little smile wrinkling the corners of her mouth. She hadn't smiled this much in years, not ever in the Baptist Church, hardly ever at home, not even at the Heritage Festival at the school when Dad made her get out on the floor and do a little flatfoot dancing. But she was happy now, her hands held over her heart as if she were going to reach in and grab it, then give it away.

The other parishioners whispered to each other, as agitated as Tim. Something was up. You could feel it in the air like a mild dose of electricity, sort of like the shock you got when you touched a wire between the posts of a car battery. Not bad enough to hurt, but enough to make you uneasy.

This felt like one of those turning points. Ronnie didn't like so many turning points popping up in such a short period of time. If you turned in too many different directions, you got twisted up in knots and couldn't tell which way you were headed.

Mama Bet turned around in her seat and smiled back at the Days. She was missing three of her teeth, and the grin looked like that of a sick jack-o'-lantern. "Glad you could make it tonight, Linda," she said, her words liquid and snuffy.

"Wouldn't miss it for the world," Mom said, smiling in that empty and satisfied way.

"See you brought the boys." Mama Bet nodded at Ronnie, then reached out to pat Tim on the head. "Little Timothy Day. What do you think of the church?"

Tim shrank back from her gnarled fingers, then shook his head from side to side as if to shed himself of her lingering touch. "It ain't so scary," he said in that defiant nine-year-old way. "They said it was scary."

Mama Bet's eyes narrowed, and some of the Mathesons at the other end of the pew stopped whispering and stared.

Tim went on. "I mean, it's supposed to be haunted, but it's just like the Baptist church, only it smells funny. Like wax and old meat and—"

Ronnie elbowed Tim in the side.

"Your mom did a lot of work on it," Mama Bet said. "Cleaned it up right good, along with some of the other folks. Made it worthy of Archer's glory."

Ronnie frowned. Archer's glory? In the Baptist church, they always talked about the glory of Jesus and God. *People* weren't supposed to be glorious, at least not until they were dead. But here was Mama Bet saying bad stuff right in the middle of the church. And God didn't come out of the woodwork and strike her dead.

Mom's smile faded. "What's wrong, honey?" she asked Ronnie.

"Preacher Staymore says that everything is for the glory of Jesus."

Mom and Mama Bet laughed in unison.

"This church is a little different," Mom said.

"You mean like the Methodists and Catholics and all those other people that Dad says don't know any better?" Tim said.

"Sort of like that, yeah," Mom said. "Only here, when the plate is passed, you get to take instead of having to give."

"Cool," Tim said.

Ronnie had a bad feeling in his stomach, as if he had swallowed a boot. "Mom?"

"What?"

"You ever been to California?"

Mom and Mama Bet exchanged glances. The Mathesons had gone back to whispering among themselves, but suddenly fell silent again as the little door off to the side of the pulpit opened. Mama Bet turned and faced forward. Even the candles stopped flickering, as if not daring to absorb any of the preacher's precious oxygen. The night beyond the windows turned a shade blacker. A stillness crowded the church like water filling a bottle, and thirty pairs of eyes fixed on the man in the doorway.

Archer crossed the stage like an actor. Mom's mouth parted slightly, as if she were witnessing a miracle. Ronnie studied the preacher's face, trying to see what the others must see, the special quality that held the congregation rapt. Archer met his gaze, though surely that was Ronnie's imagination, because the preacher was looking everywhere at once, meeting every eye in the church.

Ronnie had seen eyes that intense only once before. Painted eyes. In the color plate of his Bible, on the portrait of Jesus. Sad, loving eyes. Eyes that said, *I'm sad that you must kill me, but I forgive you.*

Ronnie shivered. He wished Preacher Staymore were here. The preacher would tell Ronnie in a calm yet strong voice that Jesus was the light and the truth and the way, that the Lord was aknocking and all you had to do was open up. But Preacher Staymore was miles away, and this wasn't even Sunday. Ronnie didn't even know if you could be saved on any day besides Sunday.

If only Preacher Staymore had told him all the

rules. Then this new preacher with his peaceful face
and wise eyes and graceful hands gripping the lectern wouldn't scare him so much. If Ronnie knew
the rules, if he didn't need the preacher to help show
Jesus the way into his sinning black heart, then
maybe Ronnie wouldn't dread the words about to
come from the preacher's mouth. If Ronnie could
be positive that Jesus was still inside him, then nothing else would matter. Except Mom and Tim and
Dad.

But he wasn't sure.

Archer smiled from the lectern, his teeth gleaming
in the candlelight. And twenty-nine people smiled
back, Mama Bet and Whizzer and Lester Matheson
and Mom and even Tim. Only Ronnie doubted. It
seemed in all the world, only Ronnie failed to understand and believe.

And Ronnie wondered if he was the only one who
heard the stirrings and scratchings in the church belfry.

"Sacrifice is the currency of God," Archer said to
the flock, gathering the prepared communion from
a shelf beneath the lectern. The plate was covered
with a dark cloth, but stains were still visible on the
fabric. Archer inhaled its sweet aroma.

Conducting the ritual was Archer's favorite part of
playing messiah.

Rituals were important to the congregation. It was
as true for the Catholics and the Baptists and the
Jews and the Muslims as it had been for the unfortunate members of the Temple of the Two Suns, and
now, the fold of the red church. This was the act that
bound them together and bound them to Archer,
that made them willing to pay the currency of sacri-

fice. And the preacher's job was to make the show worth the price of admission.

"And God sent the Son, who led the world astray," Archer said, lifting the communion. "And that Son, the terrible, blasphemous Jesus, who was called the Christ, gave his flesh to the people, that they might be tainted. And God looked down, and saw that evil had been set loose upon the world."

Archer looked out at the congregation. The "old families." The living flesh of those who had murdered Wendell McFall so many decades ago. They deserved their cleansing. Anger burned his chest, but he kept the beatific smile on his face. One corner of his mouth twitched, but he doubted that anyone noticed. The lambs were too intent on the offering.

"And because we have been tainted, we must be cleansed," he continued, raising his voice, working toward the payoff.

He sensed the stirrings in the belfry, and knew that his shadow had chosen a new victim. Tonight it would be the boy.

But first, the families must taste the bitterness of their treason. They must know the depth of their iniquities. They must prove themselves worthy of cleansing. He would feed them. Matheson, Buchanan, Potter, Day, all.

He looked down at his mother in the first row. Even dear Mother must be cleansed. Perhaps she was more deserving than anyone. The ritual was his sacred duty, the reason he had been fashioned into flesh. He would not disappoint her.

Archer held the plate before him and gazed upward.

For you are a jealous God.

He bowed his head to hide his smile, then stepped off the altar and gave the plate to his mother. He removed the cloth, and watched her face as she took some of the communion in her fingers. She opened her mouth and slid the host between her rotten teeth.

Outside, the world slithered toward midnight.

Frank and Sheila were on the roadbed below the church when the congregation fell silent. Then a sermon began, filling the wooden shell of the church, and though the words echoed together into an indecipherable wall of sound, Frank recognized Archer's voice.

Through the trees twenty feet ahead, the washed-out flesh of Frank's brother floated among the bright tombstones. In the still night, Frank could almost hear the whisper of the clouds that brushed the face of the moon. The sheriff gripped Sheila's hand tightly, as much to reassure himself that she was real as to ease his fear. She squeezed back.

Samuel turned, Frank's dear, departed brother, Frank's greatest failure. "You gotta kill me again, Frankie," Samuel rasped. Though the ghost smiled, the blue eyes revealed nothing.

"Kill you?" Frank stumbled into the border of weeds and saplings that surrounded the cemetery. He knew where Samuel was now. He recognized the curve of the granite marker, the two tombstones beside it. Home. Samuel's home.

"Samuel?" Frank said, keeping his voice low. He had talked to his dead brother many times, kneeling in that lush grass whose roots were fed by his brother's decay. But he never dreamed that Samuel would one day talk back.

"Kill me, Frankie," pleaded the ghost, and suddenly Samuel was a small boy again, not a thing to be feared, just a scared and lost and lonely little boy. A brother. "You got to set me free."

"Why me?" Frank said.

"Because it will hurt you," Sheila said. Samuel's mouth parted in a wicked grin as he nodded agreement.

"What the hell does that mean?" Frank said, angry at his own helplessness and confusion. Guilt and fear were in a battle that rivaled the great blood fests of the Old Testament.

"Because it's the hardest thing you can ever do," Sheila said. "Killing Samuel again would be your greatest sacrifice."

"And sacrifice is the currency of God," Samuel said.

"You got your gun?" Frank asked Sheila.

"No. Lost it in the river."

Frank crashed through the brush, not caring if the congregation heard him. Sheila was right behind him. Frank felt foolish, thinking of killing a ghost. But what else could he do? He finally had a chance to fix a past mistake, but all he could do was repeat it. He had to kill Samuel for real this time, up close and personal. He had to take Samuel away from whatever or whoever owned the boy's spirit.

Samuel spread his arms in supplication, awaiting whatever would happen after the afterlife. His mouth writhed and bulged with the worms that crawled among his teeth. One slipped out and poked its sightless head around, and Frank fought back the revulsion that curdled his stomach. He crossed the grass, weaving between grave markers and monuments. As he came nearer he could smell Samuel, the odor of maggots and loam hot in the air.

He reached Samuel's grave, saw the shadow of the bas-relief lamb engraved on the marker, read the words *May God Protect and Keep Him,* felt the coldness radiating from his dead brother's flesh as he reached his hands up to grip Samuel's neck. And his hands met empty air as the apparition flickered and faded before his eyes.

Frank fell to his hands and knees and ripped at the grass, heedless of his shoulder wound.

"Samuel," he yelled, his voice breaking. He clawed at the soil, ignoring the pain as his fingers raked over small stones. He dug like a starved dog after a buried bone, throwing dirt high in the air. Finally he collapsed on the marred grave, the deep reservoir of his tears overflowing, the water of pity and self-pity backed up for too many years.

Archer's sermon was building in intensity inside the church. Frank listened to the mad rhythm of the words as his sobs subsided. After a long, slow thunder of heartbeats, Frank felt a hand on his head.

"It's okay, Frank." Sheila's voice was as soothing as an evening summer breeze, silk on a sunburn.

He lifted his face from the mud he had made. "I failed him again."

"What could you do? Just then, or twenty years ago? It's not your fault."

He met her eyes. They were understanding, forgiving, sympathetic. All things that he had never seen in a woman's eyes. All the things he had never looked for, until now.

"I don't know why, but Samuel still needs me," Frank said.

A shadow fell over Sheila as a dark hulk blocked out the moon. Frank stiffened. What madness was the night sending next?

"You have to kill these things more than once," said the looming figure.

David Day.

The barrel of David's rifle caught the moonlight and sent a menacing glint into Frank's eyes. Sheila tensed beside Frank, ready to attack. The sheriff clutched her arm to restrain her.

"Only, I can't be the one who does the killing," David said.

Frank suspected the carpenter had a screw loose. David had already pulled the gun on him once today, had already proven himself dangerous. But there was something conspiratorial in David's tone, and his eyes were focused on the church instead of on Frank and Sheila.

"What are you talking about?" Frank asked him.

Sheila interrupted. "He's crazy, Frank."

"And what ain't, around here?" David replied, crouching behind a concrete angel whose wings were so rain-worn that the feathers had lost detail. David aimed the rifle toward one of the windows of the church and squinted through the rifle's scope. He seemed to have forgotten all about Frank and Sheila.

Inside the church, Archer's voice rose to a fevered pitch, though the words were unintelligible. It reminded Frank of those old film clips of Adolf Hitler's speeches he'd seen, the same thundering and maniacal tirade. He'd always wondered how people could be so stupid as to fall in with anybody so obviously insane. Now he knew the kind of odd power and charisma that could totally pull the wool over people's eyes, power that could make them forget their own hopes and hearts and even humanity.

It was the kind of power that Archer possessed. Or that possessed *him*.

Power that no human should have, because no human knew how to wield it. But then, Archer wasn't human. Frank looked at David's form huddled around the rifle and wondered if *anybody* was human. Then he felt Sheila's hand in his.

Yes. Somebody was human.

Somebody lived and breathed and loved.

"What did you mean by 'You have to kill these things more than once'?" Frank asked David.

The man turned from his aiming, the shadows eerie on his eyes. "Remember what I said to you out at the house today? About killing Archer as many times as it takes?"

"Yeah?"

"When he took all those local girls out to California, he set up the Temple of the Two Suns. Don't know if you knew that part of it, but I expect it was just more of the devil's work. I went out there to bring Linda back. She was eighteen. Hell, she didn't know what she was doing. I guess I didn't, neither. All I knew was that I loved her, and I wasn't going to give her up without a fight."

"Some people don't need to be saved," said Sheila.

"No offense, Detective, but them twenty-dollar opinions won't buy you a dirty cup of water in these parts," David said. "I went out to California for Linda's good, not my good. That's when I saw what happened to one of them girls that went out there with Archer."

Frank's stomach tightened. Archer's voice ranted, roared, reached heights of frenzy that even a Baptist evangelist at a tent revival couldn't match.

"He killed her," David said. "Cut her up. Took her heart, and maybe some other things. I shut my eyes after that first part. But not before I seen them pass around the plate of meat."

"Just like he did the ones here," Frank whispered. Then he remembered the odd taste that had filled his mouth after attending Archer's service. What had happened during those lost hours?

"No," Sheila said, shaking her head in disbelief.

But nothing was beyond belief anymore. They had both seen Archer McFall change shape before their eyes. They both had watched as Sheila shot him five times at point-blank range. Yet here the preacher was, tending to his flock, culling the stray lambs, feeding them the Word.

"That's why I shot him," David said. "Killed him, or so I thought."

A thick cloud passed over the face of the moon, momentarily darkening the hill. The candles burning in the church cast the only visible light. There were no streetlights in Whispering Pines, and the scattered houses were hidden by the hills. Frank felt as though they were the only people in the world, that everything outside the cemetery and the surrounding mountains had fallen away into a dark emptiness. And all that remained of civilization, of humanity, hope, and sanity, resided right here. Frank and Sheila and David. Archer and the congregation.

And the church.

The red church, with its golden eyes.

The church that had swallowed Samuel.

The church that also claimed Frank's father and mother.

The church that held secrets in its stained and stubborn boards.

The church that had hoarded the iniquities of the old families, that had leered at their weddings and eavesdropped on their funerals and absorbed the soft, spirited seepage of their prayers.

The church that housed the ghosts of memories.

The cloud drifted on and the moon again gave its baleful glare. The steeple thrust toward the sky, the awkward broken cross barely visible against the night sky. The dogwood's branches dangled in the gentle breeze, brushing the steeple like a mother caressing a babe. The shadows shifted in the belfry, the darkness dividing itself.

"You see it, too, don't you?" David said.

Frank nodded.

"What?" Sheila said.

"The Bell Monster," David said.

"The thing that killed Samuel," Frank said.

Yes, the *church* was to blame, not Frank. If the church hadn't stood all those years, gathering legends like a stone gathered moss, then Frank, Samuel, and the others wouldn't have been there that fateful Halloween night. If not for Wendell McFall's sins, none of the tragedies would have occurred. If, if, if.

If Samuel were still alive, he wouldn't be dead. If Samuel were still dead, he wouldn't be a ghost.

David's next words interrupted Frank's thoughts and brought back the river chill that he'd been trying to ignore.

"You're the one that's got to do the killing, Sheriff."

"What are you talking about?" Sheila said.

"You're of the blood," David said, ignoring her. "You're of the old families. That's why my bullets don't do nothing. It's got to be done by one of Archer's own."

Maybe. Sheila didn't say anything, but Frank knew what she was thinking. Her bullets hadn't killed Archer, either. Maybe that was the way this thing worked.

Wendell McFall had been killed by his own people. And if Wendell was behind this, if Wendell was a restless spirit that was tied forever to the church, then maybe the scene had to play itself out again. . . .

Frank balled his hand and ground his fist into his temple. The pain drove away the foolish thoughts. What was the use of trying to figure out why Whispering Pines was go-to-hell inside out? The important thing was to make it all go away.

"He's right, Frank," Sheila said. "I know it sounds silly—hell, you know I don't believe any of this—but if there are rules to this game, that one makes as much sense as any. That's what Samuel was trying to tell you."

"My boys are in there," David said, nodding toward the church. "You've got to save them. And Linda, too. I reckon if the Lord can forgive her, I can, too. I guess when you save somebody once, you owe them."

David handed the rifle to Frank. He glanced at the belfry, at the quivering fabric of darkness. Frank took the rifle.

It was heavy and awkward in his hands. He'd never liked guns much. He'd hunted as a boy, had shown enough targeting skill to earn his police certification, but had rarely fired a gun since. He'd stopped wearing a holster piece when he'd been elected sheriff eight years ago.

"What if you're wrong?" Frank said to David.

"He's not wrong," Sheila said. "Archer says sacrifice is the currency of God."

Frank's jaw tightened. "What did you say?"

Sheila fell silent, her face pale in the moonlight. Frank was about to ask her again, to slap her, to do something to drive her words from his memory, to make her take them back and swallow them, but the day died as he stood before her.

Midnight.

The air screamed with the first toll of the bell.

TWENTY-TWO

This is just like the Baptist church, Ronnie thought. *Nothing to be scared of here. They're just passing the plate, taking up money for God. So what if Reverend McFall's sermons are a little wacky? When you think about it, Preacher Staymore's gone off the deep end a time or two.*

In the pew in front of him, Mama Bet took the plate, her hands trembling. The reverend pulled the cloth from the heaping plate. Tim wrinkled his nose, then pinched it closed. Other members of the congregation craned their necks, trying to see the offering.

"Shoo," Tim said. "Something smells like donkey crap."

Ronnie elbowed Tim at the same time that Mom squeezed Tim's forearm. "Ow," he yelped.

"Shh," Mom whispered. "Show some respect in church."

That was just what Dad always said. This place was getting more and more like the Baptist church with every second. If you could forget that it was the middle of the night and that the red church was haunted, why, you might as well be in any of them. You still had to be quiet whenever somebody performed some ritual or other. You had to pretend like you were paying attention, and you couldn't talk or laugh. You had to sit up straight and stay awake.

And sitting up straight was getting harder and harder to do. The pain pill Ronnie had taken before bedtime was kicking in. His thoughts spread fat and happy, the joy juice was sloshing around in his brain, the hard wooden pew felt like cotton candy under his bottom. He was almost having fun in church. If old Preacher Staymore could see him now, then Ronnie would be in for a serious session of heart-opening, head-bowing penance.

Mama Bet held the plate, then bent and mumbled what sounded like prayers. Becca Faye's and Sonny's faces both curdled in disgust. Stepford held his nose closed as if he were diving into a swimming hole. If something stank that bad, Ronnie was glad his nose was packed with gauze. He almost giggled. That pain pill was sure doing a number on his head.

Mama Bet reached into the plate, and Ronnie leaned forward for a closer look. Mama Bet was putting whatever was in the plate to her mouth. Dad said that the Catholics ate bread and pretended it was Jesus' body, and drank wine pretending it was the blood of the Lamb. But this looked even weirder than that.

A string of thick fluid escaped from Mama Bet's fingers. It glistened in the candlelight, looking for all the world like . . .

The happy pill was definitely messing with him. Because it looked like *blood* dripping from her hand, but before he could get another look, she had put the stuff in her mouth and started chewing.

"Gross," Tim said.

Mom didn't even pinch him this time, because she was gripping the back of Mama Bet's pew so hard that her fingers were white. She had a strange smile on her face. Mama Bet smacked her lips as she worked the offering.

"The body of God," the reverend said.

"Amen," Mama Bet responded, the word sloppy because of her chewing.

Archer McFall took the plate from her and stepped to the end of the next pew. Mom eagerly looked up at him, and he held out the plate to her. Tim edged away from her until he was pressing against Ronnie. Mom reached out, her eyes bright as ice, and Ronnie saw what was in the offering plate.

Clumps of tattered meat.

Moist, raw, and stringy.

Barf out. She's not eating *that stuff, is she?*

Mom took a morsel between her fingers and brought it to her lips. She bit down and turned and smiled at Tim and Ronnie. Bits of the pink meat dangled between her teeth. Ronnie's stomach tumbled and knotted.

"The body of God," Archer McFall said. He reached out and patted Tim's head. Then he looked at Ronnie. McFall's eyes were as deep as quarry holes, black and hiding secrets. Ronnie shivered and tried to look away, but the man's gaze held him hypnotized.

It's the pain pill, dummy. You've fallen asleep and you're just having a stupid dream. Little snakes are not *squiggling in his eyes.*

"Amen," Mom said in response to the reverend's blessing. She passed the plate to Tim, who slid back in his seat away from it. Ronnie moved away, too, but Sonny Absher pressed against him from the other side.

"Where you going, runt?" Sonny said, his lips curled in menace.

Ronnie looked wildly about the church. Whizzer

made a chewing motion with his mouth and leered at him. Mama Bet nodded encouragement, her rheumy eyes like pails of rainwater. McFall leaned forward, his mouth hanging open.

Worms. Worms between his teeth.

"Come on, Timmy," Mom said, her voice creepy and soothing. "It's good for you."

She nudged the plate against his arm. Some of the grue slopped over onto Tim's flesh, and he stared it. He looked at Mom, eyebrows raised.

"Do it, honey," she said. "Let the reverend bless you."

Tim reached toward the offering plate.

No. No. Noooo. Ronnie reached out and slapped Tim's hand away. The plate flipped out of Mom's hand, hitting the back of the pew and splashing into Mama Bet's face. The viscid blood clung to her wrinkles, small tatters of pulpy flesh on her cheeks.

McFall roared, his voice thundering, the wooden shell of the church vibrating with his rage.

And the bell struck.

The coppery, heavy taste of the communion filled Linda's mouth, her heart, her soul. She felt strong, reborn, just as she had in California in the Temple of the Two Suns. Just like always.

She lovingly held the offering out to Tim, and he was almost convinced, almost saved, almost *there,* when Ronnie knocked the plate away.

Archer's anger was radiating in waves of heat beside her. He wasn't angry over the spilled offering; no, there was plenty more where that came from, and a little dirt never hurt the sacramental flesh. But Archer couldn't abide betrayal in any form.

Neither could Linda.

God knew, she loved her boys, but Ronnie was getting to be a real pain in the rump. Ronnie was displeasing Archer. Ronnie was sitting there with that defiant look in his eyes, looking so much like his dad did when he set his mind to something. It was that same stupid Christian stubbornness, the look that said, *Don't tell* me *there's another path to God.*

Well, she wasn't going to let Ronnie get into the clutches of that devil-worm Jesus without a fight.

But she wouldn't have to fight alone.

She smiled as the bell's long arcing note rattled her eardrums.

Now would come the cleansing, the true reason Archer had been sent to this earth.

Perhaps it didn't matter that the vessel had not been fully prepared, that the sacred meat had not passed his lips. He still needed to be given to God.

Ronnie needed to die for the glory of Archer, of Wendell McFall, of the old families. He needed to pay for the iniquities of the Days. Most of all, he needed to die for the greater glory of herself. God would surely smile upon this great sacrifice she was making.

Around her, members of the congregation were rising, some heading for the door, some shouting in anger at Ronnie's betrayal. Sonny Absher grabbed Ronnie's sleeve, but Ronnie pulled free and scrambled to the floor.

"Come on, Timmy," Ronnie screeched, tugging on Tim's right arm.

No. He can't get away.

She grabbed Tim's left arm and held on with all the strength borne of desperate love. A mother's love.

For a brief moment, Tim was caught in the middle of the tug-of-war, and Archer reached over, talons extended, to take the boy. But then Tim was gone, stolen by the meddling Ronnie.

The boys scurried underneath the pew as Linda's anger rose to match Archer's. She wouldn't let Ronnie rob her of this chance to win Archer's favor. She'd wanted the reverend for so long. Not just in the lustful flesh, though that would be fine with her, but she wanted to join in spirit.

And now Ronnie was depriving her of the gift that would buy Archer's undying love.

Her oldest son had always been a troublemaker, now that she thought about it. Always reading books and getting ideas and asking dumb questions when there was really only one question. And the answer to that question was Archer.

She added her voice to the clamor and vaulted over the front pew, where the boys had gone. She lost her balance and slammed against Mama Bet, and the old woman fell heavily to the floor. Mama Bet moaned in pain, but Linda ignored her. Mama Bet may have given birth to Archer, but she was just another vessel, just another piece of meat used by God to bring Archer to Linda. Mama Bet mattered no more than rain mattered to a river.

Ronnie pulled Tim to the dais and helped him over the railing. Linda followed. Where was Archer? Didn't he see that Tim, the youngest descendant of all the old families, was getting away? Didn't he care? Didn't he want to accept the sacrifice as badly as she wanted to offer it?

Wasn't sacrifice the currency of God?

She crossed the railing and looked down at the shape on the old boards. Wings, claws outstretched, a terrible angel of dark blood.

Back again.

The work that Wendell McFall had begun was now

nearly complete. Only one more sinner's blood needed to be spilled to flesh it out and bring the Bell Monster's spirit from shadow to fully formed life.

Only one more cleansing.

She yelled at the boys to stop, but they didn't even look back. They ran into the vestry and the door slammed shut. Linda clenched her fists until her knuckles ached, then turned to look back at the congregation.

The Buchanans had spilled out the front door, their spell broken. Sonny and Becca Faye were edging toward the side of the church, away from Mama Bet, who had risen to her knees and lifted her arms.

"Look what you done to me now," Mama Bet yelled to the ceiling. She paused to lick at the offal in the corners of her mouth, then said, "You ain't made me suffer enough, now you got to go and mess up my Sunday-go-to-meeting dress. I can't wait to get my hands on you."

Linda glanced across the rapidly thinning crowd. Where was Archer?

"Let's get the hell out of here," Sonny yelled to Becca Faye. "This bunch is crazier than a bug in a bottle."

Mama Bet chanted again, a toothless prayer: "I can't wait to get face-to-face with you, mister. Then, by God, there'll be hell to pay. 'Cause you owe me big."

Oh, them of little faith, Linda thought, but Archer would deal with them later. After tonight's sacrifice, Archer would have all the time and power and anger in the world.

She shivered with rapture and went to the vestry to fetch her boys.

* * *

"Holy hell and D-double-damned," David muttered.

The bell's clangor rolled across the hilltops, slapping the mountain slopes and reverberating back in a trapped tide. The vibrations wriggled against David's skin, a thousand live things.

"There's no rope," Sheila said to herself.

She was starting to get on David's nerves. Damned woman ought not be a cop, anyway. Women were too sensitive, too caring. Too easily fooled. And that thing she'd said about sacrifice being the currency of God, why, she'd said it exactly the way Linda did.

Kind of worshipy and dreamy, in-love, like.

But she was the sheriff's problem, not his.

Because his problem was *What in hell do I do about that shadow-shape thing coming out of the steeple?*

But maybe that was everybody's problem, because the thing swooping down was full of sharp edges.

The shadow swerved and skimmed across the roof of the church, then tangled in the branches of the old dogwood. David glanced away to look inside the church. The congregation was scattering and shouting, and for a brief instant David saw Ronnie and Tim scrambling toward the front of the church.

And behind them, Linda.

He saw Ronnie lead Tim into the vestry.

"Get Archer," David shouted at the sheriff, who stood as stiffly as any of the stone angels around them, the rifle like a weight in his hands.

Sheila said, "It's not Archer's fault. He's just doing God's work."

"What in hell?" David shouted at her, and now the church door had slammed open and people were spilling out onto the cool dewy grass.

Sheila had turned. Archer had gotten to her somehow. Softened her up. Fed her the big lie and shut the door to her heart away from the saving grace of Jesus.

But the sheriff . . . well, the sheriff would take care of business.

Except he was from one of the old families.

Same as Linda, same as Mama Bet, same as Donna and Zeb and Boonie.

Same as them that was running away from the church like rabbits from a brushfire.

And David had seen Sheriff Littlefield at last night's service.

Chowing down with the rest of them.

Eating what Archer offered.

Damn.

Was *everybody* on the side of Satan?

And David had given him a rifle.

About the smartest thing you ever done, Mr. David Day. Now you'd best forget about him, forget about all of them. Save the only things that matter.

Save the boys.

And to hell with the rest.

He raced across the graveyard to the rear of the church, keeping one eye on the dark branches of the dogwood and the other on the sheriff.

Frank watched David disappear into the shadows behind the church.

The congregation, Frank's constituents, the people who had once been his neighbors, scattered across the graveyard, some getting into their cars. Others disappeared into the trees. Haywood and Nell Absher crouched behind a large marker near the sheriff and Sheila.

"You've got to kill him," Sheila said.

"Haywood?"

"No, *Archer.*"

"I . . . I don't know if I can."

"That's the way it has to be done. For God so loved the world, He gave His only other begotten son. Kill Archer, and set Samuel free. Set all the sinners free."

Frank shook his head. His clenched his jaw to keep his teeth from chattering. His wet clothes gave off a mist in the moonlight.

"You got to, Frankie," came a muffled, hollow voice from the ground, the sky, nowhere. Samuel's voice.

Frank gripped the rifle, stood, and strode toward the church. Stepford Matheson ran toward him, saw the rifle and froze, then fled in the opposite direction. The night was filled with the gargle of car ignitions and excited shouts. Twin beams swept over Frank as the Buchanans' pickup turned around. Frank didn't even blink as the headlights pierced his eyes and the truck growled its way to the main road.

He came to the foot of the old dogwood and stared up into its black branches, to the scattered white blossoms at its top.

Where is that damned brother-killing shadow?

But he knew that the shadow wasn't the real monster. The real monster was the one who cast the shadow.

The Reverend Archer McFall.

Frank climbed the steps and entered the church foyer. He heard Sheila behind him. She would want to see. She was part of it now. Though she wasn't of the old families, she had been touched and changed by Archer.

In Archer, they were *all* one big, happy family.

Frank entered the dimly lit sanctuary. Some of the candles had blown out because of the open door, and it took Frank's eyes a moment to adjust. Someone moaned near the front of the church. Another person—looked like Linda Day—stood to one side of the altar, her back to him.

"You got to do it, Frankie," said Samuel.

He spun, and Sheila smiled at him. "Sacrifice is the currency of God," she said in Samuel's voice.

"What the hell *are* you?" Frank said, the muscles in his neck rigid.

Sheila batted her eyelashes. She spoke in her own voice this time. "Just a woman, Frank. Just somebody else for you to love and lose. Just another piece of God's great puzzle."

Her face twisted, dissolved, shifted into Archer's.

"Just somebody else for me to take away from you," Archer said.

Frank swung the butt of the rifle at Archer's smirk, wanting to drive the bright, secretive glee from the monster's eyes. Just before the wood struck flesh, the face shifted back into Sheila's.

Her eyes widened in surprise and anticipated pain.

Dark.

So black that Ronnie couldn't see his hand in front of his face.

He was in a box, a coffin, with nothing but the hard thud of his heart to mark the passing of time.

"I'm scared," Tim whispered.

"Shh," Ronnie said. "They'll hear us."

Though *they* already knew the two of them were locked in the vestry. It wasn't as though there were a whole lot of places to hide inside the red church.

Ronnie finally opened his eyes. The weak gleam of moon fought through a small window set high in the back wall. He could barely make out Tim's pale face, though his eyes and mouth were steeped in shadows. He pressed his ear to the door again.

She was out there.

Waiting.

Wanting.

Ronnie shivered, remembering the deep and creepy look in his mother's eyes as she ate the raw meat, as she passed the plate to Tim, as she screamed at them for running away from Archer McFall.

Mom knocked again. "Let me in, boys."

Ronnie put his hand over Tim's mouth before his younger brother could cry out. Tim's hot, rapid breath passed between his fingers.

"Mommy won't hurt you," she said.

Ronnie put one finger to his lips to shush Tim, then slid quietly around until his back was against the door. To get inside, she'd have to bust the old metal lock. But they couldn't stay here forever. Some of the other church people might help her. Like Mama Bet. Like Whizzer.

They'd have to find a way out.

The window was too high to reach. Ronnie wasn't sure if he could even fit through it. But maybe Tim could.

The door rattled. "Come out, my honeys. I'll protect you."

Said the spider to the fly.

But that was Ronnie's *mom* out there, the one who had raised him and burped him and kissed the scrapes on his knee and stood up for him when the school counselor said Ronnie wasn't playing well with others.

This was the only mom he had.

He fought back the tears that burned his eyes and wet the bandages on his nose.

Think, think, think. You're supposed to be smart, remember? At least, that's what all those tests say.

What would Dad do?

Something shuffled in the corner, a light, whispery sound.

A leaf?

A mouse?

This was supposed to be a fancy mouse motel, after all.

That was what Lester Matheson had called the church. But Lester also said, *It's people what makes a church, and what and all they believe.*

The people here believed some pretty weird stuff.

People like his mom. And he was so scared of his mom that he wouldn't open the door.

The soft, dry rattling came again, so quietly that he barely heard it over his pounding pulse.

He'd have to do something fast.

"Ronnie," Mom said from the other side of the door.

He tensed.

"Listen," she said. "It's Tim that Archer needs. Open the door and let me have Tim, and you can go. Mommy promises."

Tim gasped.

Mom usually kept her promises.

Ronnie looked into his brother's face, saw the glint of tears on his cheeks, the weak reflection of the moon in his glasses.

This was the dingle-dork who pestered him and tore the covers off his Spiderman comics and said that Melanie Ward wanted to give him a big, sloppy kiss.

Tim was the biggest pain-in-the-rear of all time.

And this moment, this choice, was another of

those turning points that were popping up so often lately. This was some kind of test.

Everything was a test.

And to win, to make an A-plus, all he had to do was stand up, turn the brass catch, and let the door swing open, let Mom give Tim a big, bloody hug and carry him off to Archer. And Ronnie could walk right down the road to the rest of his life.

Yeah, right.

Mom knocked again, more firmly. "Ronnie? Be my big boy."

"Mommy," Tim whimpered, a bubble of mucus popping in his nose.

"Tim?" Mom said. "Open the door. Come to Mommy."

Tim's hand snaked toward the door handle, trembled, and stopped halfway. Ronnie reached out and caught it, then pulled Tim to his feet.

The thing in the dark corners shuffled again.

Mice.

He led Tim underneath the window, then put his mouth to his brother's ear. "When I boost you up, break the window and crawl out."

Tim's glasses flashed in the moonlight as he nodded.

Ronnie stooped and cupped his hands, and Tim put a foot in them. Ronnie grunted as he lifted, and Tim grabbed the small, splintered ledge and pulled himself up to the glass.

"Close your eyes and hit it with your elbow," Ronnie commanded. "Hurry."

Ronnie didn't worry about remaining quiet, because whatever was in the corner was growing louder and larger and darker than the shadows. Tim hit the window once, and nothing happened.

"Harder," Ronnie yelled, his voice cracking.

Tim smacked the window again and the brittle explosion was followed by the tinkle of showering glass.

"What are you boys up to in there?" Mom shouted, banging on the door.

Ronnie pushed Tim higher. "Watch out for the glass," he said, as Tim scurried through the small frame. When Tim had tumbled through, probably landing shoulder-first on the grass outside, Ronnie jumped as high as he could. His fingers scratched inches short of the window ledge.

At least Tim made it.

He leaned against the wall. Alone. He would have to face the darkness alone.

The darkness moved away from the lesser darkness, and the moon fell on its face.

His face.

Preacher Staymore.

Ronnie exhaled a lungful of held fear as the preacher's voice reached and soothed him. "With the Son of God in your heart, you're never alone."

The preacher stepped forward, calm and smiling.

TWENTY-THREE

Wait a second. What's the preacher doing here? During the First Baptist services, he said time and again that all the other churches led people straight to hell.

Ronnie stepped back from the man's broad, grinning face and fervent eyes.

"You're wondering what I'm doing here, aren't you, my child?" Preacher Staymore spread his arms and held his palms upward, like Jesus in those Bible color plates.

"Let me in, Ronnie," Mom yelled, rattling the door again.

"I hid back here so I could help save you, Ronnie," the preacher said, ignoring her. "God sent me special just to watch you. We knew you'd be tempted."

"Tempted?" Ronnie glanced at the window.

"Yes. You know there's only one true way."

Mom pounded on the door.

"Can you hear Him aknockin', Ronnie?"

I can try for the window one more time. Maybe if I get a running start—

Mom flailed at the door. "You boys had better get out here right this second," she said, her voice a mixture of anger and hysteria.

"Escaping won't save you, Ronnie." Preacher Staymore took another step closer. "You can run to the ends of the earth, but you can't get away from your own sorry heart. Only one person can cleanse you."

Ronnie pressed against the wall, clawing at the wood behind him.

The moon bathed the preacher's face, almost like a dramatic spotlight on some crazy stage.

"Can you hear Him aknockin'?" the preacher repeated.

Mom pounded on the door. "Ron-*neeeee.*"

The preacher reached out to touch Ronnie's forehead, just as he had done the dozen or so other times he'd helped Ronnie get saved. Ronnie closed his eyes and bowed his head slightly, the way he was supposed to do.

At least I'll get saved one last time before Mom and Archer and the Bell Monster get me. And dear Jesus, when you come in this time, please stay awhile. Please don't let me have more of those sins of the heart that make you so mad. And please, please, please, let Tim get away.

"You got to throw open the door, Ronnie," the preacher whispered, his hand moist and cool on Ronnie's forehead. "You got to let Him in."

The feeling came, that mixture of warmth and airiness expanding in his chest.

The good feeling.

The kind of feeling he got when Mom hugged him or Dad mussed his hair.

A feeling of being wanted, of being loved.

Of belonging.

He smiled, because he was going to tell Preacher Staymore that the door was open, that the Lord had come right on in and then slammed it shut so that no sins could sneak in behind Him.

Ronnie opened his eyes to thank the preacher, but the preacher wasn't there.

A slick stack of something that looked like gray mud stood before him. Touching him.

Some of the mud slid down his forehead and clung to his bandaged nose.

The mudstack made wet noises, a bubbling like snotty breath.

Ronnie choked back a scream. The darkness took shape, the shadow behind the mud gaining sharp edges.

The Bell Monster.

Ronnie slapped away the branch of mud that stretched to his head. It was like punching a giant slug.

Mom screamed his name again from behind the door.

The mudstack jiggled forward, the shadow looming behind it.

It's moving, oh, sweet Jesus Christ, it's moving.

Ronnie tried to tell himself it was the pain pill; this was a stupid dream and he'd wake up with a pillowcase tangled around his head. That he'd wake up and the only problems he would have were Mom and Dad's arguing, Tim's pestering, Melanie Ward's hot-and-cold flirting, and all the hundreds of ordinary problems that boys across the world faced every day.

Oh, yeah, and the big one: whether Jesus Christ was going to stay with him and help him get through it all, or whether He was going to cut and run at the first tiny sin of the heart.

But the mud monster moved again, pressing against Ronnie, and he could no longer lie to himself. This was real.

And the worst got worser, as Tim would say.

Because the thing *spoke.*

"Come into me, Ronnie," came the slobbery,

mumbling voice. "Give it up. It's the only way to get cleansed forever."

Ronnie didn't ask how getting smothered in a nasty, creepy mound of walking, talking mud would make him clean.

"I need you," the mud-monster said. The shadow grew larger behind it, filling the room, blocking the window. "Give yourself to me."

Yeah, right.

It's all about sacrifice, ain't it? I give myself up, and you let Tim go. That's the deal, huh?

Ronnie struggled against the crush of mud.

But then you'll be back, and it will be Tim's turn to sacrifice. And then Dad's, and then everybody else's. And everybody loses but you.

Because you don't have to sacrifice anything.

All you do is take and take and take.

The weight of the mud pressed Ronnie to his knees. The slimy fluid soaked through his clothes. Mom called again and pounded on the door, the sound a million miles away.

All he wanted to do was sleep. He was so tired. It was so much easier to just give up than actually try to fight.

So much easier.

Frank tried to pull back on the rifle, but his swing had too much momentum.

Sheila's eyes widened as the rifle butt struck her cheek.

Oh, my God. No, no, noooo.

The wooden stock glanced off her jaw, and for a split second, Frank had the illusion that the butt had passed *through* her skull. But he'd been suffering a lot of illusions lately, and the slapping sound echoed off the church and tombstones.

Sheila dropped like a sack of wet seed corn, and Frank dropped to her side almost as rapidly, calling her name.

A red splotch spread across her cheek. Frank put his fingers gently against the bruise. "You okay?" he whispered.

Her eyes fluttered open and she groaned.

"I didn't . . . you were Archer. . . ."

She gripped his shoulder, the one she had shot hours earlier. Frank winced but swallowed his grunt of pain.

She worked her jaw sideways twice, then said, "It still works."

So maybe he'd held back enough.

"You were Archer," Frank repeated stupidly.

"Gee, thanks for the compliment," she said. "Have I told you lately that you're apeshit crazy?"

"Not in the last five minutes or so." Frank glanced into the branches of the dogwood above, making sure nothing sharp and black was moving around up there.

Where *was* Archer? And how was Frank going to kill something that couldn't be killed when he couldn't even trust his own eyes?

Sheila sat up, rubbing her jaw. "Guess that was payback," she said, pointing at the blood seeping through his bandage.

"Yeah," he said, gripping the rifle. "Now we're even, but somebody else has a debt to settle."

He rose and headed for the church. Most of the congregation had scattered, and the church was silent except for Linda Day's shouting. Frank stood before the door and stared at the belfry, then into the dim interior of the church.

Twenty-three years ago, at Samuel's funeral, Frank had entered this structure with only one comfort: that God would take care of Samuel in the afterlife.

And that comfort had kept Frank going all these years, even though a tiny niggling voice in the back of his mind never let him forget what the Bell Monster had done. God had been with Frank then, had helped him deal with the sorrow of losing his family, had laid by him and with him and inside him during a thousand sleepless nights.

But now, as Frank entered the church, he knew the kind of tricks that God liked to play. And that God's closeness was only another illusion.

This time Frank walked alone.

Mama Bet crawled on her hands and knees across the floor to the altar. The muck that had been Donna Gregg's internal organs soaked into Mama Bet's Sunday dress and coated her skin. She didn't mind the sticky blood on her face or the rank, coppery taste that clung to the inside of her mouth. This was an offering, after all. A sacrifice.

There's nothing as glorious as the flesh of one of the old families.

The others had fled, those of little faith who shied from the brilliance of Archer's power. But not her. No, she would follow to the end. And the others were only delaying what was meant to be, what was ordained by God. The only thing that heavenly son of a snake ever did right was to give Archer to the world.

To her.

She licked her lips and raised up in worship of the crooked cross. The wood caught the dying light from the candles, standing as defiantly as a true believer on a devil's playground. The Jesus-demon had been nailed to such a cross, and people had fallen all over themselves to get on the bandwagon. But when the real thing, the true messiah, came unto their midst, they scattered like a bunch of hens running from a fox.

Except Linda Day.

The woman banged on the vestry door like there was no tomorrow, screaming Ronnie's name over and over again. Mama Bet chuckled to herself.

I reckon faith is either all or nothing. Linda's gone whole-hog for Archer, giving up her boys without a second thought just so Archer will pat her on the head and flash that television smile. And people think I'm crazy.

She wiped a fleck of flesh from her chin and stood on trembling legs.

I'm getting too old for such foolishness. About time I took Archer up on that eternal peace he keeps promising. As long as God stays way over to the other end of heaven, I don't think I'll mind one bit. I believe I've earned a little rest.

But first they had to nail down one little piece of unfinished business. Business by the name of Ronnie Day. Mama Bet looked at the dark shadow on the dais, at its flickering edges, at the blackness that seemed to burn through to the belly of the Earth.

She started laughing.

Linda turned from the door, her face wet with hysterical tears. "He won't let me in."

Mama Bet was enjoying the woman's misery. After all, the blood of the old families ran through Linda's veins. Linda was one of *them*—them that had hung Wendell McFall, because they were just as blind to glory back then as they were today. Them that deserved all the suffering that Archer could dish out.

You showed them the way, you lit the path, you spoon-fed them the truth, and they spat in your face.

People didn't change.

"You didn't say the magic words."

"Magic words?" Linda blubbered, her eyes roaming wildly over the church as if a message might be written on the walls. "What magic words? Archer didn't say anything about magic words."

"I believe the words are 'let me die,'" boomed a voice from the back of the church.

Mama Bet turned.

Sheriff Frank Littlefield strode up the aisle, carrying a rifle, his eyes narrowed and his face clenched in a strange smile. Blood soaked the left half of his uniform shirt. In the foyer behind him, the detective woman leaned against the wall.

Mama Bet laughed again. "You think Archer will fall down for a bullet? You're crazier than a liquored-up Absher."

"Archer *wants* to be killed. And it's got to be done by one of us. One of us who belongs to Archer."

Maybe so. Maybe Littlefield's been chosen. Though he didn't seem all that gung-ho at the service the other night. Just nibbled on a bit of old Zeb's stringy flesh like it was a piece of black licorice. Didn't put a whole lot of gumption in it.

But Archer had his own ways, and who was she to question his workings? One Judas was as good as any other. Let the sheriff come.

"He's in there," Mama Bet said, pointing past Linda to the door. "Doing a little holy work."

Linda gasped and put her hand to her mouth.

As the sheriff stepped before the vestry door, Mama Bet said, "You ain't got it quite right, Sheriff. The magic words ain't 'let me die.' They're 'Let me die for *you.*'"

The sheriff pounded on the door. "Open up, McFall. I got a message for you. From a boy named Samuel."

Mama Bet rubbed her hands together, smearing the coagulated blood. This was going to be good.

The old brass handle turned and the door swung open.

David crept from the woods behind the church, keeping his eyes on the dark canopy overhead. But one of those hellholes might be under his feet, one of those gateways that allowed the devil to crawl up out of his hot pit in the center of the Earth and stir up a ruckus. God had kicked the devil's hind end a thousand times over, but still the red-faced son of a skunk kept on trying. You had to hand it to the devil: long odds never dampened his enthusiasm one bit.

David almost felt guilty about sending the sheriff into battle. You couldn't fight a holy war unless you were serious about the *holy* part. The sheriff hadn't been to church of late, and never had been a regular. David had seen the man baptized when they were both children, but sometimes the water didn't soak completely through.

Branches snapped about a hundred feet to his right, and he tensed and crouched behind a thick oak. The sound faded. Probably one of Archer's folks. One of the stray lambs, bolting the pen now that the gate was unlatched.

David reached the clearing behind the church just as glass shattered. The moon flashed on the jagged pieces that flew from the high window. Then he heard Ronnie's frantic voice.

David ran from the trees, not caring that he was out in the open where the devil could strike him down. All he cared about was that his two children, the dearest things a father could have, were inside that church with the devil's incarnation. And, almost as bad, they were with Linda, who was so cross-eyed over Archer that she couldn't tell right from wrong.

He almost shouted, but the devil's keepers were all around. Some of those stray lambs might have a few teeth. They might just want to get a good bite of God-fearing flesh, so they could chew it up in mockery of dear sweet Jesus. Just like they had in California, and just like they had in the red church.

And then David put it all together.

The boys.

Linda was going to give them to Archer as an offering. As soul food.

He ran, sweat bleeding through his pores faster than the night could chill his skin. Tim's head appeared in the broken window, then his shoulders and arms, and he was falling headfirst ten feet to the ground.

Tim gasped in expected pain.

But David was there to catch him. He'd always be there to protect his boys. Him and Jesus.

"Shhh," David said, putting his hand over Tim's mouth before the boy could scream. Tim's glasses bounced away, settling softly in the graveyard grass.

"It's me," David said, then moved his hand away.

"Ronnie," Tim whispered, his throat tight. "It's got Ronnie."

"Who?" David said, though his heart sank like a stone down to his belly.

"The preacher."

Littlefield had better have enough faith. Littlefield had better do what the Lord required. Littlefield had better make the sacrifice.

Because even though God always won the battle of good and evil, sometimes innocent blood was shed. That much was plain through all the books of the Bible.

"Ronnie will be saved," David said, as convincingly as he could manage.

Slurping noises from inside the vestry spilled through the window. Talking. Ronnie and someone whose voice was familiar.

Naw, couldn't be.

"You said the *preacher* got Ronnie?" David asked.

"Yeah. Preacher Staymore."

Staymore. David smiled and looked to the sky. God always sent a champion when times were tough, when the good guys had their backs against the wall.

A *real* preacher, a bathed-in-the-blood Baptist preacher.

Ronnie would be all right.

"Mom's in there, and she's acting really weird," Tim said. David set him down and the boy knelt to retrieve his glasses.

"She don't know what she's doing, son. The Lord will set her straight."

Just like He had twice before. Once when Linda was young and pure, and once after she had returned from California. *Third time's a charm,* they said.

David led Tim past the gray tombstones to the edge of the woods. They could wait there, in the safety of shadows, for the battle to end and the Lord to come out on top.

Just like always.

Frank nearly dropped the rifle as Ronnie came from the dark vestry. The boy's face was pale, his eyes feverish on either side of the soiled bandage that covered his nose. His lips moved as if to speak, or maybe he was whispering something to himself.

It was the same look Samuel had worn the moment he realized that the Bell Monster was behind him and was going to get him, get him, get him. Frank's heart twisted in rage, but he instantly forgot Samuel.

Because behind Ronnie shambled a creature that was the crowning glory of a day full of impossibilities. The mud and clay of the thing's flesh glistened in the candlelight, its limbs an awkward and perverted imitation of a human's. Worst of all were the black slits that hinted at eyes and a mouth.

The mouth flapped, the edges like cold gray syrup.

Mama Bet and Linda gasped in unison, and Linda grabbed Ronnie to pull him away.

"Welcome," said the thing, and even though the word was drawn-out and slushy, Frank knew it was Archer's voice.

"Archer?" Mama Bet said, her withered face taut.

"Mother," the thing said. The clay rippled, shifted, and for a split second, the preacher's face appeared, the powerful eyes sweeping over them like a light-house beacon over a troubled sea.

Linda drew back from the preacher, Ronnie tucked behind her. The preacher turned his smile to her and then the flesh fell back into corrupted mud.

"Linda, give me the child," the thing commanded.

She shook her head, speechless and numbed.

"Give me the child," it repeated.

Frank lifted the rifle.

"You got to kill it, Frank," Sheila said from behind him.

How could you kill . . . *this*?

But he pointed the rifle anyway, lodged the stock against his shoulder and looked down the barrel. The rifle weighed a thousand pounds, and he felt as if he were still underwater.

"Give me the child," the thing said a third time.

Mama Bet fell on her knees before the mudstack.

"You . . . you're not Archer," Linda said.

"Does it matter what face God wears?" the thing said in Archer's smooth and seductive voice. "You promised. And I ask so little, after all."

Linda backed away another couple of steps. "Not like this," she said. "You're not Archer. You can't have my baby."

The mudstack trembled, dropping bits of itself on the dais. The tiny clods writhed like worms on the blotched dark angel that stained the boards.

"Sacrifice is the currency of God," it said. "And Ronnie is the sacrifice."

"I won't let you kill him," Linda said.

The thing gurgled a laugh. "Oh, *I'm* not going to kill him. *You* are. That's what sacrifice is all about. Blessings are better given than received."

Linda looked at her son, whose eyes were wet with tears.

"Mom?" Ronnie whispered. He gulped.

Frank fought the strange gravity that wrapped him like a thick skin. He could kill it. Sure, he was of the old families. He had a right. It was his job.

"Do it," Sheila whispered in his ear, a little too gleefully.

Frank remembered how the rifle butt had seemingly passed through her cheek, how she had been underwater for far too long. How she recited Archer's words in a chilling and worshipful way.

He glanced back at her. For just a moment, so briefly that before this recent madness he would have chalked it up to illusion, she wore Archer's eyes, deep and brown and brimming with secrets. She blinked them back to blue.

"You heard what Samuel said," she whispered, her eyes never leaving the quivering pile of clay. Her doting eyes, her eyes hot with a faraway and deep and inhuman love. A fervor that went beyond the flesh.

She was Archer's now.

Frank's throat tightened.

They were all Archer's. They always had been. Frank had tasted, and found it sweet. He had swallowed his way into the red church and he had let the monster into his heart. And he hated his own weakness almost as much as he hated Archer.

Yes, he could kill it.

But as his finger tightened on the trigger, the mud rippled again and shrank. Samuel stood before him with pleading eyes.

"You can do it, Frankie," his dead brother said. The boy pulled a worm from his mouth and held it up. It squirmed between white fingers.

Samuel put the worm back in his mouth and chewed noisily. "Archer ate me, you know. He eats all of us."

Then Samuel blossomed hideously into the mass of putrid clay.

Archer *wanted* to be killed.

As if somehow being killed by one of his own would give him great power. Just as Judas had given up Jesus. The sons of God always needed a betrayer. Even though Frank no longer believed in God, it was just the sort of logic that ruled in an insane universe.

And he wouldn't obey. He wouldn't give Archer what he—or *it*, whatever it was—wanted most of all. Frank wouldn't make the sacrifice.

He dropped the rifle and it clattered across the hard floor.

The thing let out a damp moan, its thick arms reaching for Ronnie.

TWENTY-FOUR

Mama Bet gazed up at the thing she had made, birthed, delivered unto the world.

A flawless monstrosity.

Her perfect, sinless child.

She reached out and touched the moist clay. This was the flesh of her flesh. Had she ever dreamed she would be part of something so glorious, so big?

And I done it all by myself. I brung it out myself, taught my Archer all about the wicked ways of the world, about the evil of the old families. I passed down the story of Wendell McFall, about how preaching was in the blood, how it was Archer's job to bring salvation to these heathen Jesus followers.

She slid her hand down the slope of the mud shape. Dimly, she heard Archer's golden-throated voice demanding the Day child.

Let them be cleansed, young and old. Then, when we're done with the Days and the Mathesons and the Potters, we can go on to bigger work. Because Jesus is legion. A whole lot of hearts got to be plucked out of tainted chests. A whole heap of iniquities got to be paid for.

The Archer-mud shook and became the boy, the one whose corpse she had dug up and pickled and then canned in glass jars so that young Archer could have offerings throughout the year. There had been other corpses along the way, a Day here, another Littlefield there, the whole graveyard like a fresh, sacred garden. Even the embalmed ones were worthy.

But getting them fresh was so much better.

The cold mockery of flesh rippled again and changed back into the mud shape.

The rifle that the sheriff had been carrying landed on the floor beside her. The sheriff was weak. That was just like a Littlefield, to fold like an accordion when there was work to be done. Well, he'd get his in due time.

Mama Bet sank her fingers into the mud and pulled a clump free. She put it to her face and rubbed it over the blood that had coagulated on her cheeks. Her boy. Her son and savior.

She pressed it against her lips, savoring the humus, this flesh of the earth.

It was between her lips, her tongue probing the holy matter, when she recognized the texture. She froze.

That night.

Nearly forty years ago.

When she gave away her virginity and took the seed.

And she remembered how, the next day, she'd found the stone rolled away, the stone that sealed off the hole in the back of the pantry. The hole that led down into the dark, moist tunnels of hell.

The clay squirmed between her gums. She tried to spit it out, but it thrust toward the opening of her throat, wriggling toward her belly.

As its rank flavor flooded her mouth, she tasted the bitter truth.

It wasn't God that had impregnated her.

It was . . . *this*.

No.

Archer was her flesh, her body, her blood. He was born of the heavens, not the earth.

Not like this thing.

But this *was* Archer. Her only son.

The word made flesh.

The flesh made mud, from that which crawled up through deep holes in the ground.

How could she ever have loved this thing?

This *thing* that walked among humans like some gift from above, throwing off lies and laying out tricks that made Jesus look like a two-bit street magician.

This thing that stood at the pulpit, slick and foul and throwing off a fungal rotten smell. The odor of the grave.

A deceiver.

Just another in a long line of false prophets and God-pretenders.

May God forgive me, I helped it. I gave it life.

She clamped her legs together, as if she could change the past and keep the thing's head from appearing, to prevent its birth. But it was too late. It had always been too late.

The McFall secret was even more secret than she had known.

The thing, the hideous coalition of accumulated sin and pain and sorrow, moved toward Linda and Ronnie.

It wanted a last supper.

Mama Bet looked at the thing that was its own father, the thing that had fooled her more deeply than it had fooled anyone, and anger burned her from the inside out. It began in her chest, where the small clump of mud had lodged, and expanded out to her skin. Her head felt as if it were glowing, as if some power from beyond had lit her hair like a torch.

Strength flooded her aged limbs, a strength born of self-loathing.

Sacrifice was the currency of God.

And damned if she didn't know what sacrifice was all about.

Ronnie stepped in front of his mother, protecting her, though the creepy mountain of mud was the worst nightmare ever made.

Mom tried to pull him back, but he shrugged her hands away. "I got to do this, Mom," he said, trying to keep his voice from cracking, but failing.

"No, Ronnie," she said.

"If I give myself to it, maybe that will be enough. That's all it wants."

So I hope and pray. Because if it takes me in, and I'm full of Jesus, then it will be filled with Jesus, too.

Though Ronnie's vision blurred with tears, he knew he was doing the right thing. After all those sins of the heart, all those selfish things, this was something he could do for the whole world. He would give himself so that the world could live. And if Mom loved him enough, she would give him up, too.

His heart, which had been shriveled with fear, now felt light and warm in his chest. A strange calmness came over him. This thing could eat him, smother him, rip him apart, whatever it wanted to do, but it could never touch the *real* him.

The part of him that floated in his heart.

With Jesus.

Because Jesus was there, all right, big and happy and brave. Jesus had always been there, only Ronnie realized sometimes you couldn't see Him because you got caught up in your own little sorrows and worries and dreams. All your little selfish things.

But Jesus stuck right there with you, no matter what.

And Ronnie knew that Jesus wouldn't step in and save him from the monster.

Because Jesus had already saved him.

He twisted away from Mom and stepped forward to meet the monster's embrace, a smile on his face, the pain in his nose and heart now as far away as heaven was near.

Mama Bet picked up the rifle.

She had no doubt that Archer could die, *would* die. And only she, who had given it life, could free it. Hers was the greatest sacrifice, after all. She was giving up her only begotten son.

Her cataracted eyes fixed upon the mass of mud that was only inches from taking the boy.

Sure, that boy deserved cleansing—he had that awful and tainted Day blood in him—but the sins of the old families were nothing next to the blaspheming joke of an angel that slopped before her.

Angels didn't fall from heaven. They rose up from the meat of the earth.

Her guts ached at the thought that this *thing* had been harbored in her belly, had grown by sapping her strength, had come forth under the lie of a miracle.

"Archer," she called with all the strength she could muster. Her diabetic limbs trembled as she aimed the rifle. The mud shape turned, its slab of face rippling. The mud changed, slid into Archer's human features.

"Mother?" he said, eyes wide and pleading and

oh so damned innocent. Like he'd never had a nasty thought in his life. Like God was the one lighting up his eyes, a holy filament burning inside that glorious, handsome head.

Mama Bet wavered. She'd suckled this thing. She'd told it bedtime stories. She'd fed it from a hundred worthless sinners. Why, surely there was *one* good thing about it, one thing worth a mother's love.

"Archer," she whispered. The rifle tilted down toward the floor, and she saw the dark stain moving, rising up like a fat and sinuous snake, draping Archer like an oversize shadow. Something else moved out of the corner of Mama Bet's eye—the sheriff jumping over the railing.

"The Bell Monster," Ronnie screamed.

The Bell Monster.

The *real* evil.

Because evil didn't wear flesh. Evil didn't *need* substance.

As the black shape settled over Archer and sank into him, soaked through his smooth suit and styled hair, Mama Bet's son smiled at her.

"I love you, Mother," the preacher said, though his teeth said exactly the opposite.

His teeth said, *You're about due for a turn in the offering plate, you stupid blind bitch. And let me tell you something: you're worse than all the others put together. Because you served me, and you loved it. You loved having your face pushed into the corrupted flesh of the old families. You swallowed the body of God like a pig snorting at the trough.*

And the horrible truth of it slammed into her like a twenty-pound Bible dropped from the heights of heaven.

She lifted the rifle and pulled the trigger, and the

stock kicked against her shoulder as the report
bounced off the wooden walls of the red church.

Frank eased over to the railing. The others had
forgotten him, all except Archer, who knew everything and seemed to always have a gleaming eye on
the sheriff. Even in his mud incarnation, the
preacher owned the red church.

But when the shadow of the Bell Monster had
risen, Frank knew that Archer had always been here,
in many forms, troubling the people of Whispering
Pines since the first family had settled in these hard
hills. Maybe it had been here since the first sun rose.
Maybe it was an evil older than hope, older than religion, older than everything that people thought
they understood. And since Frank no longer believed
in God, he no longer believed in the devil, either.

Those things didn't matter. Who cared about some
nameless, faceless eternity? What counted was that
he could save Ronnie, right here and right now.
Frank had failed Samuel, but maybe this was a chance
at redemption.

The sheriff jumped over the rail and grabbed the
boy, lifted him and carried him away from the
preacher. Archer didn't even glance at them, his
hands spread wide in acceptance as he spoke to his
mother. Linda stood in shock at the edge of the altar,
slowly shaking her head as if someone had told her
that the emperor had no clothes, and she had just
noticed the nakedness.

Shoot it.

Frank couldn't kill it, because that would only
bring the thing back, more powerful than ever. But
Mama Bet was its creator, in a way. At least in the
human way. If the Archer-shadow-thing was an an-

cient evil, it must have started somewhere. And everything that had a beginning also had an end.

Ronnie was light in the sheriff's arms as they fled from the altar and down the aisle. Sheila, or whatever Sheila had been, was gone. Frank thought of her touch, but only briefly. He was getting better at forgetting.

The shot exploded when he was in the middle of the church, and he couldn't help himself. He had to turn and look.

Archer, arms wide, palms up, eyebrows raised, mouth stunned open, a messiah on an invisible cross.

A small red spot appeared on his white shirt, just to the left of his tie.

Shot in the heart.

Archer's lips moved, but no words came. The face shifted rapidly, to mud and mountain lion to Samuel and then to a dozen, no, a hundred, faces that Frank didn't recognize. Then it settled back into Archer's face.

"Jeez," whispered Ronnie.

Archer's eyes rolled heavenward, as if looking for some large, compassionate hand to come down and collect him. But above them was only the dark ceiling of the red church.

Then the bell rang, a belch of hellwind ripping the night.

"Mom," Ronnie called, struggling in Frank's grasp.

Linda looked from Ronnie to Archer, then back again, as if making a hard choice.

The wound on Archer's chest blossomed wider, leaking a gray, gelatinous substance along with the blood. Frank thought he saw bits of stone and root in the seepage. Archer lurched toward Mama Bet as the bell rang a second time.

"Why hast thou forsaken me?" the preacher-thing said to its cowering mother. The words were as thunderous as the tolling bell, but Archer was *smiling*. As if getting killed was all part of some perverted sacrament.

"Come *on,* Linda," Frank shouted.

"Ronnie," she called, holding her arms up and running from the altar. This time they were a mother's loving arms, not the snatching arms of a conspirator.

Frank set Ronnie down, and the boy hugged his weeping mother.

"Let's get the hell out of here," Frank said, leading them down the aisle.

He turned one last time, just before they went out the door. Mama Bet had stood and was meeting her son's embrace. Except her son, her savior, her hope for the world, was a glistening mass of clay. The mudslide swept over her and suffocated her screams. Frank's feet were in the graveyard grass when the bell rang for the third and final time.

This is it, Ronnie thought. *The all-time, Whopper-with-extra-cheese turning point, the up-close-and-personal end of the world.*

And the weirdest thing was, he was no longer afraid. No matter what happened from here on in, he knew he wasn't alone. Because when Jesus came into your heart, He signed a lifetime contract with a no-trade clause. Ronnie wished someone had told him how simple it was, that you didn't need Preacher Staymore or an angel or even Dad to tell you that God was right there all the time.

He gripped Mom's hand as they ran across the graveyard. A smattering of starlight and the half-faced moon threw the shadow of the dogwood tree over them. The black branches swayed in an unfelt breeze like fingers reaching to grab them.

"Are you okay?" Mom asked.

"Yeah," he said.

"I-I'm sorry," she said, but Ronnie barely heard her, because the bell rang for a third time and the ground trembled beneath his feet.

"Over here," someone shouted.

Dad!

Ronnie dashed for the trees at the edge of the woods. Dad stepped from the darkness and grabbed him, hugged him, and pulled him into the underbrush.

Tim squinted from behind a laurel.

"Timmy," Ronnie said, his heart lighter than it had ever been. Prayers *worked*. Prayers kicked ass.

"What happened?" Tim asked.

"Did the sheriff kill him?" Dad asked, before Ronnie could answer Tim.

"*She* did."

"She? The detective?"

"No, Mama Bet."

"Did they hurt you, son?"

"No," he said, wanting to tell Dad about his new discovery, that Jesus was a pal and an ally, and who cared about an old stupid Bell Monster when you had the top gun on your side?

But he forgot about Jesus.

Because Mom was standing in the graveyard, and so was the sheriff, and the grass stretched open and the ground cracked and tombstones shivered.

Archer appeared in the doorway of the red church, the hole in his chest miraculously healed, the shirt unstained. He was bathed in a strange light, a sick yellowish orange the color of a dying fire. His face was sad and peaceful, and once again Ronnie was reminded of Jesus' face in the Bible pictures.

Ronnie swallowed hard. Because what if this *was* the Second Coming, only this time God did it in a roundabout way, the ultimate big-time test of faith?

"What's happening?" Tim said, nearly blind without his glasses.

"God only knows," David said.

Archer walked—no, *floated*—down the steps. Mama Bet was behind him, looking nearly the same as she had, the dried blood and dirt streaking her face. But her eyes were somehow *wrong*, looking past the seen and known world.

Then the ground quivered again. The dirt at the base of the grave markers roiled, and pale, wispy shapes slithered up into the night air.

Arms topped with clawing, grasping hands.

Arms followed by heads, whitish lumps that were half skull, half milkish vapor.

Then more, rising up from the ground like heavy fog. A sound like a hurt breeze wended through the forest.

The shapes solidified, became translucent people. Some wore old clothes, long dresses and bonnets, some of the men in Confederate Civil War uniforms, their blanched faces stretched and sagging, mouths yawning mournfully as they moaned. Others wore clothes of more recent vintage, suits and cravats or ties, with or without shoes. Ronnie recognized some of the more freshly dead.

There, Willie Absher, who had been crushed to death while working on a truck last year. Jeannie Matheson, an old schoolteacher who had finally given in to cancer. And Grandma Gregg.

The same Grandma who used to perch Ronnie on her knee and tell about the old ways and the old stories. Now she shook the dark dirt from her burial gown and moved forward, feet hovering above the ground, vacant eyes shadowed.

A dozen, a hundred dead, all rising up from the grave, answering the call of the bell.

Summoned by Archer.

The preacher was beneath the dogwood now, reaching out with his luminous hands to rip the air in front of him. A separate entity shimmered into being.

"The Hung Preacher," whispered Ronnie.

"May the good Lord protect us and keep us," Dad prayed aloud.

"What about Mom?" Tim whimpered.

"She bargained with the devil. Now she's got to pay the price."

"No," Ronnie said. "She changed. When Archer got shot, she became one of *us* again. We can't give up on her now."

Ronnie couldn't explain. Mom was Mom. Mom belonged to *them,* not Archer. And Archer wasn't the devil, anyway. For the first time ever, Dad was wrong.

Ronnie looked for her in the herd of haunted figures. At first he saw only the aching dead collecting around Archer. Then he saw Mom, hiding behind Grandma Gregg's tombstone. The sheriff was with her.

"There she is," Ronnie said. "You got to save her."

"Only Jesus saves, son."

"But you *love* her. You can't let Archer have her."

"She was more than ready to give *you* up. She thought she was making *that* sacrifice for love."

"What's happening to Mommy?" Tim said.

"Please, Dad," Ronnie said. He was nearly ready to run out there himself, out in the middle of those dead creepy things, to help Mom. "Jesus will run with you. Archer can't touch you if you're carrying Jesus in your blood."

Dad said nothing. As they watched, the Hung Preacher materialized, his plump, bloated face beaming with joy. Archer embraced his ancestor, lifted him as three of the new congregation removed the noose. The sinuous threads that comprised the Hung Preacher's revenance collapsed onto Archer, and the two coalesced into one body.

Then the crowd of corpses parted, and Archer headed across the corrupted cemetery. The others fell in line, a ghostly caravan.

The sheriff shouted and ran from his hiding place. He caught up to one of the figures, a young boy.

"Samuel," the sheriff screamed. "Don't go."

The sheriff grabbed at the apparition, tried to embrace it, but he might as well have been harvesting the air. The boy didn't even turn, just kept marching in that solemn regiment. The sheriff fell to his knees, weeping.

When the last of the dead disappeared into the brush, Dad said to Ronnie, "Stay here with your brother. I'll get your mom."

Ronnie looked at the dark gaps in the bushes where the dead had gone, wondering where Archer was leading them. Then he looked at the belfry, at the unmoving shadows that filled its hollowness. The candles burned low in the red church, the eerie flickering making the building seem alive.

"I can't see nothing," Timmy said. "My glasses broke. Tell me what's happening."

"Exactly what you see," Ronnie answered. *"Nothing* is happening."

* * *

The sheriff crawled into the shrubs. Below him, the road and the valley lay spread beneath the grim moon. The congregation drifted down the embankment, and there, near the end of the speechless column, was Samuel.

His dead brother, now and forever Archer's.

Frank watched as Archer reached the great stones bordering the river. The monstrosity stepped into the water. No, not into—*onto*. Because the preacher walked on water.

Archer turned and waited as his congregation followed, first Mama Bet, then others old and new, including Frank's grim parents, all entering the black river. The water swallowed them, took them under its frothy tongue and carried them back to the ancient belly of the Earth.

Frank hoped Samuel would look back and wave, do anything to show that he remembered, that part of Samuel's human life would remain even in this bleak new eternity. But Samuel slipped beneath the currents as silently as the others had, and when the last ghost faded, Archer himself dissipated and sank into the water.

Only the river mist remained, like the shroud of a final burial. The water laughed as it carried Archer's people to the deadest sea.

TWENTY-FIVE

Frank returned to the red church three weeks later.

The cemetery was quiet, the grass thick from gentle rains, the earth undisturbed. Birds chirped in the nearby forest. Wildflowers erupted along the road, black-eyed Susans and Queen Anne's lace and winding morning glories. At the feet of the giant slumbering mountains, the river rolled on.

They'd found Sheila's body two miles downstream. Hoyle said that sometimes fish or turtles nibbled on the flesh when it became softened by prolonged exposure. Frank tried to believe that. At the hard edge of midnight, as he convinced himself that haunted congregations didn't exist, Hoyle's little forensic tidbit gave a tiny comfort.

But right now, he didn't need comfort.

He pulled the cord, and the chainsaw leaped to life, its racket drowning out nature's blissful stirrings. As he dug the spinning blade into the base of the dogwood, his teeth were clamped so tightly together that his jaw ached. The sawdust was bitter on his lips and in his nostrils as he sliced into the wood. Finally the deformed tree fell, and the sun bathed the red church with its cleansing rays.

He'd filled out a missing-persons report on Mama Bet and Archer McFall, writing that he suspected they'd moved to California. He also postulated that Archer had murdered Boonie Houck, Zeb Potter, and Donna Gregg. Never mind that no solid evidence had ever been recovered, and that the state medical examiners were left as baffled as everybody else. Who cared if the FBI spent ten years tracking down a person who no longer existed, who may never have lived?

Frank sawed the dogwood into smaller lengths, then carried the brush to the edge of the forest. The work raised a good honest, sweat. Lester rode by on his tractor, gave a neighborly wave, and kept driving. The people of Whispering Pines were good at keeping things to themselves. Sonny Absher had tried to blabber, but everybody chalked it up to liquor-induced delusions.

When Frank was finished, he took off his gloves and went into the church. A pile of dry, gray dirt lay in the spot where Archer had been shot. Frank kicked at it, and dust spun in the air. The stain on the altar was gone.

He had thought about burning the church. Arson was a difficult crime to trace. But a church couldn't be good or evil— only people could. Or things that walked as people. Without people, and what they believed, a church was just a bunch of wood and nails and stone and glass.

Maybe someday God would return to this church. Maybe pure-hearted people would take up psalms and hymns and prayers here. Maybe a preacher would come here as God's servant, not as a jealous rival.

Maybe.

Frank went outside and gathered some wildflowers. He put some on the grave of his parents, then knelt before the stone that contained the engraving of a lamb.

If only God truly did keep and protect people.

If only.

Forgiveness.

That was something Jesus taught.

So Ronnie figured it was only right that he forgive Mom for trying to sacrifice him to Archer. Besides, Dad said that Jesus had already forgiven her. If Jesus, with all His problems and worries and duties, had room in His heart for Mom, then surely Ronnie had room, too. It helped that Mom and Dad had made up, and that Mom had joined the choir at Barkersville Baptist, and life was almost back to normal.

His nose was healing nicely, though he suspected he'd have a small hump on the bridge. Gave it character, Mom said. He looked forward to being able to smell flowers again.

Because he'd also forgiven Melanie. They sat together every day at lunch, and maybe in a week or two, he'd be able to smell that sweet little smell that her hair gave off. Melanie had asked him several times about what had happened at the church, but he'd never told her. At least, not yet. Every time she batted those long eyelashes and made his heart float, he weakened. Maybe someday he'd tell her, as soon as he figured it out for himself.

Summer was coming, the days long and full of sunshine. And the sun had a way of killing darkness and dark thoughts. He still walked past the red church, and he still shivered when he was near it. The Days didn't talk about what had happened at the church. Forgetting was part of forgiving.

But sometimes, when the sun was burying itself in the cut of Buckhorn Mountain, Ronnie couldn't help glancing at the belfry. And he couldn't help remembering how, that night of the ghosts when the Hung Preacher moved into Archer, the black shadow had slipped away and seeped into the old dogwood tree.

But surely that was only his overactive imagination trying to get him in trouble again. The sheriff had cut the tree down. Besides, Ronnie had Jesus, didn't he? Jesus would protect him. Doubting would be a sin of the heart, and Ronnie had suffered enough of those to last a lifetime.

So he kept his eyes away from the shadows and looked ahead to a life where dead things stayed dead, except for good things like Jesus.

These humans were the source of endless joy, endless fascination.

The thing had played many games throughout the billion passages of the sun, but this new one, the one of godhood, was the best.

With their belief in miracles, with their faith, with their frailties and failures, humans were a rich and abundant playground. From the beginning, when it had first burrowed up from the core of the Earth, it had inspired awe among those who wore flesh. The thing had taken many forms, many faces, and they had given it many names, but most of all, they had fed it fear and worship, and it craved those things that had been reserved for the gods.

And though it had been many things, trees and rocks and wind and meat, all those things were of the Earth. As it settled into the sandy riverbed and seeped back toward the hot magma of the earth's core, it considered the human thoughts it had stolen.

The time as Archer McFall had been pleasurable, as had its venture as Wendell McFall. But so had a thousand other forays into the flesh. So had many other possessions. Perhaps it would return one day, to shape clay into human form, to breathe life into hollow vessels and again bring a McFall among the people who lived in those old mountains. Or perhaps it would rise somewhere else, to play havoc in a new place, or revisit the site of other former miracles.

Because miracles never ceased.

Sometimes, when it owned thoughts, it wondered if its own existence was a miracle.

No. That would mean that greater things, greater forces, existed.

And the thing did not believe in anything greater than itself.

In the riverbed, it surrendered thought.

The master of the world returned to the dirt from which it had arisen.